The Rooting of Evil:

Book Two of the Trencit Legacy

The Rooting of Evil

Paul Melniczek

King's Way Press

Atlanta 2016

King's Way Press

3721 New Macland Rd.
Suite 200-141
Powder Springs, GA 30157
http://www.kwp-books.com

ISBN-13: 978-0-9814748-6-1
ISBN-10: 0981474861

The Rooting of Evil

The Rooting of Evil

The four companions made their way quickly past the vast fortress of Gorothagled, the empty streets silent and shrouded within the pervasive mist which consumed the entire valley. Alayian remained in the lead, the bodies of Charadan and Rundin strapped to one of the great warhorses of Trencit.

Sarion felt incredibly weary, his body aching from the bruises and cuts he'd sustained in battling the ogre and the predators hunting the vale, but more painful were the emotional wounds; the loss of General Charadan and the other brave warriors. Tears moistened the corner of his eyes and he felt the muscles in his jaw clench, tightened to ward against the raging despair which longed for release. But he couldn't let it happen. Not here in the dangerous valley, and certainly nowhere within the confines of the unpredictable Grammore Lowlands. He doubted sorrow would ease the hurt, but that path was denied to him regardless. Caution simply would not allow for it.

He looked forward at Chertron's tall frame as the man kept himself directly behind Alayian's slenderform, the vigilant warrior unready to trust the na-dryad, just as he mistrusted everything else in the Lowlands. And wisely so, Sarion knew.

Forlern brought up the rear, moving catlike several yards behind him, soundless and alert to anything which might be onto their trail. Sarion had learned firsthand the hazards which patrolled the valley as he'd encountered a host of prowling Grimhounds before entering the ancient citadel. Alayian had treated his wounds, but they would remain sore for days. He fervently hoped that the girl's ability to avoid detection would bring them out of the vale without further mishap. He didn't want to think about the prospect of facing another skirmish while in their fatigued condition. And he couldn't forget that a Killworm still lurked somewhere within the city...

At times Alayian paused, her head moving to either side, her delicate chin lifted skyward, as if sniffing the air. Sometimes she would reach into her pouch, grabbing what looked like fine brown powder, and scatter it around. An herb to confuse their scent, Sarion surmised.

They passed several mounds of the blasted rock which he'd seen on his approach to the fortress in pursuit of his companions. Alayian steered them well clear of the strange protrusions. Obviously she knew something of their origin or purpose. Sarion had avoided them earlier out of sheer instinct. The group picked their way across shattered rocks and small boulders, gradually angling upwards towards the lip of the valley. There was no way to be sure of their exact direction, but Sarion's tracking skills confirmed her choice of path. He was confident they were heading in the right course, and the ground became steeper as they trudged through the fog, which thinned somewhat as they left the depths of the valley behind them. The mist grew less, but it still remained with them. It never seemed to leave entirely, always prevalent in some form throughout their travels in Grammore. The air was continuously damp, the mist often blanketing the landscape in thick, sluggish clouds, obscuring vision and permitting only a window of several feet. The mist was almost a living entity in itself, existing only to thwart the warriors' movement and poison their spirit. Oppressive and repulsive as it surrounded them, effectively cutting the group off from any chance of glimpsing the sun, or the celestial sky at night. And it made the Lowlands appear even vaster and more formidable than it already was, concealing so much of the life and landscape it held beneath its strangling, remorseless cloak. It was an enemy. Sarion had felt its touch constantly since their initial entry into Grammore. Just one more obstacle which needed to be confronted and overcome, he realized...

He slipped on loose shale, swallowing heavily and pushing forward with renewed determination as the slope grew sharper. They had to be nearing the lip of the valley, and several moments later Alayian turned, speaking to Chertron. The big man nodded, peering ahead into the gloom. Sarion could scarcely make out Alayian's lithe figure within the haze, and she looked like a forsaken wraith, gliding smoothly, effortlessly along the stones as she led the horse. Chertron looked over one shoulder, checking on his companions and whispering.

"We've reached our camp, she says." He paused, then quickly added, "She also gives warning, that something follows us from behind."

Both men turned around, watching as Forlern skipped towards them, peering at them with wary eyes.

"What is it?" He shrugged, carrying a long knife in one hand. "Trouble?"

"I don't know." Chertron answered. "The girl says we've reached the spot of our descent." He pointed, and they saw her disappear into the mist.

"Well, let's be out of this cursed vale all the quicker then." Forlern spat, gazing down the path they had come.

"Alayian believes we're being tracked." Sarion's face was grim, but no trace of fear showed. Weary he felt, terribly hurt by the loss of Charadan and the others, but his frustration over their misfortune would not turn into fear. He would not permit it. He had faced death too many times, knew the guises it could take, and knew yet another thing -- that like the mist, it was a constant, unwelcome companion, patiently waiting to strike. They all needed to be ready for whatever form it decided to mask itself within for the next encounter.

"Did you hear anything?" Chertron pressed him, nervously looking towards the ledge of the valley.

"No." Forlern shook his head. "Maybe she's wrong."

Sarion shook his head. "I doubt it. To remain alive in this land requires incredible skill and instinct. She's a native to the Lowlands...I think we need to gather our belongings and clear out immediately." He rapped the hilt of his sword. "Flight is our only option, regardless of what follows."

"Let's be off then, the quicker the better. Already the girl has vanished." Chertron stamped one booted foot, dust swirling lazily upwards from the harsh ground.

The three men hurried forward, finding extra strength from hidden reservoirs deep inside themselves. But Sarion knew they would need rest soon.

Very soon.

The Rooting of Evil

The men quickly packed up the remaining items that had been left before embarking on their assault of the valley and the formidable fortress. Sarion questioned Alayian about her comments to Chertron.

"You're sure something tracks us?"

She nodded, her long auburn tresses spilling like silk along her slender shoulders.

"What of its nature? Can you tell?"

"No. My skill possesses many forms, but not to that extent. Much can be learned from sight, smell and sound. Odors carried on the wind, and some I can detect from very long distances..." Her voice softly trailed away.

Sarion glanced over at the warriors who were restlessly awaiting his signal for them to depart. The bodies of their fallen comrades had been strapped across their steeds, the powerful war horses serving a final tribute to their warrior masters, bearing them away past their last battle from the fateful expedition into Gorothagled. It had been a costly one indeed.

"You won't be able to take your comrades all the way to your homeland, as you know."

Sarion nodded. "They deserve the highest regard from their countrymen in burial, one that our need will prevent because of the return journey." The bitterness welled deeply within his chest, but he fought it back. "I was hoping to find a suitable area to leave them. But *not* in that place of evil."

Alayian gently shook her head. "No. And neither can they be left within any grave, shallow or otherwise. Predators would dig them up quickly. Come though, we must hasten. I fear pursuit will swiftly find us. I know of somewhere close by which will serve your fallen comrades well enough."

Sarion held her wondrous emerald orbs in his gaze for a moment, then waved a hand to his companions. "Let's hurry. The evil within the valley won't let us off that easily."

Their belongings gathered and packed, they left behind what they could spare, extra clothes and blankets, several utensils, and other items they wouldn't need. Sarion felt a slight dilemma, as they now had the extra war horses from the fallen warriors. He realized they might need to set them loose at some point, if pressed or attacked. He mounted his own steed and the great beast galloped past the crumbling remains of the ancient stone wall and into the woods, the landscape growing ever darker at the onset of nightfall.

The forest here was not as thick as the deeper jungles of Grammore, and they were on a higher elevation, the past two days carrying them upwards, and hopefully, Sarion thought, towards the border. The company moved stealthily forward with Alayian in the lead, Chertron now at her side. He wasn't taking any chances. Forlern remained directly behind Sarion, and he gained a measure of comfort in the fighter's presence. He recalled his words to the fearless warrior before their tragic descent into the valley and citadel. Sarion had told him to find strength within, and to trust in himself. Forlern had been convinced of impending disaster, exclaiming a resignation of his own fate along with the other warriors. But he had survived once more. The youngest of the group, he also was perhaps the most skilled, barring perhaps only Charadan. Sarion was amazed by the man's quickness and master of weaponry, and his hunter's instincts. His potential to move upwards through the ranks of the Trencit army was limitless -- that is, if Forlern could manage to restrain his fiery temper.

The group rode onwards, continuing for more than an hour since leaving the dread valley, and Sarion whistled ahead, signaling for a halt. Chertron and

The Rooting of Evil

Alayian paused, looking back and turning their mounts, Forlern hesitating as well, but remaining several yards behind, peering into the forest, the visibility now greatly diminished.

"We need to rest for a while, and decide our plans for the night. Do you think we're still being pursued?" Sarion stared at the girl, trying to read her thoughts, gauge her motivations. Who *was* she really?

In response, she merely nodded.

It wasn't enough for Chertron, his face dour and uncertain. "How can you be so sure? We are warriors, trained to face challenge and violence -- in whatever shape it confronts us. It's our nature to question everything, and trust does not come easy for us, especially in a foreign land." He paused. "And another thing, why are you even helping us? Where are we headed? I think it's time for some answers."

Sarion waited, not interfering. They needed to hear Alayian out before they went any further. Although he trusted her not to endanger them, he was extremely wary of her intent. If Chertron was right -- that she was a na-dryad -- little was known of this race, except that they were reclusive and mysterious, another legend lacking any proof of their existence. The great annals of Trencit might contain further knowledge, but Charadan, the only one who had read the tomes, was no longer with them. That thought stung him fiercely and he forced himself to banish the memory of the brave leader. He was still reeling from the events, his mind lacking sleep, his body aching and weary to the point of numbness, and his heart was heavy with doubt and sorrow.

Alayian spoke softly, but without any hint of impatience or hesitation. "You were in need. Despite what you have experienced in Grammore, there are others which dwell here, and hold no hostility to men.

Perhaps there exist only a few of us, but we have long respected and even welcomed those who find themselves ensnared within the evils of the Lowlands."

Chertron said nothing.

She continued. "You need to return swiftly to your homeland. Sarion spoke to me when I first found him above the valley. He told me of your quest and the dangers you've had to face. I read the truth of his words, the passion in his heart. And yes, I can lead you to the edge of Grammore, although there are no safe paths within the Lowlands; all are fraught with hazard and unpredictability."

Alayian turned to him and smiled, her eyes enchanting. Sarion found it hard to look away from the green pools of ice. He answered, carefully choosing his words. "An enemy would surely have attacked me earlier. I'm convinced that you bear no ill intent. You helped us leave the fortress. But I also realize you're not quite like us -- human." He swallowed heavily at his revelation, but she merely laughed in reply, her voice soothing, like rain falling softly upon a meadow among high, rolling hills.

"And so I am not! Wisely spoken. I'm a na-dryad as your stalwart companion has already guessed. But we are not a violent people, and never have been. We live in unity with the earth and its creatures."

"Even within this foul land?" Chertron wrinkled his face in wonder, his tone laced with skepticism.

"There is much beauty here as well." Her face turned serious. "It's a magical, wonderful, and incredibly dangerous country. It has always been so. Many of these hazards are natural. The creatures which live in Grammore are not all necessarily evil, but only unique to the Lowlands, their ancestral home. But to anyone from outside the region, I understand the dread it invokes."

The Rooting of Evil

Chertron interjected. "And others, like the ones we pursued and were attacked by?"

"Corrupted, and there certainly exist more which have always been evil. Seeking power, destruction, and death..." Alayian's gaze lifted, looking somewhere far beyond where they stood. "A shadow has fallen over Grammore, and wicked, ancient things are stirring from slumber. Cataclysmic events are taking place, and the Dark Mage is trying to enact change inside here, and stretching further perhaps. We face black times."

Sarion nodded silently, wishing to pursue the matter, but realized they first needed to reach an area which offered protection for the night. "Is there anywhere we can stop? And be secure from predators -- and what follows?"

"Yes, not much further. Rivening Well is nearby, and it is there that we can leave your friends." She pointed towards the horses holding Charadan and Rundin. Chertron grimaced.

Sarion waved back to Forlern, who waited impatiently. He gave a curt hand signal, communicating that nothing was amiss, and they again continued, the forest dark and mysterious around them. In the distance they could already hear cries and howls as the predators of Grammore awakened from slumber in search of prey. Although they had grown accustomed to it by now, it was chilling and ominous, a constant reminder that violence and death lurked beneath leaf and branch, waiting to snare the weak and careless -- the snuffling of beasts foraging through the underbrush, grunts and snarls of creatures at hunt.

Monsters.

Alayian was a native of the land, and these things appeared as normal to her, but to Sarion and the warriors it remained a haven of nightmares. An embodiment of death walking in twilight beneath the shadowed eaves and vales within a terrifying, perilous land. Oppositely Trencit was a unified, stable monarchy, ruled by King Gregor Rellanion, along with the High Council, and they needed to return in great haste with grim tidings -- a story of horror and heroism, but foremost of despair. The loss of General Charadan, King's Champion and commander of the Trencit Armies. Sarion shook his head, thinking of the tremendous repercussions that would surely threaten to unbalance the country and elevate the level of uncertainty higher than it already was, ravaged by the war in the east.

Plagued by such ill thoughts, Sarion remained vigilant to his surroundings as they picked their way through a rocky area, the trees becoming denser. The ground rose, and they appeared to be entering a region of small foothills. It wasn't long before a new sound reached their ears now, the distant rushing of water. Visibility was rapidly diminishing, and mist swirled sluggishly between the trunks and scattered boulders. Somewhere to their left a harsh cough rang out, alarming the men, and Alayian spoke to Chertron, urging greater speed.

Sarion nudged his mount towards the fighter. "What did she say?"

Chertron's face was dour in the twilight. "She spoke the name of some beast, but said it wouldn't pursue us, saying it doesn't travel far from its lair. But very dangerous if confronted."

"Not very reassuring regardless." Sarion peered over one shoulder at Forlern, who constantly looked to either side, occasionally chancing a quick glance behind himself into the dark maw of the woods. Everything appeared all right, and he nodded to Sarion.

Within several minutes the sound of water grew dramatically, and the forest opened before them, the area brightening a bit. Alayian came to a halt, pointing towards the horses carrying Charadan and Rundin. They reined in their mounts, Forlern remaining behind within eyesight, turned towards the trees.

Sarion joined Chertron as they stood before a ravine. A considerable drop opened at their feet, a steep and narrow cliff pocked with bushes scrambling for purchase against a rocky slope formed of broken rock and loose pebbles. A wondrous waterfall lay almost directly beneath them, a raging river spilling between the gaps of a chasm which jutted out from the living rock of the earth itself. The waters formed a wide basin before it entered a series of thundering rapids, churning off into the black distance. It was a spectacular sight, and Alayian smiled sadly at their expressions, speaking in a tone of reverence.

"Rivening Well, a place my people have always held sacred." She held her arms high. "Behold its beauty and be at peace, for you look upon an area which brushes against the ancient power of the earth itself. Few among any race have seen this vision. It is here we must say farewell to your courageous comrades, a fitting place for fallen warriors. The pool is deep, the waters charmed. No beast wanders this valley. The sides are too steep to climb, and there exists no path downward."

Chertron agreed. "We can't take them back to Trencit with us, that's certain. At some point we may need to abandon the other horses too. Hopefully we won't be engaged anywhere along the way. Aye, but this is indeed a suitable place to end their journey. That such incredible beauty can be found within this hostile land." The warrior gazed in admiration at the pristine sight below, shaking his head and clasping his hands together.

Several moments later, Sarion helped Chertron untie their friends from the horses, gently lifting them as they were held tightly within blankets wrapped about their frames. The waterfall sat before them, the drop a straight line into the mysterious depths. The men held first the body of Rundin, letting him fall soundlessly into the pool, and then Charadan. No words were spoken, although the men locked gazes briefly before completing their last act of respect. Swallowed by the dark waters below, they disappeared with a small splash, and Sarion felt his chest ache upon seeing them vanish. He knew the finality of their deed and what it meant, the reality taking hold and threatening to overpower him. He would never see them again...

Captain Grundel -- General Charadan. The same man. The revelation was staggering. The deception had been absolutely perfect. King Gregor had sent his best man to forage into the westland, attempting to uncover the source of rumor and unrest. And within their secretive plans had been a decision for Charadan to proceed beyond Trencit's borders, into the dark land itself if he deemed it necessary. Sarion was fully convinced that King Gregor had already known it would come to that, as Charadan had sought out the former captain in the Western Watch in advance of the venture into the wilderness.

Sarion recalled their first meeting, the company of warriors approaching him on his farm, seeking out his assistance. He could not have refused, despite leaving his nephew Edward behind. He wondered how the boy was, and smiled to himself. The youth was tough, a survivor, and showed tremendous potential. He missed the boy's cheerful face. Sarion's musing was short-lived, though, as he remembered Charadan's words concerning his own family. A wife and children, somewhere back in Trencit, whom he hadn't seen in over a year. And now, he never would again...He swallowed heavily, fighting back the tears which yearned for release. But he must not give in, he knew. Not now.

The Rooting of Evil

Alayian noticed his discomfort, and she reached over to him, squeezing his hand. A thrill of excitement ran through him at her touch, and he wondered if it was not somehow magic. Who was this magnificent girl, a child of the forest, her own natural beauty easily a match to the marvelous waterfall below them…

He gazed deeply into her eyes, which held him fast, and it felt as if she could read into his very soul…

Someone coughed.

"Well, that's done. Trencit has lost some of the greatest men in the land. There's nothing else to be said." Chertron's voice was husky, but he remained steadfast, pressing Alayian on where they should go next. "We need to rest somewhere, at least for part of the night. I don't think we can continue on much further, even if the entire hordes of the Lowlands are in pursuit."

"I don't think our situation is that dire," the girl replied. "But there are a series of hidden caves around that outcropping, and they offer shelter. We'll make for them."

They mounted the horses and were quickly off. The only sound they heard was the roaring of Rivening Well, which dominated the landscape. With the water on their left, they proceeded along the ravine, angling inwards and away from the treacherous drop. Within a few minutes they reached a wall of rock siding a large hillock. The footing grew uncertain as the horses slowed, and they shortly dismounted, leading the great beasts by hand. Climbing ever higher, they soon entered a narrow cleft which led downwards into a small cave. It widened before plunging into the cliff, leaving enough room for the horses.

"I'll take first watch," Forlern volunteered.

Alayian had entered the cave, and now emerged from the opening.

"I hope she's not leading us into the lair of some

monster," Chertron whispered to Sarion. "Perhaps she's in alliance with some creature, luring prey for this very purpose."

Sarion scowled. "I'll go first then, just in case." He trudged ahead, leaving the skeptical warrior silently watching him.

"It's safe," the na-dryad smiled to him. "This area harbors few predators. Rivening Well is somewhat of a sanctuary, you could say."

Sarion rummaged through his pack, bringing out a pair of lanterns. Lighting them, he entered the cave, which was wide enough for a small number of people. The back of the cave ended several yards from the entrance, and he nodded in satisfaction. His wounds ached, his stomach growled in hunger, and he felt emotionally savaged. The events of the past day had pushed them all far beyond the limits of physical and mental ability, not to mention the terrible loss of their companions in Gorothagled. It was too much for any man to face.

"This will do." Sarion collapsed onto the ground, slumping against a wall.

Chertron's grim face appeared at the entrance, the fighter chewing on a piece of smoked meat. He yawned, sitting down next to Sarion.

"Why do you think something pursues us yet?" Sarion questioned the girl as she stood before the cave entrance, her slender figure silhouetted in the dusky light.

"I have the ability to identify other life; it's inherent in my people. I detected something which emerged from the dark fortress shortly after we left. It's been following us ever since then, and has not given up."

It was a chilling thought. Both men stared at her for a moment before Chertron spoke. "What manner of creature is it, do you think?"

She shook her head. "I know not. It's something unfamiliar to me. But its purpose can only be evil, coming from that city of corruption."

"This Dark Mage. It must be a servant of his then, sent out to track anyone that entered, and managed to leave. I don't know what else it could be." Sarion drank from his water pouch, resting his head against the cave wall.

"But if it doesn't need rest, then it will surely catch us at some point, maybe even tonight." Chertron stretched his arm. "We can defend this area from attack."

"Depending upon what form that attack might take," Sarion added. "We're all too exhausted to fight another difficult battle; we need rest ourselves, and badly. Maybe this place will offer the protection we need. It must suffice."

"Rivening Well has its own natural magic. I don't think the creature which follows us will enter this area until tomorrow. We traveled quickly, and it needs to track us through dangerous country." Alayian's words were cautious, but honest, Sarion thought.

"And maybe it doesn't intend on harming us, or at least until it decides otherwise." Sarion looked over at Chertron, the warrior's eyelids fluttering.

"We can only hope. And one of us needs to relieve Forlern for the next watch."

"I will." Alayian smiled. "I have better skills in detecting threats in Grammore than others. I'm going to retrace our path, and see what I can find as well."

Sarion frowned, but she stopped him with a quick shake of her head. Chertron was silent.

"Do not argue, Sarion. How easily you forget that this is my homeland. Do you think I would have survived all these years if I were helpless as you might think?"

"I don't think you're helpless at all..." He replied, sharper than what he'd intended.

"Rest while I go, I have little need for such as your people do." She hurried off, her form swallowed up by the shadows.

When she left, Chertron prodded him further. "Still trust her?"

"Yes, I do. And what choice do we have? Sometimes you find help in the strangest of places, discover hope within the darkest nightmare. She has done nothing to convince me otherwise, at least."

"Not yet, you mean..." Chertron finished. Pushing himself off the ground, he stood. "I'll bring some food to Forlern, and see if he's all right. I don't like the idea of not being within sight of each other while we remain in this foul land."

"I feel the same way. But he's one of the most capable men I've ever known." Sarion smiled in admiration at the warrior's unpredictable temperament.

"That he is," Chertron agreed. "And he'll probably be angered when he sees I'm not resting."

"Not as angry as when he sees me with you too," Sarion chuckled. Even Chertron had to laugh at this, and they both walked out to check on their friend.

After returning with Chertron back inside the cave, Sarion immediately fell into a deep slumber, his sleep filled with tortured nightmares, of nameless beasts and hideous shades, all pursuing him relentlessly across a vast plain. He neared consciousness several times, his fighting instinct bringing him back, but then the terrible

dreams finally receded and he found more genuine rest
at last. He opened his eyes at one point and spotted
Forlern slumped against the far wall, a blanket thrown
about his shoulders. All seemed well, and Chertron was
missing, evidently having taken up the next watch.
Sarion wondered about Alayian, if she had returned.

The hour was late, and he wanted to check on the
other warrior. He closed his eyes for a moment, feeling
incredibly weary, but determined to rouse himself and
see how Chertron was, but he never had the chance.
Sleep overcame him swiftly and he remembered no
more.

It wasn't until morning when he awakened,
finding a pair of emerald orbs gazing at him.

"Rested?" A wonderful smile greeted him, as
Alayian hovered before the cave entrance. There was no
sign of the others. "Your companions are outside, fear
not. All is well."

Sarion stretched, yawning deeply. "And you?"

"I'm fine, of course. You underestimate me,
Sarion."

"I don't think so. It's more a lack of
understanding, I would say."

"That also."

"Where did you go last night?" Sarion crouched
forward, looking for his water pouch.

"Drink this instead." She offered him her own
pouch, an amazingly light but durable sack the color of
forest green. Her face beamed with pleasure, and she
laughed softly. "You'll find strength in the draught of
the na-dryads."

"What is it? You gave me some of this before, if
I remember..."

"A blend of herbs and roots, fresh spring water
from clean streams, powders known only to a few. It
sustains, and makes burdens appear lighter. It also heals

wounds of limb and spirit alike."

Sarion's face grew dark. "My wounds are so deep I fear they will never completely heal."

"I'm sorry for your loss; it's not the first, or the last you'll have, I'm afraid. I can read your thoughts inside the depths of your eyes, Sarion. You're like a vessel to me, filled with a clear liquid."

"Am I that easily comprehended and conquered?" He savored the taste of the cool drink, the flavor slightly sweet and altogether pleasant. He felt immediately enriched, although sore from nearly every part of his body. Groaning, he lifted himself from the ground.

Not answering his last question, she said instead "I wandered back to Rivening Well last night, and beyond. The forest was subdued, and nothing malevolent prowled nearby. I caught no sign or scent of what follows us."

"Have we lost it then?" His words were hopeful, but he had a sinking feeling inside that they had been marked by something in the service of the Dark Mage.

"I don't know, but my heart and instinct argue otherwise. My abilities to detect other life forms are keen, but not all-reaching." She stared at him, and he felt nervous before her incredible gaze, as if his very heart was laid bare to her.

"How far are we from the edge of Grammore?"

"Not very far at all. We're nearing it now, already having left the Lowlands behind. You ventured in further south, and the foothills lead into the bordering Ridgeline itself. Another day and you'll glimpse the frontier."

"None too quickly for us." Sarion moved about, warming his limbs, trying to get the stiffness out.

"Sarion, there is something else I must ask you now."

He smiled. "I'm in your debt; how can I turn you down after your help?"

But Alayian's face was serious, and he wondered if he'd said something wrong.

"My people have natural talent, in various ways, as I've already told you. We are masters of secrecy and detection, able to travel quietly and unnoticed to all but the most deceiving eye."

"But even *you* aren't totally safe here, you're saying."

"Nothing is. Na-dryads are among the most elusive, though. No human could ever find us unless we wanted them to, or revealed ourselves first."

Sarion looked at the cave entrance, catching a glimpse of one of the horses. "Hmm, I won't ask you to give up your secret then. Although I would like to think I could find you when I wanted," he smiled.

Alayian returned his look mischievously, then continued, appearing more serious yet. "We also can feel traces of magic in its different forms."

Now it was Sarion's turn to grow concerned. "What are you talking about?"

She lifted a slim hand towards him in a solemn gesture. "I detect magic from *you* -- subtle, but extremely powerful. Enough that I fear for your welfare, and those around you."

Sarion stared at her in astonishment.

The company soon left the cave behind, leading the horses onward across the rugged terrain. Sarion was quiet, considering Alayian's strange words. Their conversation had abruptly ended as Forlern entered, greeting him and asking if he should gather belongings in preparation to leave, which he strongly advised. Sarion agreed and they had soon left, despite his unspoken reply to Alayian's revelation. She detected strong magic on his person, she had told him.

Surprised at first, this quickly led to suspicion. It had to be the wand given him by Charadan before his venture into Gorothagled. The general had suspected something latent about the item, and if Alayian's talent was to be trusted -- of which he had no doubt -- it was an item of hidden magical ability. It also confirmed Charadan's notion. And where did that leave Sarion now? Did he indeed possess an artifact of unknown power and origin? A discard from some past age from a hapless victim found within the lair of a Killworm? Perhaps a great treasure indeed...But to what end? Magic could take many different forms, and not all of them pleasant.

As they traveled forward beneath the veil of mist, he tossed the idea around in his head. He would certainly have to keep the rod close, and be careful to whom he revealed it to, if anyone. He hadn't told Chertron or Forlern about the item yet, as he carefully took it from Charadan earlier. He'd nearly forgotten it.

Continuing onwards, the morning passed without mishap. The elevation climbed briefly, and then at some point they reached the height of the hill and began a gradual descent. The footing remained challenging, and they proceeded to guide their steeds. The trees were tall and thin here, a mixture of evergreens becoming more prominent. The lower jungle, which made up the greater part of Grammore, had been left behind as they neared Gorothagled. Sarion realized that no part of the Lowlands was secure from danger, but this region seemed to have a smaller presence of predators. Perhaps Alayian was right, that Rivening Well was anathema to them for some reason. It certainly appeared to have its own type of beauty and natural magic.

As noon passed -- from what he could gather without seeing the sun -- they descended into a heavily wooded valley, and his trepidation grew once more as the landscape closed about them, but nothing threatening emerged. They halted for a few minutes at the fringe of a narrow clearing shaped like a bowl. Sitting on a fallen log, Sarion spoke to Alayian about this area, and if there were any hidden dangers. Chertron remained standing, keeping a watch despite the girl's assurance.

"Wolves prowl at night, and other beasts forage throughout the vale. Normal creatures, smaller than what lives deeper inside Grammore. But some things hunt in packs, and can be extremely dangerous once they find prey. There is a simple form of existence inside Grammore, one of hunter and the hunted, life and death. This land is an untamed wilderness, frightening and powerful. Man has never been welcome here."

Sarion nodded thoughtfully before replying. "And what of the giants? Can you tell me anything about them and their lost culture?"

Alayian sighed. "I know little. A fierce race of beings which dominated Grammore in ages past. Their legacy endures. Fortresses like Gorothagled are scattered throughout the Lowlands. All of them formidable, with secrets and hazards within. Some from the Dark Mage as he discovers and makes them his own, some of other origin. But the shades of the dead yet walk the streets and empty corridors. This land has not forgotten them, even long generations since their destruction."

Forlern leaned close to her. "How many of these cities are there?"

She shook her head. "I don't know. I live mostly in this part of Grammore, and have not ventured too deeply." She waved her hand in a loose circle for emphasis. "My skills can't protect me from the darker parts of this country, where there exist predators which can easily find even myself. And they migrate. One can never tell what path you may cross." She paused unpleasantly. "Or what might cross your own..."

Sarion stared at her auburn hair, wondering as to what she really was. It might not be exactly magic, but her entire body radiated a sense of *health* which was staggering. He'd never seen anyone who seemed so fully alive. Everything about this girl amazed him. Who she was, *what* she was. And just the fact that she could even survive within Grammore. But he caught himself, thinking of her in terms as being what he was familiar with -- human. No, she certainly wasn't that at all...

Forlern stood, fingering one of his long hunting knives. "This land is so wild and immense. Trencit is a large kingdom, but this..." He stammered, trying to emphasize his question. "How large *is* Grammore?"

"Larger than you can imagine."

Alayian smiled, her eyes sparkling like tiny emerald gems. "There are depths which have never seen the glimmer of daylight. And never will," she added. "The mist clings to everything, but the deeper jungle is vast, dark and impregnable, filled with unimaginable creatures, whispered legends even among my own people. Harsh terrain, immense, black mountains. Tales among my folk speak of a great vale, encircled by unassailable hills. And inside are the crumbling remains of an ancient stronghold. There is no way of knowing...The Glefins at one time were the most traveled race, wandering throughout the Lowlands, nomadic, and when their numbers were greater they ventured beyond, into your frontiers. And even they possessed no knowledge of the inner country. Maybe it has no end..."

Her voice drifted away, and the two men stared

into the forest. Sarion had felt vulnerable and threatened at every turn throughout their journey, and now the feeling was magnified as he listened to her profound words. It was magical and frightening, as he tried to imagine the dark valleys and dense jungles of inner Grammore, where man had never entered, even within his blackest nightmares. The scope of it was incredible, and he knew that the Lowlands would never be conquered by any race. The giants might once have dominated certain regions of Grammore, but their hold could not possibly have been all encompassing. Even the mysterious Dark Mage, however powerful, would always face limits. No, Grammore would forever be its own keeper.

Forlern, next to him, was silent, nervously peering into the shadowed eaves.

"We should be off. The afternoon grows long, and I would very much like to see the Ridgeline before the end of this day." Sarion stood, adjusting the bow strapped across his back. He had a large stock of arrows now, as they had all taken some from the supplies of their fallen comrades.

He waved over to Chertron, the vigilant warrior holding his broadsword out, parrying in the air, honing his skills. Alayian suddenly stiffened, looking towards the hill behind them.

The sound of howling echoed down from above, a blood-curdling scream of several beasts -- an unmistakable cry of predators on the scent of prey. Sarion felt his heart grow cold at the sound, and the horses nickered restlessly around him.

The hunt was on...

The companions raced to the horses, gathering the reins and packs. The creatures of Grammore had found them once again...

"Is this what pursued us from the fortress?" Sarion shouted to Alayian as he leapt astride the great mare.

"I'm not sure. It's a pack of Greelvon, but I've never seen signs of them this far north."

"That's encouraging," said Forlern. "What about the other horses, they'll slow us down, Sarion."

Nodding, Sarion reluctantly agreed. "But I don't want to abandon them; they're strong and have served us well." Indecisive, he felt bad about letting the horses run free; in his mind an easy target for the beasts of the Lowlands.

"Wait." Alayian brought her mount over to the riderless steeds, grabbing the reins in one hand.

"What's she doing?" Forlern fingered his bow, counting the number of arrows in his quiver. "Time is against us."

Sarion held up a hand for patience. The hunters were still a good distance away, although he had no idea of what they faced, or how quickly they traveled. He watched as Alayian touched each of the horses on the head, calming them, whispering in their ears. Sarion caught snatches of a strange tongue, and he realized she spoke in her own language. But what was she doing? The girl then reached into her pouch, sprinkling dust upon their bodies. Chertron was already at the far edge of the clearing, looking nervously in every direction. Alayian then shouted, and the horses as one kicked away, neighing and stamping their great hooves. They ran off past Chertron, and quickly disappeared into the forest.

The Rooting of Evil

Sarion hurried to her side, a curious look on his face.

"Some of my own magic. It will give them protection from the hunters for many days, erasing their natural scent. A mixing of herbs, making them as one with the trees and plants. I think their instincts will lead them safely to the edge of the Lowlands, perhaps again into friendlier meadows. It was the best I could do."

He nodded. "Then it's good enough for me. Now to our *own* survival..." Sarion gestured questioningly, but she was already galloping away, passing Chertron, the lean warrior shaking his head in wonder and skepticism. Forlern again brought up the rear, and the small company was off. They plunged into the light underbrush, making better time now that they were no longer burdened by the other horses. No words were spoken for long minutes, and they moved forward at a brisk pace, the mist lessening in this region.

If their situation wouldn't have been so trying, Sarion might have felt more comfortable in their present surroundings. The trees were more familiar to the ones in the westland; a number of tall pines, aspens, and several hardwood varieties, but there remained still others which were unknown, and he eyed these cautiously. Even the brightly-colored birds of the jungle seemed to avoid certain species. One of these now reared before them -- a sprawling, massive tower, with hundreds of branches jutting outwards, dozens of yards long. The upper reaches were invisible, obscured by mist trailers and enormous yellow leaves. Alayian was already looking at it, steering them well away from its grasping limbs. She pointed to it with one hand, and Chertron nodded as she spoke to him. Sarion didn't need any further warning, and knew there was something strange about it. Strange and most likely perilous as well...They rode on for another minute, but then Alayian called for a halt.

They had put a good distance between themselves and whatever pursued, and Sarion had not heard any cries since they'd left the clearing. But he also felt fairly certain that they were far from leaving the hunters behind. Alayian rode up to him, her dazzling eyes boring into his own. Chertron drank from his water pouch, taking advantage of their rest, while Forlern remained a dozen yards to the rear.

"Why have we halted? Are we near the borders yet?" Sarion questioned the girl, and in reply she reached into her pouch, pulling out a clear stone, traces of blue shimmering within its mesmerizing depths.

"This is for you, Sarion." She smiled, placing the jewel in the palm of his hand.

"It's beautiful, but what is it?"

"A stone of searching. Keep it with you always."

Sarion sensed something important was about to happen, and the others listened with curiosity, Chertron staring at the na-dryad intently.

"I don't understand. A gift?" Sarion gently shook his head.

"Yes, you may call it that. When you enter Grammore, I will know where to find you. I'm attuned to the stone, and carry another with me."

"But that would mean..."

"It's time for us to take different paths. Your quest needs to be fulfilled, and the frontiers of your homeland are very close. Through this wood, across a depression, and you'll reach the Ridgeline."

Sarion felt a sinking feeling in the pit of his stomach, and he stared at her with concern. "We're not going to just *leave* you here. What about the creatures hunting us?"

Alayian's eyes flashed, the wondrous smile deepening. "I'll take care of them. You noticed that odd-looking tree we passed by? That is the home of the Grerlock, a powerful creature that lives in the forest canopy. They don't like the jungle, but have migrated north over the years. I smelled it from a distance, but it's hibernating."

A look of surprise crossed Sarion's face, but he already knew the answer to his question. "What do you intend to do?"

"I'm going to awaken it, right before the pack of Greelvon draws near. The beast will be greatly angered, and it will fall upon the predators. They will hunt you no more. Indeed, they'll be overcome themselves."

"Must be a formidable creature." Chertron remarked from astride his horse. "And you're certain that you'll be safe?"

She nodded in reply, the circlet of leaves upon her head giving the girl the appearance of being a woodland queen, beautiful and quietly majestic. And Sarion realized that she *was* in a sense...

"This is my home, remember?" Still smiling, she took Sarion's hand. She leaned close to him, and he felt a rush of exhilaration. She was by far the most astonishing girl he'd ever seen.

"Sarion, we'll meet again. Bring word to your king of the danger. I have no other advice to give, for there are many things I can only guess at. My people are scattered and few. There can be no help from them. Indeed, many of them have become so closely entwined with their habitats that they are unable to free themselves. Sadly, I may be one of the last of my race that can still travel."

Sarion was shocked by this revelation. It was a profound statement of the incredible difference between them and Alayian -- na-dryad and human. He wondered what others of her kind were like, then he realized that he might not want to know...

Alayian whispered then, words meant only for him. "Be safe. Trust no one, and expect danger where you might not otherwise. Remember what I said about the talisman you bear. I would keep it secret from any besides your king. Do not try to use it. I fear its power and origin."

"Must you leave us?"

"I am unable to pass beyond the borders of Grammore. Chertron knew the truth." Her smile was dazzling, and he was enthralled. Whether it was natural or magical, Sarion felt she could have asked him anything then and he would have been helpless to resist. She held both his hands and without warning kissed him deeply, her lips tasting finer than any vintage known to man.

Embarrassed and surprised, he was at a loss for words. His face flushed, and his skin tingled with excitement. Forlern quietly chuckled in the background.

"I would like to keep the horse, if I may?"

Sarion nodded to her in reply.

Alayian smiled to them all. "Farewell, friends. We may meet again, although the time and place is yet to be known."

She turned back, moving past Forlern, and looked over her shoulder once before vanishing in the woods.

"And farewell, Sarion. Keep me in your heart."

Alayian was gone.

The men were silent, Chertron finally breaking the spell. "A remarkable creature -- beautiful, and enchanting. I've never seen the like in all the country

I've traveled. As I said, she has her eye on *you*." He stared hard at Sarion.

"Aye." Forlern galloped towards them. "There may indeed be other reasons behind her gesture of friendship."

Chertron interrupted him. "Well, let's be off. Our need for haste is dire, and I would like to leave this forsaken land far behind. If the ridge is nearby, then it will certainly be reason for hope, although danger may yet pursue us into the westland."

Sarion agreed, even though he remained staring back the way they had come. He felt a great measure of concern for the girl's safety, despite telling himself that she was quite capable. Alayian had demonstrated her skills a number of times. Grammore was an inhospitable region though, and disaster loomed at every turn. But he also realized that their quest was paramount, and they needed to return safely to Trencit. Too many people now relied on them. And too many others had given their lives in the hope of a brighter future...

They moved forward, Sarion and Chertron riding side-by-side again, as Sarion once more fell into his role as tracker and leader. Alayian's ability was uncanny, and he wondered how much about herself she *hadn't* revealed. Much, he believed, although he placed a lot of trust in her intentions. She also looked too healthy and *alive* to be anything other than what she proclaimed -- a forest child, a na-dryad. There was no question that legends walked the waking world within the Lowlands.

They rode onward without mishap, the forest appearing identical even after the passing of several miles. The most heartening sign was a gradual lifting of the fog, now reduced to thin wisps of trailing vapor. The afternoon grew, spilling into evening, and they finally reached a point where the terrain changed noticeably. The trees broke apart into scattered copses, and before them lay a depression, the foothills of the Ridgeline behind it. It was an incredible sight and they paused, sighing inwardly. The day was quickly fading, but with good speed -- and fortune -- the night might find them at long last sheltered outside the treacherous reach of Grammore.

They exchanged weary glances, and Sarion called for a brief halt.

"I would have sworn we'd never catch another glimpse of our own frontiers," said Forlern.

"Well, it's not quite the Trencit border," answered Sarion, leaning on his horse and chewing a handful of red berries. "The westland is a broken country, loosely organized at best. Scattered settlements, small villages, trapping cabins, trading posts, and outlying farms; it never has been anything other than a protectorate of Trencit, in a sense. The people are fiercely loyal, but prefer to live without the interdiction of the central kingdom. The bordermen are very independent minded."

"I would think that geography alone has lulled them into thinking the war in the east is a faraway problem to be handled by the king's armies and the greater cities of Trencit. But if they fail, the rest of the kingdom will eventually collapse, leaving them all enslaved to the Devlents or forced into exile." Chertron swept the valley with keen eyes, watching as an enormous hawk glided earthward, disappearing behind a patch of trees in the distance as it searched for prey.

"Some maybe, but not all." Sarion replied thoughtfully. "Many serve in the Western Watch, and of these, a number of companies have been called to the central kingdom. A few of the more seasoned fighters."

"There's much good use for them." Forlern sharpened one of his knives on a whetting stone. "My own regiment consists of hand-picked men to infiltrate troublesome areas on the front itself."

Sarion and Chertron both looked at him in surprise.

Forlern grinned. "I guess I should tell you both. I'm a member of the Homeguard."

Chertron whistled. "What? I had no idea..." The fighter looked his companion over as if seeing him for the first time. "Young as you are, yet I believe it. Your skill as a weapons master is great, and at your age. Tis' an honor indeed that few ever reach."

Sarion questioned him now. "And you had *no* idea, even being in that position, of Charadan's identity?"

The warrior shook his head sadly. "I don't know of too many people that have ever actually seen him. His travels are a tightly-kept secret. I think King Gregor held him in such close confidence that only a select few could even have recognized him if he wished it that way. It's impossible for any to gain access to the High Council, where he sat as King's Champion and General of the Royal Armies. To think of the protection surrounding him, and then realize that the king ordered him on such a dangerous and secretive mission..."

"My heart tells me that Charadan has been on many such ventures. Who can say?" Chertron patted his horse, feeding the animal a tuft of high grass.

Sarion nodded to himself. "And the repercussions of his loss...It's staggering to think about it. Charadan held two of the most prominent seats in Trencit."

"The king will be devastated." Forlern's face was grim. "And the High Council will be thrown into turmoil. The feudal Lords will be hysterical, and a power struggle might ensue, to some extent, at least."

Sarion felt the truth of Forlern's words. Although he wasn't very familiar with the politics and bickering of the Trencit hierarchy, he knew enough. The king ruled the kingdom, but he showed great deference to his Lords and councilors. Nearly all governing decisions were debated at the table, and it was not uncommon for individual houses to be at odds, and sometimes arms against each other. Sarion could recall several bitter disputes between principalities which had resulted in subterfuge and warfare, and the royal armies themselves had to quench the in-fighting. King Gregor was a fair and just ruler, by all accounts, but there was a constant power struggle to gain his influence, and to maneuver the High Council.

"And just think," scowled Chertron. "We're the ones who have to bring the terrible news before the king."

All three of the men were silent at his words, lost in their own thoughts, until they departed shortly afterwards and galloped across the valley, the dim brightness of the fading gray sky being slowly eaten by an eager twilight.

They passed across the valley, appearing like three cloaked wraiths upon proud horses of sturdy flesh and blood, the dull glint of steel from weapon and armor revealing their true identity as men, and not a nightmarish trio with ill intent emerging from the sinister Lowlands. They made excellent progress, unhindered and with the path clearly set before them. While his companions tasted hope for the first time since entering Grammore, Sarion's own heart felt heavy, his mind swirling within a vortex of emotion.

The loss of Charadan was keenly felt. That pain

would take a very long time to lessen, he realized. In the relatively short period he'd known the courageous leader, he'd developed a tremendous amount of respect and loyalty to him, and understood how Trencit had come to rely on him in such a great capacity; how King Gregor had relied on him, placing Charadan into such high office. And now they all would grievously miss him...

They had been friends. The mutual respect for each other undeniable. All of the warriors he would consider friends -- comrades-at-arms in a stricken, desperate venture, trespassing into a violent and unforgivable land, hostile to all that dared set foot within its shrouded territory. Great heroism had been displayed under the most dire circumstances; facing terrible odds and ghastly adversaries.

Sarion glanced over at Chertron, but the fighter's eyes were fixed on the ground before them. The man's focus was unrelenting, his determination proof enough to bolster Sarion's own lagging confidence. And now, with Alayian gone, he felt an incredible emptiness, such as he'd not experienced in many years, different from the loss of his companions.

Na-dryad. He tossed the word over in his head as he galloped along with his comrades, keeping alert to anything out of the ordinary. Alayian. She wasn't even human...

Chertron had warned him. Her intentions were suspect, and the warrior seemed to guess at much more. Sarion was eager to ask what else he knew, or at least questioned, but he felt very uncomfortable even thinking about it. Another time, maybe. After Grammore was far behind them, although the memories would surely remain fresh always. More scars embedded into his heart, he told himself. Deep wounds, mounted upon older ones. It was a harsh world they lived in...

The landscape appeared serene, normal. Tufts of high grass carpeted the vale, scattered copses were everywhere, and small brooks trickled beneath their feet, at times swampy, the turf yielding under the hooves of the mighty war horses. Stag bounded through the underbrush, while countless woodland animals foraged for food. The air was slightly cooler here, as they had traveled in a northern direction while in Grammore shortly after their harrowing encounter with the dread Jurvech. When they had first entered, the land had quickly become a treacherous marsh, and after a short march, had transformed into a warm and oppressive jungle. Sarion believed that the jungle continued to grow much worse, the bulk of the vast Lowlands consisting of impenetrable, dense undergrowth, home to a fantastic variety of plant and animal life. How big was it? Alayian had hinted that Grammore was incredibly large, and she had only wandered throughout the northern edges, not too deeply into the interior. She'd told them there existed places that no one had ever traveled to, or ever would...

An intimidating notion. Depths where the light of day could never possibly reach. It was difficult for one not to be overwhelmed by the fathomless dimensions of the wilderness. Few from Trencit had ever set eyes upon the Lowlands, and fewer yet had dared its misty eaves. Sarion had been one of them...And he was extremely fortunate to have returned. A survivor of two expeditions, both of them ending in disaster. His first venture had taken place somewhere between where they'd originally entered with Charadan and their present location. The details were elusive, as the land grew into itself -- formless, continuous, and terribly immense.

The horses thundered ahead, the men giving the animals their head as they wanted to leave the Lowlands behind. Dusk fell, and once again the mist reached upwards from the grass, threatening to consume everything within its grasp. The Ridgeline loomed before them, a chain of low-lying foothills varying in height and depth, some of them plunging upwards into small mountains, others broken into separate clusters splintered with rocky crevices, hidden paths, and all of them shrouded in dense forests. There were maps in Trencit which laid out the Ridgeline in rough measure, but no one had traveled its entirety. A no-man's land, just like Grammore, home to an abundance of wildlife, complete with dangerous predators; some of them native, others migrating from the Lowlands. They had narrowly avoided confrontation with a group of hunters while skirting the range earlier in their journey. And of course they had been attacked by the fierce ogre in a battle which claimed the lives of several warriors. Sarion thought back to that evening and its events, which had been the start of something far greater, and much deadlier...

    All three of them now rode abreast as the land opened wider in all directions, and they avoided the thicker regions of high grass and trees where something could wait unseen. Without warning, a large shape broke the horizon to their left, scores of yards away, emerging from the concealment of a small wooded depression, the bottom blanketed in swirling mist.

    Sarion gestured sharply but the others had already spotted the figure. A feeling of dread crept over him and he reined in his steed, moving behind a pair of gnarled oak trees, the two warriors following his example.

    "What in the name..." Chertron whispered, but Sarion grabbed his shoulder tightly, shaking his head.

    They watched in fascination as the figure flew up higher, and even at this distance they saw that it was some creature of unknown origin, ponderous and massive. Sarion fervently wished the thing had not seen them, and guessing from the direction of its movement, they were fortunate, as it drifted further from sight. He held his breath, listening carefully to the surrounding countryside. Night insects droned from the tall grass, several birds called from hidden branches, and a far-off howl pierced the valley, ending quickly.

The creature continued north until it was swallowed up by the twilight and mist, fading into oblivion.

Forlern laid a hand onto Sarion's arm. "Care to venture a guess at what *that* thing was?"

"I know not, but you can be sure it's nothing we want to meet." Sarion kept staring, unwilling to move until he was convinced the creature was not doubling around and coming back for them.

"A Lowlands predator, waiting for darkness to descend and offer cover." Chertron hefted his bow, ready for action if the thing reappeared.

"Perhaps the open fields provide a better environment for it as opposed to the more confining forest," Sarion replied, uncomfortable at the thought of winged beasts scouring the valley at night.

Forlern nodded. "More than likely. Although it's not the first flying creature we've seen..."

"Hmm. But this is nowhere close to the size of the Jurvech. I hope nothing *that* big ever comes this close to the border." Chertron tapped an arrow with one hand.

"I won't argue that point, my friend." Sarion looked around, angling his head until his gaze rested to the east, trying to gauge their distance and the amount of time needed to make the lower Ridgeline. Within the hour, he surmised. "Let's move ahead, keeping a wary eye to the sky as well. We'll reach the hills soon if we don't stop."

"Or find ourselves harried by demons..." Forlern added without humor.

"Move slower, more cautiously," Sarion said, his voice low. "If we are pursued, the trees will offer us some protection from that creature. Of course, there is no certainty we'll avoid other predators," he finished grimly, but with a crooked smirk.

"Such pleasant thoughts you have, Sarion." Forlern stared at him. "I think Grammore is growing on you. Or maybe that na-dryad left her mark upon your heart..."

Sarion scowled as he rode off, but Forlern managed a quiet laugh, Chertron echoing the fighter's mirth as they followed.

The valley passed beneath the muffled hooves of the Trencit war horses as they galloped through the evening. Sarion was taking whatever precautions he could, though their options were limited. A greater mass of darkness reared up before them, and at last they entered into the forests which acted as buffer against the approach to Grammore.

Leaving the valley and Lowlands behind them was comforting, to a degree, although quickly the trees took on a menacing appearance, and once again they felt the closer confines pressing against them, the landscape obscured by tree and bough, the mist a consistent trailer of ribbon-like wisps, the entirety combining into an atmosphere of imminent threat. And Sarion was tired, still nursing his wounds from the battle with the ogre, the forced march and ride aggravating the injuries. He

conferred briefly with Chertron, and they looked about
for a secure area to spend the night, as visibility was
poor. They lighted their lanterns, strapping them tightly
to the horses. The land was a maze of small hillocks,
dense thickets, and small watercourses. Sarion noticed a
gradual ascent, and knew they would certainly reach the
top of the Ridgeline by the next afternoon. He spotted a
small rise immediately to their left, and gestured to his
companions.

"This will have to do. The height will serve as an
advantage against any foe."

The other two silently nodded, weary
themselves, and unwilling to travel much further in the
darkness. They slowed the animals and picked their way
across a stream, more a tiny rivulet of clear water than
anything else. They halted, filling their pouches and
letting the horses graze in the thick clumps of grass
along the sides of the brook. The hillock sat a few dozen
yards before them, a cluster of tall ash trees circling the
base. Splashing water across their faces, they hurried
forward, soon dismounting and leading the animals onto
the higher ground. A few boulders lay scattered near the
top along one side, and here they camped, tying the
horses fast. A small depression ate into the ground and
they halted for the night, Chertron holding first watch.

The night was filled with a mixture of natural
sounds, birds calling, owls hooting somewhere nearby,
and the occasional howl in the distance, mournful and
eerie. Crickets and other night insects droned incessantly
from the deep grass, and Sarion felt some measure of
security in their position. He watched Chertron gazing
into the woods, his sword unsheathed, the great bow
ready at his side.

Sarion talked for a few moments with Forlern,
but both men soon quieted, the arms of sleep eager to
embrace them. The ground was soft and yielding, and

The Rooting of Evil

Sarion looked into the sky, glimpsing a few pinpricks of light far above. He felt a sudden surge of exhilaration, pondering the events which he'd faced since joining Charadan and the warriors.

A new feeling crept over him as he stared upwards into the immense arms of celestial infinity, a sensation both wonderful and terrible at the same time. He felt consumed by the magnitude of the plot in which he found himself embroiled, captured and swept away by circumstances beyond his control or desire to be a part of. He believed that he was now caught up in events unfolding within his homeland and beyond, a player (or pawn?) in the endless struggle of good against evil. At stake was the freedom, indeed the very existence, of Trencit and its people, imperiled to the east by the crafty Devlents, and to the west by a new enemy, known only by what Alayian had spoken, and she knew little. The Dark Mage, a sorcerer of hidden power and intent who might prove to be a much deadlier threat than the familiar rivals on the eastern front.

And what role would *he* play in this vast and treacherous battle? Sarion knew things were already in motion, and he had a strange sensation of euphoria mixed with uncertainty. He'd been sought out by the greatest champion of the land, General Charadan himself. The notion was profound, as he really thought about it for the first time. There had been no time to consider it earlier while they were still in Grammore, descending upon the dread fortress of Gorothagled. And in the aftermath of the disastrous battle with the ogre, and the fall of the courageous leader, everything had happened so swiftly; the intervention of Alayian and the hasty departure from the Lowlands.

Now he was alone with his thoughts for the first time with the revelation of Charadan's disguise, his seeking out of Sarion, and the General's true mission --

although how much of this was still hidden he could only wonder.

Sarion soon fell asleep beneath the stars, powerful visions claiming his subconscious; a whirlwind of events which had carried him far away from his peaceful farm and thrust him into the midst of an immense and unpredictable future.

Sarion awoke, disturbed from a deep slumber, and he stared upwards at Forlern's grim face.

His instincts snapping to immediate attention, he reached for his long knife and looked around for the source of danger, his eyes squinting in the gloom, the only light the smoky flickering from a pair of lanterns, and the gentle sprinkling of celestial brightness from the stars above.

Wordlessly, the warrior pointed to Chertron's unmoving form, who stood watch at the edge of the narrow crevice where they rested. The man was a silent statue, his bow drawn, an arrow notched, aimed at something in the forest canopy. The horses were awake and restless, nickering softly, stamping their feet in agitation.

"In the trees yonder," Forlern whispered. "He alerted me, although I slept not."

Sarion peered into the forest, searching for whatever lurked beyond their camp. His keen eyes scanned the night, and he instantly noticed the lack of sound. The woods pressed in around them, tall and forbidding, and the silence was ominous.

Then he spotted it...

Following Chertron's gaze, Sarion made out a

hulking form near the top of a broad hardwood tree of indeterminate species. It was a darker shadow among the others shadows, more suggestion than anything else. But the most striking thing about it were the eyes -- a tiny flicker of smoldering ash, unblinking, and watching them in return.

Sarion moved forward with Forlern at his side.

"It's the winged creature," Forlern whispered.

But Sarion already knew, silently cursing their luck.

The warrior continued, his voice low, but calm. The man refused to be intimidated by anything..."It had to have followed us from the valley. Spotted us when we left."

Sarion nodded, his own bow now in hand. If it wasn't for the glimmer of starlight and the first glimpse of the moon in weeks, they might well have been caught by surprise. He tried to reason the creature's motives, none of his ideas pleasant. Perhaps it was a Lowlands predator, tracking them throughout the evening and to their eventual resting place, waiting for the opportunity to attack. It could even be another of the normal creatures which hunted this particular region. Maybe this country was their natural habitat. But he shrugged away both notions, his mind instinctively gravitating to an even darker idea -- that it was an emissary of the Dark Mage, deliberately tracking them, even from the fortress of Gorothagled itself. Was this the pursuit that Alayian had spoken of? She hadn't named it, instead just confirming what her senses told her. Chills raced along his spine, but he dampened his trepidation, swiftly deciding on a course of action.

Chertron broke the silence. "It's been out there for several minutes, unmoving. I heard the flapping of wings -- something large -- and the horses were acting strange. Then I spotted it."

"It's measuring us, waiting. Maybe it's never seen men before," Forlern mused, shaking his head in wonder. "I don't like the look of this demon."

Sarion reached into his quiver, pulling out a pair of arrows. Forlern noticed his movement, nodding.

"You mean to strike it first. I agree." Forlern grabbed his own bow in response.

"I have an idea." Sarion pursed his lips. He crept towards one of the lanterns. "Here's my plan."

Chertron angled his neck to listen better, never taking his eyes off their quarry. Forlern held his own bow ready.

"These arrows are coated with oil. I'll shoot the tree, while you two aim directly for the creature. Whatever it does, we can't permit it to think us to be easy prey. We aren't...Try to hit the wings. Its body might be scaled, enough to deflect our arrows. If it attacks, shoot the eyes, maybe we can blind it. In ten seconds from now."

The warriors nodded, both of them prepared to act. Whatever the intent of the winged beast, they couldn't let it gain any advantage over them.

Sarion counted, then he lighted both arrows, firing them with amazing speed. The first one flew through the air, embedding itself in the trunk a few yards below the monster, the second one directly over its head. The creature moaned in rage and surprise, a low rumbling noise that echoed dully throughout the forest. Immediately the fighters let loose their own shafts, two of them striking the creature's right wing, one of them missing, and another smacking harmlessly off its neck.

Now it roared, the great wings flapping madly against the branches of the tree, sending scattered leaves and broken limbs in every direction. Sarion launched volley after volley towards the monster, which now flew straight towards their position. Chertron and Forlern held their ground, arrows shrieking invisibly through the night and finding purchase in the creature's wings. It continued forward, lumbering across the air, a ponderous and muscular behemoth which seemed unaffected by the shafts.

Forlern swore as the beast drew closer. "Shades! We can't stop it..."

Chertron backed away a step as the monster was only scant yards from where they stood. Sarion fired another pair of flaming arrows, one of them catching the creature's wing, puncturing deeply and remaining lighted. Frustrated, he drew his sword and crouched into a fighting stance, knowing that it was too late for anything except a direct confrontation.

The beast swooped down at Chertron, who neatly sidestepped and harried it with his blade. The creature showed surprising agility, lifting its wings and kicking out viciously with a taloned leg, the claws long and glistening in the night.

"Beware its reach!"

Sarion shouted a warning, but Chertron had anticipated a counter-strike, jumping quickly out of the way. The horses snorted wildly as the monster came near, and Sarion feared for their safety. He bounded up onto a flat slab of rock, trying to distract the predator. It hovered over Chertron for a moment, then glided straight for Sarion. Forlern swung his blade high in a wide arc, narrowly avoiding a kick downwards from the winged beast as he rolled onto the ground. Sarion waited until the monster was almost upon him, then made several quick slashes with his sword, as he knew the creature was too close to back away now. The monster saw its danger as Sarion held his ground, his weapon landing a powerful blow on the beast's right forearm. It howled in pain, the terrible eyes blazing with hatred. With a tremendous show of strength, it flapped its wings, the force nearly unfooting Sarion, surprised by the move. The creature then shot upwards and out of their reach, angling towards the thickest part of the surrounding forest and vanishing into the undergrowth.

The men remained standing for several long moments, catching their breath and hoping the fight was over. Sarion knelt down, scanning the woods for any sign of the monster, but the night was silent. "Anyone hurt?"

Forlern coughed. "No, it almost beheaded me though. That was too close. What a beast. I don't know whether we injured it that badly or not. You struck it a good blow, Sarion."

Sarion jumped down, joining his companions. "My arm feels numb from the impact. That creature's hide is like armor, but I think it won't likely shrug away that wound."

"Well done again, my friend." Forlern clapped him lightly on the back. "We landed a dozen arrows, but the wings didn't appear to be damaged from what I saw. Sarion drove it away."

Chertron nodded. "Let's hope it stays away for good, too. It knows we're not an easy meal now. It will think twice before attacking a Trencit warrior next time."

Forlern grinned wickedly in response, and the two men locked arms. Sarion managed a slight grin himself, although he didn't feel the least bit confident that the creature was gone for good. Not wanting to alarm his friends, he merely nodded and comforted the horses.

"Two of us can watch until dawn, which shouldn't be too long off. Although I doubt any of us will sleep after this skirmish..."

Sarion stared into the woods and up at the sky, wishing for the fertile soil of his farm once more, and the cheerful face of his nephew Edward. The world had passed Sarion by in recent years as he worked the land and raised the boy, helping and watching him grow into a young man. But doubt gnawed at Sarion's heart. There was so much violence besieging Trencit, turmoil and evil. Didn't he also have a duty to further serve the kingdom and its people? Charadan and the other warriors had fallen, leaving behind wives and children. And Sarion had lived in peace while others served, fighting to protect their homeland. At times he'd felt a great need to do more, return to the Western Watch, at least in some capacity. He couldn't deny that he would be able to contribute, based on his experiences and a former officer in the guard itself. And now he had been called back to service, surviving where others perished. Why did he feel such guilt? But he instantly knew the reason...It was the loss of his companions, especially Charadan, back in Grammore.

Sarion shook his head, still in disbelief. Gone. He sat there, leaning against a rock, feeling sharp pangs of pain as his recent wounds flared to angry life. The emotional wounds ran much deeper though. And he thought of Alayian's beautiful face...

He waited along with Forlern, both men quiet, watching against danger. But he remained vigilant, his hunter's instinct unfailing. The whole time Sarion wondered such grim thoughts, his heart heavy with loss and regret. He also wondered if they would last until sunrise without facing another attack.

The Rooting of Evil

Dawn eventually arrived in the Ridgeline, spreading gentle light beneath the pillared gray clouds which hovered ominously overhead. Storms threatened from the west, churning their way under cover of darkness from the Lowlands. The men ate a light breakfast and quickly made off, the horses trotting through the forest and into a landscape of dense trees, rocky outcroppings, and rugged hills. There was no sign of the creature which had attacked them the night before, and little was spoken about it, as if to ward against further misfortune. Although their spirits were lifted as they approached the borders of their own lands once again, they knew better than to let down their guard, even for an instant.

Sarion especially felt uneasy as he pondered the recent events, trying to make sense of them all. Without the shrewd counsel of Charadan, it was a far greater imposing task. He trusted his companions beyond question, but the general had been gifted in other ways. His vision was all-encompassing, and his knowledge of Trencit and its fragile position were known to only a select number of men within the king's personal confidence. Sarion realized that Charadan had told him more than what the warriors could possibly know. And now Sarion faced the same dilemma, not wishing to burden the others with some of his own fears which had been shared by the great General before him.

Was this to be his own fate? To take on a role which would require the same sacrifices that Charadan had made?

He turned his head as Chertron spoke. "It saddens me to see you in such a state, my friend. I know the thoughts which lay heavily upon your heart."

"Reading my mind?" Sarion managed a crooked smile.

"It's no difficult matter." Chertron stared skyward wistfully. "We all are plagued by ill winds, and its grip runs deep. Most of all for *you* though. Don't blame yourself for what happened. It was not within your power to decide. Charadan made his own choices. He was above the influence of anyone -- even the king, I believe. In the end, he did what he felt was best for Trencit, though it cost him his very life. He gave it willingly, and while defending his men."

Sarion was quiet, listening to the man's words, hearing the truth in them. His heart felt lightened by the support of his friend, but his chest ached from the bitterness and emptiness. "I wish I had known him longer...he was an incredible man." Sarion shook his head.

"The finest. But listen to me, Sarion." Chertron's voice turned grave, his eyes alive with conviction. "From what I've seen, *you* have much in common with him."

Touched by the man's emotion, Sarion smiled, feeling a tremendous sense of pride having this brave warrior at his side.

By early afternoon they were deep into the Ridgeline, scrub brush and dense trees surrounding them on every side, an ocean of wood and leaf. The ground continued to rise, and tall hills encircled them. At times they caught brief glimpses of the broken heights, and Sarion picked his way forward, attempting to bring them out of the vales and onto the higher reaches. Several times during the day they spooked herds of deer and stag from cover and spotted the tracks of many creatures, most of them smaller woodland animals, nothing out of the ordinary. But he *was* disturbed by a number of other prints, large and cloven. They were much too big for wolves, and they clearly indicated something unknown and certainly dangerous.

He pointed them out to his companions, and they listened in silence as he voiced his concern. None of them wanted to encounter anything else like from the previous night. Chertron muttered about his eagerness to ride within the boundaries of Trencit, but Sarion wasn't so sure. From his recent experience in Grammore, along with the general unrest and raids in the west the past year, he felt that the borderlands were no longer to be considered safe; if ever they truly were, for that matter. The shadow of the Lowlands stretched eastward as the Dark Mage flexed his power and corruption towards the powerful kingdom of Trencit.

Further dampening their spirits, a gentle rain began falling as the day wore on, fat droplets splattering on the leaves above their heads and sliding downwards from the staggered branches, insidiously finding them and leaving the men wet and uncomfortable. Donning their cloaks they rode on, speaking very little, their mood darkening as a heavy mist slowly rose from the moist earth, clinging to their limbs and tweaking the realm of doubt and possibility, as if Grammore was reaching out to them, exerting its control, a reminder that the Lowlands were a scant day's march behind.

The sun was again a forgotten memory, the brief glimpse which they'd enjoyed earlier now appearing as no more than a wicked tease, showing them a small glance of hope before the harsh land again reclaimed them as its own. A premature nightfall descended, enveloping the men in shadows and suggestion, the normal forest sounds now subdued, giving way to distant shrieks and clamors of newly-awakened predators. Sarion noticed an increase in the tempo and ferocity of the activity, and he feared that they now traveled within the midst of an extremely hostile region. The other men exchanged nervous glances, fingering their weapons as the horses walked forward in agitation, their nostrils steaming in the moisture-laden air.

"It's as if we're still in the Lowlands." Chertron mumbled to him, riding alongside, while Forlern remained a few paces behind the pair, barely visible in the diminished forest gloom. "Stay close." Chertron looked over his shoulder and Forlern nodded, his face shrouded within his cloak.

Sarion pulled out a lantern, quickly lighting it. He found them invaluable, as they remained lit despite the adverse weather, illuminating an area large enough for them to proceed even at night. He concentrated on everything around him; tracks, which were almost impossible to discern now, changes in the terrain, and especially the reactions of the horses. He also tried to gauge the cries echoing through the woods, and how far away they were. There was no indication of a suitable resting spot for the night, and he felt a growing reluctance to halt, desiring to push forward no matter how long it took them, and leave this dangerous country behind. He believed them fortunate not to have encountered anything, in fact.

Thinking this very thought, Sarion's blood froze as a huge figure appeared before them, a great shadow, formless and massive. At first he believed it to be a tree, but then it shifted as they approached, lumbering forward and appearing to be monstrously tall, its upper body hidden within the concealing boughs above.

"Beware!" Sarion shouted the warning as the creature reared close, a long appendage reaching towards them as the war horses kicked out in terror. His sword instantly in hand, Sarion ducked to avoid the blow, slashing upward and striking into the hideous arm, which was covered in moss and slime, brown and strangled with shoots of vines. The impact was deep, so deep in fact that he struggled to pull back before he became unbalanced. The creature's arm passed over him and headed directly for Chertron, the warrior's horse in great distress, neighing madly.

Forlern shouted, and events happened too quickly for them to react, Sarion still recovering himself. There was a dull smack as Chertron and his steed both went down as the behemoth struck, sending horse and rider hard to the ground. Stunned by the ferocious attack, Forlern and Sarion watched helplessly for a moment as the creature moved its bulk forward, a living mass of hairy flesh, mold and soil.

"Grab him!"

Sarion flung himself from his own horse, engaging the creature in an attempt to distract it from the fallen warrior. Forlern jumped down, rushing to the fighter's aid, and both men were appalled as the monster ignored Chertron and instead picked up the horse with one enormous hand, which lacked either digits or a distinct shape; a massive, pulpy knot of power. The animal was either unconscious or already dead as it was lifted up, vanishing somewhere overhead. They grabbed Chertron as the creature was focused elsewhere, and they quickly placed him on Forlern's horse, Sarion running back and chasing down his own steed before it disappeared.

They retreated to their right, bypassing the dreadful beast, and they heard a loud sucking noise from high above. Sarion knew the horse was gone and that the creature might still be hungry.

They plunged into the forest, holding tightly to

their steeds and thinking only to put as much distance as possible between themselves and the terrible beast, hoping desperately that they weren't carrying another victim from battle.

The men swept through the dark forest for several minutes, Chertron propped up before Forlern's watchful eyes. Sarion looked over to them at times, remaining attentive to any sounds of pursuit, from the creature or anything else which threatened. When he believed them to be at a safe distance from their adversary, he halted, leaning towards Forlern's grim form.

"He's conscious; I heard him breathing when we escaped."

Forlern gently examined Chertron, whose head was bowed, his eyes closed. Sarion gestured to the ground, and they carefully lifted him from the animal, placing him on a shallow pile of leaves. Nodding to himself, Sarion rummaged in his pocket, pulling out a packet of herbs. He crumbled them in his palm, then into a small drinking container. Whispering softly into the warrior's ear, Chertron's eyes fluttered for a moment, and he moaned. Sarion put the container to the man's lips, and he drank deeply, sighing, then tilted his head backwards. Sarion gazed into his face, listening to his breathing.

"A nasty blow to the head, but I think he'll be all right."

Forlern nodded in relief, scanning the trees around them for any sign of danger.

Sarion looked up at his companion. "I fear to

move him about to any extent. He needs rest, but our situation is hazardous -- to wait out the night, or search for a more secure location. Our options are poor."

"Do you think he'll recover by tomorrow?" Forlern's face lacked expression, his voice low and toneless.

"I'm not certain, but I'm hopeful. He's incredibly durable...like most Trencit fighters, of course."

Sarion felt Chertron's brow, and placed his hand on the warrior's chest. Satisfied, he spoke to Forlern again. "We'll wait a bit, and then move off until we find somewhere more suitable to spend the night. This place is too exposed from every side."

The fighter nodded. "What in blazes was that creature back there? It came upon us without warning."

Sarion considered. "I'm not sure, but it may have been an elemental of some kind."

Forlern's eyes widened in surprise. "An elemental? I've read about such things, but never dreamed they existed..."

"Nor I. Seems that we've dispelled a great number of myths on our venture into the westland." Sarion turned his head, hearing something far off, then decided it posed no immediate threat.

"It's as if we never left Grammore. Curse this country and all its foul beasts." Forlern sighed deeply, testing his bow.

"And what's even more frightening," Sarion added, "is the fact that such creatures roam the Ridgeline, possibly in large numbers. When we first entered, we encountered the Killworm. And then the unknown predators hunting the vale while we passed across the higher terrain. I've tried to gain the upper reaches, but there's no direct path. We can only move forward until the opportunity rises for a safer trail. The lower region is home to a much greater diversity of species. More dangerous as well..."

"I wonder if that thing will pursue us further?" Forlern now paced back and forth, the lanterns casting eerie shadows on his cloaked form. The rain had lessened, but remained a persistent and unwelcome companion.

"Perhaps not." Sarion continued to watch Chertron, whose eyes opened several times, and once he gestured weakly with one hand. "You'll be all right, my friend. You received a strong blow to your head, although the memory might be unclear."

Chertron mumbled, then closed his eyes.

Sarion turned to Forlern. "I think he'll come out well and whole, but such injuries can result in grievous circumstance -- one may fall into a deep sleep and never awaken. I'm making sure this doesn't happen."

He patted Chertron's arm, and it was obvious that the warrior understood his concern, opening one eye, attempting a weak smile. "Kick me if I do..."

"I'll pinch you first, then pour cold water on your face." Sarion smiled broadly. "We need to move soon. I'll put you before Forlern again."

"The beast?" Chertron coughed, his face lined with pain.

"I think it was a chance meeting."

They all started as a sharp cry echoed through the woods, coming from the region they had left.

"Seems something else wasn't so fortunate..." Forlern scowled, and Sarion helped Chertron to his feet, all of them eager to depart.

The Rooting of Evil

They rode off into the woods once more, moving from one point of danger into more of the unknown. Within a short time they came across a wide stream, gnarled trees ringing the low banks. The water was shallow, the bed lined with gravel and thousands of smooth round pebbles. The fog lifted somewhat in this area, and they gazed across the slow-moving waters, spotting a narrow island upstream from where they waited. A few strangled trees covered it on either side, and they hurried towards it, carefully restraining their steeds, keeping the splashing to a minimum. They kicked out a herd of stag, the creatures galloping off in surprise. In a few moments they reached the island, finding it wide enough for the animals while offering some cover from unfriendly eyes.

Sarion considered it a stroke of luck, as the water would confuse their scent from any wandering predators. When they were properly settled, he attended to Chertron, convinced that the warrior was in no immediate threat from his injury. He made sure that he stayed awake for the next few hours though, taking no chance. Forlern slept like the dead, the young fighter finally collapsing onto the spongy turf and quickly going to sleep. Sarion watched for signs of trouble, sharing some water with Chertron.

"You have quite a lump on the side of your head, but it seems you have a thick skull."

"Why Sarion, that almost sounds like an insult." Chertron chuckled, grimacing at the effort. "Oh...that hurt. Well, I'll miss my steed. It was a reliable beast, that horse."

"The Trencit animals are the finest in all the known lands." Sarion gazed dreamily across the stream, feeling a genuine sense of security on the little island, the first such feeling he'd experienced in a while, at least since Alayian had left. Alayian...

"So what think you? Will we pass through the Ridgeline tomorrow?" Chertron looked around, trying to gauge the direction of his homeland.

"We should, if all goes well. We wandered further north from where we entered. If we continue northward, the mountains become higher and the land much harder to negotiate. More wilderness and danger..." Sarion shook his head, wondering what the country was like in that region. Northern Grammore, where less was known than even the southern reaches. He continued. "Once we cross the hills, we're a few days ride from the lands of Gwerath. Lord Pralicon holds a wide sweep of western country as you know, and his stronghold is well defended. A formidable power of Trencit, to say the least, although his temperament is quite unpredictable from what I've heard."

He had traveled across the Northern Province on several different occasions, and it was home to many outlying border villages, the native country of a people who were staunch and not easily frightened. But certainly the unrest in the west had affected them also, reaching tenaciously towards their settlements.

"When we first set out on the venture, Captain Grundel..." Chertron paused. "Ah well, it's hard to think of him otherwise. Even now, I don't believe it."

"I know..."

They both fell silent for a moment, reflecting on the courageous leader, now at final rest in the magnificent valley of Rivening Well.

"Anyway, General Charadan had told us about the situation in the borderlands. Lord Pralicon sent out scouting parties to roam the outlying areas, coordinating them with the Western Watch. As you well know, many of his people serve in that force."

"Worthy fighters, proud and skilled in weaponry." Sarion had fought alongside many of them in his tenure with the guard, and he held them in a high degree of respect.

"Of course, with the war in the east, King Gregor has squeezed each of the Lords for as many fighters as he deemed necessary to reinforce the Royal Armies, which have been sorely beleaguered as of late."

"Indeed." Sarion yawned, knowing he needed to wake Forlern soon, or else he would be dangerously weary for the trek ahead. And he couldn't afford that...

Chertron continued, obviously feeling better as the night wore on. "Well, there has been much debate in Council, and several of the Lords have resisted sending any more of their own fighters. Lord Pralicon not the least. This all makes sense now, as he feels threatened by circumstances in the west."

"I would think so. His concern is justified."

"Right. But when word of our expedition spreads, there'll be chaos in the Council, and a great debate will ensue. Since there is a definite cause for worry, with the Dark Mage rising to power, Pralicon will refuse to send any more men. And his forces are substantial. King Gregor has been relying on the outer Houses to back up the main army. It's not a good situation facing the kingdom. You've been out of the Watch for a while, so perhaps you don't realize the extent of confrontation brimming around the Council."

Sarion raised an eyebrow. He *had* been out of touch for a long time, sequestered on his farm, having little contact with the inner workings of the central kingdom. Had things really become that bad?

Chertron shifted towards him. "Sarion, with the loss of Charadan, you can't begin to understand the turmoil which will soon unfold. He held the High Council together, brought rivals to bay on many occasions. King Gregor named him his Champion for countless reasons, not the least his ability to demand respect from his own council members. Not everyone agreed with Charadan's views, but I'll tell you this...they all respected him, and many of them feared to cross him."

Sarion was silent, considering the man's words. The politics of Trencit were constantly changing, many houses striving to enforce their individual spheres of influence on a monarch who tended to be very deliberate and restrained with his Lords. Sometimes to his own undoing...

"It gets even worse yet."

Sarion stared hard at Chertron, seeing genuine pain in the man's eyes. Was it that bad? What could it be?

Chertron shifted, making himself more comfortable. The stream bubbled on either side of them, and Sarion absorbed his surroundings. The night air felt brisk and clean, filled with the subtle aroma of the woodlands -- the biting smell of pine needles, the earthiness of damp soil, and a hint of flowering shrubs, delicate and aloof. He waited for his companion to speak, feeling an involuntary tightness of his muscles in anticipation of the revelation to come.

"Rumors."

Chertron fidgeted as he tried to find the right words.

"Black whispers within certain ranks. Foul tidings, especially beneath the walls of Daregil Keep, which has always been the ancestral citadel for the rulers of Trencit. And I don't know for certain if any of these are true, mind you. But aye, it's an evil thing to hear." His voice drifted lower, and Sarion was alarmed by his friend's composure.

"Assassination attempts against Charadan..."

Surprised, Sarion exhaled sharply. "What?"

"Yes, rumors of such have abounded the past

several months."

"Are you talking about forces outside of Trencit?" Sarion was chilled by the implications. "But we're at war, and this isn't difficult to believe."

"No, you misunderstand me and what I've just told you. These were from *inside* the kingdom..." Chertron held him tightly in his gaze.

Sarion whistled softly. "I've been far removed on my farmlands. I never suspected such treachery from within our own ranks. But why? And for that matter, who?"

The warrior shook his head. "No one knows, my friend. And now you understand the turmoil we'll be returning to...General Charadan has fallen. The king will be greatly affected. The Royal Armies have lost their leader, the High Council their strongest voice and most respected member. The entire kingdom will be shaken to its very roots. But worse yet, there are those who will receive this news with great pleasure. And we don't know who they are..."

Both men sat there in silence. Sarion suddenly felt wide awake, tense, his weariness quickly forgotten. There was so much going on within the Kingdom of Trencit, and the more he heard, the worse everything sounded. Even while in the Western Watch, he was primarily isolated from the inner workings of Trencit, focused on the vigilance needed to keep the borderlands safe from marauders, most especially the Glefins, which at one time had posed a major threat. And now -- if their former captive were to be believed -- the creatures were an extinct species. There was too much for him to consume all at once. He needed to think things through very carefully, and be extremely cautious as they returned to Trencit and eventually to Daregil Keep. Sarion nodded to himself. Discretion was necessary...

"Word of Charadan's fall must remain a secret

until we reach King Gregor." It was an easy decision, and he looked over at Chertron for his reaction.

But the warrior only agreed. "You're right, my friend. A wise approach. We'll let the King deal with the repercussions on his own terms, not on anyone else's."

The conversation ended with that remark, and Sarion roused Forlern a few hours before dawn, finally succumbing to sleep himself and the black nightmare wings which eagerly awaited him.

The dawn greeted them with a promise of fresh rain to come, and they prepared to leave, filling their water pouches and cleaning themselves in the cold stream. Morning birds sang cheerfully from the surrounding foliage, but contrasted with the gloom overhead. Sarion decided on a general direction which would take them to higher ground, and hopefully a straight passage through the Ridgeline. None of them wished to spend another night in the forsaken no-man's land.

They crossed the stream once more, this time reaching the far banks, and continued through the forest, picking their way across an increasingly rocky terrain, towering trees rising above them, and clusters of large boulders strewn all about. The air grew cooler, but not unpleasant, a gentle breeze ruffling their hair and rustling fallen leaves. The mist lifted away and the sky was grey, but clear enough to offer them plenty of light, something they had lived without for a span of long days.

The durable Chertron was recovering remarkably from his injuries to the surprise of his companions, although he required frequent rest. Forced to ride along with Forlern, their position was now even more precarious, lacking the third horse. It was a grievous loss, but they all realized it could have been far worse. The image of the terrible and strange creature was yet vivid in Sarion's eyes, and the thought of glimpsing one of the legendary elementals -- and getting away unscathed -- was certainly not lost to him.

Morning had come and passed, and the companions found themselves ascending a gradual rise, the trees lessening somewhat, but the ground becoming looser, covered by crumbling rocks and jagged outcroppings. By early afternoon they had reached well above the valley floor, and Sarion was satisfied by the distance they had traveled within the past few hours. He called for a quick halt and they dismounted before a narrow crevice, where a pool of water flowed quietly at their feet, emerging from the living rock of the mountain itself.

Sarion looked back down the way they had come, finding an opening in the forest canopy, and he gazed in wonder across the shrouded lands now far behind them -- the treacherous country of Grammore, cloaked within perpetual mist and uncertainty. He thought back on the events of the past few weeks, events which had managed to uproot the very foundations of his existence, changing his life in a profound manner, one which was steeped in hazy circumstances beyond his capability to foresee and perhaps control.

The Grammore Lowlands.

The name itself was enough to invite terror, stir up nightmares from the deepest corridors of one's mind and cause the bravest of warriors to give pause. That treacherous land had brought about the fall of Trencit's greatest leader and the majority of his hand-picked group of fighters, leaving them victims to the evil predators which inhabited the harsh climate, monsters of terrible power and malicious intent. Remaining in the Lowlands was also the incredible na-dryad Alayian, and Sarion couldn't deny the strong emotions which ran through his blood as his thoughts drifted towards the vision of her alluring face, the eyes of emerald ice.

The journey had indeed left him a changed man.

His skills had been called upon, and he had done his best to rise to the task, acting as guide to Charadan on a dangerous quest. Confronting the ogre on Hawker Peak, they had fought a terrible battle which had resulted in a bitter stalemate. But Charadan had remained undaunted, deciding to pursue their quarry into the horrors of Grammore, where danger lived and breathed in wood, water, and earth. A desperate mission into madness and the unknown. In the end, Charadan had died, along with some of Trencit's finest warriors.

And Sarion kept asking himself -- had it all been worth it?

The disastrous venture into the ancient citadel of Gorothagled, which had proven to be nothing more than a trap set for them by the mysterious Dark Mage. They were unwitting pawns in a game much larger than any they could have realized. But Charadan had felt compelled by honor and the deep love of his homeland to seek out the solutions to lingering questions which eluded him and the king. Ones which demanded answers, and sacrifice.

Looking down upon the dreaded Lowlands, Sarion was engulfed in a vortex of emotion. Sadness, bitterness, anger, loss.

And longing...

His throat felt parched, and he swallowed heavily.

It was a powerful moment for Sarion as he stood there, feeling incredibly insignificant and yet immensely important at the same time. Polarizing emotions, enough to cause him to search within his very heart and soul. Harsh regret because of his failure to save Charadan and the other warriors. And despite Chertron's words of comfort, the wound was fresh and painful. Sarion was a warrior, there was no doubt. And as such, he understood the losses while in the field. The tragic venture into Grammore had cost him dearly...but he also looked at his own role with a new perspective. His actions, in many ways, were central in a vast ring of events, having a substantial effect in the current whirlwind of uncertainty which threatened the very destruction of Trencit. His determination was so great that his skin tingled, the excitement coursing through his veins. He tasted the winds of his own destiny, and felt a disturbing sense of foreboding for what his part would be in the future of the kingdom.

Chills ran along his skin as he was struck by a vision of both hope and doom in the same breath, all held within the immense and terrible hand of fate, all humanity subject to its cruel and unfathomable manipulations. There was much that needed to be done, and he keenly felt the weight upon his shoulders, knowing that Charadan had placed far more on him than he realized. He recalled the words of the courageous General, uttered with his last gasp of air in the dark citadel of Gorothagled.

"Don't forget the king. Have faith in yourself, Sarion. You're the one, save us."

Sarion bowed his head. How could he live up to such an impossible appeal? He was only one man...and yet, how could he deny the brave Charadan at his death? Simply, he couldn't. His honor would not permit him. He would attempt his very best, whether it cost him life or limb. Too many men had already paid the ultimate sacrifice, and many more would follow suit in the weeks and months ahead. But the responsibility...

Grammore beckoned him, teased and tormented him with its immense power and savagery, quiet majesty, ancient knowledge, and stunning beauty. So much of his own fate was concealed within, and he knew with terrible certainty that the Lowlands held the key to the events which would transpire, involving Trencit, King Gregor, the Dark Mage...and himself.

"Sarion, anything wrong?"

He turned, shaking his head gently as Forlern called to him. "No, lost in thought. Trying to see if Grammore is willing to give up any of its secrets, even from this distance."

Forlern nodded in understanding. "You need say no more, my friend. A spectacular sight." He approached, standing next to Sarion. "I feel it too. And I think I'll always carry a part of the Lowlands with me, like a thorn embedded near my heart. We've all lost a part of ourselves in Grammore. We've buried our own back there, and I feel empty inside, incomplete." He paused.

Sarion matched the warrior's sad look with his own fierce gaze. "But we'll prevail, Forlern. It's the only thing we know how to do -- it's *who* we are." He pointed to Chertron, who lay back against a wall of rock, splashing the clean mountain water across his face.

They watched their companion in silence.

Sarion placed a hand on Forlern's shoulder, gripping the man tightly. "We need to stick together when we return to our homelands. Things are not always what they seem, people are not always whom they appear to be."

Forlern frowned thoughtfully. "Dangerous times."

"Together," Sarion repeated. "I don't want to separate. Maybe the king can place us in the same unit.

The Rooting of Evil

Perhaps we can persuade him that we can best serve Trencit as a team."

The fighter laughed. "My thoughts exactly. I have the distinct feeling that he'll agree with you, Sarion. About a great many things..."

"Let's hope." He sighed. "We're passing through the main hills, and we should come out entirely before another day arrives. I'm anxious to put this venture behind me, and look to the east. A great storm is brewing, but we'll enter it with our eyes open."

"And our swords ready..." Forlern added.

"Indeed." There was a sparkle in Sarion's eye as he spoke.

They returned to Chertron, both men striding across the rocks with determination in their step.

They pressed on that afternoon, the sun a welcome old friend hovering in the sky above the Ridgeline, the warmth of its rays invigorating them as they moved onward. Small woodland animals scurried before their coming, but they were natural creatures, living in the harbor of the protective forest. The way was difficult at times as they began to ascend onto the higher terrain which would leave them on the edge of the border regions once again. The area was a mix of hardwoods and pines, tall ashes rising above them, the lofty boughs scratching against the rock walls to either side in a way that made them appear desperate for more open air. Sarion led them into a narrow canyon between the endless chain of hills, and was pleased with their progress. They passed through the greater part of the vast landmark of the Ridgeline and would soon be entirely free of it. They never paused, instead wishing only to leave the region finally behind them.

It was time for them to return to their own country at last.

Chertron had recovered nicely from his injury, resuming his usual demeanor of alertness and caution. The day was growing late when they entered a clearing and the ground dropped noticeably. Looking back, the hills were suddenly behind them now, towering majestically from the protective tree tops.

Sarion nodded in relief, calling for a brief halt. He blinked his eyes, taking in the scenery around him, admiring the quiet splendor of the borderlands. The air was clear and clean above their weary heads, washed in pink and a faded red, as the fiery orange of the late afternoon sun sank beneath the western hills behind them. The scents of the surrounding forest were numerous and fresh, the sounds normal and peaceful. With fortune on their side, perhaps the immediate danger of the disastrous quest had drawn to a subdued conclusion.

"We've come quite a ways, but I can say we're safely through the Ridgeline at last." Sarion dropped to the ground, his boots making small indentations in the moist earth.

Chertron dismounted, followed by an exuberant Forlern.

"Shades, I thought there was no end to that wilderness!" The younger fighter slapped his gloves and stretched.

"That's not to say we're out of any danger, of course." Sarion adjusted his pack, rummaging through the contents. "The borderlands have been anything *but* safe, especially in recent times. Marauders, wandering creatures from the Lowlands..."

"...ogres," added Chertron.

The Rooting of Evil

"Let's hope we never meet up with any of those foul monsters again," Forlern finished. "If this Dark Mage has such demons in his service, he must indeed be a powerful sorcerer. Black magic, wielded against Trencit."

"Well, he certainly is that for sure." Chertron rubbed his forehead. "I don't know -- and would rather not care to know -- what else is under his sway. I wonder if King Gregor has ever heard of this necromancer before."

Sarion turned towards him, his face thoughtful. "Hmm, I think perhaps not. Charadan gave no indication in his notes of such. It's my belief that he is entirely unknown to Trencit and her people." Sarion wondered as to the origin of the mysterious figure. Alayian had spoken of the Dark Mage, declaring his power to be the force behind the unrest in Grammore and the borderlands, but she seemed to know very little else, and that greatly disturbed him...

The men tied the pair of horses, and unpacked a few of their belongings. Sarion scoured the area for edible roots and berries, looking to replenish their dwindling supply. They had not been in any danger of running out, as the warriors all carried ample food, smoked and tightly packed in field rations. Sarion's skill as tracker and huntsman assured the company that food would always be found, whether it grew under the earth, fell from bush or tree, or lurked in a shallow pool of water. The borderlands of Trencit were composed vastly of wilderness, but the territory held a tremendous amount of game and fruit-bearing trees. And in addition to this natural bounty, they would soon come across regions where hunting lodges, outposts, and even small villages could be found. No, they would certainly not starve. At times he'd been uncertain of the vegetation in Grammore, but within the Lowlands were rooted an incredible array of non-poisonous plant life, and they had made do, supplementing their own supplies.

He came across a blueberry bush, and filled one of his bags, sampling a handful for himself. The others were resting, engaged in light conversation a few dozen yards away when he stiffened, hearing a sound in the distance coming from the east but obscured by the forest which grew thicker in that direction. His hand immediately snapped towards his sword, and he eased himself into a fighter's crouch, trying to understand the source of disturbance. Chancing a quick glance back to his friends, they seemed oblivious to whatever approached. Sarion whistled sharply, alerting them as he pointed ahead. They took notice, gathering their supplies and moving towards the horses with weapons in hand. Sarion's signal was all they needed to know that something was afoot, potentially dangerous.

He now moved forward, picking a spot which provided cover behind a fallen tree, its bark carpeted in thick moss. The branches were a tangled mess, but he found a protected area where he could aim his arrow and remain concealed from prying eyes. Chertron and Forlern led the horses into the closest section of woods, muffling them and making their way towards Sarion, but he waved them back with a curt sweep of his hand. The noise grew louder, and he readily identified the source.

Horses, shuffling through the brush...

He chewed thoughtfully at his lip, excited but cautious. Men.

From the sound of it, a sizable company was picking its way through the forest and towards the clearing. Since they approached from the east, Sarion believed they were from Trencit, but he was taking no chances. He had seen too many things the past few weeks to let down his guard, especially this close to the Ridgeline and Grammore. They were too deep into the wilderness to encounter a hunting party, and his natural instincts shouted out a warning to his inner ear.

Sarion waited.

For a minute. And another.

His keen ears missed nothing. The snapping of twigs, branches being slapped. A cough. Soon he heard the snorting of horses, snatches of conversation. He made out several words, but no complete sentences. The voices were low, but measured and confident.

Within moments a pair of riders broke through the undergrowth, wearing cloaks of forest green, light helms upon their heads.

Sarion sighed wearily, and a smile of relief creased his face.

They were warriors of Trencit.

From Trencit!

Sarion thought he would never again lay eyes upon his own countrymen, but now they swarmed into the clearing, a large group of armored fighters, rugged and serious of expression. Great bows of ash were strapped upon their backs, and the animals were darker than the beasts which Charadan's party had rode into the Lowlands. Sarion wondered why a hunting unit of this size would even be this deep in the borderlands, unless something were amiss. Perhaps the King had ordered them into the field, receiving the message from some of the warriors Charadan had sent back to Nighton after their initial battle with the ogre.

Still remaining concealed, Sarion wished to take in the full measure of this group before revealing himself. He counted over twenty men, and by the look of them they were in scouting mode, but had yet to see the hidden fighters. But they bore no insignia identifying them as being members of the Western Watch. Surprised, Sarion recognized the crescent moon above high ramparts, the mark of the House of Truthilon, Lord Pralicon. Had they come this far north from their excursion into the Lowlands? Gwerath Keep was many miles away, east and north, by Sarion's reckoning. Strange indeed...

"Hail, warriors of Trencit!"

Sarion leaped from his place of concealment, springing above the massive fallen tree and holding his hands skyward in the Trencit gesture of greeting. The hunting party was startled, most of them having reached the middle of the clearing already. Weapons were raised and a few shouts rang out, but Sarion remained standing there, lowering his arms and folding them across his chest.

Chertron and Forlern also emerged from cover and were walking the horses over to join their companion. The hunters formed a protective semi-circle, and bows were held ready, but none of them were aimed. Two men rode forward towards Sarion.

"Wanderers in the borderlands? What business have you so close to the Ridgeline?" The lead man challenged Sarion, one eye covered by a patch, his face crisscrossed by scars, a thin beard covering his chin.

"The king's business," Sarion replied. The other horseman approached, and his dark eyes narrowed at Sarion's words. He looked to be close to Sarion's age, lightly armored and his face shaven, long, raven black hair cascading across his shoulders. A long sword was fastened at his waist, but his hands rested on the pommel of his saddle, away from any weapons.

Sarion continued. "My friends and I have journeyed far on a perilous mission." He gestured behind him as Chertron and Forlern came near, nodding cautiously to the wary horsemen. "These fighters were hand-picked, chosen to patrol the western borders under the command of Captain Grundel of the Homeguard."

The two hunters exchanged a quick glance, and the first man nodded. "Then you are the ones we seek. Word came from the king that a party of warriors had set out weeks ago searching for marauders, and their need might be great. We were ordered to seek them out and offer assistance as necessary. But we were also told you would most likely be found much farther south."

Chertron stepped forward. "We've been assailed and pursued for long days and nights. This morning we breached the Ridgeline, making our way west."

"My name is Virgil, Third Captain of House Gwerath, and Protector of the Westland. This is my second, Raymark."

The man with long hair announced himself, and Forlern inclined his head, a look of recognition briefly visible on his face. "Forlern of the Homeguard. This is Chertron, tracksman and warrior in the Hybril Legion. Sarion was also chosen for our group, sought out by Captain Grundel. He's a former captain of the Western Watch."

The northerners stared at Sarion. Raymark spoke, leaning low on his horse, which nickered impatiently. "You are known to us, Sarion. But what of the others? And your captain? Twelve warriors set out, although word from Nighton came that several were injured."

"We are all that is left," Sarion replied evenly. "The others have fallen."

"What?" Raymark asked in surprise. "The Captain of the Homeguard as well?"

"We've been beset by great evil and dire circumstance for many treacherous days. The tale is

long, and we have suffered recent injuries, and battle."
Sarion gazed up at the men, gauging their reaction.
Raymark's face was clouded, but Virgil looked
impassive.

"And why are you so far south?" Chertron
questioned them. "This is beyond the limits of your
normal patrols, is it not?"

Raymark nodded. "We've been requested to send
out as many hunting parties as possible, scouring the
land with all available fighters while the men of the
Watch have pushed further to the south and west. Our
meeting here is more by chance, than anything. We
intended to make a sweep along the neck of the
Ridgeline, and decided to continue this way. Seems you
were fortunate that we did."

Sarion wondered to himself about that remark.
They appeared to him as shrewd men, perhaps with
motives of their own. Curiosity? He had to be very
careful, and give away only enough to ease their
concern.

"And you've encountered nothing unusual in
your travels?" Forlern questioned them with a hint of
skepticism in his voice.

Raymark angled his head towards him. "No.
Rumors and whispers from trappers and villagers."

"Then *you* are fortunate indeed. The borderlands
are extremely dangerous these days." Forlern shook his
head, measuring the newcomers.

"Maybe on the other side of the Ridgeline, but
we've seen nothing to cause us any concern."

"Indeed that may be true, but you nearly passed
Sarion here as he remained hidden." Chertron chuckled,
and Raymark's face darkened.

"I wouldn't be so easily amused, my friend. Our
fighting skill is well-known throughout Trencit. We fear
nothing -- within our borders or beyond."

The Rooting of Evil

Sarion listened to the careful exchange, staring up at Virgil, whose face was expressionless. Sarion grew impatient, seeing no purpose for the conversation to continue -- especially knowing Forlern's quick temper. Even now, the younger man looked ready to exhale something harsh in return, and Sarion quickly interrupted before he could speak.

"We are glad to have met up with your men. Our need is urgent, and we must report directly and immediately to King Gregor. Any help you can offer is greatly appreciated, and Chertron is without a horse." Sarion knew these men were proud and independent, and he was unwilling to exert the royal orders too strongly on the northerners.

Virgil inclined his head. "You will receive our aid of course. I would hear more of your mission, and the man leading it. Your name is known among us, Sarion. I heard you left the Western Watch a few years back and never rejoined."

His words were directed entirely at Sarion, and both Forlern and Chertron remained silent, letting their companion take charge of the negotiation.

"I did indeed, thinking my part was done. Times change, unfortunately, and not always for the better."

Virgil finished the conversation, giving a quick hand signal to one of his men. "Let's be off, then. We'll head east, and offer our protection until we've reached deeper into our homelands. Sarion, ride with me if you will."

Sarion nodded, and his companions went back for their belongings, watched silently by Raymark and his warriors. After several moments, the men were mounted, and Chertron was offered a horse of his own. The gesture was accepted graciously, and the group rode off towards the east as the sun fell behind the hills of the Ridgeline, washing the evening sky in a rage of purple

and orange, a wondrous tapestry of color which defied
the violence and evil which lay slumbering in the nearby
Lowlands.

The men rode until night descended, darkness
blanketing the landscape in a sheet of dim light cast by a
bloated moon and an infinite legion of stars, a celestial
veil of tiny pinpricks dotting the heavens far above their
heads. A suitable spot was chosen for camp, and several
of Virgil's fighters encircled the main body of men, alert
to anything which might approach. A trio of fires were
set ablaze, and the overall atmosphere was one of
cautious acceptance, as warriors from both sides
perceived the other as fellow countrymen, despite the
difference in rank and background.

Virgil prodded Sarion with careful questions
concerning their mission, and he answered in a polite
tone, if rather vaguely at times. Sarion understood the
game being played, and knew that Virgil was not one to
be easily fooled.

As they settled and broke out some smoked
meat, he approached the matter directly. "Sarion, it's
obvious there's much you are not telling me here. I hope
you don't consider me to be of loose tongue, or ill
repute."

Sarion hesitated, considering his words carefully.
He didn't wish to antagonize the man, but he refused to
let all the details be known.

"Neither. There are certain facts which I've been
held to secrecy on, from direct order coming from King
Gregor himself."

This wasn't far from the truth, as Charadan was

foremost in the king's confidence. By confiding in Sarion, there had been an understanding that others could not be allowed to hear the full accounting of their quest, and the motives behind it. And there could be no conveying the fall of the King's Champion at this point. That would be a terrible mistake.

"Understood. So this Captain Grundel was under direct command from the king. And who was second in command?"

Sarion stared at Virgil, his gaze unwavering. Would he know of Rundin? Was that even his real name? He decided to tell that much at least.

"Rundin, although I never learned his true ranking. A member of the King's Guard, I'm sure."

"Hmm, never heard of him either. I know some of the king's elite, and their numbers are not great. Of course, the distance plays a role. I don't travel to the capital often."

"Don't care for Trencit politics?" It was Sarion's turn to ask questions.

Virgil raised one eyebrow, a crooked smile crossing his face, but Sarion failed to read the man's intent. Virgil continued. "There is much to do within my own land, of course, mostly the drudgery of routine, and my cousin keeps me constantly occupied."

Sarion nodded. "Lord Pralicon maintains powerful holdings among the Lords of Trencit, and his ancestry predates many of the lesser houses. How is he these days?"

"Quite well. He takes to the hunt much of the time, as there exists little in his own court which can keep his attention. He makes appearances in Daregil Keep as well, although less frequently than in the past."

Sarion kept his voice even, probing further. "And he has no concern for the unrest in the borderlands?"

Virgil's face was impassive. "Let's just say

there's little of anything which seems to really worry him. His confidence is supreme, and he's well aware of the folklore and legends which are rooted within the beliefs of superstitious people."

Sarion shook his head in disagreement, and wondered about what Chertron had spoken of earlier -- Pralicon's refusal to commit more of his own men to the wars in the east. Maybe a deeper game was being played by the powerful Lord..."Your lands are not far from the shadow of Grammore. There are horrors living inside which surpass the imagination. I've entered twice, and although I escaped without major injury, I'll never be the same man."

"I don't doubt your words. The Lowlands have long been a haven for things which live beyond our understanding. Pralicon's concerns are of men and steel though, things which walk beneath the light of day. He's very pragmatic, and is confused by the king's uneasiness. Surely your tale will reveal some truth of the matter?"

Sarion paused, staring around the camp. He watched as several patrols shifted in the shadows, among them Chertron's tall form. The three companions had agreed that one of them remain alert at all times, offering to share the guard. Raymark had seemed offended at first, but then Virgil had only laughed quietly, giving his aquiesance.

Folding his arms, Sarion leaned backwards and rested against an old stump, gazing into the brilliant night sky overhead and thinking of Edward. Word had to be taken to his nephew that he had returned and was on an urgent mission to the king himself. Edward and the others would be elated, but disappointed that he still wouldn't be coming home -- not yet, at least. Within the constellations he drew imaginary lines, piecing together Alayian's wondrous face. He felt a momentary shiver of excitement and nearly forgot to answer Virgil's question.

"Our tale is a grim one, full of sorrow and great bravery. A number of courageous warriors fell in battle to the evils of Grammore, strong men who gave their life to upholding Trencit and its people. The wound is a deep one, and these comrades became close friends to me, despite the short weeks we were together. The three of us faced the horror and the darkness which holds sway within the Lowlands. We survived, but the rest have fallen, far removed from their homeland. Trencit has suffered a grievous loss."

Virgil was silent, contemplating Sarion's words. He grabbed a flask of ale, offering it to Sarion, who accepted.

"I hear the truth of your words, Sarion. And I know who you are, the name and story familiar to me as the one who led the ill-fated venture against the marauding Glefins." He leaned towards him, his voice low. "And although you don't know me well, I understand your caution. I can only respect what you have done; to have traveled within the forbidden land."

Sarion stared at him, his face thoughtful.

Virgil nodded, continuing. "Years ago I would ride among the hills of the Ridgeline, skirting the deep valleys and roaming the wilderness. I have seen things which would frighten the bravest warrior. And so I believe in the threat. But few others share my knowledge or open mind."

"I understand. It's easy to be skeptical when the danger is far away, or hidden. *Or* fought by others," Sarion added. "In my own country we tend to forget the battles being waged in the east. Things have been a stalemate for so long, it's difficult to understand who's even winning. And if things go badly, men will be called away to reinforce the royal garrisons."

"And so it has begun." Virgil spoke quietly.

"What is Pralicon's stance on the war?" Sarion pressed him, feeling more comfortable with the man, although not eager to trust anyone at the moment. He knew better than to fall into that trap, fellow countryman or not...

"Hmm." Virgil smiled, his mouth slightly crooked. "Indeed, I have his Lordship's confidence in many things. I'll not elaborate to express his opinion though. I'm not immune to his judgement, and wrath..." He added dryly.

The men sat there in silence for a while, and Sarion held his hand up, disguising a yawn.

"Ah, I've kept you up too long. Maybe tomorrow we can speak more of your journey. I would like to hear your story, and learn for myself of the dangers which stalk that land."

Sarion stood, stretching. "Very well. And we'll share the watch with your men, as we said earlier. Forlern has the next, and he'll awaken me later. Good night."

Virgil rubbed his chin with one hand, nodding as Sarion left. He stared after him for a long while.

It seemed to Sarion that sleep had just taken him when he awoke to a sound. Eyes bleary with much needed rest, his instincts snapped to immediate attention as the cries of men shattered the night air.

Men screaming in terror...

Trying to locate the source of danger, he moved forward into a hunter's crouch, his vision adjusting to the dim firelight, his sword already in hand.

The Rooting of Evil

He was greeted by chaos.

The warriors of Gwerath were yelling, moving about in defensive formation, several of them pointing into the trees. Sarion's heart jumped as he realized Forlern was on watch.

Forlern! Please, let nothing have happened to him...

Shouts echoed through the night, and Sarion's expression was grim as he caught snatches of words.

"Devil..."

"By the Seven!"

Bows sang in the twilight, steel scraped against holders and buckles, and Sarion knew that the deadly hand of Grammore was tenaciously reaching outwards as death roamed the land this night.

"Beware! The gargoyle comes!"

His blood froze at this last description. Sarion instantly knew the source of what threatened, and his newly found hope in meeting the fighters from his homeland was now quenched, as unexpected misfortune struck them once again. It was the winged hunter...

Sarion spotted its massive form as it streaked from the concealing branches of an enormous pine tree, the branches splitting apart like dry kindling, the wood unable to thwart the power of the great beast as it made passage towards the men below. Its talons reared angrily and it slashed at one of the fighters, leaving only a headless body behind. Another man was knocked over, and Sarion now saw more figures lying on the ground. The monster must have emerged from cover, taking the unsuspecting men by total surprise. But there was no time for thought, only action...

Chertron's durable face appeared from the shadows, leaping towards Sarion in a protective stance.

"Forlern?" Sarion shouted, but Chertron shook his head uncertainly.

"I don't know where he is. The gargoyle managed to track us somehow. Cursed beast..." The warrior pulled out his bow, notching an arrow.

Sarion imitated the gesture, searching for a clear shot, but the monster was flying low, harassing the fighters and keeping them off balance. Sarion knew the creature had learned well. It was attempting to prevent the use of their shafts by not exposing its bulk overhead. And that made it even *more* dangerous...

Muttering at his side, Chertron shifted his bow back and forth, trying to find proper aim. It was no use as the beast glided above the ground, easily deflecting the few sword thrusts which came towards it. Another man fell, and above the clamor was Virgil's voice, shouting orders for them to assume defensive positions.

Sarion and Chertron were on the opposite end of the glade, and they made their way forward in an attempt to place themselves into the fray. From out of the shadows sprang a lean form, furiously flashing a long sword at the creature's flanks.

Forlern!

Sarion quickened his pace, dodging past the agitated horses which were tethered against a pair of fallen logs. Chertron fell back a step, unable to match Sarion's speed.

Sarion watched as Forlern scored a blow against the monster and it veered to the left, along the edge of the clearing, circling back towards the enraged fighter. Raymark was dangerously close to the predator, twirling his long sword over his head in an attempt to pierce its side. The creature spread its wings wide, sending a gust of air against Raymark and another warrior, and they stumbled beneath the onslaught. Seizing the moment of surprise, the monster angled towards them and scored the nameless fighter with a deadly strike and he crumbled to the ground. It kicked out at Raymark and he was flung mercilessly, crashing into a pair of warriors holding short bows.

Forlern tried desperately to reach them but the creature showed its cunning by feigning a head-on attack, instead veering off into the forest eaves. Confusion reigned as the men regrouped, led by Virgil on horseback, his own weapon held ready. The cries of the injured filled the night, and half a dozen fighters bearing lighted torches cast them into the bushes, setting them on fire to increase their vision. Sarion reached Forlern's side, clapping him on the shoulder.

"I feared the worst for you, my friend. What happened?"

The warrior scowled. "The beast came with stealth, from out of that patch of trees." He pointed to a place several yards from where they stood. "Decapitated two of the guards before anyone knew what happened. Slaughtered several more as they rose from sleep. They never had a chance..." His words were laced with bitterness, but Sarion only sighed in response.

"There's nothing any of us could have done. It chose a time and place where it could attack us by surprise, regardless of our greater numbers." It was a chilling thought. The monster clearly was unaffected by the seemingly unequal odds facing it. And the creature hunted at night, when men were at the greatest disadvantage.

"This thing tracks us with keen intent. There can be no doubt now." Forlern expressed what Sarion himself had secretly feared. The predator had been sent to track and hunt them down.

Chertron joined them, gazing warily at the tree line. Warriors ringed the entire encampment, the lighted bushes crackling angrily and providing better lighting.

"It seems this Dark Mage has his hand in our mission. Unwilling to let us go." Chertron patted his sword. "This beast is relentless, trailing us since we rode across the valley."

"Indeed," Sarion answered. "It pursues us across hill and dale, and despite the addition of other fighters. To attack us when our numbers have been strengthened shows a particular degree of purpose. And this only leaves us with more questions, fewer answers..." His voice trailed off.

"What do you mean, Sarion?" Forlern's face was impassive, and he leaned closer to his comrade.

"Why does it still follow? The meaning is unclear, and one must look past the obvious." Sarion stared over at Virgil, who now approached them. Shrugging off further questions, Sarion went to meet him.

"A bitter lesson to learn." Virgil spat.

Sarion spoke. "The Ridgeline has never offered safe passage. The lands beneath its shadow are filled with terror and uncertainty. The evil of Grammore stalks the very borders of Trencit." He leaned on his weapon wearily, his companions keeping vigilant watch behind him.

"You warned us of the danger. And you don't seem surprised by the appearance of this demon." Virgil stared intently at Sarion, his voice low with anger. "Tell me what you know."

Forlern responded for him. "We did warn you," he replied evenly. "And yes, we've fought this beast before. A few nights ago. And many others while in Grammore."

"And you survived..." Virgil was clearly surprised. "My men." He gestured over his shoulder, shaking his head. Sarion could read the loss in his eyes.

"How many?" There was a pause before Virgil answered Sarion's question.

"We rode across the northern fields a score and

five. A dozen will not be returning to their homes. Raymark is unconscious..."

Forlern whistled under his breath, and Chertron shook his head sadly, the kind eyes filled with the grief of a warrior who has lost comrades in battle.

"We mourn the loss of your men." Sarion's voice was filled with genuine concern. "Whatever we can offer you need only to ask."

Virgil was silent for a moment. "This thing hunts *you*. And now it hunts us as well." He spat.

Sarion nodded. "A predator from Grammore. Sent to thwart our return. We know not its thoughts, or origin. Only its intention, which is most certainly to kill us, prevent us from talking to King Gregor, perhaps."

Virgil gave him a sharp look, ready to say something, but Forlern interrupted.

"And we can only hope that there is nothing else which tracks us..." Forlern's voice was grim, and Virgil turned his head towards the fighter, measuring him and his words.

"Whatever your purpose in Grammore, it was surely a deadly game your captain played to have disturbed such evil." Virgil stared towards the west, but the creature had disappeared.

"A deadly game..." He hurried off towards his men.

The remainder of the night was uneventful, and there was little rest for any. Sarion attended to the wounded, and two more horses would be returning to Gwerath without a rider. Fourteen men in all had now perished in the span of only a few minutes.

Paul Melniczek

Fourteen fighters...

It was a shocking number of lost men.

Sarion was amazed by the ferocity of the attack. How they had survived the previous assault now appeared as a greater stroke of fortune than even before. Had the creature been testing them? Or perhaps it had underestimated the trio, believing them to be easy prey? The answers to his questions eluded him, and he concentrated on doing what he could, although there were few actual injuries. Most of the men who had been close enough to the winged predator had faced a grisly end. He went where he was needed, using his healing skills as best he could. His packet of herbs was always full, and he constantly foraged for fresh roots whenever they rested.

A broad-shouldered warrior named Hurgul was trained in healing, and he conferred with Sarion about the injuries. The most grievous was Raymark, who had suffered a nasty blow on the helm, and a series of gashes from the creature's talons. The metal had saved his life, but he'd been unconscious for a while, revived shortly after the battle ended. As with Chertron, Sarion recommended that he not be allowed to sleep, and one of the fighters watched over him. Raymark's good eye was attentive to everything going on around him, but the man said nothing. The scars on his face gleamed angrily in the firelight, and Sarion left him after a while.

Morning eventually arrived, and Sarion thought the new day would never come. He yawned, knowing that he needed sleep, but uncertain when he would have the chance to actually rest in a clean bed with a roof over his head. So long ago, it had been...it felt like a lifetime. Hopefully his wish would soon be granted. He knew they should be reaching outlying settlements within a day or so.

The diminished company packed up and broke

camp, moving off into the faint morning light. The forest was restless around them, filled with the singing of birds and the grunting of nocturnal animals rustling through the undergrowth, heading back to their dens until nightfall arrived once again. But these were the normal sounds of the gentle woodland creatures, and Sarion felt a measure of comfort hearing them around him now. He rode at Virgil's side, although he'd offered to share the lead and help find the best path. The captain had politely declined the offer, insisting that Sarion remain under the watchful care of his warriors. Since the attack last night he had been unusually silent, dwelling on his own unspoken thoughts. Sarion failed to gauge what went on beneath the man's stoic face, and he refused to make any conclusions, either way...

Sunlight trickled down through gaps in the forest canopy, and despite the horrors of the previous night, it was difficult to imagine that a predator of Grammore was now tracking them. Sarion remained alert, and so did his companions, although he doubted the beast would show itself while the sun was up. Such creatures were kindred of night and darkness, their power strongest when shadow blanketed the land, and the fears of men were greatest.

Forlern rode behind him, Chertron further back. They were positioned in the middle of the company now for maximum protection, Virgil had told him. Word of their mission had to reach King Gregor, and immediately. If he'd been unconvinced previously, the appearance of the dreadful winged hunter and the slaughter of his fighters had swiftly and permanently changed his opinion. His mood was dark, and he shifted his eyes across the shoulders of his men, watching their reaction. Sarion in turn observed Virgil's focus, and to his keen senses, he felt and saw the visible manifestations of tension.

Paul Melniczek

Virgil's men were proud and strong, tall and dark-haired. Dwelling in one of the furthest reaches of Trencit, they were independent and considered themselves to be self-sufficient in all capacities. But they had been assailed by something from the realm of nightmare and legend by a creature of violence and hatred which killed without hesitation. They were daunted...the warriors had seen over a dozen of their comrades struck down in a frenzied attack, under cover of night and in a land which they believed to be secure. Their superior numbers had been meaningless, the mastery of sword and bow seemingly futile against the marauder. A warrior could ill afford to lose confidence while in the field, and these men were precariously close to that brink. Heads constantly glanced skyward, necks angled backwards, snapping to the sides. Virgil noticed it, and Sarion did as well.

When they halted early in the afternoon, Virgil spoke to Sarion while the men rested and ate a light meal.

"Sarion, it's no secret that you keep things from me, details of your journey. I'll not press you on the matters you deem fit for only King Gregor's ears."

Sarion gave him a neutral look.

"But I must know *everything* about this winged pursuer. If and when it might strike us again."

Nodding, Sarion described their encounter with the gargoyle when the three men had crossed the vale, seeking the cover of the Ridgeline. Virgil listened in silence, showing no expression. His eyes darkened as Sarion recited their first battle with it, and also the harrowing escape from the weird elemental creature and Chertron's injury.

"I've been thinking much about this monster." Sarion mused. "Its purpose is clear, to track and kill us."

"There exists an abundance of prey for it to hunt

within these lands." Virgil gestured absently to the west. "Perhaps it feasted on our fallen comrades, but that doesn't explain everything." His words conveyed his great displeasure, as they had to leave behind the slain fighters. It would have been impossible to return with them from the wilderness as they were being stalked. Distasteful, it was a necessity. Virgil appeared greatly disturbed by the circumstances.

"I don't understand the creature's motives, only that it's relentless and deadly. We can't afford more encounters like last night's. I don't think it will turn back until we're all dead..." Sarion's words were grim, although he felt them to be true.

But Virgil seemed to read more of his thoughts, and pieced together the unspoken words. "The gargoyle is on a mission -- that much is clear. Your company has stirred evil while in the forbidden land. And now it hunts you...and my company as well." Virgil stared at him, his eyes intense. "What were you doing in there?" He snapped.

Sarion matched Virgil's gaze with an unyielding stare of his own. "Evil was disturbed before *we* ever entered." He weighed his words carefully, deciding what he could tell this man -- someone who was not necessarily a friend...He paused for a moment, feeling his own temper brewing. "Haven't you been listening to the voice of your own people? The king's own command? Well, now you've had a taste of what's been going on in the borderlands. The blood of your own men has now been shed. Look around you and listen. Is Pralicon that naive, sitting smugly in his stronghold that he's ignored the cries from the borderlands?" Sarion stood before Virgil defiantly, and several of the fighters watched the interchange, their eyes uncertain.

Sarion continued. "Good men have given their lives for Trencit. We entered Grammore on a perilous mission -- to discover the nature of these marauders plaguing our frontiers."

Virgil retorted angrily. "Be careful of your words, Sarion. Lord Pralicon is well aware of the possibility of danger, believe me. We would not be here otherwise."

"Possibility? Is that what he thinks? Then you'd both better open your eyes," Sarion said. "Go past the Ridgeline, see how long you can survive the terror which dwells therein."

Virgil's orbs smoldered, but Sarion cut off his remark.

"And if you make it that far, keep going...through the perpetual twilight, where the sun's warmth is only a distant memory. The horror of nightfall, when predators roam in search of easy prey. The howls and shrieks. Plants which devour the unwary, bog dwellers, massive and ferocious. Immense creatures spawned in caverns far below the earth, grown to tremendous size, existing only for bloodshed and violence. Grammore is a land of nightmares come to life. You can't *imagine*...The worst of man's fear in living form. And *we* braved these dark regions, led by our captain. You want the truth? I'll *tell* you why we entered."

Behind him, Forlern and Chertron fidgeted restlessly, holding back their own words and letting their comrade follow through with his intention.

"We came upon an ogre."

Virgil's face betrayed no emotion, but his eyes were twins pools of ice.

"In the region of Hawker's Peak, we were waylaid by such a beast." Sarion's voice lowered. "You've seen the strength and ferocity of this demon which hunts us now. We've been threatened for the last several weeks by such terror -- and things which dwarf this winged creature, monsters which defy imagination in their power and violence."

Virgil was silent.

"Several warriors were killed outright in a short but fierce battle. Our captain held the men together and sent word back to Nighton and the king. This message was circulated, hence your own orders." Sarion hesitated a moment. "Captain Grundel decided to hunt the beast. We pursued the ogre."

Now Virgil showed real surprise. "What? You hunted it? Into the Lowlands?"

Nodding, Sarion continued. "Yes. We spoke of the reasons behind his choice. He wanted to slay the monster and make sure no more of our people would be harmed. Call it bravery, folly even...but he was held in close confidence with King Gregor, so his motivation was in the interest of Trencit alone."

"That's why your company entered Grammore, tracking this monster..." Virgil leaned closer.

"Yes. Into the land of horror. There are no words to describe what we saw down there. Monstrous..." Sarion gripped the air with one fist for emphasis. Then he continued, his voice lower. "The warriors showed tremendous courage. Every step of the way we were beset by the creatures which live there, waiting for the unwary. We couldn't let down our guard. Not for a moment. By night, the greater predators are active, and we fought a number of pitched battles, avoided detection by the more powerful dwellers, and were hunted several times. Our numbers dwindling, yet we still pressed on, reaching a point where it was obvious that the ogre was lost to us. By chance, we encountered an ancient citadel to the north. And Captain Grundel decided to enter -- against my argument."

"This captain was a man who feared nothing, it seems. But the choices he made..." Virgil ignored the watchful stares of his fighters.

"Truly." Sarion winced inwardly at the thought of Charadan, forever lost to the world. He swallowed heavily before continuing. "Our group descended into a valley filled with unspeakable horrors. And inside the fortress a trap had been laid for us..."

Virgil's eyes narrowed.

"Most of the men perished, including Captain Grundel in the end. I won't speak of all the creatures which stalk those desolate and shadowed streets. Evil spawned of violence and hatred, powerful and cunning. Things exist down there which are far worse than beasts of flesh and blood..." He stared intensely at the other man before continuing. "But the trap was indeed carefully laid out. The ogre was waiting for us. We finally killed it after a bitter, terrible fight. Vengeance was ours, but it was too late to save Captain Grundel and the others."

There was a long pause, then Virgil answered. "I am sorry for the loss of your captain, a courageous leader to have taken on the nightmare of Grammore. I won't speculate as to the soundness of this decision, however. It borders on madness. But your tale answers some questions, and I think I understand more now. If King Gregor was directly involved, then his decisions speak for themselves."

"You deserved an explanation, at least," Sarion replied. "We're surrounded by a growing darkness, and the high towers and proud men of Trencit are no longer secure. But we need to face the danger together if we are to survive. If not, then in the very end, we will surely fail." Sarion measured Virgil for several long moments with an icy stare, and both men remained silent.

Sarion then turned towards his comrades without speaking, all eyes fixed on the determined outline of his back.

The Rooting of Evil

The afternoon turned into a premature nightfall as ponderous grey clouds rolled in from the west, pushed forward by an increasingly strong wind. Starting first as a gentle, prodding breeze, the air grew heavy with the promise of storms to come. The landscape was a healthy assortment of lush undergrowth and mixed hardwoods, their path leading them across small, bubbling streams and slender foothills. They did not come across any other travelers, or even a remote cabin or outpost. Virgil spoke to Sarion several times that afternoon, describing the features of the land, of which he possessed some knowledge, but admittedly was not very familiar himself. His charge was far to the north. He'd taken his patrol much further south than ever before under the auspices of the king's request, and partly due to his own desire for a trip in the wilderness. Things at home were rather boring, besides the nagging rumors, which Pralicon was indeed aware of, but far from alarmed.

But Virgil certainly had never anticipated the recent disaster which had befallen his company...

Speaking with Forlern and Chertron earlier, Sarion and his comrades had decided to press on directly to the fortress of Dwellyn, and from there send word to King Gregor that they were on their way to see him. Dwellyn was one of the major houses of Trencit, a powerful and intimidating citadel which served to guard the western approaches to the central plains, where the vast majority of people made their homes. The region was also the veritable breadbasket of Trencit, filled with countless villages and farms, the inhabitants loyal to the

Paul Melniczek

king and country. It was a gentle and comfortable area, where the men and women made an honest living in their respective occupations. Much of the royal army was comprised of men born within the central plains, and inside the hearts of these citizens was a deeply-entrenched loyalty. For if the royal legions were overcome, everything they had would be lost.

Sarion blinked his eyes as a gust of wind snaked through the trees, blowing dirt in his face. He now sat in the lead beside a fighter named Stewerd, a grizzled veteran and one of the finest trackers in the northland, according to Virgil. Sarion had no reason to doubt his words. He spoke to Stewerd throughout their ride, conversing on the easiest path and making remarks concerning the contours of the passing landscape. There were no trails this far to the west, and most trappers were a superstitious lot, having no desire to brave the hazards of the Ridgeline and what lurked there. The game was ample within the vast reaches of the more protected borderlands, and the trappers preferred to venture no further than a one or two day's ride from the nearest outlying villages.

Sarion and Stewerd slowed their pace as the shadows lengthened beneath the surrounding trees. The sun had forsaken them a long time ago, devoured by the hungry western clouds which had moved in from the Ridgeline. A light mist began to form, seeping upwards from the soft earth, and the air was damp with moisture. Sarion felt the first drops of rain land on his hair, and he shivered, pulling his hood out.

He listened to the sounds of the forest around him, his senses keyed for anything out of the ordinary. They were not yet that far from the Ridgeline, and he refused to let down his guard. He believed that the winged hunter still pursued them, although how deep it would penetrate into Trencit was a nagging question to

98

which he had no answer...Would the thing finally abandon its mission, and return to the west? Before long they would be reinforced by more fighters from Trencit, and their numbers would prove too great for even this formidable predator. It was intelligent and cunning though. Sarion would not underestimate its power or determination, but they could not afford another encounter like the previous night's disaster.

And something else gnawed at his mind...When just the three of them had battled it, he was certain they'd caused it a significant degree of injury. The thing had flown off in obvious distress, suffering from a number of arrow and steel wounds. Yet last night it had attacked with incredible vehemence, unhindered by any harm from recent battle. Did it have strong powers of regeneration? That was a very disturbing line of thought, and Sarion bit his lip in frustration. He looked skyward, but the boughs overhead obscured any possible view of the open horizon. He peered over at Stewerd, the man intently surveying the land, at times his head swaying to and fro, almost serpent-like, as he attempted to take in all possible sources of danger.

They needed to find a clearing; that was paramount. Beneath the forest eaves they were extremely vulnerable, and the gargoyle was in its element of darkness and concealment.

Rain began to fall in a heavy, drenching curtain, and the men pulled their cloaks around their shoulders, trying to ward away the moisture and chill. The fog deepened, and visibility was quickly growing poor. Sarion's unease continued to grow, and the landscape appeared to him in a more threatening fashion. A familiar image wavered before his eyes, a land of nightmares and dire threats, filled with unspeakable, relentless creatures, waiting to lure and trap the weak and unwary.

Paul Melniczek

It reminded him of Grammore, with the relentless fog, dismal weather, and pervasive atmosphere of lurking dread.

It was as if they rode once again within the forbidden land, and the seeds of doubt were spreading, finding ample root inside the hearts and confidence of the warriors, needling them with invisible fingers of fear. The horses nickered softly and the voices of the men were hushed, the mood sullen and uncertain. The trees were an endless row of silent towering sentinels, patiently watching their progress as they passed beneath the lofty branches and through the tangled brush. Steam issued forth from the nostrils of the great warhorses of Trencit, and Sarion absently patted his own mount on its side. But he kept glancing overhead, inclining his neck so as not to alarm anyone behind him. The overall tone was already downcast, the fighters nervous, and he knew better than to add more doubt to the company. He frowned, putting his mind to task on their delicate situation. Tried to sum up the recent events, and what their next plan needed to be in order to reach King Gregor as swiftly as possible. But he dare not think too far ahead. They passed through dangerous land, despite being within the sovereignty of Trencit.

And in reality, it fell under Trencit's dominion in name only. The borderlands had always been a region of uncertainty and loose communication, where few traveled, these being only those who knew and respected the threat from the west. Trappers roamed the edge of wilderness but ventured forth in pairs or small groupings. The Western Watch itself was now a guard of diminished numbers, relying partly on the few border Houses and their natural protection. To the north was Gwerath and Lord Pralicon's lands, which consisted of dozens of villages and numerous outlying farms, outposts comprised of armed companies, and roaming legions of fighters on horseback, trained marksmen who moved swiftly wherever they might be needed. Castle Gwerath was a beautiful but formidable fortress nestled in the foothills of the western Krale, a deep and treacherous mountain range which surrounded Daregil Keep on every side, the ancestral home of the rulers of Trencit. The mountains of the Krale were steep and snow-crowned in white from their lofty elevation, a great part of the chain impassable and unexplored, and also home to many legends in their own right...

The Keep itself had never been taken since its construction centuries ago. The only access was through the Grip, a narrow valley which sliced between high, challenging foothills leading to Daregil Keep. It was heavily fortified, protected by a legion of the Royal Army. Even if an enemy were able to reach this deeply into Trencit, past the forces of a number of lesser Houses, it was nearly impossible to attack the Grip with the intention of breaking through to the Keep itself. No army had ever made it that far...

To the south of Sarion's own lands was Sharield, a relatively isolated province which held sway over the rugged southern villages of the westland. It took long days just to reach the citadel from Sarion's farm, and there was little trade or communication between the region and Trencit. Sarion wondered if word concerning their venture with Charadan had even reached the ears of Sharield's current ruler, Lord Berillon. Perhaps not, and even if it had, there was a strong chance that little, if anything, would be done. Maybe another patrol sent northward. The lands under Lord Berillon included some of the most secluded among all of Trencit, virtually a province standing on its own, with virtually no activity occurring between itself and the central kingdom.

Sarion pondered the makeup of his homeland as

he scanned the surrounding countryside. The mist was growing heavy at an alarming rate. He knew, without looking back, that Chertron and Forlern would be extremely wary. And the other warriors would be feeling the cold hands of doubt and uncertainty creep into their hearts and minds...

Stewerd turned to him, his face grim within the folds of his cloak. "If this dreadful rain and fog doesn't let up we're in for a long and miserable night. And still no sign of a break in the forest."

Sarion nodded, his keen eyes probing the terrain before them. "The land seems fairly even in this region, flat, and without a change in the texture. No hills, hardly any loose rock, for that matter."

"Aye. Our patrol is far from home, and no maps exist which describe the layout of these woods. I don't know how much further we dare to even travel. The men and horses need rest."

Sarion wished conditions were otherwise, but he'd grown used to discomfort and danger the past several weeks. But now, within the borders of Trencit, he'd at least hoped for a lessening of their troubles. Instead, little seemed to have changed. "Let's press on for a bit, and pause if the trees clear out. We can't afford to be bottled up beneath the forest without room to watch and maneuver if necessary..."

Stewerd was silent, and Sarion knew the man refused to speak the name of the deadly one which hunted them. The shock of the previous night's events was fresh, as the northern warriors were still reeling from the disastrous encounter. What would another such attack bring? It was a terrible thought.

The horses shuffled forward, and there was nothing to be done but hope for a suitable campsite to materialize. The diminished company rode onward, their numbers now fourteen. Virgil's scouting party had come across Sarion and his comrades by chance as they left the Ridgeline. The northern fighters, haughty and confident, had faced something quite unexpected and violent in the form of the winged hunter from Grammore. Their training had proven insufficient against such terror. And now they passed beneath the eaves of an unfriendly forest, where death could easily be concealed within every shadow...

"It's no use, the trees seem to go on forever."

Stewerd shook his head, his eyes never veering from the forest ahead as he spoke to Sarion. Visibility had been reduced to a scant few yards in any direction. Most of the fighters had taken out and lit their weatherproof lanterns, and if anyone wandering those woods happened to catch a glance in their direction, they surely would have thought that a host of spirits was making its way through the darkened wilderness, forsaken will-o-wisps out on a dreadful nocturnal hunt.

Poorly as things appeared, their situation suddenly became worse as the land softened beneath the feet of the two lead riders.

"Ho! Have a care." Sarion felt his horse stutter as its hooves stepped on the yielding turf. "We've chanced upon a marsh." Frowning to himself, Sarion checked his steed as Stewerd also slowed down his own beast.

"Curses. A swamp..." The northern tracker muttered several oaths beneath his breath, and Sarion jumped to the ground, examining the landscape.

"That explains the heavy mist. I should have guessed it earlier." Sarion picked his way carefully forward, shaking his head in frustration. Fens were fairly common in many parts of Trencit, and especially in the borderlands. But their situation was serious, and the bog took the form of a very unwelcome obstacle to their travels. He stooped to the earth, examining the texture of dirt and plant life, but already his boots were sinking deeper into soft mud, so much that he immediately backed away, a quiet sucking noise resulting from his efforts. Stewerd was several paces behind him, and Virgil's tall form materialized from the mist like a spectral warrior, coming forward on foot to see what the delay was all about, Chertron quick on his heel.

"What's wrong?" Virgil stiffened, now entering the quagmire himself.

Sarion looked over his shoulder, responding. "Impossible to tell how large this marsh is. With the mist and rain, we're likely to run into a lot or trouble if we go further in the dark, and it might prove to be impassable. Some of these bogs are vast in the wilderness. Without a map, we're taking a tremendous risk."

"It appears we've encountered a formidable obstacle then. The edges?" Virgil's face was shrouded beneath a dark hood, his hunting cloak thrown about his shoulders to fend against the chill and growing downpour.

"I could guide us, skirt the main swamp itself, but in the darkness and under these conditions, that would be a treacherous venture. We have few choices this night. None of them pleasant." Sarion shrugged.

Stewerd agreed. "Aye. Quicksand, snakes, deep mud. Even from the edge itself, the signs are all there."

Virgil folded his arms, sighing. "We'll back off and make camp. There's nothing else to be done until morning."

He turned around and disappeared into the fog.

Chertron came up to Sarion as Stewerd followed his captain. "I like it not. This dismal bog is the last thing we needed to see on such a cruel night. Another stroke of misfortune."

Sarion grinned at the fighter. "And are we strangers to such? Hasn't bad luck hovered above our heads like an unseen cloud since we first ventured together, your patrol intruding on my peaceful farm and hoisting me away?"

The warrior nodded. "It seems like years ago, that day. I'm sure you miss your nephew terribly -- we all have loved ones behind..." His voice trailed off dreamily.

"Well, my friend, we should be used to it by now." Sarion patted the warrior's shoulder in a gesture of comradeship. "Where's Forlern? I'm surprised he didn't come forward to investigate."

Chertron chuckled. "He wanted to, but we agreed that someone needed to remain with the others. Our eyes and ears must be turned to every nook and shadow." He lowered his voice. "These northern fighters are frightened to the bone. *That* is an ill omen for men facing danger."

"Indeed." Sarion gestured for them to return. "Well, let's hope that this is the only misfortune that we face tonight."

They retreated into the fog like twin phantom warriors stalking the silent and primeval forest.

Sarion and his two comrades huddled together in conference as Virgil's men prepared camp.

They had distanced themselves from the bog, moving several dozen yards away and into the forest, in the hopes of leaving some of the denser mist behind. It was difficult to tell if there was any difference, though. The fog was a sluggish, oppressive and unwelcome companion, working to dampen spirits and hinder visibility.

Chertron yawned, glancing over at the warriors as they prepared for the night's rest. Raymark watched the three from behind a fallen log, his face grim and expressionless.

"I don't trust that one." Forlern spoke, following Chertron's gaze. "I think he holds us responsible for the attack of the gargoyle."

"He's lucky to have survived," replied Sarion. "But I think you're right. There's something about him that leaves me suspicious. I feel more at ease with Virgil, despite his high ranking and blood ties to Pralicon. He's a noble man."

Nodding, Chertron agreed. "Yes. A natural leader, regardless of his kinship to Lord Pralicon. And he's devastated at what's happened to his men."

"That's something few men can claim." Sarion spoke quietly, as one of Virgil's men passed by. "But he carries the responsibility for his fighters within his heart, as well as on his sword. It saddens me greatly to see the loss of Trencit's warriors to the evil ones. This must *end...*"

He snapped the last word, and the look in his eyes was intense. Both his friends stared at him in silence, feeling the determination held deeply within Sarion's breast.

"What do you propose?" Forlern questioned his companion, knowing all too well the direction of Sarion's intent.

"We've reached a pivotal point with this hunter from Grammore. The next encounter will be the *last.*" His words sunk in, and the others waited for him to continue. "It has harassed us many miles, relentlessly tracking us. And now, with our dwindled numbers, there can be no advantage. Indeed, the advantage has always been with *it.*"

"You think it plays us, as a cat to a mouse?"

The Rooting of Evil

Chertron raised his eyebrows.

"I'm unsure. Maybe it was surprised as we fought it off in the first engagement. And it deliberately attacked the northern fighters the other night instead of ourselves. Raked through their ranks with foul purpose, perhaps softening us up for a later assault. I can't pretend to know its mind, but the creature is cunning and deadly. Whatever its true motive, the endgame is the same -- to destroy us before we reach a fortified area deeper inside our homelands." Sarion bowed his head in thought.

"You're right, I feel this is coming to a conclusion, one way or another." Forlern fingered the blade on a wicked knife. "If it shows again, I'll slay it myself this time."

Sarion lifted his head up, and Chertron's mouth opened in surprise. "Don't do anything foolish, man. We're in this together and we've come much too far now."

"He's right. No unnecessary risks, Forlern." Sarion reached out with his arm, but the fighter shrugged it off, standing.

"No. Its days are marked, and I'm tired of being hunted. Across the Ridgeline, all through Grammore, and now back into Trencit. It's time to send a message to this Dark Mage. I fear him not -- nor his minions."

Forlern stalked away, gazing into the forest while his friends remained there watching him.

Sarion and Chertron spoke in hushed tones, sitting together for long minutes after Forlern had left, the two companions discussing their situation; one which looked increasingly grim.

"I think you should understand that Virgil's warriors cannot be relied upon in the face of what tracks us." Chertron's voice was low, and Sarion raised an eyebrow at the remark.

"They're capable fighters, loyal to their leader, but I see that's not the heart of your statement." Sarion stared at their hasty campsite, which appeared far too inadequate for their purpose. Some of the warriors had found suitable spots for rest and a pair of Virgil's men patrolled to either side of their makeshift perimeter, vague shadows standing as mute sentries against the backdrop of mist and rain. The horses were tethered together amidst a trio of tall evergreens which protected them against the heavier rainfall.

Chertron continued. "If there's another attack, those men will be extremely vulnerable. It's a terrible thing to say, but I feel it's true. Their spirit has been shriveled away, and I'm saddened to see such a thing. They've been sheltered too long from the evils of this world, I'm afraid. Despite living on the borderlands, they haven't experienced the terror of Grammore and the wilderness."

Sarion replied, his voice tinged with regret. "The same could be said of many in Trencit. Living in the deep interior, little is known about the face of the enemy. And this is different from the danger in the east. That one is at least easily recognizable. The western horror comes straight from nightmares."

No words passed between them for several moments, and they listened to the soft pattering of rain as it soaked the already moist ground. Sarion broke the silence first. "All right, we need to take action. The time has arrived for something unexpected."

Chertron's eyes narrowed. "Ah, a plan then?"

Sarion nodded. "Yes, well...more than just one

plan, actually."

"Let's hear it, my friend."

Sarion pointed towards the middle of their campsite, where a massive, ancient poplar spread gnarled limbs skyward, the hoary tree reaching out as if in supplication to an unseen forest deity. He grinned. "I need you to help me go up *that*."

Now Chertron looked surprised. "What? You mean to climb that tree? And this is part of your plan? Can I hear an alternate idea first?"

Sarion chuckled. "Come now, I'm not a desperate man. Not yet, at least...I'll need you to stand guard at the bottom. Tell Forlern that I'll be up there, waiting to see if the creature attacks. But no one else is to know."

"You'll be in the demon's own element. I like it not."

But Sarion continued. "The branches are too thick for it to reach me. I'll pick out a good location. Make sure a few lanterns are at the base of the trunk, and hang them on the lowest limbs. I don't want Virgil's fighters to notice me. If some of the men are focused on my actions, the gargoyle might see this attention. It could be lurking nearby, for all we know."

There was an uncomfortable pause as the two companions gazed across the silent forest, wondering if indeed the hunter was even now hiding in the shadows and darkness.

"All right," Chertron finally answered. "We'll make our way over quietly. You first. I'm afraid to ask about the other plan now..."

Sarion started moving off, catlike in the twilight. "As well you should be. *That* one I'm less confident about." He winked, leaving Chertron with that lingering thought.

Paul Melniczek

After several furtive minutes, Sarion made his way up the massive tree, positioning himself in such a way as to pass unnoticed by the guards. Chertron distracted one of the men who might have spotted Sarion's curious ascent, giving his friend enough time to clamber up and out of sight. The Chertron spoke to the northerner for a few moments, and then left him alone once more, promising to relieve him on the next watch. Chertron then approached Forlern who was now lying on the ground, blanketed against the weather, but remaining fully alert.

Meanwhile, Sarion crept a bit higher up the tree until satisfied with his location. The branches were plentiful and thick, although slippery. He was able to sit comfortably, nestled with his back to the great trunk, one leg propped onto a gnarled limb. He dared not go too high, as he needed to maintain some degree of vision from the lanterns. Looking down, he saw Chertron's tall form as he hung two lamps on opposite branches, throwing off a bright glimmer of light, enough to Sarion's liking. The Trencit lanterns were a remarkable asset in the field, waterproof and virtually inextinguishable. For travel at night, especially within hostile regions, they were of vital importance, and had proven this reality many times over. Sarion shifted about, making certain of his footing. He frowned at the thought of slipping from the tree into the midst of an alarmed camp. It was certainly an embarrassing possibility, and he was determined that it would *not* come to pass. From his height, he could very well break an arm or leg, for that matter. He shook his head at the grim notion.

He took out his bow, placing several arrows where he could quickly grab them, if the need arose. And that was his hope -- that if the creature attacked, he might be able to strike it clearly from his higher vantage point. But that's all it was -- a hope. Conditions were terrible, and the only sure thing was the fact that *nothing* was certain...And so he sat there, watching, and waiting.

Minutes passed, and the night dragged on. Sarion remained vigilant, but his body felt stiff, and he caught himself beginning to drift off more than once. He observed the men below, catching glimpses of Chertron who stayed close to the base of the tree. Forlern wandered about restlessly, glancing up at his hideaway several times, but staying near to the fire. Two of Virgil's fighters remained on guard, but the leader himself had fallen asleep much earlier, placing his trust in the others. Eleven northerners remained -- that was all. It was a grim thought. They all needed rest, and Sarion knew it would be a long day ahead of him, especially if he sat awake in the tree all night. His plan was to descend in the early morning hours, as the time of greatest danger was in the deep of night.

His thoughts wandered as he waited. Edward's face appeared to him many times, and he wondered how the boy was faring. He sorely missed the lad, and realized he was becoming a man before his eyes. One day he would be a young adult, something that Sarion had experienced himself not too many years past. Despite Sarion's own skill in the field as tracker and fighter in the Western Watch, he was not an adventure seeker. Even at his relatively young age, he had already seen enough death and violence to last a lifetime. He wanted no more.

Thinking such things, he instantly came alert when he heard a very soft fluttering noise, like the flapping of wings.

He stiffened, all senses coming to play, straining for an indication as to the source of movement. His hand instinctively moved to the arrows within short reach, and he carefully adjusted his balance so he could swiftly react.

The noise sounded again, unmistakable this time.

And it was to Sarion's utter horror when he located its source -- directly above him, from the unseen heights of the great tree.

It was a terrible moment for Sarion.

He notched an arrow into his bow, angling his neck upwards at the same time, peering through the misty rain and darkness.

It was in the tree!

Hardly daring to breathe, he fought the overwhelming sense of fear which threatened, his inner mind screaming at him to leap from the branch and onto the ground. But that would only serve to alert the creature, perhaps confusing the warriors below as well. But they *had* to be warned...

Indecisive, Sarion sat there and waited. There was a quiet rustling, as the creature moved its considerable bulk among the upper reaches of the huge tree. Despite its size, the gargoyle surprisingly made little noise. Sarion realized this was the reason for its swift assault, as it possessed the ability to hunt silently while stalking its prey. The creature continued to prove resourceful in so many aspects. Truly this was a formidable adversary, and the Dark Mage had certainly hand-picked his emissaries with deadly cunning. Would they be able to finally kill the deadly predator though? It was a daunting question, and sitting there with the monster scant yards above him, Sarion's mind was filled with doubt and trepidation.

Although he had faced danger countless times in his trek through Grammore, it was mostly the *anticipation* of attack, not the immediacy as it now was, and the lives of his friends and Virgil's men were hanging in the balance. He could not afford to make the wrong decision. Sarion licked his lips, and his mouth was dry. He was afraid that the slightest noise would reveal his location, and the creature would descend upon the unsuspecting fighters.

The waiting continued, and the gargoyle also waited, watching silently and unseen from above. Sarion was convinced it was still unaware of his own presence, and that in itself was at least a good thing. But how could he use this to his advantage? Despite all of his training in the field, the variety of all those experiences and skirmishes, he was unable to make a decision for action, whatever it was to be...

But he reeled in terror when a sudden noise broke from below. Forlern shouted a warning, and another yell pierced the night from one of Virgil's guardsmen.

"Devil! Awaken!"

Sarion, confused and alarmed, at first had no idea what was happening. The fighters could not have seen the creature hidden in the shadowy heights of the tree. Impossible.

And then realization dawned on him, irrefutable and ghastly.

Another gargoyle was attacking the warriors below...

Paul Melniczek

Sarion felt devastated.

Shades! Two creatures!

It all made sense to him now...The violence and relentless tracking, the seeming ineffectiveness of the wounds which he and his companions had inflicted during the fight. He had felt something was wrong, a piece missing, and now clarity broke through to him, terrible and powerful. These thoughts all flashed through his mind in the fraction of a moment. His battle instincts took over, a tremendous and deep-rooted commitment to his friends and countrymen, and also a growing sense of rage at the manipulations of the Dark Mage. Forlern was more forthright in his anger, but Sarion was of similar mind. He was just able to keep his own emotions in careful check, but to lose control under such dire circumstances was a sheer invite to disaster.

Sarion knew that he couldn't join the fray. He had a slight moment of advantage now, the first since they had been pursued by the hunters, and however difficult the decision, he needed to make the right choice. He heard his name shouted from below, and he made out the forms of the men as they gathered against the attack. Someone screamed in the night, and he felt a shard of anger pierce through his chest. Another warrior lost. Please, let it not be one of his friends...It was a guilty wish, as it meant another man would die. But he couldn't change the face of his devotion.

The creature above him stirred, and Sarion knew that it was preparing to descend. His hands gripped the haft of his bow, and his fingers tingled with anticipation. His nerves felt raw and exposed, and it took every fiber of his training and force of will to remain there and not help his friends.

"Sarion!" Someone shouted his name again, and he cursed the misfortune which had once again befallen them. All the mishaps and tragedy of the past several weeks. Charadan's face appeared in his mind, but he shrugged away the memory-fragment. The captain was gone...another victim to the Dark Mage, and the urgency of the present demanded all his attention.

Wait, patience...

He peered overhead, spotting a large shadow which emerged from the mist and darkness. The creature no longer attempted to disguise its presence. The final assault had begun, and all eyes were on the ground. Sarion narrowed his gaze, hoping fervently that the beast would become overconfident.

His wishes were answered, as the gargoyle came into full view, snapping small branches in its wake. Although Sarion had seen the predator in close quarters before, he was still amazed at its appearance. The wicked talons, capable of beheading a man where he stood. The thick body armored with a strong coating of scales, which covered it completely. The durable wings, its surprising ability to move quietly and quickly for a thing of such size and mass. In all, a creature which could attack equally from the ground or in the air. And now, it was gliding effortlessly through the huge tree, angling away from Sarion and outwards where it could join the fray, except that Sarion had no intention of letting the gargoyle complete its foul purpose...

He waited for the right moment. The creature approached an opening between two thick tree limbs, and Sarion let loose a pair of arrows. The first one struck behind the monster's left ear, which was little more than a pointed flap of toughened skin. It didn't have time to react as the next shaft pierced the left orb, and now the creature roared in pain and rage. Thrown off balance, it crashed into the branch which held Sarion, and he braced himself for impact. The entire tree shuddered with the force of the muscled beast as it landed hard, snapping the limb with ease. The vibration also jarred Sarion, as he had failed to consider what now occurred. Holding his bow tightly, the other hand grasping onto the wide trunk, he was able to maintain his balance for a moment as the gargoyle plummeted downwards, but then he slipped on the mossy bark, gasping as he plunged towards the ground himself.

Branches slapped mercilessly at him and he struggled to remain upright to break the fall. He felt several stabs of pain in his side, and then he hit the ground, rolling with the fall. The gargoyle was already down, howling in pain, and Sarion caught a glimpse of Chertron with sword held high. Darkness then claimed him, and he tumbled head over heel, knocking over a lantern and smacking against Virgil himself, who also went down from the collision. Images and shadows passed before Sarion's vision, shouts and screams ringing out in the night. He heard the singing of bows, and the terrified braying of the horses. His mind shrieked for him to control his momentum and gain his feet, join in the fray. The men needed him -- they were all in tremendous peril. He couldn't fail them now. Not Chertron and Forlern.

But helpless to stop his fall, he felt stinging pain as his head struck something hard, and everything went black. He remembered nothing more.

Sarion had no idea how long he had passed out, but his eyes suddenly snapped open and he blinked several times, adjusting to the gloom and shadow.

Someone stood over him, and he recognized Forlern's grim face.

"Ah, Sarion. What will I do with you? It's not enough that I declare an end to our relentless hunters, and then you climb that tree and set your own snare? Not even confiding in me?" He chuckled lightly, and knelt down to Sarion, who propped himself up on one elbow, feeling a wave of nausea coming over him.

"How do you feel?"

Sarion's throat felt dry, and he swallowed several times before replying. "What happened to the gargoyles? Are we out of danger?"

"A difficult question, but one I will attempt to answer. And out of danger, you ask? I fear that will never become a reality, based on the events I've witnessed these past few weeks, my friend. Here, now don't try to sit up already. By the Seven..."

Sarion resisted, and Forlern muttered beneath his breath, realizing that his efforts were futile. "All right, take some water at least, and here's a bit of dried meat."

The offerings tasted good, and Sarion was surprised by the hunger he felt. But then, with the chaos of the recent events, sustenance was not always a priority. He looked around, and darkness still claimed the forest. The rain had lessened somewhat but the mist remained with them, clinging to the damp ground and coiling itself between the dim silhouettes of the surrounding tree trunks. Several men huddled around the central fire, and Sarion spotted Virgil and Chertron, the two men leaning close in discussion. He also noticed that their numbers were fewer, and he saw at least two warriors sprawled on the earth.

"How many?"

Forlern knew what he was referring to, and he sighed deeply, bowing his head. "Five more of Virgil's men will not be returning to the fair woods of the northern province. We were victorious this time, but paid dearly for our valor. The hunters are both slain."

Sarion was silent for a long moment. The gargoyles had been killed. He felt a great measure of relief, but his heart was stricken by the heavy toll rendered by the deadly creatures, and his absence from the battle. They had been hunted from Grammore and into the Ridgeline, and even after, finally gaining the borders of their homeland Trencit, although for the vast part this region was uninhabited and thinly patrolled. "What happened?"

"Well, the first creature attacked, and the warning was given. I looked for you, and feared the worst when you didn't answer. I knew something was amiss, else you would have been in the forefront of the attack. I joined the fray immediately, but two of Virgil's men quickly fell, including Stewerd..."

Sarion grimaced at Forlern's words, and shook his head.

Forlern continued. "Aye, a good man there, I liked that one." He paused for a moment. "My memory fails me some. The heat of battle blurs details. I didn't have time to strike with my bow, but I made directly for the beast. It was a few moments after this when the other gargoyle crashed down from the tree, you following right behind...Chertron fell upon the monster immediately, and slew it outright. You had severely injured it already, but he gave it a fitting end. I shudder to think what would have happened if both creatures had attacked us in surprise. This was unanticipated."

Sarion shook his head, frowning. "I should have realized this sooner. I suspected something was wrong, but I believed the creature was acting on its own, with powers of regeneration." Sarion shifted, sitting up. His head throbbed, and his entire body ached. "I underestimated it, I'm afraid. And my actions also prevented me in taking part against the attack. More men have died... "

"Sarion, that's nonsense, and you know it. None of us knew the nature of these creatures, or their ultimate purpose -- except for killing us. We've gone through an incredibly difficult ordeal. Lesser men would have perished. Many have already, although I don't diminish any of their bravery – but yours not the least." Forlern paused for a moment. "Your foresight may have saved us all in the end."

"I don't know," Sarion replied. "It certainly was not my intent to take myself out of the fighting." He deeply regretted this fact. Sarion's training as a tracker required a constant ability to remain in control of events, anticipate the unexpected. It was the only reason he had been able to survive from so many deadly encounters. How many times had it been himself walking away from a trap or mishap? Was it all just a matter of good luck? Sarion had left behind many comrades in arms, and the number was ever-growing. It weighed heavily on his heart.

Forlern continued. "Misfortune has hovered over us like an unwelcome shade these several weeks. King Gregor will have much to think about. I wouldn't want the crown of Trencit to sit upon my head."

Sarion agreed. "Hmm, nor I. And Chertron is all right? Wait, I see him now."

Forlern angled his neck towards their companion. "It will take an army of gargoyles to bring him down. I wouldn't want any other by my side. After you, of course."

"And the other creature?" Sarion questioned him, eager to learn the events of the dreadful fight.

"Virgil threw himself directly at it -- he's another man with no fear in his heart. He wields his sword with deadly mastery. Held the beast at bay, while a few others rained arrows down on it. But I made due on my promise." His eyes glittered. "I found an opening as it was distracted for a moment, and then I cut off its head."

A wry grin crossed Sarion's face. "You slew the beast, then. We've gained some measure of vengeance."

"But not enough...not until we can strike at this Dark Mage. Then. And only then. Come, let's get you up and join the others. Despite this wretched, utterly dismal weather, dawn is near. Perhaps we can be at ease when we travel again."

The two men walked side by side as they made their way to the middle of the camp, Sarion's face troubled and thoughtful, his head throbbing with pain. The men looked up from their conversation, noticing their approach. Chertron's face broke into a huge grin, while Virgil nodded.

"You had us worried for a while, my friend. That plan of yours worked, although in a quite different way. How do you feel?"

"Terrible. Weary and aching, my head's splitting. But I'll be all right...I think." He turned toward the northerner. "I'm sorry about the loss of your men, and wish I could have been able to strike a blow at the other hunter."

"You've done enough, Sarion." Virgil stood, his face streaked with dirt from the battle, but his eyes were dark and determined. "Without your anticipation, we all would have met our end here. I can only wonder if both creatures have tracked together from Grammore, or if they joined at this spot."

"I don't know the answer to that question. You would think they would not have waited so long to combine their attack though," Sarion answered.

Chertron replied. "Perhaps they wanted to weaken us, sensing that at full strength, we would have been too much for them. Ah, but we'll never know the true reason, I'm afraid. The matter is finished, and too many brave men have fallen beneath the shadow of Grammore's evil. Too many..."

Forlern slumped down onto the log. "My thoughts are that this is merely the beginning. Trencit might soon be facing enemies from both sides. One we know, and the other we don't. Our kingdom will be sorely pressed to fight battles on separate fronts."

"All the more reason for us to reach Daregil Keep, and warn the outlying provinces. There remains many unanswered questions. Assuredly, forces gather in the Lowlands, hoping to infringe upon Trencit's sovereignty. We know not to what degree. Borderland raiding? But to what purpose? The motives are unclear." Sarion's voice had lost its edge of weariness, and he now spoke with confidence.

"There's no argument there." Virgil ran a hand through a strand of black hair. "Lord Pralicon will take sterner measures once he discovers the events of our venture. He'll be outraged by the loss of so many fighters. And I'll have much to answer to..."

Sarion stared at the two men who remained on guard at opposite sides of the camp. "None of this is your doing, Virgil. If he holds you responsible, then he's being unreasonable. I think your capabilities as field commander are more than worthy. And your presence might have very well saved our lives, and the nature of our mission. But yes, Pralicon will have much to think through, and worry about now."

"*And* the king..." Forlern added.

Sarion rubbed his forehead, wincing. "We need to reach King Gregor without further delay. I hope to make good time this day, but we have to negotiate the bog first. Once past this immediate region, we should experience better speed to our travels. Dwellyn is still a number of days off, but once there, we'll send word of our arrival to the king."

"And what then? That's the real question."
Forlern sighed, slapping a hand against his boot,
knocking off a clod of mud.

"But first..." Sarion turned, drawing breath, and
facing Virgil. "We part our ways this morning."

The captain's eyes narrowed. "What do you
mean?"

"There is little choice in the matter. You need to
return to your own homelands, and speak directly to
Pralicon. If nothing else, the loss of his fighters will
have some impact on his decisions. There's nothing
more you can do for us...Your company has suffered
terribly, and your duty is to the north and your own
people. I believe we're out of present danger as well."

"And what if you're wrong?" Virgil said.

"Well, if I'm wrong...then the separation still has
its merits. Any more pursuit will have to decide on
which of us to follow. Lord Pralicon will wish to hear of
these events immediately -- and directly from his Third
Captain. I think this is the best course for us all. And for
Trencit. The best interest of our people *must* come first."

The men were silent for a few moments, and the
forest around them was growing lighter, but viewed
through the mist and rain it was more a lessening of
gloom than anything else.

The northerner was quiet, rubbing his chin
absently. He then spoke, his voice low. "It's difficult to
argue the logic behind your statement, I suppose." Virgil
stretched his legs, then stood. "I'm not looking forward
to a confrontation with my cousin. He'll have many
questions to which I won't have the answers. And that
will only make him more frustrated."

"Sounds like a *very* reasonable man to me. I'm
well aware of his mood, along with everyone else at
Daregil." Forlern leaned against the trunk of a nearby

tree, the limbs offering some protection against the weather.

Virgil ignored the sarcasm, addressing Sarion. "So be it. We'll part our ways. I don't blame you for the death of my warriors. You've suffered a great deal of loss yourself, Sarion, and I fear there's much more the future holds that none of us can foretell. King Gregor's mind will be focusing on *you* and your companions in the coming weeks, and that is indeed a daunting thought...The royal scrutiny comes with a price. Don't play the same games with Gregor as you did with me."

"We had our reasons..." Forlern started to respond, but Sarion cut him off with a wave of his hand, turning his neck to the contentious fighter and frowning.

Virgil shook his head. "That one better keep his tongue close in Daregil Keep -- if he still wants to have it, that is. You should brush up on your court etiquette. Sarion, hold a tight leash on your friend, for his own good."

Forlern bristled with anger, but Sarion gave him a withering glance, and he stomped off.

"An outstanding fighter, but his temper will lead him into great mischief. It's a wonder he's gained such a ranking at his age though. Ah well, any misfortune he experiences can only be blamed on himself." Virgil stared after the man, and Sarion decided to leave it at that.

"So, we'll pack our belongings, and try to get past this dismal bog. My thanks for your help and protection, Virgil. And may the return trail to your homelands be safe. I'll speak highly of your assistance to King Gregor."

Virgil's face broke into a disarming smile as he walked away, and Sarion again felt this was a man who could be trusted. An ally. Even a friend, if the situation allowed. But of the temperamental Lord Pralicon, whom he had never met, that could certainly not be expected. Sarion wondered what the powerful Lord would now do. From speaking with Charadan and his men, Pralicon had not been very receptive to the idea of sending his men to fight in the war to the east. Indeed, he had been almost confrontational...Trouble in the west would only aggravate matters. Pralicon doubtless would focus all attention on Grammore and his own borders, and ignore the king's request. Of all the major houses in Trencit, Pralicon was perhaps the single Lord who could openly defy the King and get away with it. There had been no serious internal warring for decades, but skirmishes would take place at times, usually over territorial disputes between the numerous provinces.

Shortly, their belongings gathered and horses ready, the men from both groups shook hands and made hopeful remarks. Last were Virgil and Sarion as they stared each other down, and the surrounding warriors hushed in respectful silence.

"It's time we went our separate ways then, although it's been but a short span of days. Unpleasant ones at that. Good luck to you, Sarion." Virgil stepped forward, offering his hand. "The horses are yours to keep. I don't lightly forget any who have fought by my side. You and your friends have proven themselves as capable fighters. Although I think you *still* keep secrets from me, I sense you have strong reasons, and not ill in nature. It's in my heart that you'll have an important role to play in these dark days ahead. King Gregor would be wise to consider your advice, I think."

"Can I tell him you said that?" Sarion grinned, taking the captain's hand.

"That will be at *your* discretion." Virgil smiled. "I've never talked to His Majesty, and have been at Daregil Keep only a handful of times before. But it's a wondrous citadel, the very heart of Trencit's power and its people. May good fortune keep you near. Farewell, Sarion."

They locked gazes for several seconds, and then parted, both lost in their individual thoughts. The northerners looked on curiously, noting the similarity in poise and character between the two men. Raymark, who had been virtually silent the past two days, watched the exchange as well, merely nodding at the trio as they left, his face impassionate as he turned to follow his captain.

But more than one warrior knew they had shared company and hardship with some of Trencit's finest, and were sad to see them leave.

The three companions rode to the south, as Sarion decided to skirt the bog in hopes of finding more secure ground. The rain stopped sometime before dawn, and the day promised to be damp and overcast, as heavy gray clouds could be glimpsed through gaps in the forest canopy overhead. They kept their cloaks wrapped tightly about their determined forms, and spoke little in the early morning hours. Sarion felt uneasy now that Virgil and his men were gone. He had welcomed their company from the beginning, and found himself liking the charismatic northerner. Reflecting on their conversation, he agreed that Lord Pralicon would be furious at the loss of his warriors, perhaps holding his cousin to blame. Sarion fervently wished that Virgil would be spared the wrath of the powerful Lord, but there was nothing he could do regardless. Pralicon ruled over a province that was independent of the rest of Trencit, and more than likely viewed the fealty to Daregil Keep and the king as long-standing tradition. He

had not hesitated to balk at the request to send warriors
to the east. As Sarion considered further, he now
recalled something else -- Pralicon had withdrawn some
of his men from the Western Watch in recent years,
preferring to coordinate patrols rather than place his
fighters under the royal arm. Sarion shook his head.
Unity was needed, as the threat in the west continued to
evolve. Pralicon would have to work more closely with
King Gregor, and soon.

The morning grew into early afternoon, despite
the gloomy shroud of twilight covering the land, and the
footing became firmer as they left the swamp behind. By
Sarion's estimate they were now heading due east,
plunging deeper into the wooded region which
comprised the vast majority of the entire western
borderlands.

"We should pass several score miles north of
Nighton within the coming days," said Sarion.

"Are you familiar then with this area?" Chertron
rode to his right, Forlern bringing up the rear a few
paces behind them both.

"Somewhat...my recollection is vague, and there
are no distinct landmarks anywhere nearby that I can
recall. I've traveled throughout much of the countryside
on patrol while in the Watch, but these were routine
hunting parties around the greater villages. For the most
part, there was little consistent action when I served.
Until the marauders threatened our people, of course.
Then we ventured deeper into the borderlands, riding
beneath the eaves of the Ridgeline itself, tracking the
invaders."

"Grim times, indeed." Chertron gazed over at
him with curiosity, but Sarion was unwilling to follow
that part of the conversation.

"Yes, they were. And they're not much better now." He left it at that. Moments later, he continued.

"Unfortunately, the Western Watch is a revenant of its former glory, although the forces were never of high numbers. The strongest regiments have been recently called for service in the east. The provinces might have to fend for themselves, if things have truly worsened with the Devlents. I'm not even sure what the standing force is anymore."

"Gregor may have no choice in the matter. He'll have to send fighters from Daregil itself if the westland is threatened." Chertron's brow furrowed. "Reserves have been called up, and emissaries were scouring the villages to recruit additional men. Soon every able man will be fitted with a coat of armor and cold steel. The thunderheads of war have their eye on Daregil Keep."

"Troubled times we live in."

Sarion surveyed the land before them, a mixture of hardwoods and thin scrub bushes. A small stream lay at their feet, and the horses splashed through the rippling current, scattering silvery fish. "Let's stop and fill our pouches; mine is getting light. There's certainly no scarcity of good drink and game in this country."

Chertron halted and quickly dismounted while a watchful Forlern remained on his own horse, scanning the landscape for any danger. Ever vigilant, the younger fighter left nothing to chance.

"Would that we traveled together under friendlier circumstances," said Chertron.

Sarion scooped water from the stream, splashing it against his face before responding. "Maybe we shall yet, if fortune smiles our way. But for now, all I see is a dark path leading through shadows. Evil surrounds our kingdom, and pulls its shroud ever tighter. We must remain firm, and not despair, no matter the odds facing us."

The Rooting of Evil

He looked at his companions and they returned his strong gaze. Neither of them flinched, as he knew they wouldn't. There was not the slightest trace of fear or discouragement in these two.

"I just want one chance to strike at this Dark Mage." Forlern's voice was low but unwavering. "He'll regret sending his minions our way, of that you can be certain." A crooked smile creased his face, and Sarion smirked in return. Despite their terrible ordeal of the past few weeks, Forlern still maintained his swagger. If anything, the recent experiences had made him a more deadly adversary to his enemies. His fighting prowess was uncanny. Forlern was a match for anyone in the field that he'd ever seen. More than a match...

The companions relaxed for a while, each of them lost in their own thoughts. Sarion sat with his back against a slim birch tree, and he listened to birds singing above his head somewhere. The forest was peaceful, and it reminded him of his farm and the youth who waited back there, his nephew Edward who would be quickly turning into a young man. Sarion was going to have word of his journey sent back to Edward when the chance arose. The lad would certainly be worrying, regardless of Sarion's promise of a safe return. How Sarion missed the gentle rolling hills and wide pastures of his home. But there was also another part of him that had been awakened by the appearance of Charadan and his warriors. Sarion had not recognized it until recently, but he'd felt a quiet thrill at being out in the field once more, using his skills for the benefit of his country and its people. There had been many times over the past few years when he'd sat at home, staring out at the night sky, wondering about the men who fought a bitter war against an unforgiving, relentless enemy in the east, while many like himself were secure and content in their homes, far removed from the fighting. It had been a guilty feeling, despite his own history of service in the Western Watch. No one could ever accuse him of not doing his part to bolster Trencit, but that failed to alleviate this deep-rooted feeling. He had always known somehow that he would be called to serve again, and that was why he never grew lax in maintaining his fighting ability. Daily, he practiced and sparred with one or two of the helpers on his farm, although his prowess far exceeded their own. Sarion was a finer swordsman than ever, and his handling of bow and arrow were exceptional, and his competency had been put to task on the quest into Grammore. Not for the first time he reflected on the coming days and their eventual arrival at Daregil Keep. The news of Charadan's fall was like a physical burden on his shoulders. Sarion shook his head reflexively at the memory of the stalwart Captain of the Homeguard, King's Champion and leader of the Royal Armies. Held within Gregor's tightest circle of counselors and advisors, Sarion never had the slightest suspicion that Grundel was actually Charadan himself. Rundin certainly had known, but none of the others who had ventured forth from the great keep -- handpicked for a perilous excursion that would lead most of them to their deaths in a faraway land inhabited by cruel and monstrous beasts, a nightmare realm where shadows and legends held dominion, and men were of no consequence.

And what of this Dark Mage? Who, or what was he? A man? Alayian had named him as the enemy, but knew very little about his origin or purpose. Nothing, actually, except the name itself. Sarion fervently wished that Alayian had found safe harbor after helping them to escape. The remarkable na-dryad was another mystery -- a fascinating, beautiful one. He reached into his breast pocket, fingering the stone of searching which the girl had given him at their parting. It was attuned to the one she carried, and would help her to find him if he ever returned to Grammore. The Lowlands held such beauty and ugliness inside its shrouded eaves. Sarion had entered twice now, both times under desperate circumstances, and had hoped never to return.

But with Alayian's wondrous face glazed within his memory, Sarion knew that despite the tremendous dangers dwelling within the forbidden land, he *would* be going back again someday.

After a short rest the companions made off again, their pouches filled and spirits raised as the sky unexpectedly broke in the afternoon, glimpses of sunlight piercing the forest canopy. The mist and dampness burned off and they welcomed the warmth. The horses trotted through light undergrowth, although the trees never grew very thin. The westland was vast and wooded, and this particular region scarcely inhabited. They couldn't forget that the Ridgeline was still only a few days behind them, and its pall of uncertainty and peril was far-reaching. The border folk respected and feared it, and few dared to impose on the forbidden territory.

The day went by quickly, as time itself seemed to move swifter as the weather improved. The men spoke more, occasionally asking Sarion about the passing landscape and its features. In turn, Sarion found his thoughts turning closer to Nighton and the Western Watch, along with aspects of Trencit's interior politics, and most especially Daregil Keep and the High Council. He felt a shiver of foreboding as he considered the eventual meeting with King Gregor and his councilors. It was not something he looked forward to, not in the least.

Dusk was drawing nigh when the ground swelled upwards, stretching out towards a series of low foothills. Thick, thorny bushes were in abundance, along with many rock outcroppings, and the trees were primarily tall hardwoods, towering above their heads. Birds chirped in the boughs overhead, at times fluttering by and disturbing the foliage.

Sarion explained that the region of hills were one of countless formations common in the westland. "By my reckoning, Nighton is less than two days to the south and east. We can't see it yet, but the stronghold sits in a valley, sided by tall hills, offering formidable protection. It rests against the northern wall, which is steep and treacherous to attempt. A natural barrier." They followed his gaze in silence for a moment, imagining the fortress nestled invisibly within the deep reaches of the westland.

"We avoided Nighton on our venture with Charadan," remarked Chertron. "I'm sure he didn't want to raise any eyebrows. So I've never been to the fortress myself."

"I've been there several times, actually." Forlern nodded, fingering the hilt of his sword. "Well-maintained, and home to a strong garrison of men, although too few in these dark times."

"Is Jerol still First Captain of the Western Watch? I served with him years ago, and it would be difficult to find a more capable man. Little news reaches my lands." Sarion pictured the rugged fighter in his mind, someone with whom he'd shared many harrowing field expeditions with, and some of them were best left buried in his memory.

Forlern answered. "Aye, he still is. Gregor would never remove him from duty, that's for certain. He's very well respected in the west, and holds the king's trust."

"Well he should...few know the borderlands like he does. He held a lower ranking when I first served, but fought well against the Glefins, leading many hunting parties." Sarion leaned forward, as if trying to breach the horizon and gaze far beyond.

"But he never went into Grammore?" Chertron's question caused Sarion to straighten.

"Not that I'm aware of. He was in the south when we ventured out on that fateful mission. Jerol was often sent to spy out the far reaches of the westland, south and north. He gained much of his knowledge about the territory, and I know he explored the Ridgeline at times. I went with him on a few forays. An excellent tracksman in his own right." Sarion grinned to himself. "I'm sure he's only become better through the years. He would be a great ally if the need arose."

"Do you think we might pay a visit to Nighton, perhaps? To give Jerol a warning, and at least some knowledge of our journey...without the specific details, of course?" Chertron rubbed his chin, and his companions were silent for a moment.

Sarion considered. He badly wanted to have word passed on to Edward, and Jerol would not hesitate to send out a messenger. But their need was great, and the king must have word about the fall of General Charadan, and none but themselves could complete that unpleasant task...

The others stared at him, mistaking his hesitation in a different direction.

Forlern coughed. "Can he truly be trusted, though? Our mission must not be delayed, or thwarted. From what I see, there should be no further hindrance from here to the Keep. The lands are a bit difficult for swift travel, but they *are* under Trencit's dominion. Nighton might cause unnecessary questions to be raised;

ones we have no time to answer."

"No, it's not that. I mean Jerol can be trusted. The man I know was above reproach. I know he'll never change." Sarion turned to face Forlern. "And I would like to send word to my nephew. It's been weeks, and he must be terribly worried."

"Aye, can't blame you there." Chertron clapped him on the shoulder. "A fine boy he looked when we first visited your farm. If Nighton is so close, then maybe we should stop there, at least to meet with this Jerol, and perhaps he'll give us fresh horses. We certainly can't be faulted for warning those entrusted with protecting the frontier about the danger in the borderlands. Doubtless he's heard much more ramblings than have reached our ears of late."

Sarion replied. "Both your points are well-taken, my friend, as always. And these animals *have* been in the field for a long spell. Beautiful creatures, but they'll have Trencit stock at the fortress. I think you're right about talking with Jerol. I, for one, would rest easier knowing that the patrols of the Western Watch remain at their highest alert." Sarion narrowed his eyes, and the other two looked at each other.

"What think you, Forlern? It won't be much of a delay, and the horses will be worth the detour, if nothing else," Chertron said to the younger fighter.

"All right. We'll stick to that plan then. Perhaps Barthuk and Lerion are still there as well. It would be good to see our former comrades again. And I also could do for a drink of fine ale -- those northerners had none with them."

"That you knew of..." Sarion grinned at the scowl on Forlern's face, then urged his mount onwards. "Come, the day is nearly gone; let's make haste while we can."

Continuing, they soon came to a wide but

shallow current and entered without pause, their steeds splashing cold water against their rider's legs. The trees marched up against the course on both sides, the shadows creeping long and relentless in their quest to devour all remnants of daylight. The air smelled good and fresh, and Sarion's heart felt lighter as they went deeper into their own country. The horrors of Grammore already seemed half a world away, but he knew it was a seductive but false sense of comfort, for the Dark Mage and his emissaries were flexing their power, reaching in and probing Trencit's borders. Sarion found it extremely disquieting, knowing so little of what was merely a name mentioned by the enchanting Alayian. Even the na-dryad lacked any substantial knowledge of who, or what, this person was...The Lowlands were untamable and vast, with no structure in existence except for the unquestionable, chaotic hierarchy of the deadliest and most cunning predators. The strong preyed on the weaker -- this continued on down the chain of survival, and had been like this for countless centuries. There was little to describe the history of Grammore even within the ancient tomes at Daregil Keep, from what he knew. The Lowlands had always been the same; an immense, impregnable, and hazardous wilderness. The only surety which lay beneath the shrouded landscape was a swift promise of death to the weak and unwary.

They rode for another hour and halted when they chanced upon a cluster of logs and scattered rocks, which jutted from the ground at sharp angles. Weary to the bone, the men ate lightly and Sarion took the first watch. Little conversation passed between them that evening, the three companions focusing on their own thoughts.

The night passed uneventfully, and the next day proved to be warmer and more pleasant. Sarion found a trail which led to a small hunting cabin, little more than a one room wooden structure fronted by a large smoking pit, a small well, and stocks for skinning. It looked to be recently occupied, although it was empty. Sarion noticed fresh tracks, and believed that a company of trappers was somewhere nearby. The fighters entered the building, resting for a while and helping themselves to a stock of food and smoked meats.

"We need this more than they do," muttered Chertron, as he took a huge bite from a piece of hard cheese. The others were silent, sharing some of the other food between themselves. The king's men had the privilege of any stores of food or weaponry they saw fit to use while out in the field, whether it was in the villages or private dwellings. King Gregor made sure his warriors were treated well, and suffered nothing to the contrary.

They continued shortly, riding off into country which sloped higher, merging with the hills they had seen from a distance. Several times throughout the day they encountered travelers, primarily trappers and local villagers. They stopped, questioning these people for any news. All of them voiced the same concern, that dark things were creeping across the Ridgeline and terrorizing anyone unfortunate enough to cross their path. Word spread that several cabins had been ransacked, the occupants slain or carried off. Worse yet, people dwelling in the village of Karin, scarcely a day's ride to the south and west, had been the victims of marauding wolf-like creatures which had invaded a number of outlying farms.

Sarion's face darkened at this description, but he said nothing, deeply troubled by the grim tidings. One of the trappers had been in Nighton earlier in the week, and spoke that it was nearly deserted, most of the men out on patrol to the border villages. Forlern shook his head at the news, while Chertron pressed the man for additional information, but he knew little else. He claimed to be heading deeper into Trencit for safer hunting grounds.

They rode onwards late into the evening, passing several more groups of men, none of them offering anything else of interest. The companions tethered their horses at a split oak tree, rent asunder through the middle. Sarion was glad to end another long day of riding. His wounds were recovering nicely, but his muscles ached in several places. Stretching his arms behind his head, he yawned deeply, looking up into the forest canopy and finding an opening which revealed a veil of stars. It was a peaceful setting, and he felt relaxed within the arms of his country, although he couldn't quite shake the disturbing feeling of imminent dread which had slowly grown on him the day long. He knew it was from the unsettling news concerning the village of Karin, which he had been to on several occasions. It was one of the most distant villages in all the westland, and a fairly sizable one at that. If marauders were brazen enough to be attacking in force, then things had deteriorated since their departure several weeks past, and he couldn't help but wonder if their excursion had been a catalyst for these dire events.

They rose early the next morning, eager to reach Nighton later that day. There was little discussion among the companions, as each of them was curious to discover how the men of the Western Watch were faring beneath the shroud of the recent activity. The ride was pleasant, the air warm and the terrain a mixture of hardwood trees and scattered meadows carpeted with grass, in parts broken up by a variegated display of wildflowers.

It was well past midday when the country angled sharply upward, the landscape now giving way to fewer but taller trees, and numerous clumps of bushes and thickets. The ground became rockier, but they maintained a brisk pace. They intersected a number of smaller trails, although Sarion was unwavering as he knew the terrain well.

A broad chain of hills lay directly before them, and Sarion pointed to the south. "There, we go through the valley which holds the fortress. It's impossible to enter unseen, as watch towers are located in strategic areas. You probably came in through the eastern passage before, if I'm not mistaken."

"Aye. I've been out this way once, although my memory is a bit vague." Forlern nodded, admiring the scenery which lay before them. The hills were several miles long, wooded perhaps three quarters of the way to the top, and from their vantage the crest appeared void of any greenery. They were not high enough to be considered mountains, falling short of the Ridgeline, but they became steep at their peak near the middle.

"A number of these towers sit along both sides of the hills, and are always manned. Nothing creeps upon Nighton unawares."

"Has the fortress ever been assaulted?" Chertron questioned.

"Not to my recollection. In the history of Trencit, there's never been an organized enemy moving in from the west. Of course, recent events may test that tradition. From what we've seen in Grammore, the Dark Mage holds dominion over some very dangerous creatures. But they appear to have singular purpose."

"Such as?" Forlern leaned closer.

"Well, as guardians, for one thing. Marauders. Intent on terrorizing our borderlands. Hunters, like the gargoyles sent to pursue us. All of them deadly. But no organized grouping, enough to form an army."

"And that's a good thing then." Forlern nodded.

Sarion pursed his lips. "I'm not so sure."

"What's your concern, my friend?" Chertron touched him lightly on the arm. "I believe I know you well enough now; I can see something weighs heavily on your mind."

"Ah, many things press upon me indeed. Ever since setting eyes on that cursed citadel, I've been trying to fathom this maelstrom of events we find ourselves trapped within. It's like a vortex of water, and things are spinning about us, too quickly for me to grasp. I can't help shake the feeling that we're right in the middle, floundering." Sarion sighed.

"Grim words, Sarion," Forlern muttered.

"But with much truth in them, I fear. My greatest concern though, is in what guise the attack from the west will show us. If there exists no large amount of creatures for the Dark Mage to muster together, then the raids would seem almost pointless, and to what greater effect will they have? People are being killed and forced to flee their homes. But if there is no army to follow on the heels of these sporadic marauders, then what *is* the reason?"

"Maybe we've seen only a fragment of this mage's power. We know so little of Grammore. As the na-dryad said, the Lowlands are immense beyond belief. There could yet be an army of malevolent creatures waiting for the signal to attack." Chertron shrugged.

"But if this is untrue, and you're right -- we *don't* really know anything -- then the alternative might be even worse."

The two warriors stared at Sarion, waiting for his revelation.

"Enchantments…he might possess magic to such

a degree that Trencit will have no protection. Either that, or he's keeping in check something terrible, perhaps a dreadful predator of Grammore, held beneath his sway and ready to be set upon us when we least expect it."

They were all silent.

The image of the terrible Jurvech appeared in their minds, a reminder of the incredible size and form that monsters could take within the Lowlands. Ancient denizens of the forsaken wilderland, there was no way of knowing what else lurked inside the shrouded domain, and if Alayian was to be believed, then the depths of Grammore, both in physical magnitude and diversity of species, was beyond comprehension.

It was an appalling notion...

"Well, enough time for speculation later. It will do us no good right now for such discussion. Nighton awaits." Chertron spoke, eager to move forward.

"And King Gregor..." Forlern added.

Sarion looked south, his eyes unfocused, as he recalled his years of service in the guard. There had been many dangerous ventures back then, but it was not always so. Most of his tenure had consisted of scouting, drilling, and coordinating communication between central Trencit and the outermost parts of the western border provinces. As he moved further up in ranking, his duties became increasingly focused on strategy and overseeing the training and placement of fighters. When the problem with the Glefins had ensued, he'd been chosen to lead the campaign against them, and eventually led a hazardous foray to stop the cunning creatures, tracking them into the Ridgeline and beyond. Of course, he had plenty of incentive to hunt them down after they'd entered the village of Chorilan, where they had killed his brother Glaring and his wife...

Shuddering, Sarion gritted his teeth. No, he bore no love for the treacherous Glefins. But now was not the time to dwell on such bitter memories. He motioned his friends to follow him and they thundered off, the horses kicking up rocks and dust as they galloped along the trail and towards the waiting hills.

The distance had been deceiving as they rode for the span of another two hours, and Sarion led them through a forest which grew increasingly thicker, the ground beneath their feet angling gradually downwards, until they found themselves within the midst of a shallow dale. The hills had long disappeared from view, and the sun had sunk into the tree line of the western horizon, the sky showing a burst of fiery orange with high clouds hovering overhead, reluctant to glide onward in the still air.

The hollow was long and narrow, but the path remained sure and well-traveled. Sarion remarked that they were drawing closer to the valley which harbored the western stronghold, and would reach it after nightfall. At one point he brought his horse to a quick halt, and the others looked about curiously.

"There." Sarion pointed to a gap in the trees to the south, and they followed his gesture.

"Smoke. Something burns..." Chertron's voice was low and cautious.

"Is it normal for the Western Watch to light fires," questioned Forlern?

Sarion nodded. "In times of peril we would set watch fires to warn travelers and nearby villages." He felt a chill trace along his back at the implications as to what the ominous smoke signaled. There could be little doubt that the troubles in the borderlands had reached a new level of concern.

"We must make haste." He turned away, his companions grim-faced and determined.

Paul Melniczek

Sarion led them to a brisk gallop as they rode through the lip of the valley, the hills rearing up to their left as the ground swelled beneath the horses' hooves. Long shadows swallowed the remaining daylight, and the terrain appeared in a more sinister vein, as their minds focused on the danger threatening their homeland. The path narrowed, and the trees ahead parted as the trail ran straight into the broad trunks, gnarled branches held out in welcome.

Once again surprising his companions, Sarion slowed his horse, his bow appearing in his grip with amazing speed, an arrow notched and another already waiting. Chertron grunted, looking about and trying to determine the nature of whatever threatened, but Forlern was equal to the task, quickly handling his own bow.

"Horsemen," Sarion whispered. "Two there, another pair further south."

The valley suddenly echoed with galloping feet as riders exploded from the forest, their bulky forms heading directly for them.

In a moment's time, however, Sarion's face changed to one of relief, and he lowered his weapon. "Patrol from Nighton. We're among friends."

"By the Seven," muttered Chertron. "Your action was so swift I was certain that demons were waiting for us within the shadowed eaves."

"Caution cannot be idly thrown about, regardless of our location anymore. The westland is no longer safe." Sarion held an arm high, giving a quick salute. It was a gesture known throughout the Watch, and was shortly duplicated. The riders approached within several yards, and Chertron and Forlern looked on with great interest. These men were not heavily armored, but wore light brown cloaks, woven with such material that they blended well with their surroundings. All of them had arrows strapped to their backs, their other weapons concealed.

"Hail, hunters of Nighton. Well met in troubled times."

One of the horsemen came forward while the others stayed back a few paces. His hair was acorn brown, long and flowing, and he looked to be close to Sarion's age. A trimmed mustache and light beard covered a face which appeared handsome despite the shading of dirt from travel.

"Hail, warriors of Trencit. I hope fortune keeps you and your comrades in good faith. My name is Captain Karrol, Third Forester of Nighton. I need your name and rankings."

Sarion nodded. "My companions Forlern and Chertron, members of Trencit's Homeguard and Hybril Legion." His companions nodded respectfully, the gesture returned by Karrol. "We've traveled long and suffered great hardship, and need your aid in reaching Nighton and speaking with Captain Jerol without delay."

Karrol's eyes widened. "Jerol is away in the field. And several days overdue..."

Sarion frowned. "Those are ill tidings. Regardless, we must be swift; we're returning from a quest and are on our way directly to King Gregor."

Now Karrol was surprised. "Are you indeed the ones led by Captain Grundel from Daregil Keep? Word has spread along the borderlands to assist and seek you out, and hunting parties have been abroad for the past several weeks. Two of your company reached our fortress, and hence have returned to Trencit. But where are the rest of your comrades, and your Captain? Also, your own name?" He leaned forward in his saddle.

"Ah, that is good that they found your walls. We

worried about them. But we're all that's left. The others we've left behind, fallen within the shroud of the evil that threatens our homeland."

The other riders murmured between themselves, but Sarion continued as Karrol's face darkened.

"I might be known to you, as I served in the Western Watch a few years past. My name is Sarion, and I led Grundel's company into the Lowlands."

Karrol straightened. "Sarion!" He exclaimed. "Indeed, you are known to us all -- and your skills have been sorely missed, I might add. Into Grammore you've been? I cannot imagine what dire circumstances caused your company to venture forth into that accursed land."

"Dire indeed..." Sarion whispered.

Karrol continued. "It's an honor to receive you and your companions into Nighton, although I can see there is a veil of despair hovering over you. Your journey must have been terrible to suffer such losses, and the death of your captain. Times are dark, and the borderlands are under siege by nameless creatures which prowl our homesteads at night."

Sarion felt a twinge of anxiety at the Forester's words. "Let's hurry, and we'll exchange what information we can later. It will be comforting to sleep in a warm bed after weeks beneath the stars and moon."

Karrol made a quick gesture and his men fell into a tight defensive posture, forming a ring about the others. They rode off, heading towards the end of the vale and the trail which plunged into the undergrowth. Little could be said, as conversation was muted by the passage of the beasts, and Sarion had no desire to forestall their stay at Nighton by further distraction. Eager as he was to hear any news, he also wanted to put this part of the journey behind him. He felt a strong longing to once again be surrounded by the strength of Trencit's fighters, the durable and honest men of the

Western Watch. He was also worried about Jerol, and missed his old comrade-in-arms much more than he cared to admit. The company rode briskly beneath the shrouded forest, and they only halted once when another group of riders approached, numbering half a dozen. Sarion caught a brief snatch of conversation, enough to find out that these men were relieving Karrol's patrol and were expected. The newcomers eyed Sarion and his companions with interest, and exchanged a brief salute before galloping away and disappearing into the twilight.

They continued onwards for nearly an hour without seeing any travelers on the path, whether they be fighters from the guard or otherwise. Karrol remarked to Sarion that most travel was done on the eastern side of Nighton lately, as word spread across the westland that marauders were scouring the borderlands. Sarion knew these lands well, and he recognized that they were at the end of this section of the trail, the main valley somewhere ahead of them. The trees separated, and the sky opened above their heads, the glittering of a million stars greeting their weary forms as they halted.

Before them lay a narrow gap between tall hills. Fires burned in two locations, and Sarion spotted the pair of watchtowers which guarded the western entrance of the valley. A large wooden gate had been raised as a barrier, a formidable door notched with iron fastenings as the only way through. The towers were surrounded by a stone structure, at level height with the gate and fortified with slim windows, their purpose to allow protectors to rain arrows down upon any would be attackers. Although it was impressive in its own right, the small fort paled in comparison to other strongholds of Trencit, the larger ones consisting of fabulous citadels backed by sheer mountains in some locations, enormous and forbidding.

But the western borderlands had never been under siege by an enemy, and Sarion felt a twinge of regret because of the defenses in front of him. They seemed vulnerable and inadequate in the event of an assault by some of the creatures they'd seen in Grammore. And what could possibly stop one of the winged gargoyles which had pursued them so relentlessly past the Ridgeline? He shook his head, silent and thoughtful.

They trotted ahead, Karrol holding up his hand and shouting orders. They crossed the path several hundred yards leading up to the structure, and Sarion spotted furtive movement to either side, where clumps of boulders and scattered trees concealed hidden fighters. The organization of Nighton had always been fluid in structure, consisting of numerous hunting parties as opposed to larger and bulkier forces such as the Trencit Royal Armies, which were vast and filled with a full complement of cavalry, archers, and foot soldiers. The Western Watch was equipped for speed and stealth, and had served their ward well in the history of its inception, but could it withstand an adversary such as what had emerged from the Lowlands?

Led by Karrol's men, they galloped forward, the gates opening silently. Sarion spied other fighters within the towers, which rose several dozen yards into the air. Skilled archers had always been positioned there, and he was certain that little had changed. A voice hailed Karrol as they passed beneath the entrance, and the Forester answered in reply. Chertron and Forlern nodded at the men who waited inside, tending the gates. All were dressed in the same garb as Karrol's men -- Sarion knew their clothing was appropriate for their calling, the purpose of which was to blend in with the great forests of the westland.

"Excuse me for several moments as I need to

confer with my men. We're maintaining a tight measure of security and communication in these troubled times." Karrol nodded to them, about to walk off, but Sarion held up a hand.

"A word of warning for your men, captain. Tell them to beware the skies above. Danger may come in odd disguise. All directions are suspect."

"From the sky?" Karrol tilted his head, trying to understand the nature of Sarion's words. "What do you mean?"

Sarion came forward, dismounting. His companions had already left their steeds as some of the fighters approached, leading the animals away for water and feed. "We were pursued from Grammore and several days' ride from the Ridgeline by predators from the evil land. Winged gargoyles."

Karrol's face showed a look of surprise, before turning grim. "Flying creatures? That bodes ill. What happened to them, do they yet follow?"

Folding his arms, Sarion replied. "We came across a hunting party of Pralicon's men, led by Virgil, whom I'm sure you're familiar with..."

Karrol nodded in return. "They've traveled far south then, which was fortuitous for you, as I'm certain they offered protection."

"The offer was genuine, but to little avail." Sarion's eyes darkened.

"What do you mean? I hear sorrow in the tone of your voice."

Sighing, Sarion continued. "Twenty-five warriors from the north ventured forth with Virgil; a third returned to their homeland."

Karrol's mouth slowly opened, but he remained silent.

"A winged demon attacked us after we left the Ridgeline, but we held it off. After meeting up with

Virgil's war party, we were again attacked at night. They suffered grievous loss. And then again the next night, even though I had a plan ready. But there were *two* of the beasts this time. We slew them in a pitched battle."

"Was Virgil killed as well?"

Sarion shook his head. "No, he escaped with little injury. He possesses great skill of arms."

Karrol pressed close. "Such as yourself and your friends, to have come out of the darkness once more. Your mastery of weaponry has not been forgotten, Sarion."

"Swords are but little help against the predators of the Lowlands, I fear. The gargoyles are large, heavily armored. I believe there are none others which followed. But they pursued us relentlessly, with grave intent. We had been marked."

"We need to talk further back at the fortress. And it is my fear that you have no words of comfort to offer."

Sarion was silent.

Karrol continued. "I'll have my men bring some fresh fruit and drink. You know your way around, of course. You may rest inside the guard barracks until I return." He pivoted, motioning to some of the waiting men.

Sarion and his companions walked over to one of the long, stone buildings which lay behind the walls of the fort. Inside, they were greeted by a dozen or so men pursuing different tasks, some of them merely resting. Fire pits were lit in several places, and Karrol's men tended to their needs. After several minutes of eating and brief conversation with a few men of the Watch, Sarion and his comrades retired into a corner, propping their feet on stools while sitting at one of the square wooden tables which dotted the interior. Torches lighted the room on every wall, casting a warm glow throughout the building.

"To sit again on a real foundation. Horses are wonderful beasts, but I tire from constant riding," said Forlern, taking a deep draught of ale from a metal goblet. "Hmm, I'd forgotten what good mead tasted like." He smacked his lips, and Chertron hefted his own mug, drinking deeply and sighing.

"I feel more at home here inside these barracks." Chertron grinned, and Sarion felt a sudden rush of comfort in the company of these two hardened fighters. In just the short span of a few weeks, they had been through a lifetime of sorrow and ordeal already.

"A welcome respite indeed, if only for an hour or more. The life of a warrior, my friends." Forlern took out one of his knives, honing the blade on a small sharpening stone. "Well, what next Sarion? How much do you intend to reveal to Karrol, or his commander?"

"Probably not much more. Enough that they realize the extent of danger, certainly."

Chertron scoffed. "*We* can't even answer that riddle."

"No, we don't know all the facts ourselves. But I think Karrol is a shrewd man. You don't become Third Forester of Nighton without a good measure of ability." Sarion leaned back, closing his eyes and yawning.

"The Foresters...basically the equivalent of a captain, right? You addressed him as such, I remember." Chertron questioned.

"Yes. It's more the traditional name for the highest Captains of Nighton. There are normally ten such ranking leaders at any given time. I was Third Forester when I left, actually."

"Third in command? I knew you held a high position, but you were merely a pup those few years ago." Chertron grinned.

Sarion shrugged. "There were a lot of skirmishes

in the field with the Glefins, and my territory was in the area of greatest peril. Much hand-to-hand fighting occurred, and my company suffered the heaviest losses. Two captains were slain within a short period of time. I was promoted very quickly."

"They made the right choice." Forlern added his comment without looking up. "My own was not much different. I was a member of several forays going deep into lands held by the Devlents. A select group was handpicked to spy, and cause a bit of general mischief." Forlern grinned wickedly.

"Indeed. Sounds like dangerous work," said Chertron. "Nothing can be taken for granted in the east. The Devlents do not sleep."

"Aye, they're a relentless, unforgiving enemy. No quarter given. I've heard stories of men captured, and none have ever returned." He bit his lip. "Several of my comrades were taken on a raid. Nearly myself as well. That was the last time I went out. Shortly afterward, I was selected for training in the Homeguard."

"How long have you been a member?" Chertron asked the younger fighter.

"Not much over a year, perhaps. Before this venture."

"That's remarkably quick. I hear the training is intense," Chertron replied.

"Oh, it is that...but I had little difficulty. In my group, there was none that could best me. Even my weapon's master wasn't much of a challenge, I'm afraid." Forlern sounded almost regretful.

Sarion listened to the conversation with interest, offering little himself, but he felt compelled to interject. "I'm sure they knew your potential a while ago, perhaps before you first were sent to the eastern frontier. That is precisely why they chose you for such dangerous missions."

"Aye," added Chertron. "It's one of their ways to siphon the best ones from the ordinary fighters. Charadan had his eye on you, thus the reason you're sitting here now."

Forlern stared at him with a blank expression. "Don't brush over your own skills, Chertron. You're too modest."

"Unlike someone I know..." Sarion added, but Forlern shot him a perplexed look, then grinned.

"Well, it was no accident how we were brought together. We were both chosen for our particular talents. Your abilities as a tracker and swordsman are not to be underestimated." Forlern went back to sharpening his knife.

Chertron spoke. "No, I was told that from the beginning, of course, although I had no idea we would enter Grammore, by the Seven. I wonder if Charadan had this planned all along?"

Sarion opened his eyes, taking a deep breath and finding comfort in the scent of the fires which warmed the building. "I've asked myself that many times. I think the king and Charadan both intended on a venture into the Lowlands. There can be no doubt that Gregor and he knew a lot more than what we ever realized."

"Doesn't that bother you at all? I dislike when information is held back from me, especially when I'm sticking my neck out for the kingdom against an army of monsters." Forlern's voice was even, but tinged with bitterness.

"I don't hold it against Charadan for not telling us. Sometimes it's in the best interest of all. Secrecy and stealth have their advantages. And he gave his life for something which he felt strongly about -- searching for answers which could help Trencit. I'm certain the decision was not made lightly."

"No one's questioning his intentions. But look at the result. Without his leadership, both politically and strategically, the High Council will be thrown into chaos. Both of you aren't as familiar with the inner workings as I am. Being a member of the Homeguard brings you into direct contact with much of Daregil's inner machinery. They trust us with carrying out the kingdom's most important duties, whether it's on the front or elsewhere...we protect the king himself, and the Keep is under our personal vigilance. And I can tell you, things were not going so well *before* this ill-fated journey."

Sarion was somewhat irked by Forlern's mention of Charadan, although the younger fighter's points were all valid. And it was true -- a storm was brewing, closing in around Trencit. General Charadan was gone, at a time when he would be needed most.

"His loss will send ripples of unrest throughout the kingdom. Gregor's Champion and chief councilor dead. I wouldn't want to be inside the Chamber of Light once the council members start to unravel."

Sarion had never been in the meeting room of the High Council, and few others had been there as well. Situated near the very pinnacle of Daregil Keep, it was a place of great historical import, serving as the vortex of Trencit's power and royalty through the centuries, where decisions were made which affected the life and death of the country's fighters and citizens. For the first time since the loss of Charadan, Sarion felt a deep sense of awe and forbidding that he was on his way to give Gregor the terrible news. What would the king's reaction be? Outrage, sorrow, despair? All of these? The coming days would surely reveal the truth, and Sarion knew that he must be up for yet another challenge, but this one entirely different than the harrowing adventures of the past few weeks, and one that he felt far less comfortable with...

"It's much easier to look back now and question Charadan's actions," Chertron replied evenly. "But as Sarion mentioned, we don't have access to all the knowledge of the king and his closest advisers. Charadan knew the risk and weighed it against the consequences of inaction. I believe that the hunt for the ogre was his foremost concern, and the ending of the raids. Unfortunately, it seems the ogre was only the beginning of what's to come...and I think that Charadan and Gregor discussed the prospect of venturing into the dark land if the need arose. It was a decision made by one who loved his country dearly, and would give anything in the hope of keeping it safe. I can't fault him. We also have slain the ogre, which would have remained a formidable enemy if left to wander unchecked, and we have a name for the one who threatens, although this means little to us now. Things may become clearer as the days pass."

"Well, I have the utmost respect for Charadan, but this decision seems to have a tinge of desperation. But again, such matters are out of our hands. Trencit's men lead the fight, wherever it may find us..." Forlern's voice drifted off, and the three men sat there in silence for long moments.

Sarion rested for a time, actually falling asleep, abruptly coming to attention when a green-clad fighter informed them that Karrol was on his way, and apologized for the delay. Stretching weary limbs, the companions grabbed some fruit from a broad platter on the table and prepared for another hasty departure.

"How far is it to Nighton from here?" Forlern questioned Sarion.

Yawning, Sarion gazed around the room at the men milling about at various tasks. "The moon will be high overhead before we reach its proud gates. Get ready for another long ride in the dark, my friends."

Forlern scowled, grumbling beneath his breath, while Chertron merely grinned in response at his irascible comrade.

Karrol and several of his men returned and shortly they were on horseback once more, leaving the western gate behind. The valley opened wider as they rode eastward, the hills to their left rising much higher, becoming sheer and intimidating. The land itself was a mixture of open meadows and scattered woods, the ground rocky in many parts. They were accompanied by six fighters, and Karrol briefly explained that there was much activity taking place within the region, and he needed to keep lines of communication open at all levels. Riding alongside of Sarion, he exchanged several bits of information at times when the group slowed due to the terrain.

"The fortress is depleted, I'm afraid. Nearly all of our patrols and hunting parties are in the field. Another pair were sent out yesterday morning to the south."

Sarion felt a twinge of uneasiness at the Forester's words. "Has there been any news from the area east of Hawker Peak? That's where my farm sits, but a day's ride from that region."

"Nothing that I've heard," replied Karrol. "There have been mostly rumors and whispered tales, growing ever more frequently and disturbing. The news about the raiding of Karin has spread quickly across the borderlands, and a sizable force was sent out a few days ago."

The Rooting of Evil

"Any word from your men?"

Karrol shook his head.

"Is that where Jerol is then?"

"No. Grahin led the fighters, Fourth Forester of Nighton. Jerol rode off to the south with a small hunting party. When I was back at the fortress two days past, he had not returned yet."

"The men of the Western Watch are being taken to task in these grim times. We were always up to the challenge, though." Sarion smiled at the Forester, who returned the look with one of his own.

"Aye, although we much prefer peace and riding in the great western forests over any skirmish. I should have known, the past few years have been much too quiet."

"A wise man enjoys the arms of good fortune wherever he finds it. But the future is shrouded in darkness and uncertainty, and it may be long days until light breaks through again. We'll be ready. I have tremendous faith in the warriors of Trencit." Sarion stared at the clear sky above him, the wondrous hills casting a moon-shadow over the landscape.

They rode on in silence for a long time, the horses following the well-trodden fairway which sliced between the forests which grew thicker to either side. More than once they passed other men, gliding ambiguously over the ground like phantasmal specters on their steeds in the distance. Karrol talked with all whom they met, exchanging information and giving orders. Little news was revealed, and they only paused briefly each time. The other riders were primarily on relief duty, following a well-scripted rotation schedule with men in the western outposts, but their ranks were exceedingly thin, their duties more often leading them into the field and away from the protective confines of Nighton and its greater surroundings. Sarion knew the routine very well, and he was also pleased to see that the guard was in good form, the men appearing keen, focused on whatever they'd been assigned. The fighters had not become lax in the Western Watch.

During the late night hours they finally came within sight of Nighton.

The forest broke away to either side and the valley opened wide, revealing sweeping hills which reached up into the sky, the tallest part of the range nearly the height of mountains. Craggy ridges dotted with scrub brush and crooked trees and sheer cliff walls supported the vale like sleeping giants erupting out of the ground from centuries' old slumber. The fortress of Nighton was on the northern reach, backed formidably by the chain of hills, which looked impassable even from this distance. A natural barrier, the men of Trencit had chosen well in constructing the stronghold, taking advantage of the rocky slope and building upon it.

As their horses galloped onwards, Sarion felt his heart lift at the sight, the fortress a symbol of Trencit's far-reaching power, home to the Western Watch and the Foresters who guarded the vast borderlands. So many memories, he thought to himself. He had left in a time of peace, when the threat of the Glefins had been eradicated, to the best of their knowledge. The men were sad to see him go, but knew that he faced an entirely different challenge, that of raising an orphaned lad and taking over a sizable farmland to the south. Foresters could step down from their position except in times of war, or if the king spoke otherwise, but the threat in the east had not been evident like it was now.

Despite his responsibilities, he chided himself for losing touch with the guard. At times, certain fighters would visit him while out on a patrol near his home, but these had become infrequent the past two years. And now, riding within sight of his former place of service, he admitted to himself that he missed much of the routine of being in the Watch. The men were close in comradeship and disciplinary actions were rare, as the fighters boasted a strong loyalty to Trencit and their captains, such feelings perhaps greatest here when compared to the rest of the kingdom, for that matter. A tightly-knit community, the Western Watch was hailed with tremendous respect by the tough people of the borderlands, and the relationship had always been strong.

The horses thundered ahead, and details of the fortress gradually became clearer. A ring of horsemen rode out to meet them, at least a score of fighters bearing quickly down on them. Sarion knew that another such squadron patrolled the eastern section of the immediate valley, always vigilant against any manner of danger which might threaten. As the newcomers drew near, Karrol signaled them and was quickly identified. Instead of pausing, he motioned for the company to continue ahead, as these men were the standard patrol and would not have access to any news which Karrol desired.

The ground grew steeper, plunging upwards as they approached the walls of Nighton. Although falling well short of Trencit's greater citadels, the fortress remained an intimidating sight, ringed by high walls which jutted from the hillside, spiked with buttresses and round observation holds. It consisted of three great walls several dozen yards high which were angled in such a way to prevent scaling, the top jutting out further than the bottom stones. Sarion spotted the dark forms of sentries standing at intervals along the parapets. The Hold never slept.

Banners on both ends of the first wall hung proudly, flapping in the breeze, emblazoned with Trencit's royal insignia along with the Horned Stag, marcher of the Western Watch. The front gates were comprised of two heavy wooden doors, which now began to slowly open. It was customary for the entrance to be closed at night or in times of strife or uncertainty, but during the day hours there was much traffic, including the countless patrols coming and going, traders offering their wares, emissaries from Daregil Keep and other citadels of Trencit, or citizens of the westland visiting family members who served in the Western Watch. Unlike the royal armies which were much stricter, Nighton had always been very open and accommodating. Sarion knew that the history of the borderlands had much to do with this, as Trencit had never faced a concerted attack from enemies along the western frontier, only sporadic raiding and the shadow of Grammore, which was viewed more as a place of legend and rumor than anything else, like a fabled dragon which no one really believed in except for a knowing few...And knowing what he now did, Sarion thought it was better this way. If more people were aware of the true nature of the things which dwelt in the Lowlands, the horrific denizens which stalked the shrouded landscape, they would be living under a constant state of fear which might strike at any given time.

No, it was better that they didn't know...

As they drew closer, Sarion saw the yawning gap which lay all around the outer walls, a deep cleft in the stone which basically served as a moat. A small opening in the wall, out of sight and further to the east, had been carefully constructed to filter out a flow of water from one of the cold streams which originated in the living rock behind the fortress. Clear and fresh, it filled the gap effectively, eventually filling it all, and leaving through an underground tunnel near the edge of the near wall. The water was always moving along, as the builders wanted to capture some of the natural beauty of the

surrounding landscape, while creating yet another
formidable barrier to prevent an attempt on Nighton.
The water-filled gap was less than a dozen feet deep,
and iron pikes had been secured onto the bottom, a
deadly barrier for any enemy unfortunate enough to fall
into the moat. At times, the stream could be redirected
from inside the fortress, allowing men to replace the
spikes as they became rusted and weak. In all, it was a
very effective combination, serving to defend the
fighters of the Western Watch while maintaining its
picturesque setting. Nighton was a creation of visual
beauty, engineered with security foremost in mind, but
taking nothing away from its surroundings. A perfect
balance had been created, and the fortress was greatly
admired throughout the westland.

The road leading towards the entrance narrowed,
turning into a slim, stone ramp way. Crevices opened up
on either side, these holding no water, but could be set
with traps if needed. Much deeper than the moat itself, a
fall would result in serious injury, and death to any horse
which faltered. A railway acted as precaution against
such mishap, but the posts were not permanent, instead
rigged to be withdrawn so the sides were exposed;
another barrier against an invading force.

The company reached the gates, which were now
fully opened. Two sentries waited, hailing Karrol with a
formal salute which the Forester returned.

"Feels like I've never left." Sarion smiled gently,
feeling a surge of pride within his breast. His years of
service here would never be forgotten, he knew. It was
almost like returning home, in a sense.

"The walls of Nighton are indeed strong and a
wonder to behold. The designers crafted wisely."
Forlern nodded his approval. "I was impressed when I
first rode beneath the walls, and the feeling has not
lessened. But I would dearly love to sleep in a *real* bed

tonight..."

"You have my support in that one." Chertron chimed in.

Karrol gestured for them to follow. "You'll rest in the finest quarters for your stay in Nighton, as befits your rank and recent hardship. And of course Sarion is always bequeathed our hospitality due to his prior service. Come, we'll ride across the courtyard and they'll take our horses. Then we shall go to the inner hold."

The walked their steeds beneath the entrance tunnel, passing the gate tenders and a number of guards. The horses' hooves echoed along the hard stone and they entered into the open air, moving across the broad courtyard while the walls of Nighton rose about and behind them. Despite the late hour, a host of riders milled about, and Sarion knew they were a scattering of messengers and fighters ready to relieve guards and scouts. Large water barrels leaned against the interior walls which were thicker than they appeared from the outside. A few rooms lay to either side, formed as part of the main wall, and these served as storage chambers for supplies and weapons. There were no stairs leading higher, and Sarion had always admired this foresight. Any attacker which managed to somehow breach the gate would still be denied access to the upper walkway. The only entrance was further inside the keep, in cleverly sculpted tunnels which led beneath the courtyard and eventually onto the ramparts. Much care and thought had been given before Nighton's construction, and when Sarion had served in the guard himself, he had found little which could be improved upon.

They crossed the courtyard and dismounted, their horses led away. Karrol spoke briefly with a tall, lanky fighter, who appeared to hold some middle ranking, although Sarion failed to see the markings on the man's outfit. Torches were set in large brackets, spaced evenly about the area, and the aroma of burning wood was strong. The main watchfire was further east, unless it had been changed.

Two of Karrol's men remained with him as escort, and he led Sarion and his comrades deeper into the fortress, along the main causeway. They passed a number of small buildings and stables, garrisons and merchant stands as well. Nighton was a bustling community, home to the Western Watch and housing a good deal of ordinary citizens. Spacious and self-sufficient, it was alike to all of Trencit's war citadels; created to withstand a prolonged assault and offer protection for as many of Trencit's people as possible.

Normally, horses were not allowed to thunder through the middle of Nighton unless the need was urgent, and although Sarion could make such a claim, he didn't want to attract undue attention to their presence. Besides Karrol and his men, no one else would know their identities. After long minutes, they made their way through the central market square and proceeded into the interior part of the hold, which nestled against the surrounding hillside. Guards were posted at checkpoints, and the smaller buildings disappeared, replaced by additional garrisons and training grounds. Before them rose the pinnacle of Nighton, piercing the night as it plunged skyward above the Forester's Hold, a fortified building which served as home to the Captains of Nighton, bastion of defense for the long arm of Trencit as it stretched into the vast westland and unpredictable borderlands. Here the King's will would be enforced. Royal emissaries or messengers from the western provinces, all would end up here on matters of Trencit's western affairs.

A small wall surrounded the structure, dotted

with torch fires and the motionless forms of the unsleeping sentries. They walked up a flight of several dozen steps ending in an iron gate, guarded by two fighters. The entrance was open, as they were expected. Karrol greeted the men, speaking quietly with one of them. He turned to Sarion. "Jerol has not returned yet, and no word has been sent from his company. I know not what this means, but it concerns me. We'll speak more inside."

"I'm ready to fall asleep on my feet," yawned Chertron. "My apologies, my Lord Forester, but the days have been long with little rest."

The inner doors were opened and they entered, Sarion's mind filled with countless memories of his own travels inside the hold. Had it been this long already? He shook his head in silence.

Once inside, they walked through an ante-room and into the great hall. A large fireplace dominated the room, a stone chimney plunging upwards into the ceiling high overhead, which was lined with wooden beams. Instantly, several servants appeared, including a pair of young lads and two older women, hosts serving the leaders of the Watch.

Karrol spoke to them, giving orders for the needs of the newcomers.

Forlern leaned wearily against a long table, while Chertron slumped down. Sarion remained standing.

Shortly, the Forester came over to them. "They'll bring out some fresh fruit and meat, and then you'll be taken to your quarters, where a hot bath is now being drawn."

"Ah, would that my memory could imagine such comforts again. Sarion, if this be a dream, wake me not." Chertron sighed deeply, while Sarion smiled down at his friend.

"Karrol, I would impress upon you an urgent

need, if I may, that word may be taken to my nephew at my farm of our safe arrival, if you have any rider to spare in this troubled time."

"You have only to ask, Sarion. Your former ranking and present situation are not to be denied. I'll send someone over shortly, and you can tell him where to find your home. He'll leave this very night."

"My thanks, Karrol. I had intended to return myself after our mission was finished, but that's quite impossible now..." For the first time in a long while, Sarion breathed an inner sigh of relief knowing that Edward would hear about his uncle's arrival. Now he sat down, as if a great weight had been lifted. Karrol left the room while the servants brought forth the promised offerings.

"Ah, that is good news for you, Sarion. The boy must be sorely worried." Forlern grabbed a hunk of bread, taking a huge bite.

"He's strong, and is growing into a fine young man, and my servants are extremely loyal and reliable. But I worry about the raiders. I need to find out more information when I speak to Karrol."

They sat and ate uninterrupted for several minutes, and then, as promised, a young, sandy-haired man approached Sarion, bowing, and told him he would be the one sent as a herald to inform Edward and the others. While Sarion spoke to the courier, other servants came over to clean up the dishes, and lead the weary men to the promised bath.

Sarion waved them ahead. "I'll meet up with you later; I need to speak with Karrol first about some matters, and it could be a fairly long wait."

Chertron grunted in acquiescence, but Forlern nodded warily. "If you need counsel or anything else, don't hesitate. You'll find this lout snoring loudly in his sleep, but I'll be up for your call." He nudged Chertron wickedly in the ribs, and his companion scowled at him.

"I wouldn't be so sure, Forlern. Until later, Sarion." Chertron clapped him on the shoulder and they were led away, down the great hall and up a flight of steps. Sarion watched, wishing he could join them, but there would be no rest in his heart until he spoke with Jerol, or the other captains. In the end he didn't need to wait very long at all, as Karrol appeared short minutes later with another man at his side.

By his uniform he was another Forester, but older and larger than Karrol, grizzled with grey hair tied back into a long ponytail, his creased face marked with faint battle scars.

"I'm Captain Chensel, Second Forester of Nighton. Well met, Sarion. Karrol spoke briefly of your charge, and you have the full confidence of my position to offer what help I may. I would also in turn like to know more of your mission, and the fate of Captain Grundel."

They shook hands, Sarion not surprised by the strength he found. "Can we speak elsewhere in close company?"

Chensel nodded. "We'll go to my quarters. I wasn't about to speak openly here. Come."

They left together, Sarion following, although he was quite familiar with the keep, and little had changed. They crossed the hall and ascended the wooden stairs, which spiraled around in one sweeping column, overlooking the bustling main hall. The building housed the Lords of Nighton, and every respect of the office was evident. Banners and pictures adorned the walls, while torches and tall candles were fixed in brackets, throwing light into every corridor. They went up several flights of stairs, passing sentries at strategic check points. A few other men walked about on various errands, lower ranking officers and a handful of servants. They neared the top of the keep itself, passing by Sarion's own former quarters, which he commented on.

"Although I came from the south, I heard much about your service in the Watch. We have long memories here," Chensel remarked, as they climbed a narrow set of steps. Once they reached the top, they were saluted by two more sentries, and Sarion knew that these were the personal bodyguard of Nighton, entrusted with protecting the High Captains of the Western Watch and the First Forester himself. They walked down a short corridor, halting at an oaken door.

"My quarters." Chensel entered and they followed a pace behind.

The room was sizable yet cozy. A small fireplace was lighted in one corner, and a square table sat on the opposite side, accompanied by several high-backed chairs. Books and maps lay spread out on a smaller table, and the room was lightly furnished, as if the occupant spent little time there, which Sarion knew was probably true. The westland offered unpredictability, and danger emerged wearing many guises. The Foresters performed their duties rigidly and with little time for other pursuits.

"Please be seated." Chensel grabbed a metal pitcher, pouring wine into a trio of goblets for the men.

Sarion slumped down, yawning widely. "My apologies, but like my friends, I'm bone weary. But there is much to talk about, and sleep won't find me until we've spoken."

Chensel nodded in return. "Karrol told me of the fall of this Captain Grundel, and the death of nearly all your company. A terrible story waits beneath your brow, I fear."

Sarion answered. "Long and filled with dread. I'm amazed that it was only the span of a few weeks. It seems more like half a lifetime."

"Can you tell me the events which led you to stray afar? Emissaries from Daregil Keep have arrived, searching for news of your company."

"Karrol spoke about two members of our group who returned back here. I hope you found them safe?" Sarion queried.

"Yes, the one injured, the other was unhurt. They left a few days afterwards with an escort as the wounds were not too bad." Chensel held his gaze with eyes of deep green. Sarion knew the man wanted information, and seemed to be as eager to hear his own tale as Sarion was to hear news of the borderlands.

"I'll speak of our journey, and the misfortune which plagued us. It's a grim tale, and forgive me if I leave out some details. My mind lacks the clarity of a night's sleep."

The Foresters nodded silently and Sarion spoke, his voice low, as he repeated the tale from when they sought him out on his farm and their subsequent departure. As when he talked to Virgil, he deliberately avoided mentioning certain things, especially some of his own personal thoughts, Grundel's true identity, and also the rod which he kept concealed. But these men were satisfied, enough so that they didn't question anything, remaining silent until he finished recanting his tale. At times Karrol's eyes widened, his mouth opening in astonishment, and even the more reserved Chensel seemed amazed several times, although he didn't interrupt.

When Sarion ended, reciting the events up until they had met with Karrol and his patrol, he drained his mug and set it down heavily.

"That is the most incredible story I've heard perhaps in my lifetime." Karrol continuously shook his head. "There are a thousand questions I can ask of you, a thousand..." His voice drifted off.

Sarion smiled sadly. "Please, give me until the morning then, as I have not the heart or strength to respond to a thousand questions this eve."

Now Chensel spoke. "From anyone else's lips, I would say it were the ravings of a madman. But knowing who you are, and the members of your group, I can't believe otherwise than it's the truth. Such grim words. Your captain was incredibly bold by leading you into Grammore. Or should I say, having *you* lead them. And after an ogre yet..."

"Your description of the Lowlands is ghastly. Facing such desperate odds, it's a wonder any of you managed to leave. Gorothagled sounds to be a city of horrors, both alive and dead." Karrol made a furtive gesture, as if warding off evil.

"I know very little of Grammore, or the dangerous creatures which thrive there. I've been to the Ridgeline many times, but never beyond. I've seen enough that I don't wish to go any further." Chensel sighed. "I understand your haste in returning to Daregil Keep. You should depart on the morrow, with fresh horses and an escort. And I know you're eager for news of what has transpired throughout the borderlands. It does seem that events have coincided. The wheels are turning in some vast, insidious scheme, and I'm afraid we have few answers."

"Going into Grammore answered several questions, but raised greater ones," Sarion replied.

"There is much going on in the westland, and none of it yields good tidings." Chensel's face darkened, and Sarion felt a chill crawl his spine, despite the warm crackling of the fire several feet away.

"Immediately before you arrived, I received a message sent from Jerol's patrol."

Karrol look surprised. This was evidently

something he had not yet heard.

"The news is unsettling, and bodes much evil."

Sarion felt himself tense.

"It seems he's entered Sprechyd Wood."

"Sprechyd Wood?"

Karrol's alarmed cry echoed Sarion's own dark thoughts.

"Why would he want to go anywhere near that accursed land?"

Sarion leaned forward, gripping the table's edge. Sprechyd Wood... Scarcely two day's ride due south of Nighton, it was a densely forested hollow which nothing was able to penetrate, even the light of day. The trees crouched ominously at the borders of the imposing wood, as if daring outsiders to brave their hidden secrets. To his knowledge, no man had ever entered the dreadful region and returned to tell the tale. It was a patch of wilderness in the midst of the westland, very much like Grammore in many ways, but much smaller, although it still comprised a sizable area. Avoided by all, absolutely nothing was known about the ancient hollow. Legends and whispers, but that was all...If one passed along the edge, they could see things moving inside at times, furtive and insubstantial figures which never broke through the forest eave. Sounds could also be heard at night, and it was a desperate man who camped within sight of the dark land.

And Jerol had entered...

"Whatever could have driven him *there* of all places?" Sarion shook his head in wonder.

Chensel frowned. "The messenger told me that

The Rooting of Evil

Jerol came across the tracks of marauders which had ventured deeply into the borderlands, coming from a direction which might very well have originated near Karin. He made a quick decision to follow, as he had no intention of letting the raiders roam freely, and so close to Nighton itself."

"And then he tracked them into the hollow?" Karrol's face registered disbelief.

"The messenger said they were an hour's ride away from Sprechyd Wood when Jerol dispatched him to send this message. Our captain rode with two score fighters."

"But you're not certain he actually *entered* the hollow?" Sarion queried the grizzled Forester.

"The courier didn't see him enter, of course. But the message was very clear. Jerol fully intended on tracking the marauders towards the hollow and further, and would send additional word once he returned."

Silence fell upon the room, and a charred piece of kindling crackled behind them. Sarion leaned back in his chair, digesting this disturbing piece of news. Despite the irrationality of entering Sprechyd Wood, Jerol was too shrewd to go in without a strong belief that it was the right decision, and one with a high level of success. That was for certain. No, Jerol hadn't risen to First Captain of Nighton by making foolhardy choices. A calculated risk, perhaps. Sarion knew the man too well. His thoughts darkened though when he considered their own recent venture led by Charadan, sending them all into Grammore, resulting in terrible loss. It was a disturbing similarity.

"We must go to his aid. There can be no question." Karrol was again speaking. "Immediately."

Chensel nodded. "I know, that was my initial reaction as well." He paused for a moment, staring at Sarion. "What are your thoughts on this matter, Sarion?

I would value your input."

"We need to find out why he entered, of course. And lend aid in whatever way possible. However, I would urge great caution in this matter. If prowlers from Grammore are this close to the walls of Nighton, then things are much more serious than I'd realized. Our enemies grow ever bolder, and King Gregor must hear of this. I dislike the notion that the westland can be so easily maneuvered, and we need to rethink our strategy."

The men listened intently to his words. Sarion felt as if he were offering too much, as the Foresters seemed eager to absorb his suggestions. There was enough pressure on him already -- promises to uphold, from Charadan, and the king desperately needed to hear his tale. Sarion had hoped for a clear and swift passage to Daregil Keep, but as before, something else was now threatening the security of the westland, and ultimately Trencit. The more he thought about it, the darker his mind turned, as other possibilities emerged.

"A trap..."

The words escaped his lips, almost without him consciously saying it. The two men listened intently.

He stared at them both for a moment, then continued. "It might well be a trap laid by our enemies in order to undermine the leadership of Nighton."

Chensel's eyes narrowed sharply. "To lead him into Sprechyd Wood? Surely he wouldn't blindly fall into such a scheme."

"No, not blindly. But I fear a greater plan being wielded against us here," Sarion said. "With each passing moment, I imagine snares even more devious."

"This Dark Mage which you mentioned..." Karrol interjected. "This unrest originates from Grammore, certainly. And that is a cause for much alarm. If your notion bears truth, then his manipulations are far-reaching, his knowledge of our land considerable, although it's not difficult to know the machinery of our leadership and organization."

"Ah, but this Dark Mage seems to have a well-conceived plan, which I believe Sarion is leading up to." Chensel stroked the side of his face thoughtfully. "I think you strike at the root of the problem there, Sarion. Events have transpired very quickly in recent weeks. There exists an organized, powerful effort to impair our reaction. If this is indeed a trap set to ensnare Jerol, then there can be *no* doubt our enemy seeks to eliminate the leadership of the Western Watch, or at the very least greatly disrupt it."

"And the more I learn, the less I know." Sarion stared at the wall behind Chensel's head. "The Dark Mage seems to know everything about us, and we know nothing of him, despite our foray into Grammore. Nothing at all..."

His words were grim, but worse yet was the appalling secret he refused to tell them. The unutterable truth, about how terribly undermined the leadership of Trencit really *was* now. General Charadan was dead...

"We have a decision to make." Karrol stamped the table with the flat of his hand. "Jerol needs to be found."

Sarion knew he was right. The Western Watch could ill afford to lose their leader. The other captains were capable, honorable men, but Jerol had assumed the highest ranking position in the borderlands, and with good reason. They simply could not afford to lose him as well.

"I'll send a patrol to hunt for him. They'll leave tomorrow. Karrol, I want you to lead the company."

The captain nodded.

Chensel looked at Sarion. "If your circumstance were otherwise, I would ask for you to accompany Karrol on this quest. Your skill and those of your companions would be welcome. Is it possible that other messengers can be sent to King Gregor?"

Sarion matched the Forester's gaze. Measuring him, perhaps? King Gregor needed to hear from them, there was no question. Directly. And no other could be trusted with informing the king that his champion and chief councilor was now dead. But *was* there another way?

"It troubles me greatly, this matter of Jerol's absence. And I know it's imperative for us to depart for Daregil Keep at dawn, but maybe there is yet a way..." His voice trailed off, and they waited for his answer.

He closed his eyes for several long seconds. He was weary, mentally and physically. The trials of the past weeks weighed heavily on his heart and mind. There were too many things he needed to do. The vortex again...surrounding him, engulfing him. Only Chertron, Forlern and he knew the truth. But he felt these were men he could trust. They were leaders of Nighton. Strong men, loyal to Trencit. Still, he resisted. He desired to know *their* opinion of what should be done. It affected their role in the defense of the westland. Didn't he owe them this? They were his kindred, serving in his own stead, although he had been called to serve Trencit again.

Karrol and Chensel watched him, and he felt their gaze boring into him, trying to decipher his thoughts, gauge his hesitation.

Chensel broke the silence first. "I would offer you an immediate position in the Western Watch, Sarion. Your past record of service and ranking in the guard are all the requirements needed for reinstatement, as you well know already. As Second Forester of Nighton, my recommendation carries the power to make it thus. Jerol would undoubtedly see fit were he here as well, and with him missing, it is fully in my right to make such a promotion as I now command Nighton at this moment, and the Western Watch, although I wish it weren't so. You can be promoted without hesitation as a Forester."

Karrol nodded in agreement, but was silent.

Sarion was touched, and felt a surge of pride welling within his breast. Maybe this was what he needed, to rejoin his former comrades and patrol the borderlands with an organized force. After all these years again...But there was the very important task ahead of him, one which simply could not be ignored, or brushed away. King Gregor and General Charadan. And Edward and his own homelands.

"What say you, Sarion?" Chensel pressed him.

"I am truly honored, Captain. Truly. It makes my heart leap, the possibility of serving in the Watch once more. I have my nephew to consider, and my holdings, but I now realize that my place needs to be closer to the origin of conflict, where I can strive to make a difference. The lives of the entire kingdom are at stake, and I can't selfishly hunker down on my own lands any longer and ignore my countrymen. As they say, the troubles of the present day shatter the illusions of the past."

"We all have family elsewhere," said Karrol. "My own will be moving within these walls shortly, at least until matters grow less unsettled. But I can't see even a glimmer of this promise for many a night to come."

The First Captain raised one hand before him for emphasis. "Your hesitation is noble. I can see to your nephew's safety, if that alleviates your concern. The courier has left already, but I can just as easily have a patrol sent to secure your land, and bring the boy to Nighton." Chensel's face was determined, and Sarion knew that the captain was a decisive man, one who could make quick choices, however difficult.

"My thanks. But you forget the greater part of my involvement. King Gregor will be gravely displeased if he learns that we did not come straight to see him, or that we were sidelined by your decision."

But Chensel disagreed, shaking his head. "I'll make sure messengers are sent swiftly to Daregil Keep. We can place news of your company's expedition in royal script, and tell them that our need was dire with Jerol's absence. He'll be greatly concerned upon hearing that the Captain of Nighton is missing. Of *that* I'm completely certain. And if you were asked to assist, then he'll understand and respect the decision. King Gregor puts much faith in the leaders of Trencit, Sarion. I've met his Majesty already, and talked several times with him. He'll understand."

But you don't know the truth. Charadan is gone!

What to do...he thought. What more could he say without seeming aloof? The night was growing long. Choices needed to be made. Immediately...

"I agree with Chensel. Trencit calls us all to duty, and the time and place are not always of our own making. This Captain Grundel seemed to think very highly of you, and with obvious reason. King Gregor will look favorably upon you as well." Karrol sipped from his mug, his eyes never leaving Sarion's weary form.

And still he hesitated...Sarion felt that his eyelids would surely close, and that it would be impossible to lift them until the night wings of sleep were finally appeased.

"To have you serving in the Watch once again would be a great boon to us, Sarion." Karrol continued, eyeing him hopefully. "I would like to see you strike some blows at this enemy -- your swordsmanship is still spoken about in the training grounds of Nighton."

The Rooting of Evil

Smiling weakly in response, Sarion found himself increasingly liking this man. Sighing, he finally answered. "All decisions are difficult, and hold their own levels of risk. Action, inaction…we cannot know the outcome of any. But…I have not been entirely honest with you about our mission, and there are strong reasons I withhold information."

He looked into both their eyes, looking for doubt, a glimmer of mistrust. Instead he found only understanding and acceptance.

"I'm certain your motives are honorable. It is in my heart that there are things you wish to tell King Gregor directly." Chensel's gaze was powerful, and Sarion knew the man was even shrewder than he'd first thought.

Chensel spoke further. "If you believe such is the best path, then I will not question your reasons. Indeed, I feel that you hide something even more terrible than what has already been stated. And *that* gives me cause for great concern. Your tale is horrific enough -- the description of the evil in Grammore, the loss of Trencit's warriors. Nightmarish beasts emerging from the grim shroud of legend, walking the earth within the eaves of the forbidden land. How much more can a man suffer?" Chensel's words conveyed a deep feeling of sympathy and respect. Sarion wondered even more about the origin of this captain. Beneath his words lurked a greater vision of what beset their homeland. Sarion suspected that Chensel might guess, or know far more than he realized, about a great many things.

And then, based on all these things they had mutually learned from their discussion, Sarion made his decision. He realized that whatever his choices had been the past few weeks, and would continue to be in the coming days and months, that he would go with his instincts. Deep down he still felt a wrenching in his heart about Charadan's order for him to remain along the valley rim while the warriors penetrated the dead city Gorothagled. There remained a terrible guilt -- a black, yawning chasm of pain -- that he *should* have argued more fiercely, perhaps even disobeyed the command, and followed his companions. Things might have been different...But, *unlike* the courageous general, Sarion now decided to reveal the entire truth. He would accept the consequences if things went amiss. But he owed the leaders of Nighton no less.

"I've listened to your words, and pondered the heaviness weighing down my own decisions. We're all at risk, and the men of the Western Watch serve as the frontline in the defense of the westland against the dangers which threaten, in whatever form they take. I trust my instincts. And my instincts tell me to do this...I shall confide in you both."

There was a long pause.

Sarion spoke, his voice quiet, the words dredged up from the depths of his very soul. "General Charadan is dead..."

"What? Impossible!"

Chensel and Karrol were both stunned by his powerful statement, the Third Forester standing up in shock. Sarion held off their questions for a moment, raising his hand for calm until Karrol at last fell back into his chair. Chensel appeared outwardly calm, but his eyes smoldered with an inner fire. Sarion paused long moments before speaking, and then, in hushed tones, he spoke to them about the true identity of the false Captain Grundel. The room seemed to crouch down beneath the men in an unseen veil of despair, as the implications reared up in all their minds. Karrol kept muttering to himself in disbelief, and Chensel appeared even older, the wrinkles on his face tightening. Sarion's throat felt dry, his voice going hoarse from lack of rest, but he continued, filling in the details which he'd left out earlier. In the end, there was little to say, all three men lost in themselves.

Chensel finally broke the oppressive silence. "We need to further discuss the tragic events of your quest, Sarion. With General Charadan dead, the kingdom will be in upheaval. Too many things to talk about..." He sighed, passing a hand across his brow. "Charadan gone. A devastating blow to Trencit. I won't plague you with questions anymore this night though. I see that you need rest, and you appear to be near the brink of exhaustion. Karrol and I will be making decisions -- ones which can't wait until morning. Nighton's leader *must* hear of these tidings. A hunting party will be made ready for departure tomorrow."

Sarion sighed. "And I'll be coming along...Jerol needs to be found. If you can handpick a group of men to leave for Daregil Keep as escort before dawn, that would be the wisest choice as well. I'll go to King Gregor after this other matter is settled."

Chensel nodded solemnly. "Very well. We'll talk more in the morning. This night will only be growing older, and your tale has brought much sadness upon my ears. But I have a duty to perform, and will do my best to ensure the safety of the westland. Nighton will prevail."

Sarion stood, locking gazes with the grizzled captain. Inclining his head, he left, knowing where his own lodging quarters were located.

But he had one more conversation ahead of him before this night of grief would end. It already seemed like an eternity.

"You must go to Daregil Keep without us."

Forlern's eyes flashed dangerously. "Are you mad, Sarion? Why would you even *ask* me this? I will not leave you and Chertron. It was *you* who insisted we all remain together, and I agreed!"

Chertron was quiet, his face drawn. Sarion stood before them both, his own mind resolute, his orbs showing only determination.

"I don't want it this way, believe me. I know we've been through much already, and such a choice is not made lightly. Our companionship I hold dearly, and the bond of friendship has grown steadfastly. Nothing will ever change that...But King Gregor *must* know about the fall of Charadan, and with the greatest of haste. As a member of the Homeguard, your word will not be questioned. Indeed, Forlern, as the highest ranking member left from our company, it's your responsibility in this matter to go directly to the king. Charadan was your commander, and the mission is not completed. We cannot trust this to any other. Chertron was chosen as well, but he was given a temporarily leave to prepare and take part in this mission. He's not bound for additional active duty, at least until he returns...I'll come to Daregil Keep immediately after we find Jerol. You have my word."

Forlern's expression remained hard, and then he frowned, pacing back and forth. "I would not give your word unless you know what the future has in store for you. It grieves my heart to leave my comrades in such uncertainty. I like this not, but also cannot fault your reason, Sarion." He shook his head. "Ah, Shades. I know now how *you* felt thus when we descended into the dread valley before our assault on the fortress."

The Rooting of Evil

Sarion moved towards him, clasping his shoulder. "Forlern, we'll meet again soon. But it's impossible for me to continue onward without knowing what happened to Jerol. I think the king will understand. I served with Jerol in the Watch, and Trencit can ill afford to lose another of its leaders."

"That goes for yourself as well, my friend." Forlern smiled sadly. "You'll be reinstated soon if you don't watch yourself."

"That offer has been made this very hour. My burdens continue to mount, and I feel as if I'm stranded in a quagmire, sinking slowly." Sarion clapped him on the arm, slumping then into a chair. "By the Seven, this night has no end. Dawn will find us hours away, dead on our feet. But this is the choice before us, and not made lightly. If anything, let our resoluteness carry us forward in the coming days. When I come to Gregor, I'll figure some way to keep us all together. I think Charadan would have wanted it that way."

They all were silent, remembering the brave General, who none of them had *really* known, in many ways. But his character had been evident throughout their entire journey into Grammore. And they missed him dearly.

"Arrangements are being made, so we'll depart in the morning." Sarion stood, walking towards one of the beds, all which looked inviting, blanketed heavily in the handwoven patterns of the southland, where such quilts and other tapestries were created from the hands of skilled weavers. He collapsed onto the soft sheets. "Until the morrow, my friends. Seems our adventures have no end."

Chertron grunted, moving towards another one of the beds. "My only question is this -- who will look after this temperamental scoundrel without *me* around?"

After a brief moment, even Forlern managed a

weak chuckle, although to Sarion's keen ears, he heard the sadness within.

They all slept late into the morning. Despite the urgency of their missions, Chensel knew the men required a much-needed rest. The sun had climbed well into the sky when servants finally entered, informing them that hot baths had been drawn. Chertron was the first to leave, although his scowl expressed his dislike at leaving the comforts of the bed. "I wonder how long until I lay on another like this?" He grumbled to himself. "One night of reprieve, and then off for another prolonged ride. Ah well, 'tis better than the long weeks in the field guarding the eastern borders."

The three companions all made preparation for the coming day, enjoying the hospitality offered by Nighton, eating generously as heaping plates of steaming food were brought to their quarters. Their appetites were not easily satiated, but there was no shortage of helpings. A lieutenant named Hintrile looked in on them while they ate, apologizing for the interruption, but sent by Chensel for a briefing. As discussed the night before, things had already been set into motion. Messengers had left for Sarion's farm, carrying word to Edward, as well as a written letter which Sarion scripted. He didn't go into great detail for the boy, instead expressing his concern that they be wary of marauders, and wait for further word if things became worse. Sarion missed the lad, and told him that his service was required, although the situation remained uncertain, as he still needed to go before King Gregor.

Forlern's escort was waiting in the courtyard; a

full complement of a dozen fighters, fully armed and with the swiftest breed of horses in the borderlands. He would be the first of the companions to leave that morning.

It was a quiet farewell, as Chertron gripped him hard on the shoulder. "You know what to do. I don't envy your position in breaking such news to the king. But you have no fear, whether it be man or beast. Keep your head held high, and make sure you convey the urgency of our peril from the Lowlands. He'll listen to you. And he may very well wish to hear your counsel, as the three of us have seen what no others have...the face of evil in Grammore. Tell him of Charadan's bravery, and how Sarion led us through the Lowlands. We all owe our lives to Sarion."

Clasping arms with the fiery warrior, Sarion nodded at Chertron's words. "Give him Charadan's scroll. The medallion. Speak to him of all that befell us in Grammore. Tell him of our quest to slay the ogre, the mysterious Dark Mage, the cursed fortress, and the last of the Glefins. The terrible beasts and the winged gargoyles. He must know *everything*." And now Sarion's eyes blazed with an inner fire of determination. "Most of all, tell King Gregor of the bravery of his fighters, and that despite the fall of Charadan, that his men will suffer the evil rising against us. You tell him all this Forlern, and then I'll speak to him when we meet again in Daregil Keep. Trencit must not lose heart despite the loss of her general. *King Gregor* must not despair."

"By the Seven, I will tell him all these things. You have my word. And I'll tell him of our courage, hunted every step of the way in our venture into Grammore, and how we prevailed in the end. How Sarion of the westland prevailed along with the bravery of Chertron, and what Charadan saw in you, and what we know." Forlern held up the parchment, waving it gently in the air. "General Charadan will tell him in his own words," he spoke sadly. "May good fortune follow you wherever fate leads you. Be well, my friends."

He turned to leave, opening the door and then quickly pivoting. "Do not be overly long, or *I'll* come looking for you both..." His old brashness returned, and he grinned, his eyes narrowing. Sarion smiled, and Chertron only nodded, sighing.

"Try not to end up in the royal dungeons, Forlern. If we ride into Daregil Keep to find your head wedged between a stockade, I'll gladly throw the first egg myself."

Forlern laughed, and Sarion knew it was partly genuine. But he also knew the younger warrior was in much pain at leaving his friends. He saw it deeply in his eyes.

Sarion and Chertron were led to Chensel's quarters for a short meeting. They spoke of their earlier conversation, and the task at hand. Sarion also wanted more information about the deployment of forces, and the two men scanned maps of the westland. Sarion expressed concern over the increasing reports of marauders, and he suggested several points where additional hunting parties might be sent. The Forester listened to Sarion's words intently, telling him the Captains of Nighton were holding a council later that afternoon. He gave his word not to speak of Charadan's death, but instead they would rework some of their patrols, and send messages to Lord Pralicon in the north, and the other provinces to the south. Communication was vital, and the Western Watch needed to coordinate with the greater armies of the borderlands. Sarion also warned him of the winged predators, and for his men to watch the skies for the evil ones. Even Nighton could be compromised if the guards were unaware of this potential threat.

It was time for them to leave, and Chensel added a final warning. "Have a care, and beware the dangers of Sprechyd Wood. I have nothing to tell you of the hollow, save for one thing -- do not enter beneath the eaves and tempt its secrets, even if Jerol has done so. I know not what foul snare was laid, but you are well-advised against making the same mistake, Sarion. And remember my offer to reinstate you into the Watch again." At this he lifted his eyebrows. "We'll need your leadership in the days to come. Farewell."

Sarion felt a strong sense of pride from the captain's words, and he thanked him for his help. But right now, there were too many other pressing matters which needed his attention, and he was troubled by a sense of impending doom, something which bothered him greatly. Events swirled about him, and he shrugged off these grim thoughts.

They departed, led by a pair of green-clad fighters, who were to accompany them on the coming excursion with Karrol. Valadire was in command of this particular patrol, a low ranking captain of Nighton. Tall and lean, he reminded Sarion somewhat of Chertron. Valadire was even taller though, with warm eyes, speaking with a quiet voice. Roughly middle-aged, his hands were heavily callused, and he carried a brace of knives at his belt. The other man was younger than even Forlern, and his name was Quarran. His light blond hair and quick smile gave him a boyish look, and Sarion felt an immediate liking to the man. While traveling through the citadel, they all spoke freely of the fortress and its activity, and about their upcoming journey. Sarion pressed Valadire for news from the borderlands, and the captain spoke of scattered reports of marauders, but as of yet nothing had eclipsed the trouble experienced in the village of Karin.

They left on foot, walking through the midst of the fortress, which was bustling with daily activity. Warriors going about various tasks, merchants selling their wares in the stone streets, and those who lived within the walls going about with their own business, some related to Nighton, and some of it revolving around their own unique livelihood, whether it be craftsman, baker, ironsmith, or any one of countless other occupations befitting a citizen living beneath the emblem of a Trencit citadel. It was a thriving, if not enormous, fortress, and a strong symbol of Trencit's power in the westland.

They reached the main courtyard, and it was filled with men coming and going from patrol duty. Valadire led them to a side building, where they found a small company of Nighton fighters, along with Karrol himself.

"Well met, Sarion and Chertron." He greeted them warmly, and ushered them to a table. "We'll be off in a few minutes; just making some last minute preparations."

"How many are coming with us?" Sarion questioned.

"Ten hunters, plus yourselves. Valadire and Quarran as well." Karrol pointed towards the others, who were packing gear on a bench across the aisle.

"I hope it's enough, for whatever we encounter." Chertron frowned.

The Forester turned to him. "There are too few men to spare. And I think a larger party is unnecessary. We'll need speed and stealth for this mission.

Unfortunately, we don't know *what* type of trouble Jerol is in...or, if he actually is in any danger at all. It would not be unlike him to ride off for a few days, pursuing a whim. As First Captain of Nighton, he follows his own path, wherever it may lead."

"Then he hasn't changed at all these past few years," added Sarion. "But I'm worried. Dark things are making their way across the Ridgeline, causing mischief. If he's caught up in danger the likes of which *we* were, then he might be involved with something he's never experienced before."

"Aye, that's my fear as well." Karrol rubbed a hand across his chin. He nodded, standing, as Valadire gestured towards them. "We'll know the reasons soon enough, if things go well. We should be off."

The two companions followed after him, and Sarion wondered what exactly they *would* find out about Jerol's fate...

The hunting party left Nighton without delay, mounted on fine war horses, fresh and ready for a prolonged ride. They rode east, heading for the other end of the valley. The vale opened up wider here, and was similar to the western approach. Forests were scattered along the sides of the hills, which plummeted upwards, steep and treacherous. A natural barrier, it was impossible to lead horses to their high elevation. Loose rock and jagged boulders made the going hazardous for the lower stretches, and then the angle increased drastically. It was as if some unimaginably immense giant from the beginning of the world had scooped a deep, long trough through the hills, forming a valley which offered the inhabitants a perfectly devised shelter. Staying in the middle, the path was worn and smooth, consisting of low grass and firm ground. They passed numerous horsemen and other travelers headed for business in the thriving citadel. They even spotted a trio of riders wearing the emblem of Daregil Keep at one point. Sarion considered hailing them, but thought better of it. He had confidence that Forlern would go directly to the Trencit capital without delay, and was unwilling to involve any others at this moment. Their need was urgent, and nothing else would be accomplished by retelling part of their tale, even to couriers from King Gregor himself. They would know soon enough. Chensel would inform them that Forlern was now on his way to Daregil Keep bringing news of Grundel's expedition. After that, the king would have to decide on his own course of action...

The horsemen waved to Karrol's company, but showed no intention of stopping. The traffic along this part of the valley was constant, and it was unlikely they would pause for any conversation regardless. On Chensel's orders, Karrol was to remain as inconspicuous as possible. At this point everything was a distraction, and could be costly. So the men thundered ahead on their steeds, riding late into the afternoon before they reached the eastern wall.

Like its western counterpart, it was ruggedly built, the walls high and heavily guarded. A pair of fires burned from somewhere to either side, braced against the hills. Sarion knew the location, nestled firmly in hillside rooks, spaced apart to maximize the drift of the wind. The intention was unmistakable -- danger was afoot in the westland. They were approached by the warders of the gate, and Karrol met with their commander in private for several minutes while the fighters rested. The sky above had darkened, grey clouds rolling in from the Ridgeline. The Nighton hunters remained attentive even here. Sarion knew that they had been told the importance of the mission, and the identity of their new companions -- of this he was certain. And once they left the valley, things would become unpredictable. Chertron had questioned him about the terrain leading up to Sprechyd Wood earlier. Sarion explained that it was filled with trails leading towards central Trencit, with some branching away to the provinces in the north and south. Immediately around Nighton there was much activity, but then it dropped off in the direction of Sprechyd Wood, as people avoided passing too closely to its borders. The nearest village was miles away from it. Patrols from the Watch traveled mainly to its western and northern edges. To its south stretched leagues of wilderness, with few farms and towns. East, the region consisted of scattered forests until entering the central plains, which eventually led to larger towns, numerous farms and dwellings. The land also became flat, broken by occasional small hills and quiet lakes. This large area was the veritable breadbasket of Trencit, the most populated and productive region in the kingdom. The climate was temperate year-round, and was heavily protected along its northern, southern, and eastern edges by the Royal Legions.

Shortly, Karrol returned, looking troubled, coming to Sarion and Chertron. "No word yet from Jerol...The commander of the western gate, Captain Lingar, has been awaiting his return. He sent out a few horsemen to search for his party."

"That's not very comforting. I was hoping our journey would prove unnecessary, but my heart tells me otherwise." Sarion stared at the fighters guarding the ramparts of the wall.

"There's more..." Karrol's voice grew low so only the two companions could hear. "One of Lingar's men questioned a peddler coming from the south." The Forester paused. "He claims to have seen something flying in the air at night, near Sprechyd Wood."

Sarion and Chertron locked eyes for a moment.

"That is ill news," Chertron muttered. "It could be the ramblings of a fool, but we've seen enough strange creatures in our wanderings to ignore such talk."

Karrol continued. "That could well be one of the winged predators you spoke of, which followed your company from the Ridgeline. A different one, perhaps. And there's yet another thing I must speak of, even *more* worrisome."

Sarion leaned close.

"A number of travelers spoke about people missing in the area around Sprechyd Wood. And seeing other unusual things. Bones of animals, stripped bare. No signs of any struggle. I told Lingar that no one is to leave the valley alone for any reason. Men are to be paired in two at the very least, larger whenever possible. Single messengers are forbidden. Something infringes on Nighton's very borders, I feel. A great evil."

"The news continues to grow ever worse. Let's hurry then. I fear for Jerol's safety even more." Sarion straightened, and Karrol signaled to Valadire that they were again on the move. As they passed beneath the sturdy walls protecting the valley entrance and entered the woods which loomed ahead, Sarion couldn't shake the feeling that they were not riding within the friendly groves of Trencit's wondrous westland, but instead were plunging into the forests of Grammore once again.

The company from Nighton followed main trails

for a while, riding through deeply forested regions consisting of gentle, sloping valleys and rugged undergrowth. The hills were all small, nothing as impressive as the higher terrain surrounding the western fortress. The sun remained hidden for most of the day, and a premature twilight eagerly descended over the spacious westland. The sky was a vague splash of gray, heavy and uncertain. Earlier, they had passed several dozen other travelers, the majority heading to Nighton, but in the hour before dusk they were alone. Karrol made sure to question everyone they came across at this juncture. Even the slightest hint of news could prove valuable. Sarion was at his side whenever they met with others. Nothing appeared to be of interest. Everyone expressed the same concerns; rumors circulating the borderlands about dangerous creatures prowling the territory. There was a general feeling of unease, and many who lived in the area were relocating towards the larger towns, but those who farmed and had much land to care for had little choice but to remain at their homes and stay vigilant. Everyone asked what the Western Watch could do to defend their borders, but it was common knowledge that they were spread thin already.

The company slowed their pace as it became too dark to see very far. Sarion rode next to Karrol, with Chertron taking the lead, helping to scout the land with one of the hunters named Glavit, a bear of a man with a thick red beard and a keen eye. Valadire rode immediately behind them, and the fighters remained on high alert for any threat. Lanterns were brought out, and they appeared as a company of phantoms if any passerby happened to spot them from a distance. After a while, Karrol decided to camp for the night, as they had made good time. With luck, they would come upon the borders of Sprechyd Wood before sunset the following day. The hunters made a quick and efficient camp, foregoing a fire, as it might attract unwelcome eyes. When all had settled and guards were posted, Karrol, Sarion, Chertron, and Valadire sat in conference, discussing strategy for the upcoming search. The Third Forester unfolded a map, setting it on the ground before them, the parchment illuminated by a pair of lanterns.

"This is where the rider gave his last position as..." Karrol pointed to a spot near the northwestern edge of Sprechyd Wood, which was marked as nothing more than the name itself.

"What's really known about the forest?" Chertron looked up at their faces. "Even in my homelands in the east, it's spoken as a place of dread to scare children at night. Liken to Grammore itself, but within the realm of Trencit. Seems to have remained unchanged for centuries, much older than our kingdom. It was always here."

"You're right," Sarion answered. "I've lived in the westland all my life, and know nothing about it. No one goes near it. No one dares to enter. And nothing leaves the dark wood. But I *know* there's life inside. You can look at it from a distance, and feel something in there. Ancient, powerful. Perhaps evil."

"There is much similarity to the Lowlands, in this respect," Karrol added. "Not in scale, although Sprechyd Wood is large in its own right. But it's certainly dangerous. Only a fool would believe otherwise."

"I agree," said Sarion. "But I also think there's a difference between the two. I can't quite explain my feelings, having only entered Grammore. But even looking from the outside, I'm struck by what I can sense there. The whole *forest* seems alive somehow, while Grammore is more like an ocean filled with terrible beasts and other fantastic life, of so much variety and strangeness that it defies comprehension. Sprechyd

The Rooting of Evil

Wood is old, very old, slumbering. And I would not want to awaken what sleeps inside..."

The others pondered his words in silence. Valadire then responded. "I have only seen this which lies before us. I've only been to the Ridgeline once, and on this side. But your words make me again wonder what need drove Jerol to enter, if indeed he did such. We should track the edges, and look for signs of his passing. There's a wide swath of grassland which surrounds the forest on all sides. One cannot enter without knowing so. It's as if Sprechyd Wood forbids even plant life from infringing on its domain."

Chertron sighed. "Well, there's little we can do except search for them when we reach the forest. I for one have no desire to tempt its dangers. But I'll follow Sarion wherever he decides to go, even into Sprechyd Wood."

Sarion smiled at his companion. "We're seeking Jerol, and I'm not leading this company. We'll offer Karrol our aid, and I also do not wish to try the forbidden region. Uncertainty surrounds us."

Karrol nodded. "And *that* is the only thing we do know...Get some rest, my friends. One evening's stay at Nighton is hardly enough after your weary travels."

They separated, and Sarion wrapped his blankets tightly about against the dampness. His dreams that night were plagued with visions of nameless beasts searching him out, their eyes like fireflies glimmering in the shadows.

Sarion was roused from sleep by Chertron, his kindly face creased into a scowl. Fat drops of rain poured down through the forest canopy, drenching everything in sight. The cloud cover from the previous day had come through with its promise, and torrential rains had begun an early assault on the borderlands. Cloaked with his hunting jacket pulled tight, Sarion made the best of it, sharing a quick breakfast with several of the hunters and gearing himself for traveling in wet conditions. The company was packed up and soon off, heads bowed low against the hostile weather. The ground was moist and the air damp, but the fighters were used to such environments, living in the unpredictable westland.

Few words were exchanged between Karrol and Sarion, only a general review of what both already knew. Later in the morning, the captain sent out a pair of scouts to track the road ahead. The trees pressed close on both sides, and the trail they followed would lead them to their destination. Dozens of paths crisscrossed the region, but they came across no sign of other travelers for most of the day. Karrol mentioned once that they were near Fledge Rae, a small village, but he didn't want to spend time by going there. Late morning turned into early afternoon without any change in the weather or the scenery. Sarion had traveled this country before, and knew that if any outsiders strayed from the paths, they could easily become lost in the wilderness. They halted only twice for brief rests, and at times Karrol would send out another pair of fighters to relieve the forward scouts, but nothing unusual appeared. As the day grew long, a growing sense of unease fell over the company as they knew Sprechyd Wood was near. Sarion could almost feel its presence like a living thing, the great forest waiting patiently, confidently, unable to be compromised. Even the brave fighters of Nighton feared the grim forest, especially living within easy reach of its shadow.

The Rooting of Evil

Karrol consulted with Sarion several times, and the Forester believed them to be very close now. Glavit, who remained in the lead with Chertron, suddenly halted, speaking with the Trencit warrior and pointing to the ground. Sarion and Karrol came forward moments later.

"Why have you stopped? Something wrong?" Karrol's voice betrayed no emotion, but Sarion felt a twinge of warning.

"I'm not sure, Captain Karrol." Glavit glanced over at Chertron. "The rain is erasing most of our tracks, but not all. Gravil and Hurtun passed this way scouting ahead of us. See the hoof prints? And then nothing...like they simply vanished."

"It might be the rain falling heavier in this area, but it seems strange," Chertron offered, a puzzled look on his face.

Sarion dismounted, moving forward, the men waiting for him to search the ground. He avoided the middle of the trail, crouched along the sides and stooping low to the earth. There were faint markings before them, unmistakably from the two hunters. But then, exactly as Glavit said, they disappeared. Sarion straightened, a cold feeling easing its way across his back. What had happened here? Could the rain have wiped away all trace of their passing? He moved about, and there was no evidence that anything had continued further. The scouts had not been ordered to go very far from the main party. Then he saw several odd markings which he couldn't identify. A nagging doubt emerged in his mind, and he felt a sudden rush of fear. He bolted upright, heading back to the men. "Quickly, we must leave!"

Karrol's mouth opened to question him, but Sarion cut him off with a gesture.

"Now. Caution the men for silence, and muffle

the horses."

The captain gave a short whistle, and the signal was passed along. The hunters could travel with the utmost stealth when necessary, and the beasts were muzzled, their hooves dampened. Within two minutes they were again mounted, and Karrol leaned close to Sarion, his eyes waiting for an explanation. Sarion only shook his head, pointing skyward.

To the trees.

Layers of mist seeped forth from the surrounding trunks, and the forest was hushed. No one spoke until Sarion whispered over to Karrol. "We need to break from this cover. How far away do you think Sprechyd Wood is?"

"A mile or two at most, immediately to our south."

"Are you certain?" Sarion's urgent face spoke of a need for accuracy.

"As much as can be. Nightfall is almost upon us. If we continue along the path, there is a ridge which overlooks Sprechyd Wood, and the land opens up towards the vale."

"We may not have time for that. The more I think about it, the trail itself might be our enemy. Call your men. I think it best if we leave the path now."

Karrol's eyes narrowed in surprise. "The going will be difficult, nearly impassable at times. What about the scouts?"

Sarion's orbs were unblinking as he answered. "Beyond our help. They're already dead."

Karrol's face barely concealed his outrage. "How can you be so sure? I'm not leaving them to fend for themselves."

The Rooting of Evil

But Sarion only shook his head. "If you don't want to share their fate, then we *must* veer off the path. A trap has been laid, or blame it on terrible misfortune. It matters not, but the result will be the same."

Karrol considered for a moment, then nodded. "I'll listen to you, Sarion. You know something that I don't. But I'm not giving up on my men."

He gave the order and they soon entered the undergrowth, the fighters dismounting and leading the animals by hand. The gloom settled down, smothering them and making the visibility worse than it already was. Their durable lanterns were brought out, biting through the bleakness around them, enough so that the men could still negotiate the thick forest. Karrol told his hunters to keep their eyes open for anything moving about, even overhead. They continued on without speaking, their feet sliding on wet leaves and sinking into the yielding loam.

Sarion was vigilant, his sharp eyes missing nothing. With all the horrifying events of the past several weeks, perhaps the most disturbing of all was the changing face of his homeland. The west had always been wild, due to its vastness and proximity to the Ridgeline. And marauders had at times ventured into their territory, most especially the Glefins. But never *this* deeply, and to this extent. And, if his hunches were right, never to the level which now threatened them. They kept moving, dodging the branches which hovered before their faces, careful to avoid the thickest of brambles. Time dragged and night fell at last, the *real* night, piling on even more blackness against the struggling remnants of twilight which had prevailed the day long.

Sarion could not have imagined a more dangerous situation than what they now faced…

An hour of such travel passed without mishap,

when finally, to the relief of all, the woods broke open, revealing a shadowed, clear grassland before their nervous eyes. Sarion pressed them forward, looking over his shoulder constantly. "We must not delay. I thought I heard something several minutes ago."

Karrol whistled and the hunters scurried into the open night. Soon, all had left the forest behind, and Sarion urged them down the gentle slope and to the south. Below them, still a good distance off, a large and impenetrable darkness loomed, holding secrets and filling the men with quiet dread. Ancient hickory, oak, and shagbark trees squatted eerily in the half-light, aged sentinels crooked and tall.

They were all affected by what now confronted them, for sweeping the landscape less than several hundred yards before their feet waited the forbidding hollow of trees known as Sprechyd Wood.

They skirted the strange and unknown forest, keeping it a fair distance to their left. Sarion suggested to Karrol that they keep moving for a while, and that he believed the immediate threat to have passed. The fighters mounted their horses again, riding late into the night without rest. The rain lessened to little more than a trickle of annoyance, and they finally halted after going several miles.

"Tonight, the open sky is our friend." Sarion dismounted, pulling his hood tightly over his damp hair.

Both Chertron and Karrol hovered before him, questions lining their faces. Valadire organized the men for camp preparation, sending guards to patrol the perimeter. He walked over to the others, and Sarion waited to speak until he joined them.

"You have much to explain, Sarion. We've left Gravil and Hurtun behind, good men, something which is unacceptable. You of all people know this." Karrol's face was impassive, but his eyes smoldered, his distress evident over leaving behind the missing fighters.

"I *do* know, but my action was necessary. If there was any chance to help them, or any other choice, for that matter, I would have done my best to search for your men."

"Don't doubt his words, Captain Karrol. I think I know what Sarion suspects." Chertron added support for his friend, but the Forester ignored him, his gaze fixed on Sarion's resigned face.

"We were being stalked back there. Your fighters were taken by something which would have attacked us as well. We were fortunate to have escaped this far."

"What do you mean?" Valadire asked.

"Their trail was not entirely washed away by the rain. The markings were clear enough leading up to that point. There was also no sign of a pitched fight on the ground, but I saw strange marks, meaning *something* took them by surprise -- an unknown attacker with a tremendous advantage. One which used the trees."

"Two armed men taken without even a fight? Nighton hunters who know these woods like none other? I don't believe it..." Karrol shook his head.

Sarion held up one hand. "But these woods are no longer the same ones we're both familiar with. They've been compromised, at least certain parts. The men had no chance. Snatched from above, the attack came so swift and deadly that they were slain before they could even draw their weapons. Even their steeds were taken."

"What could have possibly done this?" A look of quiet horror spread across Karrol's face.

"On our journey into Grammore, we saw evidence of predators which kept to the trees. Silent and cunning." Sarion's eyes narrowed.

"He's right..." Chertron's voice was little more

than a whisper.

Valadire interjected. "But it would have to be extremely powerful to take two men and their horses and leave no sign. Into the trees yet? That's unthinkable."

"Indeed, but not so unbelievable when considering the creatures which live in Grammore." Sarion sighed, folding his arms.

"So you think something from the Lowlands has penetrated these woods?" Karrol questioned, but already knew the answer.

"I'm certain of it." Here Sarion paused. "This in itself is enough of a concern, but I have a greater fear as well. It might have been a Killworm..."

The men were silent, and only Chertron moved, nodding his head slowly to himself.

"A Killworm? They exist only in legend. And you're saying that your group encountered these monsters in Grammore?" Karrol pursed his lips.

"Yes. We've found out through our travels that legends do indeed walk the earth, and one of these monsters was on *this* side of the Ridgeline. That was shortly after our journey started. Long thought dead, when Captain Grundel entered the lair he discovered a newly-hatched egg, and the young Killworm nearly had us all that night. If it wasn't for his quick thinking we would have met our end there."

Sarion remembered the terrifying event, when Charadan had been lowered into the round hole, reappearing minutes later and ordering them all to leave quickly. A soundless, terror-stricken flight in the dark, they had fled immediately as the infant Killworm emerged, keening its dreadful call and showering the night sky with long strands of silver death, an excretion meant to cripple its prey. They had barely escaped with their lives...And yet another had been waiting inside the dead fortress of Gorothagled, a monstrous guardian set in place against intruders. Charadan and the others had managed to somehow escape its clutches as they moved through underground tunnels, but not before a pair of warriors had been claimed as they warded outside while the General searched one of the buildings. If the Killworm had found them in the open while battling the ogre, none of them would have left the dread citadel.

"I can't be certain," Sarion continued. "It could very well be another creature which also hunts from the trees. Regardless of what type, it explains the missing travelers in this area. The only trace left behind would be the bones of its victims, if someone happened to stumble across them. Whatever it is, this creature hunts our people. And until we know the nature of this new threat, there is no defense except to avoid it."

"Can this Dark Mage control such beasts even from a distance? But that would require tremendous power." Karrol was astonished.

"He possesses such magic, this is for sure," Sarion replied carefully. "But I don't think he can manipulate such a beast from far away. He may exert enough control to place them where he wants, and leave them to roam unfettered, perhaps. That seems more likely...Guardians and marauders set loose to disrupt our patrols and slay us. And another thought, which offers less comfort. It's told that creatures such as the Killworm are magical in nature, imbued with power far beyond the strength found in beasts of flesh and blood. It was said they cannot be killed by normal means, steel or flame."

"Then we're helpless against such monsters?" Sarion shrugged, uncertain himself.

"And now at least one, perhaps more, have made their way into the westland...This is ill news indeed, if it be the truth. What can we do?" Valadire looked to Sarion for an answer. They all looked at him, but he only shook his head.

"I don't know, except make sure we don't fall within its power, and avoid it at all costs."

"Do you think we're safe here?" Karrol pressed him.

"It's difficult to say. As safe as can be. I don't think it will venture willingly into the open. It was said they preferred a certain territory, with a central lair. If we move past that particular region, then we might avoid any encounter. But such a beast would have a vast area under its dominion. The men need to be vigilant. And ready for a swift departure if need be."

Chertron nodded, and left with Valadire.

Karrol remained staring at Sarion, who held off the Forester's comment before it passed his lips.

"I'm sorry about your men. If there was anything we could have done, I would have tried. I've seen too many good fighters fall in recent weeks."

"I understand Sarion. And my apologies for doubting your word. I know not what we're facing, and rely on your counsel to keep us from harm's way. But the loss of any fighters under my command is a sore blow. These men give their lives in the defense of our homeland. An enemy of flesh and blood is one thing. Nightmares which prowl at will, unseen in our own forests is quite another matter. The evidence is here which leads to such truth. And if so, then we cannot effectively protect the people in the westland."

Unable to refute the Forester's grim words or offer comfort, Sarion shook the rain from his cloak and turned away. He was only one man, without the answers. Perhaps there were none to be found. So much had fallen on his shoulders since the fateful journey into Grammore. So much frustration. Pain. Death. What more could he do? Melting away into the shadows, he slumped to the ground alongside Chertron, whose eyes were already closed, his breathing deep. Staring at his companion, Sarion longed for more peaceful times of recent years. He chided himself, knowing where that path would lead. No. He could not afford regrets. His responsibility was to the present, and immediate future. The westland. Trencit.

Thinking about their mission, and what he now understood, Sarion lacked the heart to continue his discussion with Karrol concerning the missing Jerol. But he also realized Karrol would now be having the same grim thoughts about the fate of Nighton's First Captain.

What further surprises would the next dawn bring him?

Sarion did not have to wait until the new day for anything unexpected…

Rough hands shook him awake and his knife flashed in his palm within moments. His grip eased on the hilt as Chertron's friendly eyes locked on his own. Sarion read the uncertainty in his companion's orbs, but no panic.

"What is it?" He hissed.

"I'm not sure. We seem to have company." Chertron's arms were at his sides, but he held no weapon. That was a good sign at least, thought Sarion.

"Come. Karrol and Valadire are over here. You'll see for yourself."

They walked across the grass, slippery with a fresh coating of rain. The night had not ended yet, or perhaps dawn was just as gloomy. The foul weather prevailed, cloaking the grassland in heavy sheets of mist. The entire camp was awake and at full attention, the hunters moving about like shades, gliding soundlessly in the gray curtain of darkness and haze.

Too few men.

Sarion shook his head. The dangers which threatened seemed to be numberless, while their own ranks were limited and scattered, and now lessened by two more warriors...

They reached the southern edge of the camp's perimeter, where both Karrol and Valadire waited with another pair of fighters, all of them gazing towards the impenetrable vastness of Sprechyd Wood, its presence looming in the distance like a living entity, hunkered down and watching them. But it wasn't the forest which had captured their attention. Less than two dozen yards away a light flickered like a will-o-the-wisp, forsaken and hopeless. A shadow supported the light, which now appeared to be a lantern flame held aloft by a stooped figure.

"Come no closer and announce yourself. We are fighters of Trencit, hunters from the Western Watch. Speak or consider yourself within our power." One of the guards hoisted a long bow, notched with a steel-tipped arrow. The one hailing the stranger had unsheathed his sword, holding it warily. Other fighters ringed the encampment in protective posture, warding against anything approaching.

"Such antagonism towards a harmless old peddler?" The words were thin and rough, with the hint of a suppressed cough. The stranger moved cautiously towards them. Sarion made out features now. Hooded with a dusky brown cloak, the figure held one hand upright in a gesture of friendliness.

"Speak your name." Karrol questioned the man.

"My name is Mugil. Who travels on such a dismal night?"

"I am Captain Karrol from Nighton. What is

your business this close to Sprechyd Wood?"

The man unfurled his hood, revealing an unkempt white beard with dark chasms of blackness for eyes. The hand holding the lantern wavered, as if he suffered from a trembling disease, or perhaps caused by his age. He appeared to be very old. Sarion wondered what the man was doing in the middle of the wilderness, in such close proximity to dangerous lands.

Stopping short a respectful distance from the hunters, the stranger reached behind his thick cloak, pulling out a gnarled walking stick. "Forgive me, but this staff helps support my weary limbs. I need its strength. I live in these woods." He angled his neck awkwardly, and by his gesture, seemed to be referring to the forest which they had left earlier in the night.

"So close to yonder hollow?" Valadire questioned the man.

"I have no fear of that place..." His tone sounded almost mocking, and Sarion found it strange. "I've lived beneath shadowed eaves my whole life. But what is your purpose in these parts? Your men appear ready for battle. Surely not against old hermits?"

If Karrol was annoyed by the stranger's remarks, he didn't show it. "Death roams these woods. You would best find a safer haven. Several of our men have been lost."

The hermit nodded to himself, but said nothing.

"You know of these things?" Valadire pressed him, inching closer. "If so, what can you tell us?"

"Hmm. You're right. A great evil stalks the trees."

"Have you seen that which hunts us?" Valadire continued, and Sarion stared at the stranger in silence. The old man shifted his stance, as if just becoming aware of Sarion's presence. The others seemed not to take notice.

"Seen?" He paused. "I've seen many things. Terrible and beautiful. Some which could freeze your blood where you stand," he scoffed. "Even such brave warriors as the men of Nighton."

"We don't have time for riddles, old man." Valadire grew impatient. "We seek a patrol, overdue by several days. Have you seen them in your wanderings?" His tone reflected his skepticism of the stranger, who might very well be nothing more than a madman.

"Yes." Mugil's voice was a low whisper.

The men exchanged stares. Now Karrol came forward, halting a few feet before the hermit. "Where did you see them? Time grows short. Tell us."

There was a long pause before the stranger answered. He leaned heavily on his cane before responding. "I'll do more than just tell you. I'll show you where they're at..."

"Where are they? Are they all right?" Valadire questioned the hermit repeatedly, but the stranger refused to answer, gesturing into the distance. Karrol also pressed the old man for several moments without result, but then Sarion signaled, stepping back several paces. Karrol left the questioning to his captain, sliding further into the camp after Sarion.

"What do you think?" The Forester leaned in close.

"He may know something, or it might be the ramblings of a half-crazed old man. I don't know. But we have to investigate. He could very well lead us to information concerning Jerol's whereabouts. Right now, we have no other option." Sarion shrugged.

The Rooting of Evil

Karrol nodded. "My thoughts exactly. There is something a bit strange about this hermit though. But why would he attempt to antagonize us? If my time is wasted, I'll lash him to a tree and leave him there..."

Sarion smirked, although he knew Karrol would do no such thing. But they all would be angry indeed. "I think several of us should go with him, and leave the others behind. If this hermit has traveled safely in this region, then maybe we can learn something of use."

"I'll go along, with three hunters, and yourself. What about Chertron?"

Sarion hesitated, knowing that the stalwart warrior would want to come with them. But he had other plans for his companion...

"No. Ask him to stay behind with Valadire and the rest. We should be prepared in case something unforeseen occurs."

The Third Captain agreed. "Let's be off quickly. If the hermit speaks the truth, then Jerol might be nearby. And I have a lot of questions for *him*."

Karrol called for Chertron, and the fighter joined them several seconds later. Once he told the warrior of their plan, a look of frustration crossed Chertron's face. Sarion dismissed any retort with a wave of his hand. "It's best to keep our strength in both places. We won't be gone long. If the hermit leads us astray, we'll hurry back. But I don't want to forget what stays hidden and stalks the forest behind us. Your keen eyes must protect the others. I don't think we all should ride off where this hermit takes us."

Karrol added more. "With luck, we can return to Nighton before the morning grows late."

"I don't like this idea," Chertron muttered. "And I don't have much faith in the ramblings of a mad hermit. He might lead you all into a pit of vipers."

"I think we can take care of one old man." Karrol

chided. "But I think he knows something of value. Maybe he can show us where Jerol camped. I think he *is* half-mad, though, but I feel there is some truth in his riddles. Have a care while we're gone."

"And keep *your* wits, Captain of Nighton. And listen to Sarion." Chertron slapped his friend on the arm. "Be careful and return swiftly. Needless to say, I don't like this business one bit..."

"I haven't liked it since your company of warriors plucked me from my humble farm a few long weeks ago," Sarion replied.

"Good thing we did. You might have withered away and grown fat and lazy over time."

"Now I'll disagree with you..."

Sarion wagged a finger at the lean fighter, and moved back towards his horse while Karrol went to see how Valadire was faring.

Striding through the light rain, Sarion felt a twinge of excitement as well as trepidation. He was discovering how unpredictable the westland really was in these dangerous times. Nothing was as it seemed anymore. True, it had never been the safest corner of Trencit, but not to this degree. What else would they discover? Too many surprises lay in wait, and he needed to make sure that any new surprises would find him well-prepared.

Especially the unpleasant ones.

Sarion, Karrol, and the three hunters rode silently behind the odd peddler, who refused to mount one of their horses, claiming his frail condition. They had to settle for a slow pace across the grassland, the hermit shuffling ahead with head bowed low. He refused to tell them anything more, except that it was not very far where they had to go. Soon they would know of their captain's fate. Sarion didn't like the sound of the old man's description, but there was nothing to be done except to follow him in the hopes that something promising would be revealed. Sometimes Mugil cackled quietly, humored by a joke known only to himself. Other times he whispered secrets which only he could hear. It was unsettling, and Sarion distrusted the hermit, but could not determine anything which threatened. Regardless, he remained highly vigilant, in the lead next to Fradwil, one of the Nighton trackers. They rode along for close to an hour, and Karrol questioned the hermit several times.

"Yes, very close," was all he would say.

The new day arrived, nothing more than a lessening of twilight, and Mugil finally halted, pointing to the south.

Towards Sprechyd Wood...

"What are you telling us? That the men we search for are in the forest?" Karrol frowned, his face clearly showing his doubt.

The hermit nodded, the hood once again thrown over his head.

"That is forbidden territory. No one willingly enters."

Mugil turned towards him. "Not true, Captain of Nighton. One can enter unhindered, if they know how to avoid the perils."

"*You* have entered the woods, haven't you?" Sarion leaned down, peering beneath the stranger's cowl.

Mugil stared at him for a moment, angling his head slightly to one side. "A shrewd guess, warrior."

"And you've seen our comrades in the woods? How deep inside are they? And why would they undertake such a journey?" Karrol remained unconvinced.

"Hunting. They tracked something which led them there. You will know once we arrive." He would say no more.

Sarion exchanged a cautious glance with Karrol. Both men felt uneasy, but Sarion knew they had come too far to turn back. He respected Sprechyd Wood, and believed beyond question that danger existed within its dark reaches, but Sarion had braved another forbidden land and emerged from it. Twice now... He thought things over, debating in his mind. It was a risk, a great risk, but maybe they could attempt it. Sarion had no knowledge except for his own instincts to go on. He felt that one might prevail, if wary and determined enough, and as long as they dared not venture too deeply. If Mugil had gone in and returned unscathed, then it was possible. Surely the old man wouldn't risk his own life on such a reckless whim. At last he nodded.

"All right, hermit." Karrol's voice was low but unwavering. "Lead on. But if anything threatens you'll be the first to welcome it."

Mugil was silent, but Sarion thought he was smiling inside the folds of his robe.

His uneasiness continued to increase as they moved towards the dread forest.

The small group halted before the ominous border of Sprechyd Wood. Sarion had never been this close before. The trees were monolithic sentinels, hoary and wide of girth, all of them hardwoods of some type, although many were so gnarled and ancient they bore little resemblance to the common species of Trencit. Some were pocked with round holes, possibly homes to night birds or other woodland creatures, but of either there was no sign. No sound leaked outwards from the shrouded forest, only a strong sense of *something* which waited inside, watching and listening to their every move. Unsettling as it had looked from a distance, it was much greater from this close, almost overpowering, and Sarion's instincts shrilled to him of latent danger. Where it came from and how deep, there was no way of knowing, but it was definitely there…Glancing over at Karrol, he immediately knew that the shrewd captain felt it as well.

"They entered here?" The Forester lifted his lantern into the night, long shadows quivering from the intrusive light as he questioned the hermit.

Pointing, Mugil answered. "Inside here, not very far at all."

Sarion dismounted, bending low and scouring the ground for signs of recent passage.

"You'll find no marks, tracker." The hermit's voice sounded reproachful. "You know nothing of this forest, do you now? It doesn't much like outsiders."

"Then what can you tell us besides riddles and vague answers? What happened to their prints?" Increasingly skeptical and annoyed, Sarion stood directly before the aged hermit.

"The forest has a way of swallowing all traces of unwanted life. A wise man treads lightly, a foolish man blunders forward without regard."

"What would you have us do then?" Karrol dismounted as well, joining Sarion.

"Leave the horses here, and we'll enter quietly. Less risk of awakening unfriendly eyes." Mugil leaned heavily on his staff, as if incredibly weary.

"We'll do as he says. Tie the horses along the edge. I'm growing tired of your wandering answers, though, Mugil. Our business can ill afford games or delays. There had better be something useful inside here."

The hermit only nodded in response, then plunged beneath the eaves of the forest.

Sarion felt extremely disturbed by the old man's words and actions, but few choices lay before them. If there was anything here to aid them in finding Jerol, any sign or indication of his passing, then they must investigate further, despite Chensel's warning of the dread forest. He and Karrol had already agreed beforehand not to venture very deeply into Sprechyd Wood. They exchanged a quick glance, and then followed Mugil.

Once inside, Sarion was struck immediately by a feeling of oppressiveness, the air itself stifling and uncomfortable, much warmer than outside. The dampness dissipated, and this was at least a welcome benefit, but the trees leaned close, and all sound fell dead as soon as it was heard. Their footsteps were muted, and every little noise was deafening for a brief moment, shattering the solitude before vanishing. All the men looked about suspiciously, and only Mugil appeared unaffected. Sarion dropped back to walk next to Karrol, conceding the lead to one of the hunters, with the other two fanning out several yards behind them.

"Can you feel it?" Sarion's voice contained the slightest hint of awe.

Karrol nodded. "Sprechyd Wood is very much alive. I feel a sense of wonder, and unconcealed threat within these dark reaches."

Sarion agreed. "The trees themselves seem to be aware of our presence, although I don't think the danger comes from them."

"What do your instincts tell you then?" Karrol gazed over at him, but Sarion was silent for long moments before he answered. Both men felt the quiet intensity, the ageless force which held the region beneath its sway. Unseen, unknown. But they clearly felt it, and were daunted.

Sarion answered, his voice hushed as if in respect of their surroundings. "I sense an ancient power dwelling somewhere deep inside, maybe at the heart of the forest. Secrets and nightmares are rooted in

The Rooting of Evil

Sprechyd Wood, things beyond our history and knowledge. I have no inclination of what the nature of this is. It may be evil, or perhaps something vast and elemental, uncaring of the world around it. Whatever it is, I think – and hope -- that as long as we don't venture too deeply, or stay very long, it will never become aware of our presence. We're too insignificant for whatever power lurks within here, but I would not want to alert it otherwise..."

Sarion felt a shiver at his own profound words. He relied strictly on his inner senses to tell him this, along with what he had heard of other latent powers in the world, from legends and old tales. His experiences with Grammore had also bestowed on him certain insights about things in the natural and unnatural world; entities older than man, which cared nothing for humankind's legacy. Power grew deep in the earth, forces of immense age and knowledge which burrowed through time like an earthworm through soil -- slowly, with a singular, vast purpose which could never be comprehended by the likes of men. And if men were unfortunate enough to come in contact with any of these powerful, unseen forces of nature, the results would be catastrophic.

Karrol eyed the terrain warily. "Your words are grim and offer no comfort, but I feel the truth in what you say. There's a sense of being slowly overwhelmed here, and if confronted by the source of such potency, we would be crushed like flies beneath a boot. Somehow, I don't need to *see* this to know the reality."

Nodding, Sarion eye's narrowed. Karrol possessed keen instincts. It was no wonder the man held such a high position in the Western Watch.

They continued for several hundred yards, and although the way was dark and forbidding, they found easy passage. Mugil trudged ahead, silent for the most

part, while the hunters followed cautiously. They
continued for a short time, and Karrol was about to call
for a pause, thinking the hermit quite mad, when Mugil
stopped and held his lantern high, turning around. The
forest grew thinner and the ground dropped before them,
turning into a shallow depression which arced deeper
into the woods, so deep that it looked like one long,
unending incline leading to black oblivion, and however
impressive and daunting as the landscape was, nothing
prepared them for the sight of the structure which lay
directly before them -- a broad, oddly-shaped building of
some type, with points of fire leaking through several
oval holes placed high in the front, a sweeping curl of
smoke rising from some unseen chimney or shaft and
disappearing above the forest canopy.

"There is where you'll find the answers you
seek."

Mugil stared right at Sarion, the hermit's eyes
glittering with a hint of either madness or malice, or
perhaps both.

Sarion couldn't tell which it was...

"Someone lives *here*?" Karrol's voice was filled
with amazement.

The hermit's response was strange. "At times."
He walked towards the building, picking his way
carefully between the expansive trunks and over a
scattering of dead branches.

Karrol gestured for his hunters to spread out,
with Fradwil following behind Mugil, and the other two
veering off in opposite directions. He turned to Sarion,
keeping his voice low. "You don't have to come inside.

It might be a good idea to have someone wait here in case anything threatens. I'm sure I don't need to say it, but I like not the feel of this place. Whatever lives here can't be friendly to us or our cause."

"I share your feeling, but I'm not staying behind. I did that once before, not again..."

Karrol caught the reference, to when Charadan had commanded Sarion to stay at the valley's edge while the warriors entered Gorothagled. Still he pressed the matter. "I could order you to, Sarion, you know that."

"You could," Sarion agreed. "But that doesn't mean I would listen."

The Third Forester frowned. "Yet you told Chertron to stay behind while *you* came with us."

"I did. My skills are greater than his. We both know that." Sarion said this without the slightest trace of arrogance. It was the truth, and Karrol knew it as well. He looked to his men for a second, then turned his attention back to Sarion.

"All right then. We all go." He fingered the hilt of his sword, a deadly gleam in his eye. "Let's see if anyone is home..."

The two men crouched low, making their way ahead. Already the other hunters were approaching the building, which took on a different appearance as they drew near. It was made of a mixture of stone and hard mud, but solid of build. It struck Sarion as something crude and efficient, the home of someone primitive, but he didn't know exactly what that meant. After a few moments, they reached a point not more than two score yards from the structure. It now appeared much taller than Sarion had believed. The gradual descent of the land served as a natural illusion. The holes, which looked to be hand-carved windows, were several dozen feet overhead, too high to reach, and the walls looked sheer enough to prevent scaling. Instead of a door, there was an opening, maybe five feet high, rectangular-shaped. Already Mugil stood in front of the entrance, no trace of fear in his bearing. Two of the hunters circled around, and Sarion knew that Karrol would await their report before doing anything else. Light trickled outwards from the openings, and Sarion thought that it might be from lit torches or lanterns.

They waited for a while, neither man wanting to break the silence. Sarion also noted an unusual odor about the structure, but nothing recognizable. From the height of the entrance, he wondered if this was indeed the hermit's own home. But who had built it? He scanned his surroundings, looking for anything of interest, but to all appearances nothing seemed unordinary. He had half a mind to search the other side himself, but he knew the capabilities of the Nighton hunters, and Karrol would have chosen these men for excellent reasons. Sarion looked behind him, and then glanced over at the captain. At the same time, one of the hunters reappeared from the left side, shortly followed by another.

They were both startled when Mugil reprimanded them. "Inside, quickly. It's not safe out here." The hermit disappeared into the entrance, holding his lantern aloft and shuffling through. Karrol had no time for a reply, and Fradwil looked back at him questioningly. Frowning, Karrol motioned for him to stay put. The other hunters now approached, reporting their findings.

The first man, a veteran named Luthine, spoke to them both. "Nothing around back, not even another entrance. Stacks of wood for a fire, and a crumbling well. But that's all."

"No tracks of any kind?" Sarion asked.

Luthine shook his head, the short brown hair cropped tightly against his high forehead. "No. The ground is a bit moist, but there's nothing to be found."

Nothing to be found, thought Sarion. Or *left* to be found...

Karrol was less impatient. "Here's what we came for, and Mugil doesn't seem afraid. It could well be where he lives. Fradwil first, Luthine next. Sarion take the rearguard. I don't want anything to surprise us."

Sarion spoke. "Beware of any laid traps. This Mugil plays some type of game with us, I fear. Whether his intent stems from madness or worse, I can't tell."

Sarion straightened, but the hunters were already off. Fradwil hovered before the entrance, his knife in one hand, a lantern in the other. After a moment's hesitation, he disappeared into the dark maw of the building. Luthine followed seconds later, then Karrol, the other fighter on his heels. Sarion waited, examining the entrance. The stone was smooth, nearly flawless. Something had made a clean cut when the structure had been built. He fingered the edges, looking for any sign of a trap, but nothing was revealed. The forest behind him was silent, and he scanned it for indications of movement. Nothing materialized, so he took a deep breath and followed after the hunters, his sword in hand. His uneasiness continued to grow stronger.

He angled his neck so as not to brush the top. The doorway was short, opening to both sides almost immediately. His lantern illuminated a wide room, and he saw Karrol and the other hunter a dozen yards ahead. Sarion lifted his lantern above his shoulder, looking up. He was surprised as to the height of this room. The ceiling stretched way above him, the top lost in shadows and dim suggestion. This entry room was nearly bare of furnishings, except for a small table and two chairs, the surface made of rough wood, a pair of metal goblets on either end. Nothing of significance, and already the others were moving through a corridor, much higher than the entrance, and wider as well. The whole design was unusual, and Sarion felt that he was missing something crucial here, but couldn't place his finger on it. He hesitated briefly, shaking his head. The others were now out of sight, and that bothered him just as much, so he continued.

The floor was little more than flat, packed mud. He reached the corridor, pausing to search the ground for any telltale signs, but again came up with nothing. He crept forward, hand ready on his sword. This tunnel was much longer and he wondered about who had built it. Other corridors opened to either side, causing him to frown. He didn't like this at all. Too many hiding places...He gave a short whistle, and hurried onward. Within moments, Karrol reappeared, concern etched into his face. "What is it, Sarion?"

"I'm not sure, just don't get too far ahead. Any sign of Mugil? There's no indication of anyone moving through here."

The other shook his head. "Not after he entered. He couldn't have gone much further. He certainly doesn't move very quickly."

"Captain Karrol. We've found something." One of the hunters appeared. It was Luthine.

"What is it?"

"A large room, a round chamber of sorts. Fradwil and Glared are searching it now."

"And the hermit?"

"There's no sign of him. Maybe he turned down one of the corridors."

Sarion turned to Karrol. "I don't like the feel of this at all. It smells of a trap."

The Forester nodded gravely. "Let's see what they've found, and then make our way out quickly." He gestured, and Luthine hurried off. Sarion backtracked several steps, listening for any noise. Crouching in the shadows for over a minute, he heard nothing. Shaking his head, he joined Karrol and they followed the others.

They walked another two dozen yards before the walls broke away, revealing the largest room they had seen so far. Luthine was immediately in front of them in a protective posture.

"Where are the others?" Karrol snapped.

Luthine motioned to either side. Sarion spotted them both, moving in separate directions along the wall. As his eyes adjusted, he saw what looked to be a huge, round pit sitting in the middle of the chamber. The ceiling was very high up, the roof hidden beyond the reach of their inadequate lanterns. No windows opened anywhere.

Straddling the pit was a thick, long pole, a type Sarion recognized as being used for spitting large game, such as boars or stag. Cauldrons lay to either side, black and massive. A sense of foreboding squeezed at Sarion's chest, and he scanned the room for any sign of habitation. The breathing of the men sounded harsh to his ears, and he glanced over at the Forester. Karrol signaled for Luthine to search around the pit. Sarion wanted to see for himself, but had no desire to leave their back unprotected. He had an unnerving vision of the hermit screaming into their midst, wielding a knife. Something was not right here, and he'd suspected Mugil from the beginning. More so now...

The hunters glided along the walls like phantoms. Luthine reached the hole, staring about warily. Karrol looked about in all directions, his face impassive in the gloom. Without warning a low rumble echoed from somewhere behind them in the structure, a noise which sounded like grinding stone. Sarion and the fighters instantly froze, preparing for an attack.

Nothing else broke the stillness, and Sarion edged into the opening where they had entered. He whispered back to Karrol. "That sounded like it came from the entrance. Or close to it..."

"Do you see anything?" The Forester kept his eyes on the men, who had reached the far side of the large chamber. "I fear we've been led into a trap as well, but to what purpose I don't know."

"I'm certain of it now," answered Sarion. "Call your men back, and we'll leave this place. The hermit's intent is unclear, but it's not to help us."

Luthine uttered a low oath, and he hurried over to join them. Karrol kept his gaze riveted on his hunters, letting out a short whistle for them to return.

"Captain." Luthine's voice concealed most of his emotion but Sarion heard the fear beneath the syllables, and he listened with dread.

"What did you find, Luthine?" The Forester held the man's eyes with his own piercing vision.

"Bones, Captain Karrol. Human remains. The pit is filled with them."

The Forester cursed as the others approached.

Luthine continued. "And I saw scattered weapons. There can be no mistake -- within the pit are helms and swords from Nighton."

Sarion's heart sunk at the fighter's grim words, and he realized with terrible certainty the fate of Jerol and his company.

And he also knew that they would soon learn much more as a tremendous crash sent vibrations shuddering along the wall as a panel slammed open in the middle of the chamber...

Things happened very quickly…

The Rooting of Evil

The opening of the secret door took everyone by surprise, despite their drawn weapons and alertness. On the right side of the chamber a mechanism had clicked into action, serving as an entryway for what had been waiting for them on the other side.

It was a nightmare.

Even through the gloom, Sarion saw something that was all size and ferocity. A huge figure jumped into their midst, swinging a long, wicked pike directly for Glared, pinning the hapless fighter to the ground, running him through.

Karrol screamed a warning and Sarion leaped forward, his mind seething in fury at their decision to follow Mugil into this trap. He was also astonished at the savagery of what now attacked them. To all appearances it was human-like, but of massive proportions.

A giant man, but more beast than human...

Naked except for a crude band of animal furs girding its loins, the creature towered over their heads, standing over a dozen feet high, its arms and legs heavily muscled. The face was contorted in a look of mixed rage and glee, the features distorted and horrific. Terrible as its appearance, what stunned Sarion even more were the human skulls tied around its waist.

The monster howled as it shook Glared from the pike, throwing the dead fighter against the far wall and nearly taking down Fradwil, who quickly dodged to get out of the way. Sarion's fighting instincts immediately took over, assessing their situation and searching for a plan to battle the brute and save their lives in the doing...He only needed a moment to realize that they were severely outmatched, and their only chance was to escape.

"Through the doorway!"

He shouted at the others, but Luthine and

Fradwil were in no position to turn their backs on the creature. Frantic, Sarion crouched slightly behind Karrol, whose face registered quiet shock at the brutality of the adversary facing them. The giant savage didn't give them time to pause as it leaped forward as if to charge into their midst, but the act proved only to be a feint, as it swept a wide arc with its pike, lashing into Luthine's sword, sending it spinning uselessly across the room and sliding into the pit. The fighter wailed in pain as the pike struck the top of his arm, and he staggered backwards. Karrol and Sarion braced for the oncoming assault, but their adversary changed directions with amazing agility and was now hurtling towards Fradwil, who saw the danger and darted along the wall to the far side of the chamber.

Sarion had remained partly in the doorway to ward against an attack from their rear, and he now heard a loud clicking from somewhere in the wall.

Another trap!

The only thing which saved him was the slight vibration as the ground quivered at his feet, causing him to roll forward instinctively. Sharp metal spikes hammered down from the ceiling above the entrance, and simultaneously the floor yawned wide, a twin set of traps meant to impale the unfortunate victim into a bed of pointed iron nails. He tumbled into Karrol, almost knocking him down as well. By its action, the giant clearly had anticipated the event, ignoring the three men and concentrating on Fradwil, who had positioned himself on the opposite side of the pit.

The brute waved its weapon, as if calculating the much smaller opponent. Karrol hurried forward, while Luthine leaned against the wall, his face filled with anguish as he pulled a long hunting knife out with his left hand, his fighting ability severely hampered. Recovering swiftly, Sarion pushed himself from the floor as he saw the danger and yelled to Fradwil in warning. He whipped out one of his own knives in a blur, throwing it at the giant's back. It scored a direct hit on the monster's right shoulder, but it merely stiffened, growling in hatred. The pike lifted high, and Fradwil crouched in anticipation. The giant reared back, throwing the pike effortlessly, too quickly for Fradwil to avoid, and it caught him in his left side, crushing him as he attempted to dive for safety.

Karrol now reached the brute, swinging his sword sideways as the giant pivoted. With remarkable speed for a creature of such bulk, the monster shifted to one side, but the blade managed to strike its right leg. Feeling real pain the brute roared, stumbling backwards and nearly falling. Seizing the advantage, Sarion screamed at the others. "Through the door! Beware another trap!"

But Luthine was already at the threshold, holding his arm and disappearing into the blackness. Fradwil was down, not moving. Sarion knew he couldn't just leave the man there, and he ran across the chamber, gesturing for Karrol to escape. The Forester backed away from the injured giant, never taking his eyes off it. The creature prodded the area of its wound, running a thick arm across the flow of blood. It put a finger to its mouth, licking its own fluid, and smiled hideously. Karrol now stood with sword raised in the middle of the chamber, which looked more like an underground cave than anything else, as the lanterns, discarded onto the floor, failed to scatter the encroaching shadows. Sarion reached the injured hunter but it was already too late. He quickly felt for a pulse, finding nothing. The momentum of the throw had been too much, battering the man against the floor with killing force. Cursing, Sarion knelt, pulling out a pair of arrows from his quiver. He knew there would only be one chance to shoot, as the giant now moved away from the wall, staring cruelly at Karrol, who refused to back down.

Sarion aimed high, firing the first arrow and striking the brute in its neck. The second arrow already in place, Sarion watched in horror as Karrol pressed the monster in an attempt at surprise.

"No!" Sarion yelled in warning but the Forester moved closer, swinging his sword for the giant's midsection. The brute sidestepped the blow, despite the arrow lodged in its throat. Even as Sarion let the second volley fly, the giant brought down one mighty fist, hitting the Forester squarely on the head, and he crumbled to the floor. Sarion's arrow was even more deadly this time, hitting directly above the monster's left temple. Now it thrashed madly about, swinging its arms recklessly and stumbling to the rear of the chamber. Sarion never hesitated, hurrying towards Karrol's fallen body, fearing the worst.

The Forester's neck was twisted in an impossible angle, and Sarion gasped in shock at the sight of the brave captain's eyes, still open in a look of surprise and outrage.

The brute crouched down, slowly pulling out the arrow from its neck as if it felt no pain. Sarion knew the battle was far from over, and the creature was clearly not ready to give up fighting until they were all finished. There was nothing to be gained by remaining -- the three men were dead, and if he stayed, he would end up being the next victim. With sword drawn, Sarion vanished into the doorway, hoping that Luthine was not too badly injured.

The Rooting of Evil

Having the presence of mind to ward himself against further malice, Sarion scooped up one of the lanterns, illuminating the broad doorway which curved to the side, revealing nothing of what lay ahead. There was no sign of the other fighter, and Sarion had no time to do anything but move quickly, keeping his eyes open for any snares, and his ears alert for sounds of pursuit, which must surely come. The creature possessed uncanny agility, and reminded Sarion in some ways of the ogre which they had pursued relentlessly across Grammore. There was little doubt in his mind that this had been anything but a premeditated attack, the hermit acting as a lure to bring them all within the clutches of the beast that had been waiting for them. The Dark Mage had his hand in their misfortune -- it was beyond question. Passing dozen of yards through the corridor, the tunnel was high enough to permit the giant, wide enough with room to spare.

Scanning the ground, Sarion saw fresh tracks made by the brute, along with Luthine's boot prints. But still no sign of the Nighton hunter.

Sweating from the heat of battle, Sarion moved ahead at a brisk pace, but not recklessly. He soon noticed that the tunnel descended, and he realized it was well below ground, passing beyond the end of the structure. The hunters had failed to find another entrance because none of them had thought to look past the limits of the primary building. The place had been conceived well, and he wondered as to how long ago it had been created. By its appearance, the structure seemed fairly old. Perhaps the giant, or something else, had been using it for a long time. Again, too many unanswered questions, he thought...Sarion continued like this for the span of several minutes, as he slowed down, his fear of being waylaid growing by the second. Nothing else unusual had as yet appeared, which worried him even more. He started to think the tunnel would lead him into the very heart of Sprechyd Wood when he abruptly came to a large wooden door. Surprised, he looked for tracks, and saw that Luthine had advanced this far at least, and from the scuff marks, had passed through. Examining the panel with his lantern, Sarion tapped and prodded it with one arrow, attempting to locate any traps. After a few tense seconds, he moved the bar which secured it, and slowly pushed the door open.

Gloomy light flooded him and he squinted, adjusting his eyes. To his relief, he stepped outside into the forest once more, the trees leaning close, unfriendly and patient. There was a bit of open space here, and he looked about for the fighter, hoping to find him waiting.

Instead, his heart sank as several dim shapes moved within the undergrowth, hulking figures with glowing yellow eyes. Low growling erupted from numerous directions, and Sarion realized that his situation was beyond desperate. There was no way he could outrun these creatures, whatever they were, and their intent was clear. He spotted blood on the ground in front of him, along with bits and pieces of cloth. All that remained of Luthine...the injured hunter never had a chance.

The giant couldn't be very far behind him by now, and Sarion found himself in the jaws of a deadly trap. He considered going back, but the close confines of the tunnel would prevent him from striking cleanly at the giant. He might score one quick blow, but then it would be over. And if he turned his back, the creatures would be on him in a second, tearing him to shreds as well.

It was the end of his long journey, and all the pent-up frustration and loss welled up inside his heart. All the fallen warriors from the original company, slain by the manipulations of a faceless and unforgiving enemy. General Charadan and his handpicked fighters. More than a dozen of Virgil's men. Now Captain Karrol and the Nighton hunters.

The beasts advanced slowly, their appearance one of patience now, wanting to savor this next kill. From somewhere deeper in the woods, Sarion could make out the sound of low laughter. Spiteful, mocking him.

"Mugil..." He spat the words.

How he *longed* to strike a blow at Mugil for leading them on this foolhardy chase. But he had no time for regrets. There were at least six of the creatures, which looked wolf-like, with long, pointed ears, bristling gray fur, and maws which seemed impossibly wide for the furry heads. Each limb was taloned, with claws several inches in length. They were some of the most savage-looking creatures Sarion had ever laid eyes on.

Crushed by the terrible end which fate had chosen for him, Sarion could have easily given in to his fear and dismay, become a quick victim to the hopeless circumstances now facing him. Death would have been swift, descending with its dread pall. Instead, Sarion held his chin high, his eyes glazed with anger and a hidden reserve of resoluteness, despite the impossible odds mounted against him. Despair was a thing unknown to him. He was made up of much stronger fiber -- determination, an uncanny mastery of arms, and his unwavering natural instinct for survival.

Raising his sword high in challenge, he whipped out a long hunting knife, his eyes promising death as he stared into the face of his adversaries. No, he would never concede, not while a single breath of life remained in his lungs -- a drop of blood in his veins. If this was the end of his quest, then he would die as a warrior of Trencit, and he would take with him as many of his enemies as possible...

Sarion stepped forward.

Forlern departed from Nighton early in the morning, leaving the citadel before Sarion and Chertron had even left the Forester's hold. A dozen hunters accompanied him as escort, led by Captain Kretwil, a seasoned veteran of longstanding service in the Western Watch. He also served as envoy between Daregil Keep and Nighton, a trustworthy man, well-known to all the guard posts between the two fortresses. He was quiet, relying on routine and brief commands to the fighters under his leadership. Forlern had great admiration for the hunters of Nighton. He enjoyed the structured levels of authority, and the men of the Western Watch displayed an unfaltering air of pride in their position with a high regard to their appointed leaders. Orders were never questioned, or needed to be repeated. Forlern found himself envying the fluid system of the westland, even the unpredictability of the vast borderlands.

Not surprisingly, he realized that he could be happy out here in service to Nighton.

Without a doubt, serving in the Homeguard carried an immense obligation itself, and the position was respected throughout every corner of Trencit. The members were some of the finest weapons masters in the land, skilled and courageous. Deadly fighters.

And Forlern was all this, and more.

But the Western Watch possessed a wild charm of its own, a reckless freedom of sorts, due to the immensity of the lands beneath its protection, and this seemed very appealing to Forlern.

The Rooting of Evil

The westland swept past them as their horses carried the riders through the endless ocean of trees which comprised the borderlands. Hill and dale, small villages and sprawling farmlands, they rode onwards, moving steadily out from the west and into central Trencit, the breadbasket of the kingdom. Gradually the land became flatter, the forests less thick, and the roads more frequently traveled. Within the span of several days they gained the southern reaches of Dwellyn, one of the most powerful and influential provinces of all Trencit. The citadel itself sat upon the foothills of the southern tips of the Krale, a towering, forbidding range of high mountains which encircled Daregil Keep, offering it a natural barrier of protection in every direction, the single access being through the narrow Grip, a heavily fortified valley warded by a powerful legion of the Royal Army. Dwellyn had always shown fierce loyalty to the Kings of Trencit, and could be relied upon to follow the royal nod, whatever the matter. Lord Cheston currently ruled the province, a middle-aged man who enjoyed much popularity in the general kingdom, revered by his own fiefdom. Both of his twin sons held positions in the Homeguard and Forlern knew them well, training at times with the pair. Good-natured and lovers of all things concerning the hunt and weapons mastery, they often sought Forlern out, sparring with him on the training grounds, or riding afield when their duty allowed. As the elite guard of Daregil Keep, they were permitted, even encouraged, to undertake various missions on their own, seek out new forms of skill and strategy, improve their horsemanship and all other aspects of their positions. This continuous learning and training kept them at a keen edge, well above fighters from any province in Trencit and even beyond. Members of the Homeguard were promoted quickly within the military, and often were given the option of vying for positions throughout the kingdom. The higher ranking Captains of Daregil Keep answered directly to King Gregor, and His Majesty's demands were exceptional when it came to his personal guardians.

Forlern considered the twins as he rode on the edge of Dwellyn's holdings. He hoped they were safe in the eastland, and wondered how the war was faring. Such thoughts brought him again to the fate of General Charadan, and he inwardly winced at the upcoming meeting with King Gregor. He had no idea what the king's reaction would be, or the High Council...He only knew it would be extremely unpleasant and chaotic. The fighter grumbled to himself at the thought, biting his lip in frustration. He would know soon enough...

The weather remained fair in the early days after their departure from Nighton. It was a welcome break from the dismal rain and mist of the past several weeks. Many times Forlern's thoughts drifted to Sarion and Chertron, and he wished fervently that they would not be facing any peril. He still remained angry at the decision to split up, although he admitted to himself that it was the wisest course of action, and unlike Sarion, his immediate and sworn duty was to King Gregor and the Homeguard, in the defense of both. His mission had been completed, and it was time for him to return to duty, whatever form it would now take. He was uncertain if he was to be given another assignment, or relegated back to active service at Daregil Keep. There had been talk of promoting him before he'd left with Charadan, perhaps placing him as a training master, which was unheard of for someone his age. This made him grin, and the old brashness emerged once again.

Conversation was light with his traveling escort, and regardless, Forlern wasn't in much of a mood for talking, especially the first few days after leaving the borderland. He tried to focus on what he would say before King Gregor and his councilors. He might very well be brought forth before the High Council itself. Shaking his head, he disliked the politics of Trencit. He preferred action, and the constant honing of his fighting skills over the prospect of strategy and inner-kingdom debate. Admittedly though, the mission into the Grammore Lowlands had far exceeded any level of danger he'd ever faced before, and Forlern had no desire for any other such ventures.

The company followed well-trodden trails as they made their way deeper into Trencit. These were in constant use, both by royal emissaries, traders, and citizens of the kingdom, as they walked or rode throughout Trencit's interior. Merchants were in abundance, traveling in all directions, a great many coming and going to the free city of Lastrad, a sprawling community which did not fall under the direct rule of any of Trencit's individual provinces, although it was traditionally loyal to Daregil Keep. Over the years, it had grown to such size that the nearby regions wanted nothing to do with it. Home to the Vanyair Market, the largest merchant ground in the known world, it was a unique and sumptuous metropolis, where everything had a price, *if* one was willing to pay...Lastrad was also a breeding den for cutthroats, thieves, and mercenaries, where some of the worst dregs of society were to be found. Ruled by the Gran Barshara, an electorate, Lastrad was a world of its own, with its own set of rules -- that being none. Death found the unwary or foolish in many different guises there, and Forlern had seen several of its masks. Shrugging aside his recollection of Lastrad, he concentrated on the errand at hand, determined to finally complete his mission and bury some of his own dead...

The hunters passed an increasing amount of villages, bypassing them all in their quest for haste. A few times they halted, speaking with lone horsemen, couriers on route between the various provinces. King Gregor required regular contact with his Lords and their holdings, many times sending his captains out to discuss troop deployments, rotations, and the calling up of new conscripts. Rumors were abundant in central Trencit, and it seemed everyone had another one to add. The Nighton hunters paid little heed to such talk, and never paused a minute longer than necessary, most of the time ignoring all passersby. Not for the last time, Forlern held these men in high admiration. He realized that despite the eroding situation in the westland, they were all just as eager as himself to finish their command and return to the Western Guard. *That* in itself was the driving motivation for their one-mindedness. Their homelands were threatened, and they wanted to be back with their comrades, protecting and preserving the west. Forlern would certainly make a point to tell King Gregor that the fighters of Nighton were above reproach, and they were unsleeping in their duty, faced with a nightmarish and elusive enemy. But, of course, the king knew this already, and relied heavily on them.

Regardless, Forlern would remind him...

Time passed swiftly as they rode deeper into the Trencit heartland, and Forlern couldn't help thinking about his comrades behind him. He tried to discourage such thoughts, and focus on the task at hand, but found it difficult, if not utterly impossible. All he could do was urge his mount faster, trying to hasten the others. Moving in a north-easterly direction, they entered a region of low foothills and wooded valleys, a fertile area inhabited by peasants and farmers living beneath the mighty shadow of Dwellyn, Daregil Keep's strong right arm. Riding under the silver gleam of a near-full moon, they broke out into the open on a major throughway, catching their first glimpse of the castle fortress several miles to the north, nestled against rugged foothills which were backed by the towering mountains of the Krale. Watch fires from turrets peered out at their forms like firefly eyes. Normally the area was lightly patrolled, as the citadel proper was heavily protected, housing thousands of fighters, but Forlern wondered if things had changed in recent weeks. Mounted warriors would be needed to assist Nighton in scouting the vast borderlands, as the situation in the west grew increasingly uncertain. He yawned, knowing that it would soon be time to camp for the night. The road was wide, and farmland lay to both sides, divided in long sections by tree lines to separate property. Gazing across the moonlit country, he spotted a large dark shape moving from the direction of the keep, recognizing it immediately as a heavily armed patrol of horsemen.

"Captain Kretwil!" Forlern shouted over the noise of their own mounts, gesturing towards the approaching group. The captain whistled loudly, signaling for a halt.

"Seems we have company tonight," Forlern spoke as the captain leaned close to him." Maybe they'll share some Drenchcast ale. I could use a good draught after all this riding."

"What, Nighton ale too strong for your liking?" Kretwil remarked, raising his eyebrows.

"Not strong *enough*..." Forlern chided, bringing low chuckles from several of the fighters.

They all watched as one of Kretwil's men rode forward, lifting a pennant emblazoned with the markings of Nighton. Someone hailed them from the closing group of warriors, and they were quickly surrounded, outnumbered at least three to one, Forlern noticed. The patrol was larger than he expected, and he nodded to himself at his earlier appraisal of Trencit's current situation, and the measures the principalities would take to ensure the safety of the citizens.

"Hail, hunters of Nighton." A tall rider came forward, the men all dressed in light armor, their helms crested with the blue falcon markings of the Dwellyn heirloom. "My name is Florik, second lieutenant of the Dwellyn Home Watch. Are there any among your group from Captain Grundel's company?"

Forlern was surprised at the man's announcement. King Gregor was obviously concerned about his missing captain and had placed all patrols on notice. The young fighter came forward immediately to greet the newcomers.

"My name is Forlern, companion to Captain Grundel and member of the Homeguard."

"Well met, Forlern." Florik saluted him, nodding his head in acknowledgement. "The king has been awaiting your return. Then Captain Grundel is among your party as well?"

Forlern's face darkened, and he leaned closer to the man. "He is not with us. I can't speak openly of his whereabouts." He inclined his head to the other riders for emphasis.

"I see…"

"Captain Kretwil has escorted me back into our homeland. Our group has ridden hard the past week to gain access to Daregil Keep, and I'm glad to see familiar lands once again."

Florik nodded to the Nighton hunter. "You've done well, Captain. You may return to your fortress, as I fear you can best serve Trencit in the troubled westland, although all our borders are suspect these dark days. I'll accompany Forlern to the Keep to see his majesty."

Kretwil agreed, and held out a firm hand to Forlern, who grasped it eagerly. "Good fortune in your meeting with King Gregor, my friend. Tell the king of our difficult situation, and our vigilance. He must know of the shadow which approaches from the west."

"I will. And have a care yourself. Look out for Sarion and Chertron. If you see those scoundrels, send them east with great haste."

"You have my word, Forlern. Farewell, Florik."

Without further hesitation, he signaled his men and then turned about, not bothering to pause in their eagerness to return home. Forlern and the others watched them depart, and once again the young fighter found himself with another group of strangers. But despite not knowing these other men, they were all united in at least two ways -- their loyalty to Trencit, and their uncertainty of its future.

Ignoring his own weariness, Forlern pressed Lieutenant Florik for speed and rode alongside the fighter, extracting as much information as possible, all the while remaining vague about his own mission. He suspected that the man would be curious about details of his journey, but he had no desire to open up to anyone else until his confrontation with King Gregor. Listening intently, Forlern realized that Florik had his ear in the right places. He briefed him on current skirmishes in the east front with the Devlents, recent troop deployments, and rumors which abounded throughout the powerful kingdom.

Some of these were quite disturbing…

Many hailed from the westland, of which Forlern already had firsthand experience about, related to the raids and deadly marauders which raked across the borderlands, stealing away livestock at night, at times attacking isolated farmsteads. Trappers complained of

wild beasts roaming the hinterland, aggressive and
fierce. Some stories spoke of people missing, including
travelers and even several envoys on royal business.
Other tales were new even to his ears...A few of the
provinces were engaged in heated debate, worried about
the calling up of conscripts from their own reserves. The
availability of fighting men was reaching a crucial
number, and soon these reserves would be depleted. The
regional monarchs were loyal to King Gregor and
Trencit, but were reluctant to pull additional warriors
from their own home forces, most especially House
Gwerath. At the last council meeting, the ambassador
from Lord Pralicon had been firm, that no more fighters
would be sent from their land to fight the war in the east.
The meeting had ended in a bitter exchange among some
of the lesser provinces, and King Gregor had been
unusually quiet, letting his personal councilors act as
arbitrators. Things had not gone well, according to
Florik's sources.

All this left Forlern with a cold feeling in the pit
of his stomach, as he realized the maelstrom he hastened
into, and the turmoil which would shortly stem from the
revelation that Trencit had lost its foremost General and
fighting leader.

Sometime before dawn, Forlern pressed Florik
for a pause. He was near exhaustion, and there was no
point in him taxing the remnants of his strength. All his
faculties would be sorely needed when he appeared
before King Gregor. Determined to reach the Keep
quickly, he realized that his demeanor had to be
unflinching if he were to properly convey all which had
befallen the ill-fated group led by Charadan. He lay
beneath the late-night stars for long moments, mentally
reciting what he would say at Daregil. Images of
Grammore and its ferocious denizens played relentlessly
through his mind's eye. He inwardly flinched in

recollection at the muck dweller which had seized brave Kalen. The dreaded Jurvech, immense in its power, size, and violence. The shadowy terrors of Gorothagled with its hidden mysteries, the Killworm shrilling from its cavity of rock, sending slivers of death overhead in an effort to slay them all. And lastly the monstrous ogre, which had ambushed them in the borderlands, and led them on an impossible chase into the very horror of inner Grammore. Looking back now, Forlern could see how it could have been just a terribly vivid nightmare. Their quest had been destined for tragedy as soon as they had descended into the mist shrouded Lowlands in pursuit of a creature of legend. Courageous or foolish? Most likely some of both. He wondered how Sarion and Chertron fared, his two companions off on yet another journey, seeking to aid the leader of Nighton.

Tossing about, sleep eventually claimed the young fighter, but his dreams were haunted by figments of his living past.

When he once again awakened, Forlern found that morning was well under way, warm rays from the sun splashing yellow on his face through gaps in the light forest. A fighter with a boyish face approached him with a drink and some breakfast meats which he eagerly accepted. Eating quickly, Forlern soon spoke with Florik, and the company was shortly mounted and racing ahead. Feeling rested, Forlern was ready for the final leg of the journey, to reach Daregil Keep and meet with the king. His duty would be fulfilled, but after this event the future was clouded, a haze of uncertainty, but he could not let that interfere with his obligation. What King Gregor and his councilors decided would be out of his hands. Coming to this inevitable conclusion, Forlern felt more at ease. He wasn't going to let the situation intimidate him. Few things, if any, did. He hadn't reached his position in the Homeguard for naught.

Nodding to himself, he bit his lip, his eyes narrowing. He already had other plans swimming in his head as to where circumstances might yet lead him. He would just have to see…

The morning passed into early afternoon, and eventually the day grew late. The sun sank in a blaze of orange and indigo behind tall foothills to their left which were the foremost outcroppings of the mighty Krale. Dwellyn was far behind them, the provincial capital nestled among the first peaks of the mountain barrier. Ahead of them loomed ever-higher foothills, which served as the outer ward of the Grip itself. Villages and farms were becoming less common, and the region took on the persona of ceaseless vigilance, as armed companies roamed the paths, guarding all access to Trencit's mightiest citadel. They were stopped on several occasions, and each time were quickly dismissed to go ahead. Word had been passed that they were expected, overdue, and nothing was to delay their progress. Florik was also determined to take them to the Keep himself. This close to Daregil, there would be nothing gained by placing additional men in their escort. Of course, if a high ranking officer met up with them, that could change matters, but nothing occurred.

Evening arrived, finding them once again in need of setting camp for the night. They would not reach Daregil Keep this day, even under a forced march. Forlern, although still eager to finish his mission, was not about to tire himself into incoherence. That would serve no purpose, and he was clever enough to know that information would be extracted from him without haste once inside the king's chambers.

He spoke little that evening to Florik, and the officer respected his quiet mood, permitting the fighter to hold council with his own thoughts. For the hundredth time Forlern found himself replaying the sequence of events of the journey, mentally emphasizing certain standout situations which had occurred, although it seemed virtually everything swarmed to the forefront regardless of his focus. He would hold nothing back. This night his sleep was even more restless, as the excitement continued to course through his veins, energy which had been put to constant use in the field while under the duress of threat and on the hunt, now restrained as his mission passed into another phase, one of less danger but requiring great urgency and diplomacy. At times during the night his hand would reach for the handle of a dagger, a reflex which was uncanny, swift and sure. A light sleeper, he awoke more than once, his eyes flashing open, watching as one of the multiple sentries moved to and fro along the perimeter of the camp. Night birds called in the distance, and the land was at peace. Convinced everything was normal, he would fall back to sleep, only to battle imaginary nightmare foes in field and dale.

But even long nights eventually come to an end, and he stretched forth his arms and yawned, greeting the new dawn with grim-faced determination, knowing that his quest would draw to a conclusion this day.

Florik saw the fiery eagerness in his eyes, and nodded upon seeing him. They broke camp swiftly, eating on their mounts, the warhorses of Trencit hammering across the forest trail with manes held high, their nostrils flaring with the exertion of a fresh hunt. The air gradually became cooler as the company pressed further northward, and foothills now became visible to the east, their ridges crowned with thick forests. They were nearing the Grip, angling towards the mouth of the pass and skirting the rough terrain which served as the hinterland behind Dwellyn. The main causeway which led to Daregil Keep lay due south of the Grip, plunging outwards from the hills and spearing into the very heartland of Trencit, eventually intersecting with some of the land's largest villages in the central region. Travel was light on the pass they now rode, but things would change soon as they encountered the numerous passersby on business to and from the mighty citadel.

It was nearing midday, the sky overhead painted a bright azure with flecks of clouds harassing the sun, when the men spotted a large armed company of warriors. Forlern recognized them immediately as members of the Trencit Royal Army, assigned as permanent guardians of this sector. They entered a bowl shaped valley, tall hills before them and to either side. This was the sole access way to the Grip, and Daregil Keep. Wide, ringed on three sides by small mountains, it was a heavily fortified area with several checkpoints. No enemy had ever been able to penetrate this deeply into Trencit, and if they somehow managed, they would find themselves in the midst of several thousand warriors, a mixture of fighters both on foot and mounted on horseback. Countless reinforcements were on quick call, and could swarm through the Grip from the Royal Legions harbored inside the Keep proper. Even if an army could fight their way through the vigilant guardians, they would then face the deadly passage known as the Grip, a narrow trail hedged on both sides by rocky hills, where archers waited in protective enclosures, prepared to rain a hail of arrows down on any intruders. It was a difficult ascent to the higher elevations, and paths had been carved into the side of the living rock, stairways and shafts, which led upwards to the un-scalable heights.

One of Florik's men rode ahead as a contingent of warriors quickly approached them. Forlern knew there would be a short exchange of questioning, but it was all standard procedure. The horsemen signaled and Florik's man gave the proper responses. Pausing on his own mount, Forlern looked about at the familiar sights, knowing that he had only been gone several weeks, but it felt like a lifetime. So much had happened to him since then, and the events had been profound. What he'd seen in Grammore would haunt him forever…Although Trencit was a powerful kingdom, they lived in a world of violence and horror. On both sides of their homeland existed creatures both wonderful and terrible, things which had little use, and no love, for man. They were viewed as an occupier of certain lands, and when chance contact occurred, the normal sequence of events would ultimately lead to hostility. Had things ever been that different, he wondered? The war in the east had been ongoing for long years, and for what purpose? He really didn't know. And now, on the western borderlands, terror in the form of the Dark Mage and his nightmare emissaries were plaguing the peaceful frontier homesteads, for the singular purpose of causing havoc and destruction. To what endgame? He, Sarion, and Chertron had discussed the motivation behind the raids many times, and they could only guess at the greater scheme. He was sure that in time things would certainly become clearer…Perhaps all *too* clear.

After a few minutes they were allowed to continue, and Florik waved to the officer who had come out with the armed party. He added two of his own men to accompany them all the way to Daregil Keep, as their presence would expedite further situations.

Again, Forlern kept to himself, not wishing to engage anyone in conversation. He just wanted to get this journey over with, and move on. He gritted his teeth, thinking about his comrades in the westland, and fervently hoped that they were right on his heels after finding the missing Jerol.

The remainder of the day found Forlern's company moving steadily northward at a brisk pace, stopping only at designated check areas. Soon they reached the larger main causeway, sharing it with a host of others, some coming from the Keep, and others on the path before or after themselves -- individual travelers, fighters, and merchants on horseback or trolling rickety wagons, looking to sell their wares in Trencit's capital. At times couriers on royal affairs would sweep by carrying the king's markings, alone or in pairs. This was all normal activity, and varied from day to day, but it never ceased. Even during the late night hours there were always people journeying the path. Trencit was a large and restless kingdom, and never slept.

As dusk arrived they found themselves staring at the yawning passageway of the Grip. Hundreds of warriors were on permanent station here, and the atmosphere was one of standard caution, the armed men questioning all who wished to continue onward to Daregil Keep. The two fighters who accompanied them hailed their comrades, speaking quickly as to their purpose, and Forlern's group was ushered forward.

Florik gave orders to his own horsemen, and all but two of them turned about in the direction they had come. The lieutenant gestured over to Forlern. "I'm sending my men back, although I would still accompany you to the Keep. I'm certain you're in no danger, of course, but I have some other business in the citadel. *And* an excuse to be overlong in my own return." He grinned at the younger man.

"The taverns of Daregil stock only the finest, if that's what you're referring to." Forlern smirked in response, embracing the welcome relief of any distraction from his mission.

"I never said that..." Florik quipped.

"Indeed you did not." Forlern patted his horse wearily, thinking that a good drink was well-deserved for himself as well.

The Rooting of Evil

Their escorts returned, and now the company grew smaller, numbering seven. They rode through the guard ranks, Forlern trying to remain inconspicuous. His cloak covered the Homeguard insignia which he had now placed upon his breast, the first time he'd worn it since leaving the Keep with Charadan. It was still difficult to call him by his proper name. The alias of Captain Grundel would forever be with him -- he was certain.

As the moon rose higher into the clear sky, they rode without pause through the Grip. The hills rose up on both sides, giving way to a fairly narrow passageway. Smooth and maintained, the path consisted of rock which had been shaved down over centuries to permit easy travel to the Trencit capital. The road was wide enough in most places for three wagons abreast, and at certain points it narrowed so that only one could move forward at a time. Guards and runners were stationed at several key locations, and greeted them with curt nods and waves. At times Forlern peered upwards, making out the dim outlines of fortified nooks and bulwarks overhead. He knew it was boring duty, here in the Grip, but the alternative -- being sent to the border wars in the east -- was a far greater evil. For himself, he would rather be in the field where the action was. His natural flair for adventure wouldn't allow for any contentment as an ordinary guardsman. Rotating shifts, clearing rock and debris, and other minor duties were the mainstay of these men. But in these troubled times, there was always a chance for some of these fighters to swell the ranks of the royal foot legions.

They rode on at a light pace for the next several hours, as the Grip was a long passage. Near the middle, where it had been widened considerably, a small camp had been set up, consisting of tents and even a few squat buildings. Smoky torches lined the perimeter, and guards milled about in the haze, their forms appearing like grim apparitions materializing from the living rock. Forlern and his companions paused for a few minutes, resting the horses and dismounting to stretch. They lingered only briefly, eager to push forward and reach Daregil Keep before sunrise. The next half of the path proved mostly uneventful, as they passed a number of rumbling carts and dozens of other travelers, but it was with great surprise when Forlern spotted several lavishly-colored wagons ahead of them surrounded by over two dozen tall warriors on horseback, each one holding lanterns, their helms crested with twin feathers, shields slung easily at their backs. They rode with heads held high, faces uplifted.

But even in the twilight the markings were unmistakable.

They wore the personal insignia of the Lastrad electorate, the Gran Barshara himself.

The beasts snarled at Sarion, their teeth gleaming dully in the gloom of the early morning forest. Every fiber of his trained body was taut, with one hand gripping his sword, the other gliding downwards along his side to his dagger. The odds were severely stacked against him, but he remained undaunted. His keen eyes scanned his adversaries for the attack that would swiftly come -- the one that had taken the hapless Luthine, one of the Nighton hunters. Like his fallen Captain Karrol, the courageous fighter had met his end in the forbidden wood. Sarion inwardly winced, thinking of the kind and brave man whom he had known for only a few short days, but their friendship had developed immediately.

And now *he* would be the next victim…

Sarion bristled with anger. Blood would soon be drawn, but even when it happened, it was nearly the end of him…

Two of the creatures attacked in pack fashion, springing through the air directly for him. Their speed was terrifying. Sarion rolled to the left, slashing upwards with his sword. He caught one of the beasts in the abdomen, splitting it wide, but the other creature missed him by only a fraction. Sarion was on his feet immediately, but another of the hunters leaped towards him. There was not enough time for him to bring the knife to bear, and they collided in a mass of fur and fury. Sarion ducked to avoid the deadly claws, and the monster snapped angrily, searching for his neck. With a tremendous effort, he managed to slip beneath its bulk, kicking it in the hindquarters and spinning madly about. All this occurred in a few scant seconds, and Sarion realized that his first hesitation would prove to be his last…

He now twirled his sword before him, hoping to keep the creatures at bay in a move of desperation. Breathing heavily, he watched as they paused for a moment.

They were measuring him. Judging his speed and ability.

These were instinctive hunters, calculating and patient. And *that* made them twice as dangerous.

They started circling, keeping a fair distance from him, but preventing any chance of breaking through their barrier. And despite the loss of one, they were undeterred. Sarion knew they were preparing for their next attack now.

He crouched, trying to determine a course of action, decide which side they would move from. But then something totally unexpected happened…

A soft but high sound drifted in from the deep forest behind them. The creatures growled, several of them craning their necks, caught off guard. In that brief moment of confusion, a glittering haze materialized around their muscular forms, seeping through the gaps of trees and surrounding them. Taken by complete surprise, they lurched about wildly, sensing some type of danger.

But it was too late…

To Sarion's amazement they howled in pain, their cries shattering the deathly stillness. He backed away, attempting to distance himself from the chaos. The beasts slashed at the air, looking for something to attack, but could find no target. The strange flute-like sound grew louder, and Sarion felt himself being mesmerized, and he found trouble focusing. Lightheaded, he stumbled through the trees past the beasts, seeking only to escape the death that surged forward and claimed the enraged hunters. They were soon out of sight, and Sarion fell several times, struggling to keep his balance and have his weapon ready.

Deeper into Sprechyd Wood he clumsily ran, thinking only to keep moving. He went on in this way for untold minutes. Dazed and exhausted, his instinct for self-preservation took over. He had no idea what had just transpired, but his own escape from the waiting creatures had been a harrowing one. From all the members of the group which had broken off and followed Mugil on the fateful venture to seek out the missing Jerol, only Sarion had survived the trap.

A trap which he should have seen coming...

Once again, he felt a terrible loss inside. His companions had been slain to the man, but he had lived on.

Again.

The Rooting of Evil

How many times had he survived while others died? Strong and courageous warriors of Trencit, called away in their sworn duty to defend their beloved homeland. Now they lay on the unforgiving earth, unburied, victims of violence from nameless creatures, their passion borne of something purely evil, beyond their understanding. Their final resting place lay in shrouded hollows deep in the Grammore Lowlands, beneath the long arms of the Ridgeline which bordered the land of horror, and now within the gloomy shadow of Sprechyd Wood, where only a desperate man would dare venture. Fighting against creatures of legend, fierce and unrelenting, they seemed to be at a disadvantage with every step. Harried and pursued, the hunters had become the hunted. Once again, this deadly pattern had emerged. Their enemy was devious and powerful, and Sarion felt overwhelmed by all the events of the past several weeks. It was all strikingly similar to his service in the Western Watch, when he had been the only survivor, whole of body and mind, against the Glefins. Why him? His good fortune seemed unbelievable. Was it good luck? Or perhaps a curse, watching as friends and comrades were hewn down by enemies.

All these thoughts coursed through his mind like an insidious poison, drawing upon his strength and resolve. The specters of his past reared before him in the forest -- Karrol, Luthine, Virgil's men, the warriors which had set off from his own farm, fighters such as Kalen, Rundin, and Charadan...Many others as well.

He raced past the countless ranks of silent trees, the ancient sentinels of Sprechyd Wood, moss-covered and gnarled. Eventually he stumbled and fell to his knees, overcome by his battles, and in need of rest and nourishment. He wondered what had happened to kill off the beasts, but he instinctively knew that something extremely dangerous had intervened. Whether by design

or fortune, he was spared their fate, but Sarion was
cunning enough to suspect the former reason, although
there were no answers to the puzzle. He looked around,
realizing that it was still daytime, although this meant
little to Sprechyd Wood except for a lessening of
darkness as the gloom pervaded, clutching about with
unseen tentacles.

Sarion collapsed against a tall hardwood, too
tired to search for a more hospitable resting place. He
feared there were none to be found in the dark forest
regardless. His eyelids fluttered immediately as he
slumped to the ground, and he felt the arms of sleep
swiftly approaching. Nearly unconscious, an inner
warning clamored for attention as a strange noise
brushed against him. It was the mesmerizing noise from
earlier, almost flute-like in its texture and expression. It
grew louder, clearer. He struggled to awaken but the
sound pressed him down, encouraged him only to sleep,
and not resist. With a monumental effort Sarion pitched
forward, his eyes cracking open.

He remained conscious for only a moment, but
then he saw something which terrified and amazed him
at the same time.

A tall figure stood before him, shimmering in the
twilight. Vaguely human, it resembled an old man with a
flowing beard the color of damp earth. But the
resemblance ended there...

Sprouts of green erupted from its body, thin
vines waving in the air with a life of their own. Instead
of legs, a trunk connected him to the ground itself, like
the earth had attempted to swallow him whole. His arms
looked like the branches of a hoary tree, with stick-
fingers splayed wide in place of human digits.

But worst of all were the eyes, if that's what they
could be called...Slits of obsidian they were, and Sarion
felt as if he were staring into the very soul of the forest

itself, one which did not allow for creatures of flesh and blood to intrude upon. Things lay hidden here which were far beyond the comprehension of men, secrets of origin and power that could bring insanity onto those of mortal existence. Sarion realized the grave danger and shut himself away from the dreadful revelations lurking so close to him now, closer than any man could possibly face and still live.

Wrenching his consciousness back, he averted his gaze, mentally and physically, turning away lest he be forever lost. The desire for knowledge was excruciating, but his will to survive was the stronger one, and he lapsed into a sleep which dragged him to the bottom of his most frightful nightmares.

Drifting in black unconsciousness, Sarion was in a dark and secret place. He knew it was a dream, but unlike anything he'd ever experienced. He felt his body resting among the great trees of Sprechyd Wood, yet he was aware of other surroundings as well. Towering behemoths seemed to be all around him, shapeless entities which went about on purposes which eluded his understanding. They were ancient, filled with knowledge from the ages, and to them, Sarion felt small and inconsequential. He sensed this much from vague images which passed through his mind, fleeting and ghostly impressions, the life energy of their existence, although it was the smallest of residue from their immense power.

Do not fear, you are in no danger. I have dismissed those which threatened.

The voice was like a gasp of air brushing his

face, musical and subtle. Sarion knew it was from the strange creature which had pursued him, and the words which he now listened to both comforted and terrified him at the same time.

"Who are you?"

I am the one asking questions.

The tone was mildly rebuking, although Sarion sensed the being was somehow above feeling normal, human emotions.

You carry items which belie your stature.

Sarion was confused by the remark, and he tried to sweep aside the haze, focus on what the being asked. But he didn't have time for answers.

You carry a seeking stone from one of my kindred.

Alayian! He had almost forgotten about it. She had given him the beautiful stone when they had parted in Grammore. Could this bizarre creature be a dryad of some sort?

"Yes," he answered. "I met a na-dryad in Grammore named Alayian, and she gave me the stone."

I hear the truth in your words. That is enough. Such things are handed out in free will, and cannot be otherwise taken. Her touch is all around you, although you do not understand this.

"Then you're a dryad as well?" Sarion ignored prudence, desiring his own answers.

Distant kindred, nothing more. I am a Keeper of this forest. What you sense around you are the elementals of Sprechyd Wood. Their purpose is beyond your ability to comprehend. They are not even aware of your existence.

"Is this why I can travel in these woods without danger?"

I did not say that.

Sarion felt like a child being chided by an adult,

although the tone was consistent. There was a much deeper form of communication taking place here.

You must leave immediately. Lesser things will soon have you. I cannot protect you much longer.

There could be no questioning the underlying threat in the being's voice.

"There is a great evil coming from Grammore which seeks to destroy Trencit. Do you know what this is or can you help me?" Sarion gambled that the being would pass on something of value to him. He needed hope…

I care only for this forest.

Sarion's eagerness dimmed. There was not the slightest hint of compassion in the creature's strange voice.

Evil and good mean nothing to me. The one which threatens is powerful and will defeat you if he wishes.

Sarion was stunned. How could it know this to be the truth? "Can't you offer me anything to help then? I befriended one of your own kindred. Does this mean nothing to you?" He didn't care if this being could grow angry or not. Sarion was already under its spell.

You will choose your own destiny. You carry something of tremendous power, although you understand it not. It might bring your salvation, or destruction. It is perilous. I cannot allow such a talisman to enter Sprechyd Wood. This is the other reason I sought you out. You will awaken, and I will be gone. Do not venture into the forest again.

Sarion's eyelids fluttered and he woke. The trees encircled him, and a slight breeze rustled the branches and disturbed the leaves, as if something of great size had just left in a rush and passed into the hidden depths of the forest, leaving behind only a wisp, a mere taste, of its essence.

He sat there, knowing that something fantastic had just occurred. Dreamlike, perhaps, but very real. His head swam with confusion as he tried to remember the words spoken to him by the strange creature, one which had saved him from certain death by the hunters sent to ensnare himself and his companions. Saved, yes, but not necessarily with friendly intentions. It had detected the gift from Alayian, the stone of seeking. And the wand…More unanswered questions. About everything, it seemed. The weird being had also expressed knowledge of the Dark Mage, but cared nothing for the conflict taking place between the mysterious sorcerer and Trencit. Sarion realized then that this being was of a singular nature and purpose -- and that was to act as protector of Sprechyd Wood.

Sarion looked around, feeling a quiet chill, now that he was once more alone. He felt his throat tighten at the memory of the fight against the giant brute. His slain companions...He pushed himself up, focusing on his next course of action. He couldn't afford to dwell on his sorrow. There were too many others relying on him. King Gregor, Forlern and Chertron. His nephew Edward…who he hadn't seen in weeks, and possibly many more to follow until he would meet the boy again.

He had no desire to stay in Sprechyd Wood any longer. He needed to put the dread forest behind him and move forward. He remembered the touch of the elementals, and shivers crawled his spine at the brief recollection.

"What you sense around you are the elementals of Sprechyd Wood. Their purpose is beyond your ability to comprehend. They are not even aware of your existence…"

No, it was best not to think about such things until he was safely away from the dangerous wood.

Sarion's ability as a tracker was enough to lead

him in the right direction. The entire episode was a blur -- his race through the forest and subsequent collapse, and then meeting with the Keeper of Sprechyd Wood. It was hard to believe any of the events had even occurred.

He crept along, going only on his skill, tracing his own path. The gloomy twilight surrounded him on all sides but he was determined to escape. The warning of the Keeper echoed in his mind, that he was unwelcome here, even a threat.

Do not venture into the forest again.

Sarion had no desire to ever visit these woods again, *if* he could manage to free himself from its clutches now...

Nothing hindered his progress as he moved stealthily along, a shadow passing through shadows. No living creature crossed his path, and the woods were draped beneath an immense canopy of silence and secrecy. Sprechyd Wood was nothing like Grammore...The Lowlands were filled with a fantastic variety of flora and fauna, vibrant and overwhelming in its magnitude. The breath of life was everywhere, and death waited behind every tree and rock, beneath the still marshland waters or within the blue depths of great lakes and churning rivers. In Sprechyd Wood, however, the vitality was stifled. Sarion knew life existed, but the smaller woodland creatures remained hidden from sight. Others things stalked the forests, but they kept to the deeper recesses, their purpose unknown. And yet other predators dared the perimeter of the forest, seeking unwary prey. Yes, life did indeed exist, but on several levels, and none of them had the slightest similarity. The essence of the forest itself surrounded and watched him. It had observed them when they first entered, and had been with Sarion all the way. The form of this entity was still unclear, and he knew the Keeper was only one manifestation of something far greater and more powerful. If he had somehow managed to catch the smallest glimpse of what lurked at the very core of this incredible realm, it would have been his end. Sarion had not the slightest doubt about this. Fortune once again graced him with its unpredictable presence, but for how much longer?

He continued making his way through the forest, believing that he should not be very far away from the edge. He wondered as to the fate of Chertron and the others -- something which had managed to slip his mind somehow...What if another trap had been set for those remaining behind? It was a terrible thought and he increased his pace. The darkness appeared to be growing deeper, and he wanted to leave Sprechyd Wood before nightfall.

The minutes flowed past him and time meant little. His companions were solitude and apprehension, and he felt a growing sense of urgency. Sarion suddenly stiffened then, his hand tightening the grip on his sword.

There was movement ahead of him in the trees and bushes. Something was coming directly toward him.

Forlern was taken by surprise.

The wagons clearly bore the markings of the Gran Barshara himself, the electorate of Lastrad. Could he possibly be here now, traveling to Daregil Keep? Or more likely, was it one of his top ambassadors? Regardless, it was completely unexpected.

He watched as the two lead men from Lieutenant Florik's group rode ahead to hail the other travelers. The wagons were moving sluggishly and would certainly hinder their progress, and they had been making good time. Forlern wanted this particular adventure to end as quickly as possible. His thoughts constantly led him to the westland, and he worried once again how Sarion and Chertron fared. Until he saw them both and knew they were safe, part of him would find no rest.

Florik came over to him and they spoke lightly as they waited.

"It's rare indeed to see such high ranking officials from Lastrad heading towards Daregil." Forlern drank from his water pouch, taking a moment to rest before they resumed their trek.

"I've never seen an emissary, although we have a fair amount of trade in Dwellyn. Some of the fabrics they transport from the south bring a high price in our markets. And you would be hard-pressed to match their sweet vintages. I could use one right now…"

"You speak for us both, my friend." Forlern sighed, remembering some of his own experiences in the free city of Lastrad.

As if reading his mind, Florik questioned him. "Have you been to Lastrad before? I've yet to travel that far south. But the stories I hear are quite interesting..."

"And all too true, I might add." Forlern finished the sentence for him. "It's an amazing city, you can be sure. The Vanyair Market has no equal, in variety or magnitude. The finest crafts and wares from Trencit and beyond can all be found there. Lastrad is a kingdom of its own, where all are welcome. But such a place inevitably draws the worst dregs imaginable to seek its riches. You won't find a greater haven for cutthroats, mercenaries, and bandits in the known world."

"Sounds like you have tales of your own to tell, Forlern."

He nodded. "I could hold your attention for a while, believe me. There's much to see there. Great beauty and ugliness, waiting for you at every turn. And darkness brings out a very different face. A foolish man need only say the wrong word to the wrong person and he'll have his throat sliced in a second. Sometimes it doesn't take even that much effort for trouble…"

"Hmm, I don't know if your description makes me want to travel there or stay a hundred miles away."

Forlern grinned. "That's part of the enticement. Plenty of adventure and excitement there for a daring man." He then shrugged. "Death to the careless."

"And what of the Gran Barshara?" Florik nodded ahead, where his men were talking with several of the Lastrad warriors. "Have you ever met him before?"

"No, not even from a distance. No one can get near the Horlom, Lastrad's palace." Forlern grew silent before continuing. "He's a strange figure in his own right. I've heard rumors and gossip, the usual sort among people discussing their leaders. Lastrad is ruled by a council of elected officials, who then appoint the Gran Barshara himself. I don't know the man by anything beyond his title. Not even a proper name. And I really don't know how long the current official has been in power, actually."

"Hmm, I don't know either. We have no direct communication with the leaders of Lastrad. They keep to their own affairs, and don't often meddle with Trencit politics."

"Usually…" Forlern frowned, growing impatient. "What could be the holdup here? The Keep is not that far off, but we need to pass these wagons. We could sweep right by them and leave these men in our dust."

Florik looked at him curiously, wondering if the fighter spoke in jest or in seriousness. "That would be rude, don't you think? Official protocol calls for actions a bit more prudent." He chuckled. "Although there are many times I feel the same way."

The Rooting of Evil

With his last sentence, they both turned their heads as the Dwellyn riders rushed back. Florik urged his mount ahead several paces while Forlern adjusted the strap on his own steed.

"Well, what's the delay? We don't have time for pleasantries. Forlern needs to reach the Keep immediately."

"Lieutenant, we spoke to the Captain of the Lastrad Guard. The man's name is Brawnket." The rider hesitated.

"Well, out with it." Florik now showed a bit of his own impatience.

"The captain agreed to let us pass, but he had one request, and a rather pressing one at that."

Forlern moved closer, curious as to what had just transpired.

The rider continued, eyeing Forlern strangely. Florik tapped a gloved hand against his knee. "And what could that be? We'll show the Lastrad delegation their due courtesy. I'm interested in what their mission is, truth be told."

"It seems the wagon isn't holding any emissary at all."

"No? They bear the personal markings of Lastrad and the Gran Barshara. Who else but an official would travel under such guise?" Now it was Forlern questioning the first rider.

"According to the captain, this company is personal escort to the Gran Barshara *himself.* He's in that wagon right *there.*" The man pointed with a long finger.

Florik's mouth opened and Forlern sat there in shock, wondering what possible reason could bring the elusive and mysterious electorate to Daregil Keep. And as he thought this, he felt an involuntary chill scurry across his back.

Paul Melniczek

Sarion crouched, trying to determine the source and direction of the movement. He heard a soft rustling, and knew that something was approaching from directly in front of where he waited. He slunk into the deep shadows behind a pair of ancient hickory trees, already deciding that he wanted to discover the nature of this threat rather than try a hurried escape from where he had just traveled. It was nearly dark, and he needed to leave the forest and regain the open sky once again. His keen ears picked out movement from more than one area now, and whatever approached was moving closer. Sarion hefted the handle of his sword, and held one of his knives ready. If he could maintain the advantage of surprise it might change the course of a possible confrontation, although with the recent harrowing events, another fight was the last thing he wanted.

He spotted a figure walking through the trees, not more than a dozen yards away from him. He held his breath as it drew nearer, and then realized that it was a man.

Two men.

His expression quickly changed from apprehension to relief as he recognized his comrades.

"Chertron! It's me, Sarion!"

He burst forward, feeling the first glimmer of hope since the fateful battle against the minions of Mugil.

"Sarion?" Chertron was stunned by the sight of his friend once again. "Is it really you? By the Seven!"

Chertron came forward, his weapon still raised as if expecting the grim visage of a shade and not his missing companion. Quarran accompanied him, and Sarion clasped arms with the lean fighter.

"I thought you were lost back there with the others…" Chertron's face showed immense relief. Sarion nodded sadly, remembering the fallen warriors.

"I was spared their fate, by something unforeseen..." His eyes glazed over, but he didn't finish. "Where's Valadire and his men?"

"Not far behind us." Quarran answered, gesturing over his shoulder. "They're standing guard near the house."

"Did you see anything there?" Sarion's eyes narrowed. "We were waylaid by a giant savage waiting inside for us and were outmatched. A trap was set for our arrival."

"We searched, and found the bodies of Karrol and the fighters. But nothing else. It was empty." Chertron's face reflected his anger and sorrow.

"Let's gather them and leave this dreadful forest. Sprechyd Wood is no place for men. The tales are all true."

The other two were silent for a moment, and then Chertron spoke. "You have a story to tell, my friend. One which I would rather not hear." He clapped Sarion on the shoulder. "You're right though, let's be off. Evil might have left this place for now, but I fear it lurks nearby."

They plunged ahead, returning from where the two men had just emerged. "How far away is the house?" Sarion asked.

The Rooting of Evil

"If it wasn't for this dismal gloom, we could almost see it now." Chertron frowned. "We'll be there in a few moments. When I laid eyes on that building, I had a bad feeling about the place. Nothing good could possibly live there."

"We felt the same, but decided to investigate. Jerol had to be found. And so he was…"

"The bones in the pit. We knew something dangerous dwelt there when we found the fallen hunters. Valadire led the way down the tunnel and back into the woods once more. A clever arrangement for a trap. Clever and deadly."

Sarion nodded to Chertron. "It was too much for us. I barely escaped, and found myself hedged in by a pack of creatures I've never seen the likes of."

"Then something waited for you beyond the secret door?" Quarran's boyish face looked out of place in the wilderness.

"Yes. I'll finish my tale when we put Sprechyd Wood behind us."

Soon they were joined by one of the other Nighton fighters, and then Valadire himself. "Sarion, it's good to see you alive and whole once more. We feared you were all lost. Karrol's death will be sorely felt in Nighton. He was a brave and respected leader." He wanted to say more, but instead only shook his head.

"Let's keep some distance between ourselves and the building. The edge of the forest is nearby. Stay sharp. That brute could still be lurking nearby."

Sarion and the others spread out in hunting formation, moving like shades through the woods, several lanterns held aloft to shed light. The shadows shrank back but the trees seemed to usher together around them like monolithic sentinels, warding the ancient woods. Although Sarion was certain the others felt the watchfulness, he was the only one who understood just how dangerous their position was, and he had no intention of giving them even more cause for worry. Before too long the land rose beneath them as they moved out of the depression where the house lay in darkness. No sound reached their ears and the night descended upon them, awakening fears and rekindling the prospect of nightmares once again to their embattled existence. It was with profound relief when the trees finally broke away and they spotted the horses, tethered where they had left them. Valadire had refused to leave any of his men behind. The group numbered less than ten now, and it was too hazardous to separate until they returned to safer country, if any territory was truly safe anymore. The westland remained unpredictable and increasingly dangerous.

They mounted the animals and hurried away towards the middle of the grassland. Wedged between the horrors of Sprechyd Wood and the unknown predator in the bordering wilderness, the wide grass and open sky seemed like a haven without walls. The rain ended, but the mist curled around their feet with damp clinging hands, eager to make certain that any sense of comfort remained an aloof memory. Sarion needed rest, but there were too many questions to be answered. They sat and pitched a makeshift camp with several hunters guarding the perimeter. Food was passed around and they ate quietly for a few moments. Sarion felt Valadire's eyes upon him, the man eager to hear his tale. When Sarion finally quenched his thirst, he drew his legs before him and nodded. Chertron and the Nighton hunter sat in silence, listening as Sarion narrated the events of the disastrous expedition.

The men were appalled by the ferocity of the giant savage, and incensed at Mugil's betrayal.

"A trap all along. Just as I feared," Chertron muttered, but Valadire said nothing, waiting for Sarion to continue.

He finished his tale, describing his desperate stand against the waiting creatures who had slain Luthine, and then he spoke in partial amazement about his subsequent reprisal at the hands of the strange being which called itself the Keeper of Sprechyd Wood. His recollection was clouded in some ways, and he was confused by his conversation with the forest entity as he tried to recall his fantastic ordeal.

"That is truly an unbelievable tale." Valadire rubbed his chin, shaking his head. "Yet there can be no denial. The creatures were disposed of, and here you are once more. Saved by *something*..."

"This dryad, or whatever it is, seems to have little use for people." Chertron gazed towards Sprechyd Wood, as if his keen eyes could pierce the gloom in an effort to unravel its secrets. "The woods are ancient, and dangerous. We don't know anything about it, or what might live there."

Sarion looked down the slope, following Chertron's stare. "I felt some of the power when I entered. Karrol felt it as well..." He paused. "There's something living inside that has walked the earth long before men emerged, things which are of nature itself, more akin to the land than creatures of flesh and bone. I believe we felt the presence of the elementals of which he spoke, and of which I caught the faintest of glimpses, but enough so that I was stunned."

"These events are greatly disturbing. And from what the creature told you, they have no role in the battle against the Dark Mage, and Trencit's affairs. We're too insignificant to them." Valadire considered. "Sprechyd Wood will continue no matter who rules the world around it, and if men happen to invade its territory, the consequences will be deadly."

"Yet Jerol entered, and the brute and Mugil

waited inside. Perhaps the Dark Mage has some control over events within the black wood?" Chertron stared at Sarion.

"Maybe *control* is not the right word. He's likely aware of its power. Perhaps he even knows how to circumvent its attention to some degree. I don't know...What bothers me the most is that the Keeper thinks the Dark Mage clearly has the strength to defeat us. I don't believe it would offer such information arbitrarily."

"And this talisman you hold..." Valadire pressed close, unwilling to have his voice carry towards his men, one of them passing nearby on watch. "Is there anything you know about it?"

"Little, or nothing." Sarion sighed. "Alayian detected its power, but could not identify what it was. She has acute abilities, well beyond the senses of ordinary men. She's not human." This last statement sent a chill through him. He did not like calling Alayian something which sounded...so abnormal. But it was the truth. She was a different species, despite her appearance. Different and fantastic. Her beauty was stunning, her talent for survival acutely honed to such a degree that men couldn't even begin to comprehend it. This continued to disturb Sarion much more than he cared to admit, because he had strong feelings towards the girl...He missed her. He also missed Edward and his home. Sarion missed Forlern too, the young fighter off somewhere in Trencit, hopefully near Daregil Keep by now. And he also missed Charadan, who, if only for a brief few weeks, had become more than just a traveling companion. They had been friends. But what had Sarion really known about the man? Enough, probably. Charadan, even behind his lofty titles and stellar reputation, had been gifted with a practical and intelligent mind, a generous and noble heart, with a sense of unbreakable loyalty to Trencit and its people, no matter the cost to himself or his fighters. And now he was gone...

"Sarion...Sarion?"

He stirred, not realizing his eyes had momentarily closed. "Sorry, lost in thought here. My mind swirls with memories and images from recent weeks. The past is fraught with despair, the present moves along from one hazard to another, and the path ahead is troubled and uncertain." Sarion squeezed his forehead wearily.

"You need a bit of rest, and a fresh start in the morning." Valadire patted him on the shoulder. "I can't imagine what you both have been through. We must stand together and we'll face the danger with a true heart."

Chertron was silent, but Sarion felt a growing trust in Valadire, enough so that he considered telling the man the *entire* truth. Maybe tomorrow, he thought.

"All right. I do need sleep. We'll take up the discussion in the morning. But one thing more. This matter of the rod and my encounter with the Keeper...I don't wish for this to go any further. No one must hear these things. At least until I can figure them out."

Valadire looked puzzled, but nodded.

"Any idea as to our next step?" Chertron raised an eyebrow.

Sarion locked stares with his companion. "Yes."

With that, he would say no more, but grabbed his blanket and huddled onto the grassy plain, falling asleep almost immediately.

His companions let him sleep until late the next morning, and Sarion awakened to a grey sky overhead which promised more rain.

"Feel rested?" Sarion recognized Chertron's voice, and squinted over in his direction.

"Too early to say. I'll let you know in a few hours." Sarion stretched, giving a huge yawn. "I miss the comforts of my own home and bed. Nighton was a relief after those long days in the wilderness, but I miss goose-down pillows and my hounds. Most of all my nephew though..."

"The lad will be fine. You have a strong household looking out for him, and a good roof over his shoulders."

"Those things are true, but I have a terrible uneasiness as well. We live too close to the Ridgeline for my likings. It wasn't like this before. At least not until the Glefins showed up, that is. Grammore was always there, and everyone accepted it. But more as legend, a terrible word to scare naughty children with, or to mutter around a drink in the tavern. Then when I served in the Western Watch and found myself looking down into that valley, my perspective changed immediately. The wildness and mystery of it leaves you permanently affected. Somehow, I knew that one day I would have to return."

"Hmm, maybe a foreshadowing of things to come. Strange, in most of Trencit, people give little, or no thought at all to our borders. The Devlents attack us and our warriors march forth, skirmishing against them. It's only when you see battle yourself, or lose an uncle, brother, or even father, that you open your eyes and understand that our kingdom is not as large and powerful as we might think it is..."

"Words well spoken." Valadire approached, nodding to them both. "In the westland we live beneath the shadow of yonder evil. The threat of nightmares and terrible beasts. And we give little recognition to our countrymen fighting in the east. They probably think the same to us out here. Now it's our turn to share in Trencit's peril."

"We live in unfortunate times." Sarion stood, rummaging in his pack. "All we can do is move forward and trust our instincts. I don't have any more answers now than when I set off with Captain Grundel after the ogre. What I do have are a host of questions, and unpleasant memories which will haunt me the rest of my life."

"And so we begin another merry day here in the westland." Chertron grimaced. "If I cared to dwell on all the bad things which have happened, my heart would surely wither away."

"You're right." Sarion regained some of his determination. "I won't forget those who have fallen, and will strive to strike directly at my enemy. But I will *not* give in to despair."

"We're all agreed on that, at least." Valadire's face was grim, but Sarion saw something in his eyes he had failed to notice before. An intense resoluteness. He was surprised at the strength he saw in the fighter's gaze.

"And this brings us to the next matter -- a course of action. Clearly, my duty is to return to Nighton immediately and the Foresters need to hold council with Chensel. The loss of Jerol and Karrol will sorely hurt our leadership. New commanders must be appointed, and the security of the westland is paramount. We should rearrange a number of patrols, and my thought is to gather reinforcements where we may, and group several of our smaller companies into larger regiments."

"Some of this sounds wise, but why separate smaller units? The borderlands are vast. I would think a better strategy would be to spread out the fighters." Chertron questioned Valadire's notion, but Sarion interjected.

"Actually, there's some merit in this idea. Nighton can sweep across suspect areas and do more damage if they find any large group of marauders. The greater towns and individual villages must do their part, as I believe they have already started -- and that is to organize their own men-at-arms to protect their lands. The Western Watch does not have enough manpower to secure every holding. Warnings should be issued at once, and the people of the westland need to understand that war is brewing, although one that none could have foreseen."

"Maybe you're right." Chertron said. "The masters of Nighton need to hold council and form a strong defense. King Gregor has to consider the threat to his west as well as the east. With all the terrible news coming from the borderlands, he cannot refuse to bolster the forces in some way. He also needs to bring some of these monarchs in line…I think he's never felt the weight of the crown heavier than what is ahead of him in the coming days."

"And you, Sarion." Valadire stared at him. "What's your next step? Your skills seem to be taxed at every turn, but you have much to offer."

"I've been doing much thinking…" His voice trailed off, and he sighed deeply. "Lately, events have happened so swiftly that I'm just trying to meet the growing challenges of each new day. When things can't get any worse, they do. Good men are taken from us. I had tremendous respect for Karrol. He was someone I would willingly fight next to on the battlefield." He shook his head. "This Dark Mage has been a step ahead of us since the beginning. He knows our strength. Our vulnerability. Yet we know *nothing* about who, or what he is. Until we learn something of his whereabouts, catch a glimpse of what he's thinking, we'll continue to be at a disadvantage. We'll be mismatched at every turn. We cannot allow this to go on, or else the Keeper's words will come to pass."

"Your words ring truth, but what can we do? Your companion should be at Daregil Keep soon, and then King Gregor will take action as he sees fit." Valadire shrugged, agreeing with Sarion but displaying his own loss for further ideas.

Chertron leaned close, staring at his friend. "I know you too well by now, Sarion. There's something else which troubles you. Something else you know, or suspect."

Sarion slowly nodded. "I don't *know* anything for certain. But my instincts warn me of a dreadful possibility." He paused for a moment. "The Dark Mage may have spies within Trencit, allies of some form."

"That's possible." Valadire agreed. "Kingdoms great as ours will always give rise to those whose ambition knows no boundary. Or loyalty, except to themselves."

"King Gregor must be extremely cautious how he proceeds. Those he trusts may not prove to be worthy of such faith."

"Did you speak to Forlern about this?" Questioned Chertron.

"No. It never really dawned on me. It should have…Some of our troubles can be blamed on misfortune, but not all of it. The sorcerer possesses some measure of magic which enhances his strength. Maybe it's the entire makeup of his power. But he must have limits. And those limits are filled in by his emissaries, in whatever form they take. We need to be extremely careful."

His companions were grim-faced, but remained silent, considering his words.

"After I speak to King Gregor I'll return to Nighton, and give aid where I may."

Valadire nodded, a smile breaking across his face. "You will be most welcome, my friend."

"But there is one more thing I've decided to do..."

Something in Sarion's tone caused both men to pause. They looked at him expectantly, holding their breaths for a moment.

"I intend on going back to Grammore and seek out the fortress of the Dark Mage. And put an end to him."

The Second Forester of Nighton leaned over the iron balcony outside his personal quarters and stared at the grey horizon. Rain had started to fall earlier in the day, diminishing to a curtain of fine mist, casting the valley in a veil of gloom. Nightfall came quickly, and the dreariness permeated the western fortress, the mood dampened by more than just the dismal weather. He was weary, and he felt the chill of the air reaching into his very bones. Since Jerol's departure, Chensel's own duties had grown significantly. The Western Watch was a large, organized fighting and defensive system. Although individual officers were in charge of geographic regions, everything was coordinated through Nighton and the Foresters, which meant that all decisions lay squarely on his own shoulders with their leader out in the field, his whereabouts unknown.

The Rooting of Evil

Where was Jerol? Had Karrol found him yet?

He missed both men a lot more than he cared to admit...Loyal fighters in Trencit's service, worthy comrades, but more so they were his close friends. And Sarion...his story had been equally fantastic and tragic. General Charadan dead. It sounded impossible, but the world had been turned on its head with this unexpected misfortune. Sarion was somewhat of an enigma himself. His past record in the Western Watch was impeccable, and his leadership and courage were well-known to the leaders of Nighton, many of them having served with him years ago. The youngest Forester in the Watch's history, his prowess of swordsmanship was uncanny, his tracking abilities a legend in themselves. He would be a tremendous help if he returned to their ranks now. They needed someone like him.

Sighing, Chensel took a swig from his mug of ale. The liquid was warm and soothing, and he enjoyed the pleasant sensation, willing his body and mind to ease, and take the edge off all the concerns swirling in his head. His day consisted of an endless stream of protocol -- strategy meetings, war council, overseeing the upkeep of the fortress, assigning duties to the lower ranking officers, and holding private discussions with the Captains of Nighton. The previous day he had talked with a delegation from Daregil Keep, assuring him that members of Captain Grundel's party had returned, and were being escorted back to the Trencit capital. This had satisfied them, and they had discussed the growing problems in the borderlands. Chensel's words and manner left no doubt in their mind as to the seriousness of the threat, and the envoys had listened intently, greatly disturbed by the news. These were low ranking couriers, however, and as such were not privy to King Gregor's inner council, but they gave their word that the monarch would be given a complete report.

Paul Melniczek

Chensel didn't expect anything beyond this, and knew that until King Gregor spoke to Forlern or Sarion, and knew the full story, then nothing drastic would be done. And so it was another period of restless waiting…But did the westland have such time to waste?

Instructing his guards that he was not to be disturbed, Chensel wanted to spend the evening clearing his mind, formulating a master plan on defending the westland. Not an easy task. Turning around, he closed the door which protected his room from the elements. His quarters were high up in the keep, only Jerol's remaining above it. They were based on a simple hierarchy, matching their occupant's rank in the Western Watch. He seated himself at the table, poring over the charts and graphs for the hundredth time. Patrols, encampments, lines of reinforcements, and every important scrap of military information was detailed on the large parchment. They were reworked on a weekly basis, as the westland was fluid and unpredictable. Chensel looked thoughtfully at the patrols to the north and to the south as marked on the map. He was expecting word from Lord Pralicon any day, and wondered as to what the powerful monarch would do next. There had always been cooperation between Gwerath and Nighton, so he assumed there would be no problems. Couriers were also sent into the deep south where Lord Berillon ruled from the fair city of Sharield, which sat over a mountain lake, its design both formidable as well as being a marvel to behold. Berillon was popular among the people of his province, which consisted of numerous villages and several small towns. It was Trencit's most isolated territory, and Sharield traded with others living outside of the kingdom in the southern regions, which were as unpredictable and dangerous an area as could be found, although men did live there. But it was also very isolated, with no routine lines of communication between the two cities.

Chensel drank from his mug, eyeing the goblet as if he could find the answers he wanted in its simple shape. He was a shrewd man, experienced and not easily put off by any problem, even ones as serious which faced him now. He thought ahead to the worst of possibilities -- one in which the borderlands were so besieged that the inhabitants might be forced to leave their homes. Nighton could house thousands if necessary for an extended period of time. There were many storage buildings, and under Jerol's command they had been kept stocked to near capacity. Chensel was moving forward with this plan, ordering more food stores to be taken in. If things became worse, Nighton would be prepared.

The keep was quiet at night, and at times he felt as if he were sequestered somewhere far away from the tribulations facing the Western Watch. He had served in the Royal Army for several years, off in the east, leaving at a time when the Devlents had kept to themselves. He enjoyed serving in Nighton, and loved the open wilderness. A certain part of him craved the reckless freedom which the western provinces offered. Even now he longed for a trip in the field, but the current situation demanded his unsleeping attention. Chensel walked over to the fireplace, tossing in a split log, staring as the sparks showered the sides of the hearth like fireflies. He heard a thump outside, and looked over towards the doorway where Jaken, one of his personal guards, held watch. Curious, he moved over to the doorway, listening. There was no sound coming from outside. He waited for a minute.

Still nothing.

Grabbing the handle, he turned the knob and peered out, the hallway lighted by candles in iron sconces. Jaken was missing, and Chensel grew suspicious. His guards never left their post.

Unless something was wrong…

He reached for the knife at his side, pulling the door shut in front of him as his survival instincts took control. With surprise more than fear, he heard a shuffling noise as someone moved across the stone floors.

But it was coming from *behind* him…

"The Gran Barshara is in *that* wagon?" Florik whistled, his eyes mirroring disbelief. The man nodded.

"And he wants to speak with *us*?"

The Dwellyn fighter nodded vigorously. "He specifically wanted to speak with Forlern."

"What? Why in the world would he want to talk with me?" Forlern was astonished. "And how does he even know me in the first place? I've never met the man before. No one has, to my knowledge. He doesn't know *me*, you can be sure."

"Actually, I told the Lastrad Captain that we are traveling directly to see King Gregor, and that he's impatiently expecting us."

"And what else?" By the way the man's eyes darted back and forth, Forlern knew the man was reluctant to admit to something.

"Well, man?" Florik was getting angry.

"My apologies, Lieutenant. I told Captain Brawnket that we escort a member of the Homeguard, to add some weight to my point for haste."

Florik grunted. "That's understandable. So he knows a member is in our company…That should be no great surprise to anyone traveling this close to Daregil

Keep. And how would he know Forlern personally? That's my question."

"He doesn't. But just the fact that a *member* is here seemed of great importance, for whatever reason."

"Well, now I'm more curious than ever." Forlern patted his mount. "We get to meet the Gran Barshara himself, and entertain his own amusement. Let's not keep him waiting."

He moved forward, waving off a reply. Florik signaled to his men for a rest, and followed after the younger fighter. Forlern came to the foremost of the Lastrad riders, who carried the bright Lastradian emblem in his saddle post, one depicting a yellow falcon with red claws.

He hailed the man. "My name is Forlern, member of the Trencit Homeguard, and on a personal mission to meet with His Majesty. Your Lord wishes to speak with me?" The rider remained silent as another warrior approached. He was middle aged with a clean-shaven face lined with scars, clothed in full battle attire. A wicked pike gleamed at his side, along with an assortment of other weapons. Forlern was certain there were many more he couldn't see.

"I'm Captain Brawnket of the Gran Barshara's personal escort. I'll take you to him."

Forlern nodded, as he knew this man would tell him nothing. They moved towards the largest, and central wagon, which was so wide it barely cleared the narrower walls of the Grip. Here, both men dismounted, and other warriors came to tie their horses. Forlern's eyes scanned the newcomers, recognizing them as men from the deep south, swarthy and expressionless. He knew they were of top fighting caliber. Only a fool would think otherwise, knowing who they guarded. There was a single door in the side of the main wagon, and another fighter opened it, looking neither at them or anywhere else. Forlern felt uncomfortable, realizing he was to meet the mysterious leader of Lastrad. Very few people in their lifetime would ever meet this man. Why him?

He walked inside, moving onto a set of short steps. Lanterns were lit, as the inside was windowless. A smell of spiced incense drifted through the air. Forlern looked about, quickly taking it all in. Surprisingly, it looked more like a small palace chamber than the interior of a traveling wagon. Much more…There were several chairs and small tables, all of them garishly adorned with expensive cloths that Forlern could only imagine what their value was. Drinking goblets and pitchers sat on the tables, along with bowls of fruit, meats, and cheese. The wagon floor was carpeted in a rich fabric which he'd never even seen before. The compartment was a vision of tremendous wealth, and Forlern knew that the fortunes of this leader were far above anything he could dream of…

A single serving girl lay with her legs crossed on the floor. She had long, charcoal black hair, cascading down her back. Her head was bowed. Two men sat on a pair of chairs behind her, one of them further back, against the far side of the wagon. Forlern knew immediately it was the Gran Barshara.

He wore a long robe of bright purple, with the Lastrad emblem blazoned upon his breast, and seemed to be of indeterminate age. If he had to, Forlern couldn't have guessed what it was. His hair was hidden beneath a small golden crown, and about his neck rested several long chains of precious metals. Rings adorned his fingers, and he held a long rod in on hand. He stared at Forlern, his face impassive. His eyes were steel grey, and the young fighter felt as if he were locked in a physical struggle as he strived to match the man's smoldering gaze.

276

"I am the Gran Barshara. Welcome, fighter of Trencit."

His voice was low and even, the tone one of unmistakable power and the knowledge to wield it, and something else, perhaps...

"My name is Forlern, and it is my great pleasure to meet you." He made a short bow, breaking his gaze away for a brief moment. "My escort is Lieutenant Florik, from the Dwellyn Home Watch."

Forlern took the opportunity to look over at the other man now, who remained seated as well. He was not much older than himself, he realized. His posture and expression displayed a casual laziness, as if he had somewhere else to be, or this chance meeting was interrupting him in another activity. His hair was cropped low, and he wore a short sword at his belt. His feet were stretched out, and on them were brown sandals. Forlern wondered if he was the son of the Gran Barshara, as he looked too young and disinterested to be anything else.

"I have no wish to hold you up any longer, as my men have informed me of your urgency to see King Gregor. I am on my way to see him as well, although you will certainly reach the Keep ahead of my caravan."

Forlern nodded, but offered nothing else.

"I have a question for you though. Do you know of any Homeguard members with exceptional fighting skills?"

The question took Forlern by complete surprise. He almost opened his mouth with a sharp retort, but knew immediately it would be a grave mistake. He was dealing with someone extraordinary here, and a leader of a large city aligned with Trencit. But there was something in the question beyond the obvious. The Gran Barshara surely knew the capabilities of the Homeguard. What was he getting at? Forlern felt his face flush at the possibility of being baited by this man. *Everyone* knew the Homeguard were the elite of Trencit's fighters. He must be careful in his reply...

"My Lord, the Homeguard consists of handpicked men throughout the kingdom. All are quite capable, versed in every aspect of fighting. They hold positions in King Gregor's personal escort, and many are officers in the Royal Army."

"Then how is it that someone as young as yourself became one? Are all the top men fighting in the border war?"

This time the barb came from the other man, and there was undisguised scorn in the statement. Forlern bristled with anger now. Was he called in here only to be mocked by this ruler and his bored-looking offspring?

Pausing for a second, he composed himself before answering. "Perhaps you're unfamiliar with our training and skill?"

Forlern directed his gaze at the man, who had not even been introduced to him, but this time he was more critical in his assessment. There was something in his look that spoke of incredible arrogance and supreme confidence. Even more so than the Gran Barshara himself...Caught off guard, Forlern knew there was a game being played here. He didn't know why, or for what purpose, but he didn't like it at all. If it were any other situation they would be looking down the blade of his knife by now.

The man answered. "I'm familiar with Homeguard. I've met some in the past. Sparred with a few as well. There are better..." He shrugged, refusing to elaborate further, and Forlern noticed an odd ring on the fourth finger of his left hand.

The Gran Barshara spoke again. "Do you know if General Charadan is at Daregil Keep? He would know of his best fighters, certainly."

Forlern had to be very cautious here, and not let anything slip. "Charadan is in the field; that is all I know. I'm sure King Gregor will speak more of these matters with you after your arrival."

The Gran Barshara was silent, and the other man grabbed a handful of purple grapes, popping them absently in his mouth. There was a moment of uncomfortable quiet, and Forlern felt ready to shout something harsh at both of these men. But then, the Lastrad electorate waved his hand in dismissal. "That's all. You best be on your way to Daregil Keep. I wouldn't want the king to think I held up his messengers."

Forlern made a slight bow, turning on his heel. He didn't look back. And he said nothing until the two of them had returned to their company, the Dwellyn commander hailing his men that they were off once more. After several moments they mounted, squeezing past the caravan in the narrow passage, and soon were unhindered. Florik looked questioningly over at Forlern, whose face wore no expression.

Grimacing, the lieutenant finally broke the silence when they had placed several hundred yards between themselves and the Gran Barshara's escort. "Well, what do you make of *that* encounter? They deliberately baited you, and I have not the slightest notion why, besides open boorishness." He snorted in disdain.

But instead of speaking angrily, Forlern shook his head. "That was my first thought as well, of course. But there's something else that belies the obvious. Something that has me at a complete loss."

"What do you mean?"

Forlern held up a hand, then withdrew it, as if undecided. "Things are not what they appear. Did you notice anything unusual about the bored-looking man?"

"No. I was quite taken with their trappings and mannerisms, to be honest. *And* outright rudeness."

"Yes, but you're missing something here, Florik."

Florik scowled, looking confused and mildly put off. "Tell me, then. What do you guess at? Or know?"

"The man is not what he seems. I thought he might even be the son of the Gran Barshara. But no...He's his personal bodyguard. And most likely one of the deadliest fighters either of us have ever laid eyes on."

Florik's eyes narrowed. "How can you be certain?"

"By the ring he wears; it can only mean one thing. He's a member of the Ja-Ravel."

Florik gasped, the noise audible over even the horse's tromping. "That's impossible! They've all been gone, for countless decades at least."

"*That* is the popular belief. Yes...But, as a member of the Trencit Homeguard, I have access to information not meant for common knowledge. There have been rumors of a sect in the deep south for years now, reviving the old ways. Murmurings and gossip only, with nothing firsthand. That ring is a perfect description of their talisman. I'm positive."

"Unless he found it somewhere, stole it perhaps?"

"I don't think so. The Gran Barshara is an extremely powerful and wealthy man. He surrounds himself with deadly fighters and employs assassins of the highest caliber. He would not entrust the caring of his life to anyone less."

"And you think any of this is related to his visiting Daregil Keep?"

"I'm not sure, but his questions have a purpose.

There are hidden meanings behind the words, plus the direction and yes, harshness of his attitude. He may have considered *myself* insignificant, but he seeks aid from the king. Or Charadan..." Forlern paused, rubbing his chin. "Well, he won't receive any from our King's Champion, certainly. But I think I saw something else in him that you may have missed."

Forlern stared over at Florik, knowing that this was someone he could confide in, at least to some degree.

"Don't take this conversation further than here, do you understand?"

Florik nodded.

"The Gran Barshara, for whatever reason, has the look of someone desperate. A man scared down to the depths of his very soul..."

His companions were silent. Sarion's eyes sparkled with passion as he spoke, and there was no trace of anything except grim determination. It was a bold and terrible statement, one in which he had yet to unravel any clear plan to support a future expedition to Grammore, but nonetheless, he felt certain it would come to pass. Things had been spiraling around him for weeks since first leaving with Charadan and the others. They had descended into a realm where darkness and nightmares festered, where monsters moved and lived, waited for the unwary. Sarion had glimpsed things of great beauty and cruelty, partnered uneasily in a wilderness of violence and fear, and yet he had returned unscathed. For the second time in his life he had entered the forbidden land, escaped intact, and lived to fight a new day. His conviction was unshakable now. It was not what he desired in his heart, to return to Grammore ever again...But he must. The Dark Mage was a figure with tremendous power, and his range was growing, spreading across the edges of Trencit like a seeping poison. The westland was already in upheaval. The mysterious enemy would certainly not stop there. Through his manipulations, he'd already killed two of Nighton's leaders, including First Captain Jerol. The command of the Western Watch was at grave risk. And Sarion was convinced that King Gregor would listen. He must listen...Sarion had seen much, thought things through to their eventual conclusion, and it was not very pleasant. Still there remained so many unanswered questions. How many could be found in Trencit, or even Daregil Keep? Few, if any. He would have to try. Sarion also understood that they needed to strike at the source of the black power, the very root of evil which sought to destroy them, and that could only be achieved by attacking the Dark Mage directly, and where he held reign.

In the Grammore Lowlands.

No, Sarion did not know how, or when, any of this might happen. But if Trencit was to survive, it had to be tried at some point in time, and before it was too late.

"A bold scheme, dangerous and foolish, I would deem, if spoken by anyone else except for yourself, Sarion." Valadire gently shook his head. "But I think I know you well enough that this is no brash attempt at heroism. You understand, or guess at much. I think the king will take into account your opinion. Still..."

"Tis' madness." Chertron grumbled. "Madness. Grammore is the last place in the world I would want to venture into again, especially searching for an enemy whose location is completely unknown. I don't think it very wise to consider that course of action too greatly, Sarion. Let's see what the king has to say first. After this last disastrous mission, it's my feeling that he will look for new ways to defend his wide borders."

Sarion said nothing for a moment, pondering his own words. It was true. Until they spoke to King Gregor, the next course of action would be unknown, and he would be at His Majesty's service if asked. He would have to wait and see…

He nodded to himself, picking up some of his items. It was time for them to move once again. The sky remained overcast, an unfriendly mantle of gray which seemed to exist only to dampen their already beaten spirits. The weather in the borderlands was constantly changing, and could never be relied upon. Trencit itself basked in a moderate climate, which grew colder in the mountains surrounding Daregil Keep and becoming much more temperate in its southern provinces which were ripe for farming and the cultivation of livestock and vineyards. The makeup of the kingdom was not very diverse, however. You were either a farmer, baker, merchant, craftsman, fighter, or of nobility. After that, the choices greatly diminished.

The company soon mounted and rode northward, backtracking from where they had come from. Their plan was to keep to the grassland separating Sprechyd Wood and the main forest beyond the lowland for as long as possible, and then strike directly towards Nighton. They knew that something monstrous stalked the surrounding woods, and its location was unknown. If it managed to track them, there was little they could do, but their best course of action was to avoid it at all costs. If it really was a Killworm, there was nothing they could do to defend themselves except escape its clutches. This was yet another thing which greatly troubled Sarion…They had no means to battle a creature of this nature, magically spawned from an older age. Sword and shaft could bring down anything of flesh and blood, but the Killworm was said to be enchanted, brought to life by sorcery. How could they defeat such a thing?

The wind buffeted their faces as they rode along the grassy plain, and Sarion knew the cooler season was arriving. Most of the farms in the westland were in full harvest preparation, and he wondered how his nephew Edward was faring on his own lands. Messengers had been sent from Nighton, and they should reach the boy within the next two days.

If nothing unforeseen occurred...

Not for the first time he was bothered that he couldn't be there to protect the lad if anything raided his own homestead. There were a number of men who worked on the farm, and they were quite capable, trusted friends of his for years, most of them. But protection against what crept out from Grammore was another thing. The borderlands needed to be united, communication lines kept open, the local militias organized. The biggest problem facing them was geography. The westland was a sprawling territory, diverse in makeup, and many areas uninhabited. Settlers tended to live within a day's travel of the nearest village. There were only a handful of larger towns, and these didn't compare in size to the greater cities of Trencit. Some of the braver folk, mostly trappers, might chance the very shadow of the Ridgeline itself, but Sarion didn't know of anyone who actually lived there. It wasn't safe, and only a fool would think otherwise.

Little conversation passed between members of the company, and the prospect of entering the woods where they had just fled from the day before was not a pleasant one. Sarion watched as the men suspiciously eyed the looming forest on both sides, pressing in on them silently, and on a subliminal level, they all felt the presence of Sprechyd Wood. Having encountered the strange being known as the Keeper, Sarion had a new understanding of the ancient forest, or at least a small amount of knowledge. He still knew nothing about the essence of that which dwelt inside its deep reaches, only that it was incredibly old, powerful, and surpassed the wisdom of men. And beyond that terrifying small glimpse, he knew it was sentient in a way which baffled understanding. It recognized all things which dared to walk upon its soil, although measured it as insignificant. Sarion shuddered to think what would happen if the wood decided to focus its attention on someone…

No, it was best not to think of such things.

They rode forth unhindered for several hours. A misty rain fell at times, and all they could do was grumble and pull their cloaks tighter. The landscape failed to change as their mounts thundered onward -- grassy plains and looming woods to either side. Not bothering to pause, the company was a smudge of gray against a dull horizon, wishing only for passage through this hostile country. Around the middle of the afternoon Sarion and Valadire conferred, deciding to push further east, keeping to the open meadows for as long as possible, thus avoiding the region they had previously traveled. This plan brought them to an eventual halt late in the day, and now there was little choice left. They could either ride additional miles out of their way east, or enter the forest once more.

It was time for a decision, and Sarion, Valadire, and Chertron talked amongst themselves in low voices as the hunters paused, waiting for the command. With several nervous glances all around, the fighters soon plunged into the northern woods, everyone on full alert. Valadire thought they had avoided the unknown lurker from the night before, and Sarion tended to agree, but was not overly confident. They'd traveled a long distance during the day with no sign of pursuit, but they both knew how vulnerable they would be once inside the forest again. The main trail in this area had proven deadly, and they had already paid a high cost -- a pair of Nighton hunters. No, they would cut across country this time and stay off the paths. The crucial moments would be in the next several hours until they left the thickest part of the forest behind. But until then...

And so the warriors of Trencit flitted between the trees, the horses' hooves muffled against unnecessary sound. Lanterns were in hand as nightfall emerged prematurely, shrouding the western forests in gloom. In spite of the promised threat from above, the day had mercifully remained dry, broken only by an occasional drizzle. Sarion considered the weather patterns the past few weeks. Grammore was a dense jungle the deeper one traveled, humid with frequent rain and mist. It certainly had not helped them during their excursion, and it seemed that the dismal weather had now seeped into the rest of the westland. There had been a few days of bright sunlight, the warmth and light teasing them as they journeyed through the region, but never enough though. As if in answer to his musings, a light rain now began to fall, and Sarion grimaced. Was there no end to the foul weather? Muttering to himself he kept his eyes open, his ears missing nothing. Riding in the lead alongside of Glavit, he was satisfied that this arrangement maximized their ability. The bearish Nighton fighter was an excellent tracker, and Sarion felt confident sharing the responsibilities with him. Sarion drew inward, focusing on the sights and sounds around him. Over the years, he had learned to meld with his surroundings, identify all the normal attributes of the land and recognize the ones which warned of something out of place and potentially dangerous, but the dreary conditions tormenting them now acted as an equalizer

The Rooting of Evil

while at hunt. Scents were washed away, prints erased, and sounds muffled. Predators relied on these things foremost. It was only when the quarry was chased down, cornered and desperate, that the hunter could employ the one sense which men placed their lives upon – sight -- and Sarion was determined to make sure that he would not put himself or his companions in situations such as this. No, a tracker was a survivalist, gifted with talents they shared more in common with nature and the creatures of the earth than with their fellow men. Through years of hard training, Sarion had pushed himself to the limit, never satisfied and always trying to better himself. Despite all his experience, Sarion felt little confidence at the moment. The enemies were treacherous and unfamiliar, predators of Grammore that were used to being at the top of the food chain. They killed to live and were of a singular existence, bred for violence and death. Creatures born of the wilderness, they were more at home in the forest than any tracker could ever hope to be, and that was cause for great concern.

The first few minutes passed uneventfully, and then the minutes turned into hours as they picked their way through brush and around wide tree trunks. They had decided not to halt for any reason -- the sooner they gained open land again, the stronger their chances of returning to Nighton unhindered. They came across one or two side trails which Sarion quickly examined, but the weather had cleared away any evidence of recent passage. There was little travel this close to Sprechyd Wood, as it was a no-man's land, to be avoided whenever possible. The people who lived in the borderlands were practical and industrious, but also gave heed to even the most unbelievable of legends and whisperings. Through his own ventures, Sarion now knew the unpleasant truth behind such tales; that many

287

of them were firmly entrenched in fact, and not to be ignored.

The hunters continued traveling under darkness, although most of the day was gloomy to begin with. Sarion was tired -- they all appeared tired, but they pushed on. They came across the main trail sooner than expected, and cautiously picked their way forward, staying with the road. Sarion knew that the village of Fledge Rae was nearby, and he spoke to Valadire about their progress.

"Do you think we might stop by the village and question the people?"

Valadire looked troubled. "I would rather move without delay towards the fortress. Time is our enemy, and Chensel must be told about the fall of Jerol and Karrol."

Sarion nodded. "But these woods are no longer safe…if ever they were," he added. "We may hear something beneficial from the villagers, and also warn them."

"Have you ever been there before?"

Sarion shook his head. "Close by a few times, but never within the village itself."

"There's not much to see, actually." Valadire's eyes shifted to either side, remaining at full alert. "Small place, filled with traders and a few craftsmen. Wanderers stop by the tavern there, and I've heard talk of trouble at times. It wouldn't be a surprise to run across a few cutthroats. We've had to dispatch patrols in this area a year or more past. But you may be right. Perhaps we can question some of the villagers, although it's getting late. They keep to themselves at night, and wisely so, this close to Sprechyd Wood."

"How far is it from here?"

Valadire considered. "A mile or so. Perhaps less. We should come across another trail to our left soon, and that will lead us directly into the village."

"It wouldn't be too much of a delay, an hour at most?" Sarion pressed him.

The Nighton fighter nodded. "All right, let's pay Fledge Rae a visit then. If nothing else, I'll warn the people about marauders nearby, although I doubt it will mean much. Those who make this place their home won't leave for any reason. A lot of those in the westland feel the same way."

"You're right. But if they had seen what I have, they might experience a change of heart."

Valadire had nothing to add after Sarion's grim words.

They reached the trail sooner than anticipated, only several minutes after their conversation. A smaller path branched to the left, and they quickly made their way in this new direction. The trees remained dense on every side, and there was nothing in the makeup of the land which showed any indication that anyone even inhabited the area. Valadire's estimate was accurate, however, and the path widened considerably, several structures looming ahead of them, the mist and darkness casting everything in a veil of dim suggestion as they approached the village. On both sides sat small shacks, the outlying homes of Fledge Rae, each one made from wood, all with fences and shuttered windows, many in need of repair. They clustered together as if such proximity could chase away the shadow of the deeper forest, with the long reach of Sprechyd Wood only several hours travel south. They rode along in the middle of the road, catching only small glimpses of the front sections of the ramshackle buildings. They had all been constructed with the idea of protection against anything which threatened from the outside, a grim reminder as to the dangerous land they chose to live near.

They continued moving forward, advancing toward the main section of the town where they would find a tavern and inn, the two places of any importance in the small hamlet. Nothing walked on the road, and the houses were silent and forbidding. Sarion felt a twinge of uneasiness, the first indication that something might be wrong, and he lifted a hand for the company to halt.

Valadire was immediately at his side. "What is it?" He whispered, his voice harsh in the deadness surrounding them. Nothing moved and no voice called out, the only sound the soft patter of rain falling on the leaves and ground. Sarion looked over at Glavit, his hand close to his weapon, and he searched the man's face for any reaction.

"I'm not certain, but this place seems too quiet, even at this hour. *Someone* should be out, at least coming from the tavern, if nowhere else," Sarion replied.

Valadire shrugged. "It's a small village, and people keep to themselves. I don't know the particular habits of this place better than any other, though, and we live in troubled times. Let's keep going with our eyes open."

He signaled for extreme caution, and Glavit urged his horse forward. Two fighters scattered to either side, approaching the nearest homes. They proceeded forward in this fashion, and soon reached the main intersection. The tavern was directly before them, the widows staring out at them ominously, a pair of tiny flames flickering deep inside the lower section. The surrounding buildings were all locked tight, most of them dark, some dotted with pinpricks of light from taper or lantern. Valadire signaled for the two hunters on either side to check out the rear of the building.

"We'll go into the tavern first. Sarion, myself, and Quarran. If they sleep, we'll awaken them.

Nighton's call must be heeded, regardless of the hour."

They dismounted, Sarion keeping his fingers close to his weapon. A sign dangled from nails driven into the bottom of an upper porch, but the darkness and mist blurred the name. Quarran went first, trying the door, but it was locked. Valadire pressed his face close against the single oval window, peering inside.

"Hmm, the fire burns in the corner, but it looks low. The owner has evidently turned in for the night. Lack of customers, I presume. Fledge Rae has no acting central authority, like many such small villages. But we need to speak with *someone*. Quarran, knock on the door and announce our arrival. I'll sound my horn if need be. We don't have time to linger."

The younger fighter nodded, ready to pound on the wooden frame, but stopped as Chertron hurried forward, Sarion's heart jumping at the look he saw on his companion's face. He pointed skywards. "Up there…"

"What is it?" Valadire motioned for his men to spread out, two of them already flanking the building.

"Something was on the roof. I looked up, and saw a figure slip into the shadows. I don't know if it went around back or entered into a window."

Sarion felt chills at his friend's words. There was no valid reason for anyone to be on the roof at this late hour, especially in such inclement weather. Whatever their intentions, they could certainly not be good. He stepped back onto the road, Valadire at his side. Quarran remained to guard the entrance, and Glavit joined him in seconds. Sarion and the others gazed up at the top of the structure but there was no movement, their lanterns failing to penetrate too deeply into the gloom.

"Are you certain of what you saw?" Valadire questioned the lean fighter, and Chertron nodded grimly.

"I couldn't make out details; it was more of a

darker shadow among others. But I saw something moving, quick and soundless."

"Chertron's eyes are sharp as a hawk's. Even in this dismal weather…" Sarion confirmed the man's perception. There was no doubt in his own mind that something was up there. Waiting, perhaps spying on them. "Valadire, send the others around back. I fear for your men's safety. We can cover the front until they make a sweep."

The Nighton Captain agreed, and the remaining pair of hunters dismounted, following after their comrades. The tavern was an old building, with small homes on either side, but none of them connected. On its right side was a low fence, broken in spots, a narrow gap separating the close properties. On the other side was a narrow alley leading into darkness. Other buildings followed suit, all of them small and squat, private dwellings and merchant shops for those living in the village. In the few minutes since their arrival, there had been no visible sign that anything even lived in Fledge Rae. Until now, at least…

Chertron spoke. "What if your men find nothing? Do you still intend on going inside? My heart tells me there is something amiss in this hamlet. It feels *wrong* somehow."

Sarion was silent, listening to Chertron's words. He was in total agreement. His instincts had been alerted almost immediately, although he couldn't place the source of his uneasiness. From recent experience, it wasn't difficult to see specters beneath every tree and roof, though. Their close distance to Sprechyd Wood along with the brushes against Mugil and the other creatures were more than enough to justify any misgivings, real or imagined, but he wondered as to the fate of the villagers. Where was everyone?

And then the first cry came…

The Rooting of Evil

A bloodcurdling scream shattered the nocturnal stillness, and Sarion knew with terrible certainty that one of the fighters was dead. He reacted immediately, grabbing Valadire. "Call your men back *now!*"

The captain, startled for a brief moment, yelled into the night, seconds later sounding the battle cry of Nighton, a well-known signal to all dwelling under the protection of the Western Watch. The great horn bellowed forth, cutting through the mist and rain, the echoes quickly subdued. Quarran and Glavit joined them as Valadire ordered them back. Sarion notched an arrow to his bow, searching for a target. Only moments passed when the second scream broke the darkness, as if mocking the call of warning.

"Two gone already. Shades of Grimmarch!" Chertron gritted his teeth as he uttered the oath.

Valadire's face looked pained, and Sarion knew he struggled to decide the next course of action. It was a terrible moment, but time was something they had precious little of…

"Draw back! We have to retreat! It will do no good if we all fall here. I'll search the left side." The cries had come from the right side, and he hoped it was still possible to save the other two fighters. Sarion hefted his bow with one arm and mounted quickly, steering his horse forward.

"Sarion…" Valadire started after him, but just as quickly he stopped, commanding the others to withdraw. Chertron remained, unwilling to let Sarion be the only one to place himself at risk. "I have your back," he called. His bow was held ready as he ignored Valadire's orders. The Nighton Captain shook his head angrily, but he now rode into the intersection, his men surrounding him protectively.

Sarion eyed the gloomy alley, immediately spotting movement from inside. It was one of the

Nighton hunters, running towards him.

"Hurry man!" Sarion approached, recognizing one of the older veterans from the company. The fighter had his sword drawn, his head turned to look behind him.

But the attack came from a totally unexpected direction...

Sarion watched in horror as something black melted from the shadows over the man's head, emerging from the wall itself and latching onto his face, pulling him up with amazing strength. Sarion gasped, reaching for his arrow, but it was already too late. The hapless fighter screamed in agony, his hands swatting desperately against his attacker. He was yanked upwards and into the darkness, Sarion catching a small glimpse of the deadly creature which had him. It moved in spider-like fashion, with a pair of long, thick appendages as front limbs. The head was bulbous, marked by feelers protruding from the sides. It didn't appear to be much bigger than a man, but Sarion didn't need to see more to realize that it was a deadly predator, possessing remarkable speed and agility. And there was no doubt as to where it had come from either...

It vanished into the depths of the corridor, taking its victim with it. The man was dead, and Sarion knew that nothing would be gained by pursuing it further. With no sign or call, Sarion knew that the fourth hunter had been taken as well, silently snatched away without a fight. With Chertron close behind him, Sarion thundered into the road, catching up with the others.

"They're all gone! There's no time to waste. The village might be crawling with these things."

Valadire nodded and the company hastened away, all of them looking fearfully about. The return ride was maddening, as they were suspicious of every building and concealing shrub, wondering when the next attack would come. The entire forest appeared unfriendly and sinister, a vast labyrinth waiting to ensnare them. Four of their stricken company had been taken within the span of moments by something unknown.

And now they were only five…

The first rays of the morning sun filled the massive vale before them as Forlern and his companions passed through the Grip and halted, admiring with mixed emotions the impregnable capitol of Trencit.

Daregil Keep.

The citadel itself was still some distance away and the light reflected off metal pike and iron trappings, but this was merely the slightest glimmer of recognition belying the splendor of its concealed and unsleeping might.

Directly before them waited a full legion of warriors both on foot and horseback. They were on constant vigilance, permanently camped on both sides of the Trencit High Road which led travelers to the Keep. Beyond this area jutted the twin towers of The Watch, a pair of armed turrets which guarded one of Daregil Keep's most formidable defenses; the bridge which spanned the Slarillon, a narrow canyon filled with frigid waters cascading down from The Krale and eventually pouring into the Black Lake, which, if legend were to believed, was bottomless. Once the bridge was crossed the landscape flattened and gave rise to the Royal holdings which mainly consisted of farmlands providing food and sustenance for the residents of Daregil Keep. Many homes were scattered from end to end of the broad valley, nearly all of them filled with the families of the countless fighters who swore fealty to the Lords of Trencit. The High Road split this region in half and branching off in three directions; east, north, and west, with the ground rising gradually until it stopped before the intimidating walls and massive gates of the Keep proper. Here a moat had been cut from the living rock centuries ago, adding yet another barrier against enemies wishing to gain access. The turrets and battlements above housed hundreds of warriors, mainly archers who were prepared to rain down a hail of death on any opposing army which had advanced this far, but none had ever come close in all the history of the kingdom. The walls of Daregil Keep were long and sheer, forming a large, three-sided formation built into the treacherous mountain cliffs behind.

Once inside the citadel there were three main levels. The first contained military barracks and supply warehouses, and the numerous fighters on guard rotation. The second level was protected by another wall, though not nearly as high and formidable as the outer one. This area was filled with individual homes of citizens, the market square, and other functional buildings important to the welfare of the huge fortress. The last level, fronted by yet another wall, held only one structure -- the massive Lord's Tower, home of the Kings of Trencit. This enormous building was heavily protected, spiraling skywards hundreds of feet in the air. At times the highest tier was obscured by mist due to the lofty elevation. Here the Kings of Trencit held reign, and it was said that if one stood on the utmost balcony, on clear days they could see well beyond the Grip and into central Trencit, catching glimpses of the sun sparkling off the battlements of its brethren citadels, both mighty Dwellyn and proud Crestillon in the distance.

Forlern felt his heart swell with pride. Every time

he entered the valley he was struck by the majesty and power of Daregil Keep as if it were a living entity calling silently to him, whispering of valiant deeds and deep-rooted loyalty, and he was honored to play a role in defending its name and people, for the protection of the inner citadel and its leaders was entrusted into his hands and those of his comrades, the Trencit Homeguard, the personal guardians of King Gregor. It was a demanding and highly-respected duty, and he was fully aware of his place as the youngest ever sworn to its service.

His eyes glittered with an inner fire, and for the first time in weeks Forlern forgot the hazardous journey into Grammore, instead concentrating on his previous routine at Daregil Keep. He was one of the elite among Trencit's fighters, given access to the Lord's Tower in defense of her leaders.

Forlern now had returned again, after what seemed like years. And things had changed drastically since that time…

He frowned, knowing that it was this day when he would stand before the scrutiny of King Gregor and his councilors and speak of the dreadful and disastrous venture, and the tragic fall of General Charadan. Florik stared over at him, seeing the consternation in the young fighter's expression.

"It seems you wrestle with some unseen foe, my friend."

Forlern looked at him in surprise, then nodded. "Indeed. I must hold counsel with the king himself today and deliver my news."

"From your face, it must be truly terrible. Far worse than I realized."

Forlern remained silent, unwilling to speak further. It would be difficult enough later on…

"I won't press you for anything, have no fear. But I wish you the best fortune in all your endeavors. I'll be taking my leave, seeing that you've reached your destination at last. I have a feeling that you'll be playing an important role in forthcoming days. Here comes several of your own company, I believe. Farewell, Forlern, and may fortune follow wherever the winds of fate carry you."

Forlern smiled, gripping the man's hand. "And to you as well. King Gregor will hear kindly of the loyalty shown by his lieutenants. You are indeed shrewd, guessing at much. You'll hear more about my news in the coming days though, I'm afraid." His face darkened, and Florik nodded in response.

They waited until a pair of fighters came forward, both men wearing the markings of the Trencit Homeguard. Forlern recognized them immediately, and they exchanged greetings.

"Well met Jirl and Duralong. I've returned after many long nights."

"Forlern!" An older man, a grizzled veteran with arms like saplings, rode up to his side. "The king has been awaiting the arrival of your company for many days. Messengers are scattered about in all the westland. Where's the rest of your party?"

"I'm it for now; two are in Nighton yet, investigating something unforeseen which occurred as we passed through."

The two guards locked gazes for a moment. "What of your captain and the others?"

An uneasy quiet fell upon them, and the horses nickered impatiently.

"They've fallen. My mission can permit no further delay." Forlern sighed. "I must speak with King Gregor this morning."

Jirl nodded gravely.

"And he certainly wishes to speak with *you*."

The Rooting of Evil

The three Homeguard passed through the waiting ranks of sentries, their emblems permitting them access to wherever they chose. They rode across the wide bridge which spanned the Slarillon, moving between the twin towers of The Watch. The tall forms edged them on both sides, intimidating structures which swarmed with fighters hidden within. At any moment the doors could be thrown open if travelers appeared suspicious, unleashing dozens of Trencit Royal men-at-arms geared in full battle array. There was an officer of the Homeguard inside the battlements as well, coordinating strategies from the Keep, and making sure protocol was followed rigorously. The Watch possessed its own aura of mystique, and it was a high honor indeed if one were to be assigned there for guard duty. The position was a permanent one, with no danger of being called to the eastern border wars or elsewhere for that matter. The Captain of the Watch was a man named Ikrivon, of whom Forlern had no prior contact with, and had no idea what he even looked like. It was said that he was a man who entertained no humor, and suffered no lapse of routine for the men beneath his power. His word was never questioned and he wielded great might within the limits of his small but important domain.

The three men nodded to the fighters stationed at the end of the bridge, but nothing was said between any of them. The flow of travelers was constant, and Forlern knew that they were being scrutinized from windows above them as they passed, although there was naught to be seen. The iron turrets were grim and silent, rising high into the morning air, the steel looking cold and unforgiving. The two battlements were accessed by only a single set of doors in each, and these remained closed at all times unless messengers were dispatched, or fighters were called forth to detain any travelers of interest. It was rare, but it did happen. Fighters or civilians alike could be held for questioning, and none but high ranking officers or nobility were exempted. Forlern wondered if this always held true, though. Doubts lingered as to the full power concealed with the watchful stronghold, and questions were discouraged. It was spoken among his comrades that King Gregor had placed something of great power concealed within, to be brought forth only in the most dire of circumstances. As to the nature of this thing, none could tell.

The waters of the Slarillon thundered beneath them, spray drifting upwards and curling about the edges of the bridge and the towers. It was nearly a hundred foot drop, and the canyon sliced deep into the landscape, capturing the wrath of the river and ushering it swiftly towards the Black Lake, which lay out of view nearly two miles to the west. They were soon past the Watch, and now the High Road opened wide before them, smaller paths branching off to the sides and plunging into the farmland and homesteads which stretched across the valley in either direction. This area supported numerous farms and hundreds of homes, the majority clustered together in any one of the several nearby villages. A number of travelers were within sight, most of them villagers on foot, or merchants roused to offer their wares for the new day. The three rode along unhindered, steadily making their way towards Daregil Keep. They had perhaps an hour until they reached their destination, and Forlern pressed his companions for information.

"Jirl, has there been any new word from the east in the past weeks?"

The fighter replied. "Most of the talk has been about the westland, and I'm sure you have much to add there."

Forlern grunted. "Too much. What's been said around the Keep?"

"Well, rumors of raids and marauders. King Gregor has been strengthening lines of communication with Nighton."

"The Western Watch has been hard pressed. I have ill news to add."

"That bad?" Jirl scrunched his face into a scowl, his mustache bristling.

"Yes. There are not enough men to patrol the westland. When I left Nighton, Jerol himself was missing. A hunting party was sent out to search for him. The remaining two from my company were requested to help."

"Hmm, I understand that. Jerol is a well-respected figure, even from this distance. King Gregor will be sorely troubled by this development."

And many others, thought Forlern.

"Strangely, the border has been quiet lately. Perhaps *too* quiet. The High Council has been debating this matter, and the unrest in the westland."

Forlern gambled. "I wonder what thoughts General Charadan has on these things."

Jirl shrugged. "I don't know. He's in the east somewhere, along the front again, last I heard, although some are demanding that he attend council and voice his opinion. There have been some spirited discussions of late. I spoke with Tularod yesterday, and he has ears throughout Daregil. A storm is brewing along Trencit's borders. Everyone is on edge."

Forlern nodded, mostly to himself. The whereabouts of Charadan were unknown to the general public, as usual, and King Gregor had always kept it this way. He must surely be missing the counsel of his chief officer by now. Forlern grimaced, thinking of the chaos which would swirl after his tale was spoken. He must hold firm and be prepared for anything. Before the venture into Grammore, Forlern was very much at ease with his position in the Homeguard and Daregil Keep. Now it was the last place in the world he wanted to be...But it was his duty to continue on and relate the grim news. The shade of Charadan passed through his mind and he missed the brave general, someone who remained very much an enigma even in death. He was a true leader of men, demanding loyalty not just by his rank, but through his compassion and understanding. Forlern had not agreed with all his decisions, but he respected Charadan's intentions every step of the way. The King's Champion had ignored the threat to himself in order to discover the source of evil swelling against Trencit. He had been saddened at the loss of his men, but fully understood the risk of success or failure. In the end, his own life had fallen for Trencit, and the question which now lay before Forlern and the kingdom loomed like a thunderhead ready to burst free and shake the earth with its unbridled fury -- what would the consequences be?

The minutes passed, and as they drew ever closer to the great walls of the citadel, Forlern's mood darkened until he was completely lost in his own maelstrom of thoughts, unwilling to talk further. His comrades respected his temperament, and they were all familiar with each other from their mutual service in the Homeguard. There was tremendous loyalty within their ranks, and both Jirl and Duralong realized that Forlern had endured what appeared to be an extremely dangerous mission. But such things were the norm for members of Trencit's elite. It was no coincidence that Forlern was among the handful of survivors.

The Rooting of Evil

At last they approached another bridge, this one spanning the moat surrounding the massive fortress. Again there were guards stationed, and travelers were routinely stopped and questioned. Jirl spoke immediately with one of the men-at-arms, and they were quickly escorted through the milling crowd and taken across. The iron gates were open, sprawling dozens of yards to either side, controlled by a heavily guarded locking mechanism on one of the turrets overhead. Forlern caught glimpses of archers stationed along the walls and ramparts, yet another visible sign of the mighty arm of Trencit. At night watch fires were lighted at intervals, and the city was on constant vigilance. Men rotated shifts, returning to the barracks or their own homes, but Daregil Keep possessed a powerful, thriving vitality, the streets and walls like living arteries of rock and gravel, the citizens the caretakers, everyone playing a small but important role in maintaining the vast and powerful citadel.

The companions finally passed into the city, riding beneath the wall, and Forlern stared at his surroundings. Nothing had changed since he left. Trees and flowering shrubs lined the numerous paths and walkways, and the great citadel was clean, well-kept and organized, giving one a strong sense of orderliness and discipline. Merchants were heading for the market on foot and by wagon, the wheels squeaking as they trembled along the roads. Smoke and steam issued forth from the blocky structures of smithy and craft shop, and soldiers moved about on their various assignments. Several royal couriers stormed past them, heading for one of the principalities or outlying fortresses, bringing orders from the king himself or other high ranking officers.

Their progress was swift, and they moved forwards along the High Road, traveling past the plentiful streets of the first level, the long barracks and supply buildings, although there were dozens of shops here as well as they neared the second wall. This was lower than the outer barriers, but formidable nonetheless. The guards were watchful at the gates, but merely nodded to them as they entered. Homeguard were not to be questioned. King Gregor demanded nothing but respect for his chosen protectors, and anyone going against his wishes would find himself an unwelcome guest in the royal dungeons deep beneath the city.

This part of the Keep was large, home to the central market, hundreds of homes, and countless craft shops and other buildings of varying degrees of importance. The High Road edged the borders of the wondrous Trencit Garden, a public park filled with colorful flowers and sparkling fountains, each of them skillfully carved and unique in itself. It was a place where one could escape the troubles of their occupation, regardless of rank or role. It was not unusual to find someone of nobility sitting quietly on one of the many sitting rocks, while a farmer walked the paths with his wife and family. Forlern longed to rest himself, lay back on the lush green lawn and fall asleep beneath the warm golden rays of sunshine overhead, but fate had other tasks in mind for him at the moment, none of them pleasant.

The morning was quickly growing long and he was weary when they finally reached the third wall, and the most impressive structure in all of Trencit.

The massive Lord's Tower...

It was a monolith of stone and iron, unequal in the kingdom. It raised itself high against the surrounding mountains, a companion to sky and cloud alike. The main tower plunged upwards where it broke from the bulk of the structure, and even from here Forlern spotted the great Council Room, clearly recognizing the wide brace of windows which permitted the soft rays of the sun to enter, splashing down on the long table where the Lords of Trencit ruled. Men looked out from battlements, their forms appearing small and insignificant, a mere afterthought against the ponderous granite sinew of Daregil Keep. It was a sight which gave hope to the beleaguered, and cast fear upon any potential adversary. Constructed to withstand the most powerful of assaults, it was awe-inspiring and oppressive at the same time, depending on the allegiance of whomever dared its broad gates, for here lay the very heart and soul of the kingdom, and deep was its reach.

Forlern and his companions halted before the opening as armed men approached them, all of them members of the Homeguard.

"Hail, Jirl. Back so soon? Who do I see with you?"

The man who came before them was tall and lean, with long hair clasped in a metal circlet down his back. It was Rede Edelain, Captain of the Gate.

"Captain Edelain, well met once again. My ragged appearance stands as a good disguise, or else I might receive a more favorable greeting."

Rede squinted, then recognition registered across his weathered face. "Forlern! At last...by the Seven! The king has been mightily pressed to hear word of your mission. Where is your captain?"

Forlern shook his head slowly, but only deep within his eyes could one see the extent of his real emotion. "Lost, along with many others. A shadow has emerged in the westland and threatens our kingdom. I need to speak with the king *immediately*."

"And so you shall! Lost, you say? A Captain of the Homeguard? I knew him not, as he hailed from our eastern front, but the loss of any of our comrades is a terrible thing. Your tidings are already ill…what manner of evil has taken the lives of your party? Strong men were handpicked for your quest, although I do not know all their names or faces. Each one will be sorely missed."

Forlern reached over, grabbing the man's arm for emphasis, and whispered. "You'll know soon enough, my friend. I have dreadful news which can host no further delay."

Rede considered, then nodded. "Let's get you inside; I see you have a tale which needs telling. Be forewarned, though. The council has been arguing amongst themselves as they await further news. I wouldn't want to be in your place, Forlern."

Forlern scowled, his old brashness returning. "I've been in much worse straits than among bickering nobility, believe me. I'll speak to you when I'm able. But for now…" He lifted his arms helplessly, and they entered into Daregil Keep together.

Sarion and his companions thundered along the road in retreat, knowing that the village of Fledge Rae had been overrun by a deadly predator from Grammore. If there were any survivors, they would certainly not be found in the open, easy prey for the creature which had taken the others. Maybe there were some in hiding yet, but it was a slim hope. Sarion wondered what else lurked in the shadows of the forest and dark eaves of the buildings. It bothered him that circumstances prevented them from searching for any villagers, but the demands of his quest were too strong to be denied. The greater needs of the kingdom were foremost, and he already questioned the decision which led them on the fateful expedition to find Jerol. Only a few short days later, and the war party which had set out from Nighton was a shade of its original self, an alarming number of hunters fallen victim to the emissaries of the Dark Mage.

Karrol and his brave men slain in ambush.

And worse, the terrible discovery that Jerol, First Captain of the Western Watch, was now dead.

How many of them had set off from Nighton? Sarion thought it was fourteen, including himself and Chertron. And now they were down to five.

Five...

Five weary fighters, fleeing breathlessly from one trap into another. Peril ahead of them and behind. And still they were a day's ride from Nighton. Was this the future of the westland? To become a hunting ground for marauders emerging from the Lowlands, seeking easy prey? From what Sarion had seen the past few days, it seemed a very real possibility. In hand-to-hand combat, the average man was no match for the dreadful predators from Grammore. Many of them could easily fend off a score or more fighters. And other beasts, like the dreadful Jurvech, could lay waste to a small army, destroy a major town. Armed warriors could battle some of these creatures in the open and with the strength of numbers, but these monsters were cunning and swift, possessing natural abilities which lent them several advantages over men. Their survival in Grammore depended on this, or they simply would become prey to stronger beasts. A disturbing thought crossed his mind...what if the Dark Mage was trying to extend the borders of Grammore by a controlled migration of its creatures? The notion gave him pause as he mulled it over in his head, and he nearly stopped riding. The result would be to make western Trencit a wilderness, a veritable no-man's land, the inhabitants forced to flee or be killed. Eventually, only the larger cities would remain safe havens. Patrols would have to be small armies in themselves, or else suffer the fate of the unfortunate.

Sarion's eyes glittered. Yes. It made perfect sense to him...The borderlands were the frontier of Trencit. Extensive and untamed in many parts, it was impossible to adequately ward. Without tremendous manpower, the outside structure would erode and patrol lines would grow tighter, eventually serving solely to protect the greater fortresses of the central kingdom.

And then what…

Sarion was not one to panic. No, fear would not overcome him. But his concern for homeland, family and friends was powerful, a driving force which had led him into the dark regions of Grammore and other places equally forbidding. He'd entered willingly, and would do so again if necessary. Since things had gone bad in the Lowlands, the feeling of helplessness had been with him constantly, an unwelcome companion trying to undermine his resolve, feed his doubt, to cloud his hope. The past few weeks had been terrible, fraught with death and despair. Despite everything though, it was not enough to weaken his determination, and he remained steadfast.

No, his greatest trepidation was the future, and in what form evil would take. He had a sinking feeling that things would become much worse than anything their collective imaginations could give birth to...

The hours passed as they left the village of Fledge Rae behind them, along with its horrors. They agreed there would be no halting now until they reached the eastern wall which protected one of the approaches to Nighton. Dawn was not far off and they continued to make swift progress, their war steeds galloping relentlessly, the steam issuing forth from their broad nostrils. The forest was still cloaked in mist, and little could be seen in any direction, their lanterns no match against the oppressive atmosphere. As some point in time, Sarion noticed a lifting of the shadows, and knew that dawn was not far away. The rain had ceased sometime past midnight, and the air, although yet damp, seemed to lessen somewhat. He believed the current front of miserable weather was at last breaking up, and the new day might offer milder conditions. He wished it could also promise brighter news than what they carried among themselves.

They made good time, not daring to pause and give chance to delay. Morning came and went, chasing the darkness and shadows away, and lessening the horrors of the night. The day was still overcast but the lighting was adequate, peeking through gaps in the trees above their heads. Chertron rode to his left and Valadire to his right, as they rumbled along the forest trail. The Nighton fighter talked with him as their pace was slower now, not wanting to overtax their mounts in case the unexpected occurred.

Sarion looked over to him. "I think the immediate danger is long past. The creature will probably stay within the village, seeking out any survivors, if there are any."

"A rescue party must be sent to scour the area after our return. We cannot permit such a creature loose to ravage our people."

"I feel the same way, yet I would advise against it. Fledge Rae is now a graveyard or worse, a possible trap waiting to devour more of our fighters. I would patrol the edges of the wood with a large hunting party, but only in the open air. The men of Nighton are no match for what waits inside."

Valadire considered, his face grim. "It is against my heart to leave the unprotected villagers with the cruel hands of fate. If any can be saved…"

Sarion interrupted. "Anyone who remained is already dead or gone. There's nothing to be gained by such a venture; only more of Nighton's blood to be spilled."

Valadire was silent, and Sarion felt the captain's frustration. His own words sounded harsh, but he knew the truth of them. Regardless, it would be Chensel's call. If he wanted to search for survivors or try to slay the beast, it was out of Sarion's hands, but he would argue against it.

The remainder of the day found the men growing weary and doubtful. They had left the thickest part of the woods behind them and were approaching the eastern end of Nighton's valley. It would be late once they reached it, but none of them wanted to sleep outside its protection, not with the memories of horror still fresh. Sarion felt the full weight of his own misgivings and fears. Before, he would never have hesitated to camp beneath the moon and stars of the Trencit borderlands. Near the Ridgeline, perhaps. But so close to the mighty walls of Nighton itself? The notion filled him with a terrible sense of foreboding, one that wouldn't go away.

Nightfall eventually found them as a bright moon rose over the treetops, shedding its silver glare on their tired faces. The tall hills surrounding the valley of Nighton dominated the area to the north and west. They had yet to come across any other travelers, but this was not too unusual, as the great majority of roads led to the east and the heart of Trencit. That would change soon, though. Sarion expected to find the main paths within the next hour. Valadire kept their reprieve at short length, and again they were off, galloping beneath a sky growing black. The man's face showed no expression, and Sarion knew he held his own thoughts close as they neared the citadel. He wondered as to how quick the commander might overcome the horrors of the disastrous excursion.

It wouldn't be an easy task.

The man had showed tremendous courage in the past days, and was someone Trencit needed in a role of leadership. Sarion held him in high regard, and trusted him fully. But then again, the men of Nighton had always proved to be durable and reliable as the backbone of the westland protective force, and now their skills were being challenged at every turn with no relief in sight; a future filled with hazard and uncertainty, just like his own.

The next hour passed swiftly as the company continued riding, their hooded forms cloaked within the darkness. They reached a pair of trails, each leading into opposite directions, and then found themselves on the main road which would take them towards the valley of Nighton. In the distance they spotted tiny specks of light -- the watch fires from the eastern wall. They were not more than a mile away now, and Sarion analyzed everything which had transpired in the short amount of time from when they had left. It seemed like weeks instead of mere days. He was troubled, and a burning question played over in his mind.

What would he do next?

But he already knew the answer. All roads led to Daregil Keep these days, where he would finally speak with King Gregor and meet up with Forlern. By the time they reached the citadel, the monarch would have had time to digest all the news, and come up with some type of plan to combat the western threat. What Sarion's own role would be afterwards was hard to say, but the offer to serve in the Western Watch seemed the best choice where he could try and make a difference. Shortly they rumbled closer to the east wall and a shout rang in the night, hailing the horsemen who galloped swiftly towards the entrance.

"It's Valadire and the company sent out on quest. Let us in."

The doors heaved open, metal grinding metal, and several hunters came towards them bearing torches. Sarion recognized Captain Lingar as one of them, and then he halted in surprise when another familiar face appeared from the smoky shadows.

It was Chensel...

"Only the five of you?" He exclaimed. "Where's Karrol?"

Valadire drew close to him. "Karrol and the others have fallen."

The Forester was silent for long moments, his orbs smoldering. With a wave he dismissed the guards, signaling for the doors to be closed again. "Can things grow any worse?" He rubbed a hand across his forehead. "Ah, let's go inside. The night is no place to speak such sorrowful news. Valadire, Sarion and Chertron come with me."

He turned about and the Nighton hunters went back to their previous positions. The horses were taken from them and they entered the largest of the buildings behind the protective eastern wall, where the officers were quartered. Sarion noticed that Chensel's personal bodyguard numbered four now, twice the normal amount. It seemed the Nighton leader was not throwing caution to the wind. Within a few minutes they passed through the halls and main lobby until they reached the conference room, which consisted of a rectangular oak table with many high backed seats, the smooth top holding maps and various documents. The guards were positioned immediately outside the doors, and Chensel motioned for them all to be seated. He walked to the corner where a stone hearth held a blazing fire, and he tossed in a pair of logs. He finally turned around and took his place at the head of the table before speaking.

The Rooting of Evil

"Several nights ago your group left here in search of First Captain Jerol. I deliberately chose not to mention his name in front of the guards, for I've already guessed as to his fate. Has he indeed fallen then?"

"Yes," Valadire answered. "To a snare set within the eaves of Sprechyd Wood, one in which we all nearly lost our lives as well."

"Fourteen strong and only five return, the slain including a Forester of the Watch. And Jerol is dead as well. These are the grimmest tidings I've heard my entire life…"

He hesitated for long moments, then continued. "I need to hear every detail of this sad tale. And what about my warning to not enter Sprechyd Wood? Apparently it went unheeded." There was anger beneath his words. He stared first at Valadire, and then Sarion.

"Our need was desperate. Karrol and I made the decision after debate." Sarion spoke before the other man could respond.

The Forester remained staring at them, shaking his head. "Let's hear the full story, and then I'll render my own judgment. Valadire, speak. I want to hear everything without interruption."

The Nighton hunter closed his eyes, breathing deeply before reciting the events of their tragic venture. Sarion was silent the whole time, reflecting on the disastrous mission, full of regrets, and he didn't speak on his strange encounter with the Keeper of Sprechyd Wood. He still didn't understand most of it…But at last the tale was told, and Chensel shook his head sadly.

"And so passes Captain Jerol, First Forester of Nighton, who will be sorely missed, not only as leader of the Western Watch, but a close friend. And Third Forester Karrol, respected and liked by all, who would certainly have been in line to lead Nighton one day. Oh, this is a terrible day for our kingdom. And for the same snare to be used so effectively against our finest…" His voice trailed off, and he clenched one fist.

"We've failed, Captain Chensel. Failed to see the danger, and good men have died because of our misguided choices. You can hold me to blame." Sarion's words were filled with self-incrimination and grief.

Chensel stared at him. "Sarion, I cannot hold either yourself or Karrol at fault. You took a calculated risk, and it was *I* who pressed you to go on the search for our captain. The fact that this deception claimed the leader of Nighton itself speaks volumes about the depth of treachery and power our enemy possesses. None of us can be blamed for choices made in good faith, however the outcome. We place our lives in danger, defending the land we love. What more can we give?"

Sarion bowed his head.

"Ah, but the night ages, and still there is more to tell."

They all looked at Chensel -- who was now leader of Nighton.

"There's been an attempt on my life."

Valadire gasped, and Sarion gripped the edge of the table.

"I'm fortunate to have survived."

"What happened? Who was the assassin?" Valadire looked alarmed, his eyes wide and probing as if ready for a coming attack.

"More like *what* would be the better word. Let me explain. Two nights past, I was going over diagrams and such in my quarters. I heard a noise in the hallway and decided to investigate. There was no sign of Jaken, who had the assignment, and who as Valadire knows, is one of my personal bodyguards. It was then that I knew something was amiss, and I immediately went for my knife. I was certain the attack was coming, and I heard a shuffling *behind* me, although the room had been empty

314

except for myself. I spun to the side and my action saved my life, as something dark went past my head and stuck in the wall. I rolled and turned about, and to my shock a creature stood there, something black with wings."

"A gargoyle?" Sarion exclaimed. "One of the hunters which pursued us from Grammore?"

"Of some sort, but I'm certain it wasn't the same type of creature. This one stood only several feet high, and very lean. It had a tail with a monstrous head, thin slits for eyes, and talons for hands. It had thrown a dart, intent on finishing me. But it seemed to have few other natural defenses. When I moved to engage the creature, it sprang towards the window to flee. It was incredibly agile, and I knew I only had one option. I threw my own knife and struck its spine. It screamed horribly, and I'll never forget that wail of anguish. My blow proved to be a fatal one, and it tumbled onto the balcony, falling over the rail. I can tell you, it caused quite a stir in Nighton, and word passes swiftly in the city. Defenses have been made against entrance from windows, many of them now barred. Precautions have been taken, and at night more watch fires have been added. We won't be surprised in this fashion again."

"So you weren't harmed?" Valadire asked.

"Fortunately, no. The body of the creature was burned in a bonfire, but I made all our officers look at it before it was consumed by flame. Our men need to know the face of the enemy, or at least one of its guises. So it's come to this, though I wanted it not...I'm leader of Nighton now through unforeseen circumstances. I've placed the entire valley on permanent battle readiness. We *are* at war."

His words were grim but true, Sarion realized. Things were deteriorating daily. "Any word from my farm and nephew?"

Chensel replied. "I'm having my men bring them

to the city. I'm not taking any chances. Your nephew will be here within days."

"My thanks. I'll rest easier once that happens, although I won't be here to see him. I must go to Daregil Keep. I'm overdue."

"I understand this. But you'll be going there with a new title as Second Forester of the Western Watch."

The room fell silent for several long moments, and Sarion shook his head, stunned. "How can I accept this, when I haven't even spoken to King Gregor yet? Your confidence in my ability seems overreaching, I'm afraid. It's much too generous. Disaster has loomed all about me the past few weeks."

Chensel waved off his arguments with one hand. "No, you've proven your value, and your past record is more than enough. And who knows, if you would have stayed with Nighton, you might very well be *leading* it now."

Sarion said nothing at Chensel's bold statement; one which he had to admit was a possibility.

"And we another thing to think about. King Gregor might be reluctant to retain you at Daregil Keep knowing that you're second in command *here*."

The look on his face was unmistakable. Chensel was placing his entire faith in him. He wanted to keep Sarion in the west, and thought a proactive move to reinstate him would be enough to *bring* him back to Nighton soon. It was indeed a gamble of sorts, Chensel hoping to influence King Gregor. Sarion had to admire the man's thinking.

"I accept and am touched by your confidence in my ability. I only hope I can live up to your expectations."

He nodded, feeling a sense of pride at Chensel's decision. But would he be able to make a difference, any difference? His choices so far had fallen short. He thought of Karrol's words before they left, about his family coming to Nighton. A family that would now be bereft of its father and husband...

Chensel opened a bag which lay on the table. "There have been several accelerated promotions lately due to tragedy. I really hope these are coming to a swift ending soon."

He gave Sarion a broach -- his former one. Sarion knew the custom and he stood, joining Valadire who had already risen. Normally all the other Foresters would be present, but of course that was quite impossible at the moment. The words were quickly spoken, and he responded in turn, kneeling before Chensel, now First Captain of Nighton. It was dreamlike, and he focused inwards on his past with the Watch. It felt slightly exhilarating, and emotions warred in his heart, and that quickly it was all over. He stood, but now as Second Captain of Nighton.

"Congratulations, Sarion. Although the situation is dire, and your responsibilities severe. I can think of no other as qualified." Valadire clasped arms with him.

Chensel spoke. "I'm not done yet...Valadire, come forward. You're to be elevated to Tenth Forester of Nighton. You've served the Watch admirably these past few years and our need is great."

Surprised, the other man did as told, and they again listened as the oath was recited a second time, but this time for Valadire's benefit. After several minutes, they were seated once again, and the formalities were finished.

"I wish it were under fairer conditions, but these are evil times." Chensel filled his mug, offering the pitcher to the others. "May we toast to the men responsible for protecting Nighton and the westland, and that our citadel withstand all powers which rise up against it. And most importantly for our two fallen captains and Nighton fighters."

They drank deeply, all of them lost in thought for several moments before Sarion broke the silence.

"And so here we find ourselves, and the time has come once again, and without rest, for swift action. I'll depart for Daregil Keep at the rising of the sun with Chertron, and we'll meet with King Gregor at long last. These latest tidings will only add to the grim tale that Forlern bears with him. As to the king's reaction, we'll know soon enough. I'll return as soon as Gregor releases me from service."

Chensel nodded. "Well, there's nothing else to be done about it. Valadire will make arrangements for gear and fresh horses. I've spoken to all the Foresters still within the valley concerning the attack on my life, but the rest are in the field. Word must be spread about the fall of Jerol and Karrol, and Nighton will surely be stunned by the news."

"I know you'll be able to pull the men together, Captain Chensel." Sarion leaned forward. "They'll listen to you. I would also suggest sending messengers to all the surrounding provinces in an effort to coordinate patrols, and warn them of marauders. I don't know how they'll take action, but we all need to work together."

"Agreed. I've taken steps in this direction already."

"Good," Sarion replied. "I also think it would be wise to combine patrols, mustering our strength. The creatures that have entered the westland are more than a match for our hunters. We must give them the best chance for survival."

"This I understand as well. It's an extremely difficult situation with our manpower stretched thin and the size of the region under Nighton's care. I've set into motion the strategy for a prolonged siege, although I hope this never happens. I'll be discussing the defense of Nighton with my officers tomorrow. Valadire, I'll be assigning a special squadron of hunters under your command. You'll be given the swiftest horses in the westland, and I want you to act as a tactical strike force, going wherever needed. We need speed and flexibility to combat new threats which arise."

Sarion nodded in approval, and Chertron offered some advice. "I would equip your regiment with a variety of weapons. Carry enough flint and oil for your shafts. These Lowland creatures are deadly adversaries, and sword and metal alone do not suffice."

"Your recommendation is well-taken. I'll speak with our weapons-master to see what else is available in our stores. And now *I* must leave, duty calls. There will be no rest for me tonight. I must return to Nighton immediately."

"Have a care, Captain Chensel. Do not go anywhere alone." Sarion voiced his concern.

Chensel smiled softly. "I've no wish to encounter more of the Dark Mage's assassins, especially alone...I've handpicked several of our most trusted hunters as my personal bodyguard since the attack. *Each* of our Foresters will be looked after with a greater eye from this time on. Jerol and Karrol will be gravely missed. I don't want anyone else to suffer their fate."

Despite just receiving word of Jerol's fall, Sarion realized that Chensel was unquestionably a man of decision. He was taking no time in grabbing the full reins of his new office. Sarion also believed that Chensel had somehow expected the worst, planning ahead if Jerol died. Yes, he was going to be a capable leader for the men of the west. And there was another fact of great importance. Chensel was his immediate superior now, a comrade-at-arms in the Western Watch. He owed his allegiance to Chensel, along with his honesty.

"There is one other matter I must speak of before

we leave."

"Certainly."

Sarion looked at his companions, and then he gently brought out the rod, laying it on the table. He filled the gaps in his original story now as they listened in silence, and when he was finished, they all sat there in wonder at what could possibly be an ancient talisman of power.

"The king must learn of this and he can decide what to do about it. For now, keep it safe. I have nothing more to add."

"Forlern will tell him everything. If it can be of use, then Charadan made a great find."

"You could be right," said Chensel. "Unfortunately, we have no time to give it much thought now. The Keeper of Sprechyd Wood you encountered is beyond my knowledge, or anyone else's that I am aware of. I don't know what to make of it except that the world is full of countless marvels and mysteries, and we must leave it at that for the moment." He shrugged. "Good fortune, and return swiftly, Sarion. We have much work to do here."

They shook hands, and Chensel clasped Chertron's arm. They said their farewells to Valadire, and the new Forester shortly left, seeing to their lodgings and travel preparations. Minutes later one of the Nighton hunters escorted them to a windowless room where they could draw a hot bath before retiring. Sarion sat by the small table, eating fruit from a wooden basket while Chertron changed into fresh clothing. Things had spun rapidly out of control, and he wondered when he would find escape from this vortex. He hoped Edward would reach Nighton quickly, and here he would be looked after. And how would King Gregor react to Forlern's terrible news?

He didn't envy Forlern. The irascible fighter

would have his hands full...

It was time...

Forlern sat before a long, oblong table in the Waiting Room. It was here that King Gregor chose to speak with high ranking members of the Trencit army, or ambassadors from other provinces. It was bright and comfortable, with an array of food and drink always on hand. A huge fireplace sat in the middle of the large room, and the blaze was in full fury. It was a chamber of great importance, and few people in all of Trencit were allowed this far into Daregil Keep. Facing him on the far side of the room was a pair of oak doors, adorned with markings and emblems. It was a profound structure, as it led into the Inner Keep, the personal quarters of the king and his closest councilors. Beyond the door was said to be a great hallway, eventually leading to the Lord's Tower and the highest pinnacle of Daregil Keep.

Forlern had never been past those great doors...

As if on cue the panels opened, and a pair of Homeguard stepped through -- Kalorn and Henschel, both of them personal attendants of Gregor. Forlern rose from his seat, and the fighters nodded to him.

"Forlern, welcome back." Henschel spoke. "King Gregor will see you now."

The men stood aside and a tall figure entered, but it wasn't Gregor. Forlern recognized the black robe, sweeping white beard, and gnarled staff immediately. It was Barimon, Mage and chief councilor to King Gregor. Forlern had only seen the man once or twice before, as he rarely left the Inner Keep. He stared hard at Forlern, then stood behind a chair near the end of the table.

Another man entered then, handsome of face, fair haired and lean. It was Lord Galivon, Ward of Daregil Keep and the Homeguard. He was second in command only to General Charadan, and was directly responsible for the defense of Trencit's capital, along with being one of King Gregor's chief military advisors. He'd been the one who had actually promoted Forlern, along with any other Homeguard members, as Charadan's role had always been focused on the larger picture, playing a part in all the major decisions affecting Trencit. Although his title had been Captain of the Homeguard, he was rarely involved in day-to-day activities, delegating them into the trustworthy hands of Galivon and others.

"Be at ease, Forlern." Galivon spoke. "We've been eagerly awaiting news of your venture since two of your companions returned. Now it's time to hear what has befallen your mission, and to learn the whereabouts of your captain."

It was a neutral statement, and the full impact of the disastrous fortune of the expedition now sunk in...They'd been expecting Charadan to have arrived with him. They still played the game of secrecy.

Forlern nodded, but said nothing. He didn't have to wait much longer, because King Gregor himself now entered the room, his gait slow and methodical. He was well-past middle age, but appeared strong and confident. He wore a purple robe proclaiming the state of his office, but that was the only apparel designating his powerful status. Forlern saw light chain mail beneath his tunic, and riding boots on his feet. Everyone at court knew that he kept physically active, and cared little about the luxuries of his office. All of this played a role in his popularity, and the general public looked to him as a fair and just leader. Forlern bowed deeply, going through the formalities.

"Your Majesty."

The Rooting of Evil

"Be seated, Forlern. I know you've come a long and treacherous way, but I must hear your tale."

The fighter nodded, waiting to sit until Gregor had seated himself. The others followed suit and the two guards left, shutting the doors behind them with a dull thud. Forlern felt three pairs of eyes boring into him, and he fell back on his training, trying to maintain his poise and keep his mind clear, but he had only a second of preparation...

"Where's your captain who led the mission?" Barimon didn't even give him a chance to start.

Forlern swallowed heavily, his throat dry. "My Lords, it's with a heavy heart that I'm the one to bear these dark tidings." The room was deathly silent.

"General Charadan has fallen in Grammore."

Galivon stood, slamming the table. "It's not possible! Are you certain? Were you separated?"

Gregor placed a hand across his brow and rubbed his eyes wearily. Only Barimon appeared unaffected, but his orbs grew wide, his pupils black as night.

"Lost, when I need him most. My worst fears have come about to plague me...We should never have taken the risk." Gregor's voice was low, filled with sorrow. "Galivon, sit. We must hear Forlern out. I want to hear everything which happened to your company from the time you entered the westland. Leave nothing out."

Gregor stared at Forlern, and the young fighter nodded.

"Yes, my Lord."

And the tale was finally told, from when Charadan and his men first entered the westland, going to Nighton, asking questions, then moving into the countryside, eventually searching for someone who could lead them to the Ridgeline, someone experienced as a tracker. And their path had led them to Sarion. Gregor and his councilors listened intently, at times interrupting Forlern with a hail of questions. It was by far the most grueling experience he'd ever faced outside of the battlefield...The leaders of Trencit missed no detail, asking countless questions about the creatures and landscape of Grammore, what had guided Charadan's decisions, and the role Sarion played in all of this. There were times when Gregor and Galivon appeared amazed at certain things -- the vastness of Grammore, creatures like the Killworm and the monstrous Jurvech, and the treachery of the Glefin, claiming to be the last of its kind. They barraged him with queries about the dark fortress of Gorothagled, and the last battle of Charadan and his men against the ogre. Forlern described Charadan's final resting place, Rivening Well, then he led them through their escape from the Lowlands with the help of Alayian, who first called the enemy by name. He spoke of their confrontation with the winged hunters and chance encounter with Virgil and his men. He finally ended with the separation of their company, himself riding to Daregil Keep while Sarion and Chertron went in search of the missing First Captain of Nighton, Jerol. When he finished, he pulled out Charadan's scroll and handed it to Gregor, along with the silver medallion which had belonged to the fallen General, one which could only be worn by the King's Champion.

Gregor took both slowly, setting the medallion on the table, and then he read the scroll. Once finished, he passed it to Galivon, and he in turn gave it to Barimon. Only when all had read it did Gregor finally speak.

"It's true then. He's dead." There was a long

pause. "Your story is filled with sorrow. Charadan's loss will be sorely felt, his council gravely missed. Trencit has lost its finest leader. And my close friend as well…"

Gregor stood, pacing the floor for several moments and rubbing his brow, the other men mulling their own thoughts.

After a long span of silence, King Gregor finally spoke. "Ah, tis' no time for sorrow at Charadan's loss. Trencit is beset by a great evil, and we need to see Sarion immediately. I'm also curious as to this rod he bears. It might prove to be a valuable weapon of some sort."

"Or a bane…" Added Galivon.

Ignoring him, Barimon pressed Forlern for more information. "And you know *nothing* else of this artifact? Did either Charadan or Sarion try using it?"

The fighter shook his head.

Barimon looked unconvinced. "And a Killworm is loose in the borderlands. That bodes ill for any coming across it. The creature will destroy anything in its path."

Galivon turned to Forlern. "You've acted bravely on this quest, and I'm not surprised you survived to stand before us now. Good men, strong men, have died on your journey, and you've proven beyond doubt your worthiness to be in the Homeguard. It will not go unrewarded, Forlern."

The young fighter nodded, but didn't chance any words. He wondered what it meant, though.

Barimon spoke again. "And Sarion as well. I remember his service at Nighton and was curious as to whatever happened to him. His skills have only grown sharper, it would seem. Charadan spoke very highly of him."

"Yes." Gregor eased into his chair. "Charadan's recommendation will be fulfilled. I may have plans for him." He paused. "Ah, but Charadan's fall. How will we bear it?"

"We must. There are no other choices in this." The mage ran a hand through his beard.

Gregor continued. "I shall be haunted to my grave at the decision to enter Grammore. It was too great a risk."

"And I wonder about Charadan's command to leave Sarion outside the fortress," Galivon added. "Would his talents have prevented the final trap, perhaps saved Charadan's life as well? And did he foresee his own end, leaving Sarion behind?"

Barimon waved him off. "We'll never know that. Best to leave such musings alone. Gregor, the kingdom needs the full attention of its monarch. You can spend time later regretting your decisions, or Charadan's."

Forlern noticed the lack of formality in his tone. By his words, the mage was very close with the king indeed.

Gregor said nothing.

After several moments, Forlern told them about his strange encounter with the Gran Barshara. This was news to all of them.

Gregor then spoke. "I was told that an ambassador was on his way, and gave it little thought. But the Gran Barshara himself? This is unheard of. He's kept his arrival a secret."

"...at least until his meeting with Forlern." Barimon remarked. "Seems more like design."

"And you're certain of the ring?" Galivon injected himself into the discussion, his eyes intense. "A member of the Ja-Ravel, still alive?"

"They were always a source of great trouble," said Gregor. "Hired assassins to kill off the rivals of their benefactors. High ranking officials, royalty even. Their cult is one of deceit and death, and uncanny fighting prowess."

Barimon agreed. "And it was said there were many deaths blamed on them in the past century, but couldn't be proven. This man must not be allowed into Daregil Keep. Galivon, you need to have your finest men watching over him. He should be arriving shortly. Messengers need to be sent to warn Rede. If left on his own, he could cause great mischief."

"But what of the Gran Barshara's coming? Only a drastic event would make him leave Lastrad for any reason. I saw something in him when we met. It's only a hunch, and I could be wrong…" It was the first time Forlern had offered his own opinion. He decided to push further, and gauge their reaction.

"Speak without reservation, Forlern." Gregor added. "I place value in what you have to say. You've proven your skills many times over. Now what do you guess at?"

Forlern nodded. "Fear, my Lord. I saw it in his eyes. Something's scared him badly. He's desperate."

The others were silent.

Barimon spoke. "It's possible, fighter. His presence alone confirms that something extraordinary is afoot. I like not this Ja-Ravel assassin either."

"Maybe I'll confront him directly. Place him under guard." Galivon offered.

"I don't know," said Forlern. "If we play our hand too early, we give away our advantage. I would wager that this assassin thinks he's undetectable, that I didn't recognize his ring, or that anyone else will, for that matter."

"Well spoken." Gregor sighed. "We'll watch him, certainly. And none of the Gran Barshara's guards will be allowed to enter the Keep. It's protocol here, and my Law. If any question my orders, then it will only make them suspect. And if he wants my help in some way, it would be foolish to contradict my command. Either way, he won't enter Daregil Keep."

"Fair enough," said Galivon. "It's time I best get on this immediately. And many other things as well."

Gregor nodded. "I'll call for the council to meet tomorrow. They must be told of Charadan's fall and the treachery of this Dark Mage."

"They'll panic, demand action." Barimon's tone was laced with distaste. "As usual."

"They have great cause to be concerned. Barimon. I want you to search the archives, look for anything which might connect past history with recent events. We need to learn as much as possible about our enemy."

"We'll find nothing about this Dark Mage. Other things, perhaps." Barimon's answer allowed for no discussion.

"Regardless," Gregor replied. "And we must consider our options in combating the creatures he commands. We are not without our own weapons." His voice was grim, and Forlern felt there was something important being discussed here.

"No, we're not." Barimon tapped his staff.

"But they carry their own risks, and ones which I would rather not pursue..." Galivon added.

"We'll discuss this later." Gregor finished. "Forlern, you're now a Captain of the Homeguard, under my direct command."

The young fighter's eyes opened in astonishment. "My Lord?"

"Agreed." Galivon said.

"And as such, you're above any assignments unless ordered by myself. You'll be sitting in at council as one of my advisors from here on."

Forlern sat there in amazement.

"And you'll learn things which very few men in

Trencit have knowledge of. Things which you can never speak to anyone else unless so ordered. Do I have your sworn word, on threat of imprisonment and death?"

Forlern nodded, knowing that he was being offered something of incredible importance, but it also carried a tremendous price -- he would be held accountable to the highest Law in the land. "I swear, my Lord."

King Gregor rose, and the others followed suit. "Come, we have much work to do."

Four horsemen thundered from the east wall of the Nighton valley, their steeds carrying them northeast.

To Daregil Keep.

Chertron rode next to Sarion, and a pair of Nighton hunters were placed in front and back, acting as protectors. True to Chensel's word, each Forester would be granted personal guards from here on out, although the new First Captain of the Western Watch fully realized that he would not be able to find anyone under his command who could surpass Sarion's own skill at arms.

Regardless, two fighters had been chosen. The first was Bertilik, a huge bear of a man, larger than even Rundin had been. A massive shield was slung across his back, and he was armed with bow and sword. He now brought up the rear. The lead rider was Piril, lean and tall with a boyish face free of hair. He carried shafts and sword, but also a wicked spiked ball which could be whipped around with deadly speed.

Sarion knew these men were held in close confidence with Chensel, and he was taking no chances.

Their unique skills complimented each other, and were
chosen wisely. They were to defend Sarion to the death
if necessary, their own lives forfeit at the expense of
saving the freshly appointed Second Captain of Nighton.
Sarion was still trying to accept his new role. It wouldn't
be easy...But here he was now, traveling to central
Trencit while the men of Nighton rode through wood
and field, defending the people of the borderlands while
being hunted themselves, outmatched in power and
cunning by creatures from Grammore, stirred up and
controlled by the Dark Mage, marauding their lands and
killing all in their path.

Nighton hunters were dying.

His kinsmen and countrymen. Being killed in
alarming numbers. The most Sarion had ever seen
before in all his years with the Watch, even when the
Glefins had mustered their strength, attacking
relentlessly from the Ridgeline.

And now he moved in the opposite direction
from the turmoil where he was needed. Every stride of
his steed took him further away. It didn't feel right. It
wasn't right...His sworn duty was to defend Nighton
and the borderlands.

But Charadan had also placed his trust in Sarion,
asking for him to return to Daregil Keep and meet with
King Gregor. It had been the General's last wish, his
final dying breath.

You're the one, save us...

Sarion felt his eyes moisten at Charadan's
memory. Sarion was under tremendous pressure, and
now was torn between sworn duties, and he felt more
than a little reservation at his upcoming meeting with
King Gregor. Not so much intimidation, but something
else. There existed a very real possibility that he could
be facing a conflict; possibly being offered with a
position in the Homeguard, and not be able to live up to

his new office in Nighton. Chensel had been swift to promote him, but if King Gregor wished otherwise...

So what could he do? Technically he wasn't under any direct command from the king at the moment. Not like Forlern, and the other men who had accompanied him on his venture. No, the temperamental fighter was bound to return to his guard, like all members of the royal armies. He had no choice in the matter. But himself?

He rode silently, his thoughts swirling about. The vortex raged all around him, and he was caught in the middle, fighting for purchase. Too many decisions, and his lack of foresight had already been costly. The ambush which had led to Karrol's fall. He should have known...His indecisiveness at the valley of Gorothagled, when Charadan had ordered him to stay behind. The disastrous events of the past few weeks plagued him, a waking nightmare without end.

So what should he do now?

Well, he would listen to his instincts first from here on out. It might have made a difference if he'd done so before. He couldn't afford to make any more mistakes. Lives depended on it, including his own.

They had only been riding for a few hours when Sarion called for a halt. He was tired, restless, and needed to gather his thoughts before sleeping. The men made a makeshift camp next to the main road, Bertilik taking first guard. They were all in agreement as to remaining watchful, and Sarion trusted no roads anymore. They were still in the westland, with Sprechyd Wood less than two days off, and unknown marauders wandering not far from its dark reach.

The night passed uneventfully, and several men on horseback rode past at times, including a patrol returning to Nighton. None of them paused to question Sarion's company, but late in the night they all awakened as another group came from the west and headed directly for their camp, voices shouting in the night.

"Hail travelers, we're looking for Captain Sarion. Have you seen him?"

"You've found him." Bertilik walked towards them, a torch blazing in his grip.

The men numbered half a dozen, and the leader dismounted. "I'm Torrik, on orders from Captain Chensel, new leader of Nighton."

"What is it?"

Sarion, roused from sleep, approached cautiously, shaking his head in surprise. These men had ridden swiftly to find them. They themselves had only left the east wall several hours ago. He knew immediately that something was very wrong.

Torrik pulled out a sheet of paper and handed it to him. "Second Forester Sarion. I have ill news."

Everyone listened intently, and Sarion braced himself.

"Captain Chensel has commanded you to return to Nighton."

"What?" Sarion questioned. "I've just *left* Nighton for Daregil Keep."

"There's been an attack on the western wall."

"An attack!" Chertron exclaimed.

"Captain Chensel was riding to Nighton when he learned of the assault. He sent messengers to pursue your company before you could ride further. I must take your place and relay this latest set of news to King Gregor, or at the very least come across heralds from Daregil Keep. Either way, you must leave now."

Sarion nodded grimly. Nighton was *already* under attack? It seemed his decision had now been made for him. He simply couldn't leave the westland under such circumstances.

"What's the nature of this assault?"

"Captain Sarion, all I know is some type of creature prowls the western wall. You *must* leave immediately."

Chensel had been firm with his orders. Sarion gestured to his companions. "Let's pack up and be off. Captain Chensel is taking no chances, and I agree with his decision. Nighton's walls must not be compromised or the westland is defeated."

After a few minutes the men were on horseback once again, and the patrol wished them well, Torrik urging them one final time for haste.

"Captain Sarion, Lord Chensel gave me little details. Maybe he had no wish for me to know more. But he was clearly in distress about this change of events. We have many armed groups which use the passage as an entrance into the westland. It's of great strategic importance, as you well know."

"Yes. It's an attempt to undermine our effectiveness. We'll ride with all speed back to Nighton and give our aid."

"Good luck."

And then they left, Sarion's companions moving westward, and the patrol heading towards Trencit. Sarion was amazed at how quickly things had changed once more. It seemed each new day became more unpredictable than the last. *And* more dangerous...There was no end to it all, no end.

They rode hard for hours and the sun rose behind them, a cloudless day forming. The air felt fresh on their faces and the great warhorses were up to the challenge. When they finally reached the eastern wall, the guards looked nervous. More men had been called to the fortress, and everyone appeared on edge. The news had traveled quickly, and uncertainty loomed over Nighton. They were ushered through without delay and Sarion

paused to speak briefly with the Commander of the
Gate, Captain Lingar. He told Lingar to fan out their
patrols, make sure that nothing was waiting to ambush
travelers from this side of the valley. Sarion wanted
bonfires lighted at night at various intervals of the main
Trencit Fairway. They could ill afford any disruptions
on this side of Nighton. Lingar listened to his words, and
the companions were soon off again. No additional news
had been sent to Lingar about the source of the attack, so
he could only offer good fortune to the company. They
quickened their pace, as it was a ride of many hours
until they reached Nighton, and then hours still to gain
the western entrance. The weather played favorably
upon them, the air warm and the sky remaining clear.
They passed countless groups as they thundered through
the large valley -- patrols on both horse and foot,
peddlers, families, and couriers from outside the
borderlands. Sarion and his companions hailed them but
never stopped, urging their steeds eagerly forward. Rests
were few and short, and Sarion felt his impatience
continue to grow, knowing that something terrible could
be waiting for them at the western edge. When they
finally reached the capital they never slowed, rushing
past in a flurry of hooves, the warhorses straining from
the prolonged race. When the fortress was out of sight,
they came across a large patrol which moved towards
them. They were glad to see Sarion, and told him that
Chensel was expecting them, ordering fresh steeds.
After only a few minutes their belongings were strapped
onto their new mounts and off they went. Twilight was
descending, and Sarion had known from the start that
they would arrive during the night. The going was
difficult on the men, as they were all tired from lack of
sleep and the prolonged ride, but they were seasoned
fighters, used to such conditions. They needed to rest,
but Sarion pushed onward, feeling his trepidation grow.

The Rooting of Evil

It was late into the night when they finally arrived at the western wall, the watch fires blazing in the distance like the eyes of a dragon. The last leg before them, they urged the horses for renewed speed, and the mighty animals answered the call. Horsemen loomed ahead bearing torches, and they recognized the company.

"Hail Captain Sarion, Lord Chensel awaits!"

They rode on until they reached the barracks and finally the western wall itself. The gate was closed, and ranks of Nighton hunters were everywhere. Leaving their horses to a pair of fighters, they entered the fortress where a guard approached them.

"Captain Sarion, Lord Chensel is on top of the right turret."

"Very well. We're on our way."

Although the fortress was mobilized, it didn't appear as if any damage had been done to the wall. Sarion wondered again as to what had happened, but knew he would find the answer soon. They rushed upwards, climbing the spiral staircase leading to the right tower rampart, the passageway lighted by dozens of iron sconces set in the wall. When they reached the top, they found it swarming with Nighton hunters, primarily archers and runners for communication. They spotted Chensel immediately, surrounded by his personal bodyguard, seated at a small table.

"Sarion, well-met." The First Captain rose in greeting. His face was drawn, and he looked as if he hadn't slept in days. "I'm glad you stayed on the Fairway, else my messengers wouldn't have found you."

"Captain Chensel, what has taken place? We came as swiftly as possible, and heard the walls were under assault, yet it appears quiet now. Is the attack over?"

"Let me speak. Have a seat, and take some food and drink. I know you've ridden here on little rest.

We're under no immediate danger at the moment."

Sarion glanced at Chertron, who looked as confused as himself. The other guards backed away, giving them privacy. The walkway was wide, and archers were placed at regular intervals, all of them peering intently into the gloom. Ignoring them, Sarion sat down, drinking deeply from a goblet. He stared at Chensel for long moments until the Nighton leader finally broke the silence.

"One of our patrols was within sight of the gate nigh on two days ago. The warders saw them coming, and one of them spotted something moving in the copse, over a hundred yards yonder." Chensel pointed in the direction. "The guard shouted a warning to the men, who were riding at a slow gait. A dozen hunters returning from a patrol, under the command of Huyurin."

Sarion nodded. "I rode with him years ago."

Chensel continued. "The company halted, trying to discover the source of attention. They looked to the woods, and approached with caution. Something had moved through the brush, but then nothing. They fanned outwards, trying to surround the area. The men were twenty yards out when the attack came."

Sarion's hands gripped the table's edge, knowing something terrible had happened.

"A huge beast erupted from the underbrush, something monstrous. Large, maybe fifteen feet in height. Bear-like, massive and covered in brown hair. The closest rider went down with a swipe of its paw. The horses panicked, and several of them were thrown to the ground where the creature quickly finished them. Some of the men shot it with arrows, but they had no effect. It lunged at them with speed which defied its size, and soon the company was scattered. When the beast first attacked, it reared up on its hind legs, but as the men rode off, it went down on all fours and pursued them."

Sarion bit his lip. "How many escaped?"

"Two, including Huyurin. The monster hunted them down like a wolf after its prey. Although I did not see the attack, I was told that it nearly had them all, and only the swiftest horses could outrun it."

Chertron uttered an oath. "Such speed, by the Seven!"

"And then what happened?" Sarion asked.

The men passed through the gates while archers rained arrows down on the beast. It shrugged them away and then headed back to the trees, where it still waits."

"You're certain of this?" Sarion pressed him.

"I had our swiftest riders go out, and the creature gave pursuit whenever someone drew close to the woods. We have failed to get past it." Chensel's eyes narrowed. "We heard screams yesterday. A patrol was scheduled to return. They were ambushed before they could be warned. This monster has us trapped. We cannot allow it to keep us penned in here. More patrols will be arriving soon."

"How soon?" Sarion felt his spine grow cold, anticipating the answer.

"If they're on time, within hours."

"Hours," Sarion muttered. What could they do? Whatever their course of action, it had to be swift and sure. And then he stiffened as if in pain.

Edward!

"Has word from my nephew arrived yet?"

"Nothing. I sent men out immediately, and it will

take a while as you know. But they'll be coming this way eventually. Their party, and many others. We *must* drive this creature away to protect our people."

Sarion leaned back in his chair, arms folded. Chertron was silent, but the fighter moved to the edge, gazing into the night. One of the guards pointed, and Chertron looked in that direction.

Another dilemma...Sarion tried to visualize the beast in his mind, gauging its size and speed. The ogre had been over twelve feet tall, and by Chensel's description, this thing was larger yet. Over fifteen feet in height? That was incredible. He shook his head. It would prove to be a fearsome creature which awaited them. What to do about it though, that was the question...Chensel was absolutely right. They couldn't permit it to remain here, where it could pick off returning hunters who would be easy prey, unwarned. Some had already perished...The creatures from Grammore were beyond the experience of the Nighton fighters. Their natural abilities made them more than a match for a patrol of men, even a medium-sized one. They possessed stealth, speed, and ferocity. Aggressive predators, they had been chosen wisely by the Dark Mage, and his plans for conquest were succeeding daily, it seemed. They were hedged in at every turn, and the death toll continued to rise at an alarming rate.

Chensel spoke. "I wanted to wait for your arrival before launching an attack, Sarion. You have experience with some of these creatures, and I value your opinion."

"What would have been your plan?" He responded, his head still angled downwards.

"Wait until dawn. Ring it in with archers and spear throwers with a mounted assault."

Sarion said nothing.

"You don't approve?"

"I don't know."

The Rooting of Evil

Chensel frowned. "I like it not myself, but it's the best idea I've heard. We've discussed our options, believe me. Against such might, we have few weapons."

"I don't question *that*. It's just that we need to go ahead with something which has the greatest chance of success."

"Of course."

"But maybe not the most obvious…"

Chensel shrugged. "Time works to defeat us. We're moving against the beast come dawn. That's the latest I'll wait."

Sarion now joined Chertron at the wall's edge, and both men stared at the nearby woods which were virtually invisible, merely a smudge against the darkness. The only reason they saw anything at all was because of the bright sky overhead, the moon nearly full. The landscape was painted in white, and a herd of stag shuffled along to their left, oblivious of the lurking creature. The animals suddenly stiffened, and started trotting back the way they'd come. Sarion knew their actions confirmed that the beast still waited within the shadowed eaves. Without warning, he turned on his heels and looked directly at Chensel.

"I require a swift steed, the fastest available. I need to get a good look at what we're facing."

"Are you mad? Do you think to go out there alone?" Chertron shook his head in disbelief. "A poor plan at best, Sarion."

"Nevertheless…" Sarion shrugged. "I'm doing it, and that's all there is to it."

Chensel eyed him thoughtfully. "Have you forgotten that you're now Second Forester of Nighton, and next in the line of command? Much responsibility weighs on your shoulders -- including staying alive -- and you can't take needless risks. I can order you to stay here, Sarion."

"You can, but you won't do that, I think," Sarion answered without scorn. "Captain Chensel, you waited until we arrived before taking action. Now we're here at your bidding, and it's time for action, and I need to be the one to act. None other is more capable. You know this. I don't want to place anyone else at peril...not until I know what we're really up against."

Chensel sighed, turning his back on them for a moment. He then pivoted around to face them, his face grim. "Very well. And what is your plan then?"

Sarion tightened his belt. "I'm making that up as I go..."

They all watched in surprise as he descended the stairs, their eyes fixed on the determination in his stride, Piril and Bertilik shadowing him immediately. Chertron muttered angrily, and followed after them.

"Good luck, Forester." Chensel remained there, calling his men for council.

"Stay at the gate, Chertron. When I'm ready to come in, I don't want to be trapped out there with that thing."

Already mounted, Sarion listened as Langstern, Captain of the Western Wall, spoke. "Vats overhead are filled with hot oil. If you can lure it close, we'll dowse it and set the beast to flame."

"I have a feeling that the creature won't let itself get in range. It halted before coming too close before, right?"

"Yes."

"It's aware of danger then, and that makes it twice as deadly. If we *don't* figure out a way to kill the thing, it could stay out there indefinitely, effectively blocking off passage through the west," Sarion replied grimly. "Not an option."

"Let's also hope we're not attacked from the east."

The voice came from behind them, and a familiar face appeared in the smoky twilight carrying a brand in one hand. It was Valadire.

"Tenth Forester of Nighton, well-met." Sarion greeted his former companion and he leaned down, clasping his arm. "I'm glad to see you haven't left on patrol yet."

"Aye, my friend, I share the feeling...my company is still being organized, and won't be ready for another few days. So of course, I'm here to lend aid."

"I'm comforted knowing your presence is near, but I'm going out alone."

Valadire was clearly unaware of the plan, having just arrived. "What are you talking about? You're heading out to confront the beast? From what I've been told, this creature is savage, and runs swiftly. You truly mean to go out there now? You should rethink your strategy, Sarion."

"I'm not changing my mind. I want to try and test its limits, see how fast it can move, and for how long. Then we'll attack it directly using knowledge of what I discover. Wish me luck." Sarion patted his mount.

Valadire shook his head. "You know these creatures from Grammore better than anyone, perhaps. But *beware*, my friend. We don't know the full extent of its power. Don't risk your life on a whim. The Western Watch can't lose any more of its leaders."

"But I must take the chance," Sarion replied sadly. "The element of surprise has been used against us time and again. We need to take the offense."

The Rooting of Evil

He was done talking, and with that he urged his horse towards the gate, signaling the warders that he was ready. The ponderous doors opened and in seconds he was through, the men quickly pulling them shut again.

"Come on, let's move." Chertron smacked Valadire on the arm as he hurried for the stairs, pushing through a group of Nighton hunters who were on their way for relief duty.

Sarion galloped into the night, comforted by the bright sky. Dawn was still a ways off, but there was enough light for his keen eyes, although no doubt his adversary overmatched him in natural abilities. He needed to exercise extreme caution. The woods were not far away, and he slowed his mount to a walk. He then reached to his side, where several spears had been strapped by the Nighton warders. They were coated in oil, and he quickly lit one with a small lantern fixed to his saddle. The trees loomed before him, dark and menacing.

Sarion halted.

His senses on full alert, he scanned the landscape, looking for movement, listening for any telltale sound.

Immediately he sensed that he was being watched, more an instinctual feeling than anything else. There was plenty of cover within the thick forest, enough to conceal something large. But he also knew that the lurking predator must give itself away first, being a creature of great bulk. All he needed to do was listen.

And he didn't have to wait long...

There was a soft rustling from inside the woods, as of something scraping against brush and leaves, and now he knew the beast was watching *him* from somewhere just inside the tree line. Sarion tensed, waiting to see if it would move closer.

The night was silent. The noise lasted a brief moment, and then stopped.

Sarion edged the horse closer, and it began to fight him, trying to retreat, smelling the dangerous creature which waited. The Trencit war steeds were proud and strong, trained to obey their riders in every circumstance. It was rare when they acted against the will of its master.

But this was one of those times...

It buckled, kicking high in the air, and Sarion lost control. He had excellent skills at riding, but the animal was on the verge of complete panic, wanting only to run from the certain death that waited. It was all Sarion could do not to be thrown. Knowing how vulnerable he was, Sarion pulled the reins, giving in to the horse's desire to flee. He turned it about, letting the animal back away, but the moment of confusion was the perfect opportunity for the hidden enemy, and the forest erupted with a howl of fury as the creature broke for the attack. Hearing the cries of the predator proved to be too much for the horse and it reared high, surprising Sarion, and he felt himself lose balance. He knew his situation was desperate and he grabbed for one of the spears, knowing that if he fell weaponless, he was a dead man. His survival skills kicked into play, and he rolled with the fall, tumbling head over heel, gaining his feet in seconds...

...and that was all the time he had as the creature made for him, towering overhead on both feet. One mighty limb came crashing down at Sarion, all hair and fury, and he dove to the left, saved by sheer instinct. The monster was quick, but not fast enough as Sarion went immediately on the offensive, knowing that without his horse it wasn't enough just to avoid the creature's blows -- he now had to *kill* the thing.

His action paid off and he struck it in the ribs, shoving with all his strength, driving the spear deep into muscle and tendon.

The beast was startled, and let out a cry of rage and pain, not used to having its prey still alive after its initial attack. It swept out one great arm, and Sarion lacked the power to retrieve the shaft and save himself at the same time...

He jumped back, barely avoiding what would have been a lethal blow. The thing remained standing on both hind legs like an enraged bear, lashing out at its much smaller opponent. Sarion understood that the monster was well-equipped to fight on either two or four limbs, but figured it was more vulnerable while upright. He again took the advantage, whipping out one of his long daggers and throwing it into the beast's underbelly. He dodged to the right now, anticipating the surge which would surely come, and it did, as the monster came directly at him once again. Both spear and knife were embedded deep within the creature's hide, but despite these wounds, it didn't appear to be seriously hurt. Sarion cursed beneath his breath, moving left and right, trying not to give his enemy a fixed target. From somewhere behind him, he heard shouts and a great horn ringing in the night, as the Nighton hunters gathered for a rescue attempt.

But would he last that long...

Sarion had his sword in hand now, clearly not the best weapon against such a beast. It was savage and powerful, something which survived by killing any other creature it encountered with overwhelming savagery. Sarion also knew the thing was cunning, avoiding the western wall where it could be attacked and defeated from its weaker vantage. These thoughts all passed through his mind in the span of a second, as he was in a fight for his life. He had been through other such confrontations before...The ogre on more than one occasion, the creatures outside of Gorothagled, the winged gargoyles, and the lurkers in Sprechyd Wood. But not in hand-to-hand combat against something of such size and strength.

The monster waited, measuring him. It lunged again, slower now, not committing all its weight. It was exactly the kind of move Sarion was hoping that it *didn't* make, as it now relied on its own cunning instead of just its sheer mass and power. It growled at him and then went down on all fours, churning forward. Sarion feinted to the left, then dodged backwards and to the right, but his adversary wasn't fooled this time. It snapped at him with its jaws open wide, using its bulk, trying to knock him down. Sarion scrambled but the creature rammed into his shoulder, sending him sprawling into the dirt. He coughed a mouthful of dust, trying to catch his breath as the air was pushed from his lungs. He didn't have time to think, knowing that the creature would try to finish him. Luck was with him as he rolled to the left -- the monster brought both its forelimbs to the ground, scant inches from where he'd moved from...

Sarion regained his feet, but was too winded to do anything but place a few more yards between himself and the monster. The battle ensued and the creature lunged towards him. This time Sarion was quicker, and he grabbed at the spear as the beast missed him. He threw his weight fully onto the shaft in a desperate gamble, and his adversary howled in real pain now. It stopped, scratching at its side, attempting to dislodge the weapon, but it was in too deep. Sarion never hesitated, taking out another dagger and launching it at the creature's face. It struck with deadly accuracy, all his years of training coming in to play as the blade hit the monster's left eye, blinding it. It hunched over in rage, lashing out madly, trying to kill its prey with pure violence. Sarion backed away, and from the corner of his eye he saw dozens of cloaked hunters storming towards him, bows singing in the night, countless shafts striking the great beast. Chertron and Valadire were in the forefront, and the Nighton captain held a great spear before him, driving it into the monster's back.

"Have a care! Don't get too close!" Sarion screamed a warning, but the Nighton fighter had already pulled his mount away. A few of the horses kicked and fought their riders, but most of them held steady, dart and shaft nailing into the mighty beast as it retreated, making for the cover of the forest.

"Don't let it escape!" Valadire shouted the alarm, signaling the men to press on. The riders struck it with dozens of arrows and a handful of flaming spears, and the creature gave a great roar, collapsing to the ground.

"Finish it!" Valadire led the charge, and from a safe distance, the hunters continued raining arrows into the monster's hide until it finally lay still.

"Sarion, are you hurt?" Chertron came up to him, dismounting.

"Bruised and tired, but I'm used to that by now. The thing was savage."

They watched as the men circled the great creature, examining the dead body. Valadire shouted to have it burned, and he rode over to Sarion now.

"We thought you were finished, my friend! When your horse bucked we came swiftly. Chensel had a pair of riders shadowing you."

Sarion nodded. "It's a good thing. I don't know

how much longer I would have lasted, although I scored a blow to its eye."

"And I think from now on that a risk of this type should *not* be taken." Valadire's face was grim. "No one questions your bravery or skill, but we all have our limits. You need to understand your own."

Sarion was silent, weighing his words. He felt the truth in Valadire's statement. It *had* been an extremely dangerous decision to come out alone, despite all the warnings of the creature's might. Perhaps even foolish…Was he taking too much upon himself? The past few weeks had been fraught with loss. Fellow companions, men he'd known only briefly but already considered friends. Charadan, Rundin, Karrol. Was he letting his emotions take over his reasoning?

Maybe he was…

But then who else would answer the call? He was confident with his own fighting skills, and was also willing to place himself in harm's way to protect the people of Trencit. The Dark Mage had to be stopped, there was no question. His responsibilities had indeed grown as a captain of Nighton, but he would do no good if his brashness got himself killed.

"You're right, Valadire. The beast nearly had me. One of these days I might not be so fortunate."

Chertron clapped him on the shoulder and was about to respond, but the words never left him as a terrible noise echoed through the night, freezing them all; a piercing drone which promised certain death.

Sarion screamed a warning. "Fall back to the fortress!" He pushed Valadire forward and jumped on the Forester's own horse, pulling him up. A number of the Nighton hunters looked confused, staring into the woods where the noise had come from.

"Flee for your lives!" Sarion yelled to them, himself and Valadire already heading back, Chertron on their heels, knowing what lurked unseen.

Chaos ensued...

Men leaped to their steeds, scrambling to place distance between themselves and the forest, unaware of their grave peril, but the desperate action of their captains explained enough. Sarion had the horse in full gallop, Valadire holding onto his cloak. Sarion glanced over his shoulder, looking skyward and he recoiled in horror, as vast strands of webbing glinted silver in the moonlight, covering a huge expanse of land.

The first scream of anguish reached their ears as one of the hunters fell victim. It was quickly followed by another shout, and another. Sarion gritted his teeth, his worst fears materialized.

"What is it? Can we do nothing to help them?" Valadire gasped from behind.

"We have no weapon against such an enemy. A trap is set for us -- another creature waiting for the right moment to attack!"

Valadire was silent, his head turning back to watch the fleeing riders. Several other screams rang out, and soon they were within earshot of the wall. The doors were flung wide and they moved quickly through, Chertron and a half dozen others with them. More hunters entered, and Sarion jumped off the horse, heading for the upper turrets.

"Prepare for battle!" He yelled to the waiting guards, who scrambled everywhere, reinforcing their positions. With his two companions on his heels, Sarion flew up the steps, shouting for Chensel, who he found at their earlier post.

"Sarion, what is it? What comes?"

He approached the Nighton leader, then leaned wearily against one of the chairs.

"Something which we have no defense against."

Sarion paused for breath, Chensel's face pressed

close.

"A Killworm."

Forlern sat before the fireplace in his new quarters, drinking ale from a huge goblet. He felt out of place...

He paced around the room, still trying to get used to it. It was impossible for him to relax, and he found himself wishing for his old routine; normal assignments as a member of the Homeguard. That was all lost to him now. Gregor had seen to that with his promotion to captain and councilor. It certainly had benefits, though. But was it worth it all?

The past few days had started chaotically, culminating with the meeting of the High Council, where King Gregor informed his leaders that Charadan was dead. The tale had been retold, but by Gregor himself this time, sparing Forlern the dreaded task. Gregor had deflected all questions from his newly-appointed young councilor, commanding him previously to remain silent. And so he'd sat there, under the scrutiny of some of Trencit's most powerful leaders. Although most of the Lords were not present, every province was represented by their chosen ambassadors, some kin to their lieges, and word spread quickly throughout the kingdom. The High Council had been stunned by the news. Forlern had seen the fear in some of their eyes as they learned of the Dark Mage and the threat from Grammore. And there were some who had eyed him suspiciously, a few unfriendly.

Galivon had warned and prepared him for this beforehand. He would be watched carefully, being so young and new to court politics. Some would not like him from the start...

But King Gregor's will was not to be challenged. Forlern now sat within the inner circle of Daregil Keep, and he would never be able to go back now. It was quite impossible.

"Ah, what will Sarion think now when he sees me?" Forlern shook his head. "Chertron will call me a fool, certainly." He grinned wickedly.

He took out one of his long daggers, sharpening it on a stone. He'd gone down to the sparring grounds whenever possible, trying to stay active physically. Forlern could go where he wished, but he needed to alert the king's messengers at all times so he could be located. It was a high privilege, but also a confining one. He'd spent a lot of time with Galivon lately, and they had grown closer as comrades-in-arms. Galivon conferred more and more with Forlern on the structure of the Homeguard, and they spent many hours traveling Daregil Keep, once even riding through the Grip and going over defensive placements. Forlern was eager to accept this knowledge, taking in all the details and doing his best to rise to his new position. He realized that it was all a part of his training as he learned the battle aspects of the fortress on a much larger scale. He embraced it, but it was all very intimidating as well.

There was a knock on the door and he pivoted. "Yes?"

Jergen entered, one of his assigned guards. "Captain Forlern, you've been summoned to the Waiting Room. King Gregor is holding conference with the Gran Barshara and needs you there immediately."

The Gran Barshara! He'd forgotten about him during the past few days. What had happened?

"I'm right behind you. Let's be off."

The two men walked down the hallway while

Forlern's other guard, Brakith, fell in behind.

They quickly made their way through corridors and down several flights of stairs. This part of Daregil Keep was mostly unoccupied, housing the private quarters of King Gregor's elite, and Forlern was now numbered among them. The fortress was immense, and there remained parts he had yet to see, including the mysterious deeps rumored to lay beneath the great citadel. It took several minutes for them to reach the Waiting Room, and this time Forlern approached from the inner side, the doors flung open in anticipation. Gregor's personal guard nodded to him and he was ushered inside. The king was already seated, talking with Barimon. Galivon arrived at the same moment as Forlern, but coming from the opposite direction, and sitting at the far end of the table was none other than the Gran Barshara himself, alone. When Forlern entered he narrowed his eyes, clearly surprised by the young fighter's presence.

"All right, be seated." Gregor waved to the newcomers, Galivon nodding to Forlern in recognition.

"Our guest here is the Gran Barshara, electorate and Lord of Lastrad, which is allied with Trencit. A rare visit from him to our city, where he is quite welcome." Gregor continued. "You know Barimon already, and this is Captain Galivon, Ward of Daregil Keep, and now First Captain of the Homeguard, replacing General Charadan."

Forlern heard the sadness in Gregor's tone. Controlled, but still there.

"And this is the newest Captain of the Homeguard, Forlern, whom you've met already, I hear."

The Gran Barshara spoke. "We have indeed, on my journey through the Grip. It was I who insisted on bringing him inside, wishing to meet a member of your elite corps."

Galivon interjected. "And what was your impression?"

Forlern started. He knew they were trying to press the Gran Barshara into speaking his intent, or at least to call his hand.

"Hmm. That he was too young to be a member of the Homeguard. I know the war in the east has diminished your rankings, but I hope it hasn't lessened the quality." The electorate clearly wasn't to be intimidated, and Forlern bristled at the barb.

"You're wrong on that point, and I blame it on your lack of knowledge on our criteria for promotion." Galivon wasn't about to let the insult go unanswered, but Gregor cut them both off.

"Enough of this. Forlern is now one of my councilors, and his word carries weight worthy of his office." He stared hard at the Gran Barshara.

"My Lord, I hear you. Please forgive my hasty assumption. Congratulations on your promotion, Captain Forlern."

The young fighter nodded, believing none of it. He also wondered what had happened to the assassin. He'd pretty much forgotten about the entire episode since his meeting with King Gregor, and his adjustment to his new role.

"I've come here to Daregil Keep with a personal request. This is the first time I've ever been to your fair city, and I hope that the alliance between our respective domains remains true."

"Of course," said Gregor. "Lastrad remains a free city, but it's still under our protection. Nothing will change that."

"My thanks, and the gratitude of our citizens." The Gran Barshara nodded, inclining his head. His rod lay on the table, and he absently rubbed the handle. The man looked nervous, and Forlern knew he was leading up to his reason for coming here.

The electorate continued. "Lastrad is a large and powerful city, and as you know, our resources are many. Our defenses are strong, and my personal guard consists of some of the finest fighters in the southland."

And deadly assassins included, thought Forlern.

"My office requires that I keep my city wealthy by maintaining fair trade policies, provide for all the needs of the population, and most importantly, to keep my people safe."

He was silent, and they all waited.

"We are being hunted."

Forlern gripped the table's edge, and Galivon shifted in his seat.

"My people are being killed, and we've been unable to locate the source of these murders."

"You have *no* idea who it is?" Galivon said.

The Gran Barshara stared at him, his face expressionless. "*Who* it is? That might not be the proper word, Captain of the Homeguard. *What* it is seems more appropriate...The victims are being found everywhere, and they're being slaughtered -- *torn* to pieces, as if by some wild beast!" He slammed the table, his hands trembling. As if to conceal his emotion, he folded them in his lap, soon continuing. "Rumors circulate Lastrad, dark whispers in the taverns and markets, the hallways of the palace. There have been reports of something moving stealthily in the night, climbing walls like a cat, then disappearing without a trace. I don't know whether to believe any of this."

Gregor spoke. "And what is it you ask of me?"

"Protection."

Forlern was surprised by this, and from the look on the king's face, he was as well.

"Protection? But how? Do you wish for us to send patrols into your city? That would go against our long-standing agreement, plus I don't think this thing would show itself to a large group of armed men."

"No, it wouldn't. It seems much too cunning for such." The Gran Barshara shook his head. "That's not what my request is." He paused for a moment. "No, I ask for handpicked men to help my personal guard in tracking this thing down. Hunting and killing it."

"That is possible." Gregor responded.

"These killings have increased significantly the past week."

"How many people have died?" Barimon spoke for the first time.

"Reported, over three hundred."

Galivon let out a low whistle. "Three hundred?"

"And numbered among the dead recently are some of our elected officials, officers of the Lastrad Guard. The killings are premeditated. We have been unsuccessful in stopping this massacre."

Now Forlern understood the root of the Gran Barshara's fear...

"No one appears safe. My belief is that it will eventually come for myself as well."

The electorate's eyes narrowed, and Forlern saw that look again, one he'd glimpsed inside the Gran Barshara's caravan. *This* is what he was so terrified of, and for good reason. Could that also explain the presence of the Ja-Ravel assassin? A high-priced personal guard? It seemed likely.

King Gregor now stood, everyone else rising with him. Forlern knew the monarch had already come to a decision. Had he known of this situation already?

"Your request will be fulfilled. It will not be said that our two provinces are lax in their mutual friendship."

"Thank you, my Lord."

"You are welcome to seek asylum here, if you

wish to do so."

The Gran Barshara hesitated. "Your offer is most kind, but alas, I cannot accept. My office requires my constant presence, and there are those who would seize the opportunity of my absence to further their own ambitions."

Ah, thought Forlern. He fears the loss of power over the threat to his own life. Lastrad politics were widely known to be a deadly game. Forlern wasn't aware of the recent history, but his imagination could fill in the gap.

Gregor continued. "Very well then. You will be given men chosen by myself to accompany you back to Lastrad. Their mission will be of great importance. To seek out and find this person, or *thing,* which kills your people. They will work together with whomever you choose in this task. Cooperation *must* be paramount in order for this to succeed. I suggest a small task force only, combine our best men."

"Agreed."

"My men will receive all the courtesy of their office, as personal envoys of myself, and all their needs must be answered. They will be granted permission to go wherever they wish in the pursuit of this adversary. Nothing will be off limits -- no barracks, private home, watch tower, or even the palace itself. Do you understand?"

"Yes, my Lord." The Gran Barshara nodded, but Forlern thought his face showed no sign of relief. Was the man convinced of failure already? Even with the exceptional skills of the Ja-Ravel assassin, was it that bad?

Gregor looked at his councilors, then back to the electorate. "We need someone with great skill and proven ability for this undertaking. A weapons master with experience in the field, along with knowledge battling against unfamiliar creatures. It's my belief that you're facing an enemy from the Grammore Lowlands, sent to undermine your leadership and terrorize your citizens."

The Gran Barshara shrugged. "That is quite possible. Our people live in constant fear, afraid for their lives and the lives of their family. Trade is starting to suffer, and the morale of our city continues to decay. We cannot allow this to continue."

King Gregor pointed across the table. "This I understand, and I've made my decision. I'm commanding Captain Forlern to lead the mission, and he will remain in Lastrad until this thing is found and *killed*."

"A *Killworm?* Shades!"

Chensel scowled, his tired face lined with care. The responsibility of his recent promotion weighed heavily on him, and it was evident in the slump of his shoulders. Sarion knew he keenly felt the loss of his men and the troubles in the westland. It was not an enviable position to be in. Of all people, he surely understood this the most...

"Yes. It waited for us in the woods. After the beast was destroyed, it took the opportunity to attack. It was another trap. I don't think there can be any doubt of this."

They all stared west, looking for any indication of what lurked in the dark, but there was only silence.

Chensel gestured to a pair of his waiting messengers, giving the signal for an impending assault. "Make sure we strike the creature with everything we have." He hesitated, looking at Valadire first, then Sarion. "And if the Killworm enters the valley, everyone is to fall back and flee towards Nighton."

The men nodded, heading off in opposite directions. The battlement was already on full alert, but now they would be told exactly *what* they were facing.

Valadire spoke. "What can we use to protect ourselves from the creature? Can it be slain in some way?"

"I guess we'll find out soon enough," Sarion answered grimly. "Legends say that the Killworm is bred with great magical power, and can only be defeated by such means."

"We have not such means in Nighton." Chensel's voice was low. The men stared at him.

"Then we must *discover* the means to destroy it. What you're saying is that it could overrun all our defenses, break into the capital itself?" Valadire had the look of a man ready to fight an army of monsters without hesitation.

Sarion shrugged. "I don't know. It can certainly climb, and approach silently for something of such bulk. If it goes around far enough it will find easier passage in the foothills somewhere. The walls are much higher in Nighton than here. Perhaps we can hope to keep it at bay if it reaches that far."

"There are other things at our disposal in the city." Chensel answered. "We must not let the thing enter."

"Well, let's see if we can first stop it *here*." Langstern slapped a gloved hand against one of the chairs for emphasis. "Nothing has ever conquered Nighton, and nothing *will* if I have anything to do about it."

Chensel nodded. "You've served honorably as Captain of the West Gate. I appreciate your determination. Unfortunately, our foe is something unnatural, beyond any of our experience. It is a creature from the old world resurrected by the enemy. I would rather face an army of Glefins then something spawned from the abyss of Grammore. Maybe there is a way, though…"

Sarion stared hard at him. He knew Chensel enough by now to know that the Nighton leader would be the last person to give up, and the first to pursue all options. What did he have in mind?

Chensel snapped orders. "Captain Langstern, take a position on the other side. Signal if your men spot anything. Use fire arrows and hot oil if it comes within range."

The grizzled veteran nodded, and was quickly off. Chertron paced restlessly about, speaking with some of the fighters.

Sarion came close to the Nighton Captain. "The monster also secretes a powerful acid. One strong enough to bore through rock. If it uses this against us, the western wall will be lost."

Chensel gazed past him, at the turrets surrounding them, but Sarion knew he didn't see them, instead focusing inwards. He remained this way for long moments, and Valadire soon joined Chertron with the fighters.

At last Chensel spoke. "Sarion, there's something I want to consider…"

His words were abruptly cut off as cries of alarm came from several points at once.

The Killworm was coming towards the wall.

Paul Melniczek

Forlern sat in Galivon's chambers, his arms crossed and his legs stretched in front of him. It had been two days since the meeting with the Gran Barshara, and this evening he would be leaving with the electorate back to Lastrad.

And embarking on a perilous quest.

Things tended to change drastically here, Forlern mused. One day appointed as a counselor to the king himself, the next ordered to lead a mission that could possibly end in his own death. Oh, he wasn't worried about his own safety; he was used to it and it was a part of a fighter's daily role, but he'd been taken by complete surprise at Gregor's decision. The king was placing a high amount of trust in him. The situation in Lastrad was reaching a crisis. Indeed, it may already have...And someone had to track this thing down. Hunt, find, and finish it off. King Gregor had spoken with his advisors after the meeting with the Gran Barshara, and Forlern had been given an incredibly difficult task -- to succeed where the best of Lastrad's elite had failed, and Forlern well knew the capabilities of the city's fighters. They were the best that money could get, and the city possessed profound wealth. But what about the assassin? What role had he played in this strategy? The Ja-Ravel were masters of weaponry, supposedly unmatched on the hunt. This adversary, however, was far different than whatever even they'd been trained for. In the end, the assassin had been unsuccessful as well. There had been no sign of him yet, and Forlern realized that he was hidden somewhere, staying away from Daregil Keep's watchful eye. Galivon's belief was that the man had considered the possibility that Forlern had recognized him, and so the Gran Barshara had ordered him to remain in hiding until his business in Daregil Keep was finished.

So Forlern had been given his orders, and was

prepared to leave soon. But more worrisome yet was the message that just arrived. It seemed that Sarion and Chertron had been delayed because of an attack on Nighton, and their rendezvous was not to be just yet...Forlern missed his companions, and a part of him regretted the events which had led him back to Daregil Keep instead of fighting at Sarion's side, where he really wanted to be. It was too late for that now. Gregor had other plans for him, and you couldn't thwart the will of the king. At least not without paying the consequences.

Galivon entered the room, holding a plate of fruit. "Hungry?"

Forlern shook his head. "No. Just eager to start this trip off. I really don't know what to expect once I reach Lastrad."

"Always fall back on your training. Expect the unexpected. Trust nothing and trust no one, only your instincts. I shouldn't have to remind you, of all people."

The young fighter sighed. "No, you shouldn't. But this news from the west is disturbing. I was hoping to see Sarion and Chertron again, but now it will have to wait."

"Things never transpire as you would wish in our position." Galivon sat down. "Your role has changed dramatically. It has its benefits, and challenges, of course. Gregor bestowed upon you a high honor taking this assignment, and I'm sure he would rather keep you here to listen to your advice on matters. But as the ruler of Trencit, he has to make difficult decisions. It's not much different than when Charadan journeyed into the borderlands. We all discussed the problem, and it was actually Charadan's idea to pursue the mission -- even into Grammore, if necessary."

Forlern stared at him, remembering the first time he'd met the fallen General of the Royal Armies as he took on a false identity to keep his whereabouts a secret.

"You'll be leaving under a cloak of secrecy yourself. Gregor doesn't want it known how serious things are in Lastrad. Rumors have been spreading across the kingdom about the killings. None of this is real news."

Forlern hadn't even considered this.

"So you see, you're being introduced into the inner workings of the kingdom now, Forlern. And quickly. Your life will never be the same again. I have as much faith in you as Gregor does, and I can tell you, it's not an easy thing to gain. You proved your worth in Grammore, surviving where even Charadan could not. I think you'll overcome whatever you face in Lastrad as well."

"Thanks for your words of trust, but I just wish I knew what it was I'll be facing…"

Forlern turned in surprise as the door to the chamber opened, and in walked Barimon, King Gregor, and Thustan, the king's younger son, whom Forlern had seen on a number of occasions at the Keep, although he was normally in the field on the eastern front.

"All right, be at ease. We need to discuss some things before you leave, Forlern."

The young fighter nodded, and he looked over at Galivon, who appeared to have been expecting them. The men all took seats, Gregor sitting beside Forlern. He was becoming a bit more comfortable in the king's presence, although it was impossible not to feel the intimidation. The responsibilities of his new office were a constant burden, as he now had an active role in major discussions concerning the kingdom's welfare, something he'd never dreamed would be possible only a few weeks earlier. And Forlern certainly had never wanted any part of it as he was content with his ranking in the Homeguard.

"You'll be leaving soon, and I wish to offer you

good fortune on this mission."

"Thank you, my Lord. I'll do my best."

"That might prove to be insufficient." Barimon spoke, and Forlern had to control an urge to scowl at the mage.

"Peace, Barimon. And don't underestimate Forlern." Galivon spoke in defense of his new captain.

"I underestimate none. I measure a man's ability, then consider the odds against him. In this situation they're formidable indeed, and we lack knowledge of the enemy's full power."

"Then can you tell me what it is I face so I can better prepare myself?" Forlern raised his hands, seeking support. Barimon had only succeeded in adding to his trepidation.

"We're unsure, Forlern." Gregor said. "Barimon guesses at much, although he has an uncanny ability to recognize the truth, grim as it may be."

"And he also has a tendency to be overly sullen…" Galivon added.

Gregor frowned, and Forlern had already seen enough of the king's advisors interacting to know this was a drama that had existed for a while.

Barimon continued, ignoring the remark. "There are things written in the archives from ages past. I've studied them for years unnumbered. And there are few alive who can decipher the Dark Script. I've been schooling Kexel on the histories, but there's much to learn."

The Dark Script…Forlern had heard rumors of this before. Supposedly there were ancient texts hidden deep inside the keep containing languages of an older time; books filled with lost knowledge, and some said magic as well…

"Know this then, Forlern. We speak of things which you have no understanding. These books *do* exist, and we have them locked away in the Hall of Twilight, the deepest chamber in Daregil Keep. This is known only to a handful, of course. Most of them are in this room now...It must remain that way."

"Of course, my Lord." Forlern tried to absorb everything he was hearing, but the implications were becoming more profound with each new revelation.

"There are facts that have been handed down from generation to generation. Knowledge bestowed upon us from previous mages and rulers. We've also discovered things on our own which give us a partial picture of the old land, the way it was before the kingdom of Trencit ever existed.

"Things were very different then, although some things haven't changed at all." It was Galivon who now led the discussion, and the others appeared content for him to continue. "The Grammore Lowlands were *always* there. Even then, it was a vast and dangerous country, home to the deadliest predators in the known world."

Forlern nodded with interest, although this was nothing new.

"The ancient Giants were the dominant species at one time, and within the books are descriptions of their civilization and their culture, along with the great cities they built and ruled from."

"Gorothagled." Forlern said.

"Yes. And others as well."

The map Charadan had referenced, thought Forlern.

"We also have learned of the terrible guardians that the Giants created to ward their outposts and protect them against dangers from both inside and outside Grammore."

"Who were their enemies?" Forlern asked.

"We don't know. The descriptions are vague at best." Barimon now answered. "But what we *do* know is that their strongest guardians, things like the Killworm, were created with powerful magic, harnessed by their masters. Magic which originated in the earth, tapped into and controlled by the Giants."

Forlern remembered the terrible city of Gorothagled, still under the shadow of their dread masters generations later.

"They forged great weapons to better utilize and wield this magic." Galivon said. "Talismans of immense power."

The rod! Charadan had found it within the Killworm's lair, and now Sarion had possession of it...Forlern felt an involuntary chill at the thought of something so powerful in his companion's keeping. He stared at the men seated before him and they returned his gaze, as if understanding his fear.

"When you first told us about the rod, we suspected it might be such. Barimon has read extensively through the texts these past few days and is now convinced of it." King Gregor inclined his head.

"Sarion possesses something beyond his understanding," Barimon said. "We need to have it in our hands *immediately*."

"But what can it do?" Forlern asked.

Everyone was silent, and he looked at them all in turn. Thustan had yet to say anything, but Forlern knew him as an even-tempered, thoughtful man, not someone prone to quick decisions. He now spoke, answering for the rest.

"We're not certain of anything. Their uses varied. But *some* of them were rods of summoning."

Forlern grew cold at his words.

"The most powerful could summon creatures of tremendous violence, ones which could not be controlled even by the wielder, it was said."

"What? Why would they have made something

so dangerous even to themselves? That makes no sense..." Forlern couldn't believe it.

Thustan's blue eyes never seemed to blink, and he matched Forlern's gaze with one which lacked expression for several moments, but then his own apprehension surfaced, so briefly that Forlern nearly missed it.

"We think that the Giants had foresight, that something ultimately would threaten their reign. They prepared for the possibility of defeat, and if this came about, they could wreak destruction on their conquerors, but at the cost of dooming themselves. In the end, they didn't want to leave their legacy to an enemy which had conquered them." He shrugged.

The whole idea was incredible. Forlern sat there, trying to fathom all the events which had transpired, and all the terrible possibilities which faced them. And then he had another thought...

"Do you think the Dark Mage has discovered any of these talismans?"

Barimon responded. "Certainly he's found at least one, or several of these. It gives him the power to control a number of these magical creatures. That would explain much."

Forlern didn't want to ask his next question, but Barimon looked as though he knew what was coming. "And if the Dark Mage has found the most powerful of these talismans, then he might already have in his grasp the means to our destruction, even his own?"

"It's possible." Gregor answered.

"But would he even realize the danger to himself?"

"Again, we have no knowledge of this. We guess at much, understand little. Many passages are vague, indecipherable. And realize that when these scripts were originally written, the crafters did not possess complete knowledge themselves. Adding to our lack of knowledge is this new enemy, one of whom we have never heard of before. We know nothing of the Dark Mage's past, or anything else about him." The king's tone didn't sound encouraging.

The young fighter followed to his own conclusion. "And Sarion might be holding one of these talismans right now. He must be warned swiftly."

"And so he shall." Gregor responded. "I'm sending Barimon with Thustan to seek him out. They leave this evening with a patrol to support the borderlands, so he'll be heading to Nighton, yourself to Lastrad."

"The dilemma before us remains..." Galivon spoke. "*What* do we do with this rod once we hold it? I say we can ill afford to use it, not knowing the outcome."

"But in the end, if we have no other choice before us, do we then take the risk?" Barimon challenged the First Captain.

"If we're to prevail, then we will do it with our strength of arms and the warriors of Trencit." Galivon's eyes smoldered.

"You'll change your mind if you chance on one of these creatures. Steel and fire is not enough to kill them."

"We don't *know* that for certain!" Galivon pounded on the table.

"Remember, there are such weapons at our disposal already." Barimon was conceding no ground.

"But even *these* can have unpredictable results. And they're not nearly as strong as what Sarion might have." Galivon stood, clearly not intimidated by the mage.

"*Might* have..." Barimon countered.

"We possess nothing which would come even

close to the greater talismans of power. The warnings
are written in the ancient script. You've told us as much
yourself." Galivon stared at the mage, his eyes glittering
with an inner fire.

"Enough." Gregor now left his chair, motioning
for silence. "We have time before us to discuss these
matters, but *now* is not the time. Forlern, Thustan, and
Barimon must leave Daregil Keep shortly. Their
missions are equally important. Once we have the
talisman in our hands, we'll study it, see what we can
learn. Cautiously, not putting it to use. Barimon, you're
to seek out Sarion, and carry this rod to me. I'm very
reluctant to summon him back to Trencit, knowing what
he's facing there, but I look forward to his counsel."

"He's been promoted to a Captain of Nighton,
father." Thustan spoke. "They require his leadership,
especially if an assault is underway."

Gregor nodded, looking uncertain. "I know. It's
not an easy decision. Forlern has told us everything from
the quest, but I still need to hear Sarion's *own* words and
mind. Charadan relied heavily on his opinion, it
appeared. And I certainly can't leave for Nighton
myself, even for a few days. The High Council is still
trying to recover from hearing the news of Charadan's
loss and the threat to our west. It's bad enough with the
ongoing war against the Devlents, and now this..."

Thustan shrugged. He looked very much like his
father but at middle-age, his black hair gray at the edges.

"So, back to Forlern's mission...We suspect that
something under the Dark Mage's control stalks the
streets of Lastrad. A creature of unknown power, with
the capability of eluding an entire city's army. Whether
it's natural or of magical origin, you must be prepared to
fight this thing either way." He turned to Barimon.
"Give him the blade."

Barimon reached into his cloak, pulling out a

long knife which had strange markings on the hilt.

"What's this?" Forlern stared at the weapon.

The mage narrowed his eyebrows, almost smirking. "Some of our *own* magic. This knife has the power to neutralize the magical ability of another."

"I don't quite follow you..."

Barimon continued. "If you come across a creature formed with magic, something like the Killworm, then it negates the power that makes it invulnerable to normal weapons -- steel, fire, or shaft. The Giants bred these monsters as indefensible guardians, a select few which could protect them from enemies seeking to destroy their cities. However, they also created the means to destroy them as well if the need arose, with devices such as this. We are fortunate to have some at our disposal."

"So...if I strike with the blade, I'll kill any magical creature that I encounter? If I'm not slain myself in the process..." Forlern held the knife, expecting to feel some flicker of the latent power, but it was cold in his hands.

"No." Barimon stared at him.

"No? But you said..."

"Listen to my words, fighter. The knife will neutralize the *magic*, not destroy the creature. You'll still have to defeat it by normal means, and its capabilities will most likely be formidable."

"What?"

Forlern felt his heart sink...He visualized the dreaded Killworm. Even without magical protection, what man could hope to slay such a monster? It had the strength of dozens of warriors. One had slain a number of his comrades, killing them with stealth. Areck and Cerestin had been taken without a struggle, awaiting their return inside Gorothagled. He remembered his anger at Charadan, then called Grundel, concerning the quick decision not to look for their missing companions. But the general had been right all along. They couldn't hope to defeat the monster, only to escape. They had eventually done so but fortune had been with them. If the Killworm had caught them while battling the ogre, none of them would have left the Lowlands alive...

Barimon raised his hand and pointed to him. "One other thing, Forlern. After you stab it, discard the blade."

"Why?"

"It has only a single use. If it strikes anything else, the magic inside is immediately discharged, wasted. Be certain of your target."

Be certain? Forlern's head swam with doubt. They expected him to hunt down something which had proven impossible to catch, and then he would have to fight and kill it in hand-to-hand combat? It was outrageous...Who did they think he was?

"As I said before, have faith, Forlern." Galivon moved towards him, squeezing his shoulder. "You have the skills to succeed. Use your training, but in the end trust your instincts. Few possess the ability you have. The decision to send you is a wise one. You *will* prevail."

The young fighter was silent, not feeling any of his normal confidence. His old brashness was buried somewhere deep, and he wondered if he would ever feel it again. Most likely not, if he even *lived* to find it...

"We don't know what terrorizes Lastrad, but remain vigilant. Beware the Ja-Ravel assassin. I know not what role he plays, but use extreme caution with that one. You'll be given escorts, and the Gran Barshara has promised to look after all your needs," Gregor said.

"I don't think he has much faith in me."

"Nevertheless, it is not his decision. Prove him wrong. Be strong."

The Rooting of Evil

Forlern nodded, sighing. "By life or limb, you have my word."

"And that is answer enough for me. Everyone must be ready soon. Preparations are finished. May fortune smile on you Forlern." Gregor turned to leave, and both Thustan and Galivon spoke words of encouragement. Then they were gone.

Several minutes later Forlern was back in his own chambers, gathering what he needed for the journey. The future was unclear, and in the coming days he would face an unprecedented challenge. A seemingly impossible one, if he were to be honest with himself.

What would be the result?

Grim as his thoughts were, he shuddered involuntarily, thinking about Sarion and the power his friend unwillingly might be holding, power so great that it could destroy them all...

The Nighton hunters were all in position, looking west for signs of movement. Cries echoed along the wall, and several moments later a great horn rang in the night, the warning for an attack to come. The sky grew brighter as dawn approached and Sarion sprang forward, gazing into the horizon. He spotted the creature immediately, still a long way off, but there could be no mistaking the intent as it made a line directly for the wall.

"If it sends webbing into the air, the men must avoid touching the strands." Sarion looked over at the Nighton leader standing to his right.

"I'll pass word along." He gestured to a nearby runner and the man nodded, quickly leaving.

"The beast is massive. This is the best view we've ever had of it." Chertron cursed beneath his breath at what approached, a monster believed to exist only in legend, and there it was now, in clear sight before them.

"I can't believe it, but there it is. Shades, what a monster." Chensel exhaled sharply, mesmerized like the rest of them.

Sarion fingered his sword in anticipation, his mind racing, trying to formulate a defense. When they had encountered the creatures before, the only option was to escape. Outside Sprechyd Wood he'd feared that one was loose, hunting the area, and two Nighton fighters had been lost. He wasn't certain, but he suspected that a Killworm had been responsible. How many of these things were under the Dark Mage's control? He was ready to suggest a plan of action to Chensel, but without warning the Killworm stopped, still scores of yards away, the great feelers waving in the air. They all listened in horror as a high droning issued forth, and Sarion grabbed Chensel's arm. "I think it prepares to attack us with its strands."

They both watched in silence, but no threads issued forth from the beast this time.

"Maybe it must rest before producing more of the deadly webbing?" Chertron offered.

"Perhaps you're right," Sarion answered. "We know nothing of this creature save its name and old tales."

"Look. What's it doing?" Chensel pointed, and they all stared intently.

The Killworm angled its head downwards, and they watched in fascination as smoke curled up from the earth. Its numerous limbs moved back and forth rapidly, the feelers waving in the air.

"It's using acid, and burrowing in the ground, I

think." Sarion shook his head. "Wait. Now it's sinking...The creature's making a lair. It's nearly out of sight already."

The Killworm sank into the ground and in moments had disappeared entirely. Smoke rose upwards, but there was no further sign of the dread monster. It was gone.

"Amazing." Valadire spoke. "What a beast. To dig a hole that swiftly, and vanish like that. Its acid must be potent indeed."

"Well…" Chensel turned to face them. "It seems we've received a brief reprieve for the moment. It appears that the Killworm is making a den for itself. But for what purpose? Does it need to rest before it attacks us further?"

"Perhaps it does," said Sarion. "Or there's another possibility. Maybe this action is the intent of its master. To guard the west wall."

Chensel frowned. "Your words carry truth, I fear, grim as they are. What the first creature failed to accomplish, the second is meant to fulfill. We can only speculate that it merely wants to block this entrance, but we also can't assume it still won't attack us."

Valadire agreed. "This could be true. Effectively seal off the western wall, and kill anything that approaches. We have to warn away all that draw near. We need a strategy to protect our returning men."

"What we need is a strategy to drive the thing off, or find a way to kill it…" Sarion said.

Chensel motioned for some of his messengers to come close, and he spent several minutes explaining his plan. There was nothing more he could do at the moment, so Sarion went inside the interior wall and sat down at a table, looking around for some food and drink, and shortly the others joined him. Sarion needed rest for when the time came for action, as he knew it eventually would.

"I like your idea. We need food and drink." Chertron said.

"There are men enough to watch the fortress. I'm weary, tired to the bone." Sarion rubbed his hands across his face. "The new day arrives, but what will it bring us besides light?"

"Hmm." Chertron grumbled. "You've done your share as usual, my friend. Your sword helped us slay the first beast. Who would have thought another Killworm was waiting nearby? Shades."

They both looked up as Chensel joined them, several of his couriers and guards hovering close.

"Nearby…" Chensel said, repeating Chertron, speaking almost to himself. "You said nearby. I wonder about something."

"What is it? You have an idea?" Sarion peered over one hand, interested in what the Nighton leader was thinking.

Chensel shrugged. "Perhaps. Chertron mentioned it was nearby, that's all. But could there be something else we've overlooked?"

They stared at him, none of them willing to interrupt his line of thinking.

"We know this Dark Mage controls these creatures with some form of magic. Independently, these beasts are savage predators, dangerous and untamed. As it's told, the ancient race of Giants manipulated them to use as guardians, or even antagonists. Exactly as they're being used against *us* now." He paused.

"Agreed. We know this. But what are you getting at?" Sarion asked.

"It would take power -- great power -- to keep these things under control. And we already know who is behind this, the enemy called the Dark Mage. But the question we've failed to consider is *where*? It seems reasonable to believe that the wielder of such might needs to be in close proximity to his strongest emissaries. These monsters possess incredible ability. Their predatory instincts would give them a high sense for survival when threatened, yet these things show a singular purpose, focusing on limiting our actions, killing our men. In the wild, they would surely act differently. They would try to escape if overmatched, like other predators."

Sarion now understood what the Nighton leader was getting at. A shrewd observation, but typical coming from the First Forester. "You think someone is close by then, to control such powerful creatures?"

Chensel nodded. "I think exactly that."

"And if we can find them, it would give us a chance to strike directly at the wielder of magic and not just the marauders. It's long overdue for this Dark Mage to answer for all the blood on his hands." Sarion's tone clearly reflected his emotion. He'd been thinking the same thing for a while now, but events had prevented him from pursuing such a course. Maybe this current threat could also prove to be the opportunity they sorely needed.

The others were silent, considering, but Sarion took the initiative, his mind churning with possibilities. "We need to attack swiftly. While the Killworm is occupied."

Valadire and Chertron looked startled, but Chensel agreed. "Yes. We must try and snare the beast in its own lair."

"How will we do this? We don't even know if we're able to hurt it or not." Valadire looked to the First Captain.

"Nevertheless, try we must. I have an idea. It won't be easy, but our need is desperate. Once the monster decides to advance, we'll have lost the chance for surprise, and our initiative will be gone. Valadire, I want you to make for the woods where the creatures emerged from. Two score hunters, all on horseback. You're to scour the forest, look for signs of anyone. If indeed someone hides, perhaps you'll be able to flush them out and capture them. That seems to be the most likely spot, if indeed they are nearby."

"And what if they bring magic against us?"

"You'll do your best to avoid it. I can't give you any advice on this matter, but I trust your ability."

The fighter sighed, but he looked determined. "Very well."

Chensel turned to Sarion and Chertron. "Again, Nighton relies on its newest captain. Much will fall upon your shoulders, I'm afraid."

Sarion shrugged. "We all have our roles to play."

Chensel continued. "I'll send men with you, and carts filled with oil. They must be the first ones to the Killworm's hole, and the liquid will be poured into the lair and set to flame. I don't know if this will harm the creature or not, but at the very least Valadire will be able to look for our enemy without being hunted by the Killworm. This diversion will hopefully give him the time and cover he needs. Valadire, your command is to warn anyone you come across to stay clear of the west gate. Unless we find success, of course. If we fail to stop the creature, you're to act on your own, patrolling the area due west of here and avoid closing with the beast. At all costs you must avoid battling the monster."

"Very well, Captain Chensel. I'll gather the men now, and pass word of our plan."

"Hasten, then. I want everyone to be out within a few minutes. Take light supplies along, but not enough to slow you down."

"It will be done."

Sarion approached him. "Good fortune, Valadire.

The Rooting of Evil

Beware of anything you meet in the woods, and flee if you're overcome by something too dangerous. I'll come looking for you when our work is done."

"Don't be overlong then, Sarion. May fortune smile on both of our hunts. And it's good having you back in the Western Watch. Maybe we can have *that* one transferred here if we ever get out of this mess…"

He grinned fiercely while Chertron gave him the Trencit salute in reply, and then he was gone, his guards following quickly behind him.

"All right, things are set into motion now. Our plans are laid out, and the future of Nighton is in the hands of our men. Let's hope my idea doesn't end in disaster. We can't afford anymore setbacks."

Chensel slumped into a chair, and Sarion knew the man desperately needed rest. They *all* needed rest. But would they find any ever again? There wasn't much left to say and he was ready to take his leave, but the Nighton leader spoke.

"Sarion, there is one other thing we have available to us which may prove of some consequence."

"And what is that?"

Chensel looked about, but the guards remained alert but outside earshot.

"Magic."

Sarion and Chertron stared at him.

"The rod you carry. You were told twice now that it possesses great power. From beings who know far more than we do."

Sarion nodded. "This is true. But of its nature, I have no knowledge, and I have no idea how to put the thing to use regardless. I'm a fighter, not a mage."

Chensel persisted. "Time flows against us, and our enemies seem to grow stronger with each encounter. If they use magic against us, or send creatures which are enchanted, then we have no true defense, and can only fight a prolonged battle -- one which we will eventually *lose*."

His words were grim and Sarion knew that it was no wonder he didn't want them to fall on any other ears. They also sounded uncomfortably identical to what the Keeper of Sprechyd Wood had told him. Chensel had obviously been giving the matter some thought, thinking beyond what Sarion had even pondered. Using the rod as a weapon...Since becoming the bearer, Sarion had given it little thought himself. Was it deliberate? Had he subconsciously been ignoring its presence so he wouldn't think *about* using it himself? Afraid he might try it? He didn't know the answer...

"I see it in your eyes, Sarion. You're torn about trying to use it."

"I'm unsure. Maybe it's true. I don't know…"

The Nighton leader straightened. "I mean to ride out with the assault. And if things go against us, I'm going to try and use the rod."

Both Sarion and Chertron looked stunned.

"Do you know something you're not telling us?" Chertron demanded.

Chensel shook his head. "No, nothing at all. Call it an act of desperation if you will. Perhaps it will prove to be a wise decision, who can say."

"Or a disastrous one…" Sarion added.

"It might be a gift. We'll never know unless an attempt is made."

Sarion shook his head. "The risk is great. Too great...But if you insist, then let it be *me*."

The Nighton leader stared at him.

"It was given to my trust by Charadan. Nighton cannot afford to lose its leader again. *I* must be the one to try it, none other."

Chertron looked at them both in turn. "We haven't the slightest idea of what we're dealing with.

Desperate or not, I would not attempt its use, Sarion. Or Captain Chensel. Something terrible might happen."

"And something terrible *will* happen if we can't defend ourselves." Chensel stared him down. "Enough. If our situation becomes bad, then it will be tried. That's my decision. Sarion, it will fall upon you to decide when to use the rod since you're leading the attack. Use your discretion and trust your instincts. And you're right, I should remain out of the direct fray. Jerol took too much upon himself. I can't make that same mistake."

Sarion nodded. He knew Chensel was not trying to force the decision on himself, but circumstances demanded that *someone* had to wield it. Chensel would not hesitate to use the rod in his place -- or anything else he deemed a necessary risk -- to help save Nighton, and Trencit, and he could do no less himself...

"Very well. I'll have it ready, although I promise no results. If it comes down to it, then I will try the rod against the Killworm."

The Nighton leader nodded. "If that seems to be the *only* option, then you must attempt its use. If there's a way to master this talisman, then there is no other more capable, Sarion. Myself included."

They all stood, and Sarion knew that Chensel had given him the highest compliment possible.

Sarion was in the courtyard speaking to some of the men. The first group, led by Valadire, was in front of the gate, prepared to make a dash for the tree line. Sarion spotted him, but the new Forester was giving last minute orders to his men. Chertron was mounted several yards to his right, Bertilik and Piril shadowing him to both sides. He was already used to having the personal guards, but so much had happened that he paid them little notice for the most part. He did fear for *their* safety, but he didn't have time to dwell on it. He feared for all their lives...

The company he would be leading was soon gathered, totaling two dozen horsemen. The animals had their hooves muffled, and the carts with the oil were in place. The fortress had a compliment of catapults, and they were pulled taut. Everything looked battle ready, and Sarion spoke words of encouragement to those waiting for his command.

"Have a care, hunters of Nighton. The Killworm is a deadly creature, swift and aggressive. Throw everything you have at it. Arrow, spear, dart. Try to blind it, hit its flanks. I'll be honest with you all." Sarion hesitated for a moment. "We are faced with a monster of the old world, one formed with magic. I don't know that it has any vulnerable part. If our efforts fail, retreat to the gate. Save your lives. We can live to fight another day."

The fighters nodded, and Sarion saw the determination in their eyes, even after his grim words. He looked back to his left, where a slim hunter rode a dusky gray horse. Sarion opened his mouth in surprise when he saw a long shock of golden hair spilling from beneath a Nighton war helm.

A woman!

She stared at him in silence and Sarion matched her gaze for a long moment, then he moved towards Flegand, the ranking hunter who was riding with his group.

"Has the Watch permitted the women of the westland to now enter its ranks? Things have changed in the few years since I've left, if this be true."

Flegand didn't need to look where Sarion stared.

He chuckled instead. "That's Lassel, Captain Sarion. You would be hard put to find a better rider in all of Nighton, and one possessing a sharper eye with the bow."

"She's that good?" Sarion asked in surprise.

"Better…" Flegand answered. "Take my word."

"I still don't like the idea of any woman following my lead into such danger." Sarion frowned.

"It's your order if you like to have her removed, but I would not agree with it, Captain Sarion. Nor would she… Lassel has proven her worth. She's the best to come out of the training grounds in a long time."

"Perhaps, but this is no training ground. We ride against a deadly predator from Grammore."

Flegand shrugged. "Captain Chensel made the decision to move her forward. She's gained his respect."

Sarion waited a moment, and then shook his head. If Chensel had placed her here, then he had good reason. Still…

"All right. She'll ride with us then. Signal the gatekeepers to open. It's time."

The word was passed ahead, and shortly the great doors which prevented access to the valley of Nighton were opened. Valadire and his men went through first and split immediately, trying not to have their entire force pinned in case the creature arose from its new lair. The question remained though -- what would the Killworm do?

Then it was time...

Sarion and Chertron led the company, escorting the slow-moving carts. Dawn had arrived, and the men welcomed the light, the day promising to be heavy with cloud cover. Nothing moved on the horizon except for Valadire and his hunters. Sarion stared intently at the area where the Killworm had disappeared from, but there was no sign of the monster. The yards passed them by slower than he cared for, the ponderous carts moving clumsily across the grassland. With each groaning wheel, he felt a shiver of anticipation that the monster would usher forth from the hole and attack, but nothing happened. He gave another signal and the company fanned out, their strategy to encircle the lair and diminish the chance of loss if they were attacked.

They moved closer, and Sarion saw Valadire's men as they swiftly approached the forest. He nodded to himself. *That* part of their plan had worked, at least.

The carts rumbled closer to the hole, and Sarion finally got a good look at it. The opening wasn't as wide as he'd thought. Wide enough to admit the creature, but the Killworm was long and sinuous, able to squeeze through narrow gaps. They were scarcely a dozen yards from it now, and still no indication of the dreaded beast. He motioned the cart bearers to advance, and they went right up to the hole without hesitation. A number of fighters had lighted torches, and Sarion pointed. In unison, both carts were heaved forwards, the oil spilling into the hole.

"Hurry!" Sarion was right there with them, anxiously staring into the black opening, all his senses straining for signs or sound of movement. The oil was soon gone and torches were thrown into the lair, instantly lighting it. Flames licked up and the company backed away, waiting for the inevitable.

"Maybe the lair runs deep." Chertron offered. "The creature can move quickly as we've seen."

"Perhaps," answered Sarion. "But we don't have any idea what the creature was doing down there. If it keeps tunneling, there might be separate branches…"

He didn't finish his sentence, and Chertron looked at him strangely. The fighter opened his mouth to speak, but was abruptly cut off when they heard a cry of alarm from behind them.

The Rooting of Evil

They both pivoted, but Sarion already knew what had happened.

The Killworm was inside the wall...

Sarion was the first one to move, nearly colliding with Bertilik.

"Shades! Back to the fortress! It's tunneled beneath the walls!"

Sarion rode past a number of hunters, so focused on returning that he failed to see the look of horror on some of their faces. They had all overlooked the possibility that the Killworm wasn't merely content to keep them at bay, but instead was actively seeking to outflank them, and the distance it had tunneled in so short a time was amazing.

The hunters raced back to the fortress with Sarion in the lead, and everyone heard the cries already coming from within.

Sarion urged his mount forwards, giving the animal its head for the fastest gait it could muster. He cursed beneath his breath -- how could they not have anticipated the Killworm's action? But who would have dreamed it could burrow in the ground so quickly? Just moments ago there had been a surge of hope, that perhaps they'd taken the monster by surprise, dumped the oil into its lair and killing it without a fight. Sarion shook his head. He should have known better. He, of all people, who had fought these creatures before, and each time learned that they were not to be underestimated.

But there was no time for regret. There was a pitched battle being waged ahead of him and he would soon be in the fray. Even now he heard the screams of anguish as Nighton hunters were being killed. He ground his teeth together, determined that he would find a way to destroy the monster and avenge his brethren. He *had* to find a way, no matter the cost to himself.

Sarion reached the gates, but they were still closed. "Open!" He shouted, as others came behind him now. Sarion saw movement on the wall, and one of the guards heard his call, waving with one hand.

"Flee while you can! Save yourselves! The monster will have us all if you enter!"

Sarion raised his spear in the air. "No! I command you, open the gates now! It must not be permitted to take the western wall!"

The man looked indecisive, then looked behind him. "Very well, but have a care, it's at the far end of the courtyard! By the Seven, what a beast! We'll all be lost!"

Moments later the gates swung open and Sarion warily led the company inside, not knowing what to expect.

He was greeted by chaos...

Men were scattered everywhere -- some on foot, others on horseback, screaming warnings. He saw the Killworm several dozen yards away, its bulk surrounded by fighters it had already slain. They numbered many...

Arrows and shafts rained down upon the monster, deflecting off its natural armor of thick scales. The situation looked hopeless. Sarion looked for Chensel, and he spotted the Nighton leader to his right, ringed in by his personal guard. He was much too close to the fighting for Sarion's comfort. If the Killworm decided to move in that direction, Chensel would come under direct attack. Although Sarion and his companions had encountered more than one Killworm in their travels, they had successfully eluded them by escape or fortune, so this was the first time he'd seen one of the creatures in combat.

It was a terrifying sight...

Clearly outmatching the fighters, the creature darted left and right, the terrible pinchers closing in on anyone daring to attack. Another man went down before Sarion's eyes, beheaded by the dreadful beast. To see such a monster from the old world living and breathing was something that none of them were prepared for.

It was a killing machine...

If the ancient Giants had indeed bred Killworms as guardians for their strongholds, then they had perfected death itself. The thing was far more dangerous than Sarion could have dreamed possible...

It never let up, never left its guard down. Constantly moving, the appendages acted in unison, pivoting it wherever the creature wanted to go, also serving to strike out at anything which got too near. The feelers waved madly, and Sarion thought it used senses other than sight, because it seemed to have the ability to know where an attack was coming from, even in the rear. Several men found that out too late as the Killworm spun about, striking three fighters dead where they stood. Sarion watched as several Nighton fighters withdrew, fleeing, knowing that to hold their ground would only bring certain death.

Sarion's company was shocked by the massacre, demoralized at seeing their comrades hewn down so easily.

"There's no way to defeat the beast!" Chertron yelled from his left. "Chensel must give the order to fall back now!"

Sarion nodded, moving his mount closer to the action, his mind racing to find a plan, anything that might stop the monster. "Chertron, go to him. Tell him to retreat now. We must live to fight another day!"

Chertron veered off to find the Nighton leader.

Piril drew close to Sarion. "What's your command? Can we do nothing to fight the monster? Our men are being slaughtered!"

"Follow me," was all he said.

Sarion waved for the rest of the company to form a large circle, keeping a respectful distance from the creature, but he rode straight towards the fighting, placing his spear at his side.

He knew there was no other choice before him now. Chensel was right -- all options had to be pursued, no matter the risk. Sarion reached into the small bag he carried at his waist and brought out the rod. Despite their dire circumstances, he again marveled at the beauty in its craftsmanship. Such a wondrous thing, but what was the nature of its power? Had the ancient Giants created it to harness their magic in some fashion? How could he awaken it to help them now, when their situation was desperate?

He held the rod in his hand, getting dangerously close to the fighting. The Killworm seemed to have an endless amount of energy and was ceaseless in its assault, hardly giving the men time to breathe, and offering no chance for any organized counterattack.

Not knowing what else to do, Sarion held the rod in front of him, pointing it towards the creature. He closed his eyes, focusing inwards, trying to compel the talisman to come alive, react to his need. For a moment, he sat on his horse motionless, his guards looking at him strangely, but then he opened his eyes in shock as he felt a surge of power welling from somewhere deep inside his chest.

The rod was working!

But his surprise immediately turned to dismay as he felt the full weight of what was starting to happen, the old magic flaring violently to life. He was shocked, unable to keep his mind focused. Overwhelmed, he felt himself drifting, becoming lost in a fathomless void, surrounded by something so strange and consuming that it defied comprehension. It was too much...he felt like he was being pulled apart, his flesh searing with pain.

And then he caught a glimpse -- faint, tugging at the corners of his mind -- an image of what the talisman was capable of, what power he could wield. The lure was appalling, both wonderful and terrifying in the same breath. The *power* he now held within his hands, what he could bring forth...

The struggle he felt in the span of mere seconds was incredible. He was torn between claiming it as his own to wield or letting go, saving his identity and refusing. He hovered on the brink of collapse, and then with a tremendous effort of will power he shook himself free of the talisman's grip...

He couldn't do it! The rod was too powerful! It could destroy them all!

Sarion's horse buckled beneath him and he was thrown off, the animal frightened by the crackle of power coming from its rider. The world spun around him and everything was lost in a whirlwind of confusion. If he would have fallen unconscious that would have been the end of him as the Killworm surged forward, the dangerous pinchers closing for its prey. Sarion rolled on his side, trying to avoid the killing blow. Shouts went out all around him as the Nighton fighters scrambled to protect their new captain. The Killworm's massive pincher missed him by inches, but one of its legs caught him in the chest, pinning him to the ground. Winded by the vicious attack, he reflexively went for his sword and blocked another leg with his weapon, the claw clicking at him menacingly. Shafts and arrows bounced off the monster's scaled armor, and something metallic flashed above him as Piril whipped his spiked ball directly at the creature's face.

The Killworm backed off in a flurry of limbs, trying to shake away the effects of the blow.

Sarion was free, and he looked up in amazement. The Killworm was injured....

Injured!

Was it possible? Did they really have a chance against it? Encouraged by Piril's efforts, more fighters closed ranks, trying to get close enough to strike at the multiple appendages while the creature was off balance. Lassel rode into the fray, hurling a spear at the monster's face, but the Killworm was hardly defeated. It knocked the shaft out of the air, at the same time lashing out at a pair of riders attacking its flank. Both men were scored by the deadly talons, collapsing to the ground. Sarion pushed himself up, grabbing the rod which lay next to him, dull and lifeless. There was no time to think about it now. This was a battle to the death, and despite Piril's valiant charge, it was far from over.

Sarion shouted to the men, trying to shake off his pain. "Have a care! Don't get too close to the beast!"

On foot, he reached and drew his bow, aiming for the creature's eyes. The twin stalks waved madly about, and the monster never remained still, the long sinuous body constantly moving and shifting, warding off blows and striking out when someone got too near. Another man went down, and Sarion cursed, firing a pair of volleys. The first missed entirely as the creature changed directions, but the second stabbed one of the feelers and it scuttled backwards, trying to avoid this new danger. Dozens of other arrows soared down on it, and Sarion saw Chertron's lean form to the right, the fighter trying to reach him. Piril and Bertilik never left his side, both men taking shots from a distance. Lassel remained on her steed, and she let fly numerous arrows, all of them aimed at the monster's face. She then scored a hit, and the Killworm reared up on its back legs, whipping about in a frenzy.

"Back off! Keep striking at it!"

A cheer went up and the Nighton hunters tasted victory, renewing their attack, sending a relentless storm of volleys at the predator. Without warning, the Killworm scurried to the right, plowing through the ranks and crushing three men were they stood. It retreated back into the courtyard, and Sarion knew what it meant to do...

"Beware! It tries to escape!"

Men hurried after it, spear and shaft finding a mark, several of them embedding into the flesh beneath the appendages. Hindered by its countless injuries, the Killworm struggled along, blood dripping from over a dozen wounds. Sarion saw Chensel in the rear, speaking words of encouragement to his fighters. Lassel was closest to the monster, her mastery of horsemanship evident as many of the other fighters were having trouble with their steeds, the animals terrified of the dangerous predator. She was close on its rear, focused on pressing their advantage. The Killworm was heading for the hole which had given it access beneath the walls, and now it was desperately trying to escape the same way. The Nighton hunters swarmed after it, hitting the beast with everything they had. It finally reached the rim of the hole, vanishing into the ground, but it looked severely injured, barely gaining the opening.

"Get the oil, it mustn't be permitted to return!" Chensel motioned for his men to surround the fissure, and in moments carts were pushed forward, their contents emptying into it. Chensel wasn't satisfied, and he waited until several more carts had been dumped before signaling the torches to be dropped.

Flames licked skywards, and the First Captain sent riders beyond the wall, looking to see if the Killworm would attempt to escape elsewhere. Several men were wounded, but many more were on the ground, and would never ride with their comrades again. The entire fortress remained vigilant, but it appeared the worst was over for now. It was time to regroup and care for the injured and fallen. Sarion went around, giving aid where he could, but the healers of the western wall were already tending to the most severely hurt.

After several minutes, Chensel approached him with a concerned-looking Chertron at his side, and Sarion slumped to one knee, hardly able to stand himself.

"Are you injured, Sarion? I saw you go down before the monster and feared the worse…"

His companion hurried over to him but Sarion shook his head, grinning weakly. "Sore ribs, but I'll be alright after some rest."

"We slew the beast! Can you believe it? The men of Nighton fought a courageous battle, although our ranks are thinned. Too many good fighters will not return to their families again." Chensel's face was etched with loss. "A terrible price we have paid for this victory."

"How many?" Sarion asked, but already knew the number would be high.

"Over two dozen at least. The creature came upon us in stealth. We never considered that it would tunnel so quickly. My lack of foresight has failed us."

"Who could have known?" Chertron said. "We've all been surprised by these creatures from Grammore. But think…We've *defeated* it! I believe it will not live through the day. Shades! We killed what couldn't be killed! There's still hope, my friends. By life and limb, we will not be so easily overcome."

Sarion was silent, thinking things over. Everything had happened so swiftly that there was no time to consider the events, only react. "I need to rest soon, but we have much to speak about. And we need to find Valadire and see how he fared."

"I've already sent riders looking for him. Hopefully they'll find him and his men shortly."

They walked towards the furthest building in the fortress, one which housed the officers of the west wall along with a stock of weapons. Piril and Bertilik trailed behind them along with Chensel's escort, all of them unscathed, but tired and hungry. They entered past the guard, and Chensel sent all the personal escorts away to rest. They followed into the council chamber, a small room which served as a private area for the officers to discuss war and strategy. Servants brought trays holding fresh fruit, meat, and goblets of wine. They all took their fill, and only after several long minutes did any of them offer to speak.

"I need to tell you about the rod."

Chensel stared at him over the rim of his goblet, his eyes intense.

"I attempted to use it when we returned. Our need was desperate, and I saw no other choice before me."

"It's as we spoke, then. I placed my trust in your hands, Sarion. You know that. I believe you tried your best, but we cannot pretend to understand such things. My expectations were not disappointed, I can assure you. And I know of none other that could have found success."

"You misunderstand me..."

"What do you mean?" Chensel placed his drink on the table.

Sarion paused, remembering the terrible feeling of power which he'd experienced, something unlike anything he could have dreamed of.

"It worked!"

"What? The rod worked? But nothing

happened."

"Yes, something *did* happen. Something I can't explain, but one thing I do know -- I felt an incredible surge of power. It was terrible, beyond my comprehension. Only for the briefest moment, but I was daunted."

He stopped, trying to figure out how to make Chensel understand.

"So it worked, but then what happened? What did you feel?"

"It's difficult to find the words. I'm still confused, and I don't see any easy way to describe what I went through…"

Chensel nodded. "Sarion, try to explain. I know there's no way to prepare for what you attempted to do."

"True words." Sarion paused for a moment, formulating his thoughts. "I pointed it at the Killworm, because I had no other plan on how to summon the power of the rod. I concentrated, and in a few moments it flared to life. Just like that. I was stunned, but it truly worked. I focused inward, going deep inside myself, trying to seek out the nature of what it held. And I was…astonished." Sarion paused, and the others waited for him to continue.

"It was overwhelming. I sensed a terrible feeling of immense power, something so great that I feared we would all be destroyed if I unleashed it. I don't understand *how* I knew this, but by summoning the energy stored within the talisman, I received some glimpse of its nature. It was vague, incomplete, but a glimpse all the same, like a dream fragment one has after waking, but one which quickly is gone. Do you understand me?"

Chensel nodded, but was silent.

"And you turned away from it?" Chertron asked.

Sarion replied. "Yes. Before I could bring it

entirely to life. I don't know what would have happened, but I felt it was too great a risk, dire though our situation was. I made the choice -- right or wrong -- to quench the power of the rod before it was unleashed. There's no way of knowing what *might* have happened."

Chensel rubbed his chin for several moments. "That's fascinating. You were able to bring the rod to life, and felt an incredible surge of energy coming from it. There can be no doubt as to its magical nature then. The question remains -- *what* is it capable of? Sarion, I don't fault your decision not to use it. There can be no blame. You tried, and did indeed have success, unlike my previous thought. What we do next with it is the question."

Chertron shook his head. "Let King Gregor make that decision. It's not for us to resolve. We've fought our enemy at every turn for the past few weeks, with no reprieve in sight. What more could be asked from us? This is a matter for others to worry about."

Sarion closed his eyes, listening to their responses. They spoke their heart, and their opinions were valuable. But...they had not felt the power contained within the rod. It was perilous. *Too* perilous, he believed, to ever use again. By anyone.

There was a knock on the door, and one of the sentries peered inside after Chensel gave permission.

"Lord Chensel, I have good news to convey."

"Ah, that is always welcome, especially in these troubled times. Speak."

"Forester Valadire has returned unharmed."

All of them smiled, Sarion feeling greatly relieved. "Is he coming here now?"

"He's on his way…"

"Excellent," said Chensel. "Any sign of the Killworm?"

"None. The oils on both sides have been tended,

as per your command. And there is no indication of it trying to escape elsewhere."

"All is well. Then we'll await Valadire's coming."

"There's one other thing which I must mention, Lord Chensel."

Sarion could hear excitement in the man's tone. What was it?

"Let's hear it, then." The Nighton leader spoke, his tone neutral.

"It appears that Forester Valadire returns with a prisoner."

Sarion sat up straight in his chair, and all of three of them looked at the sentry in surprise. A prisoner, he thought? This was an unexpected turn of events, as well as a tremendous stroke of fortune...

A prisoner! Who could it be?

"Who is it? The Dark Mage?" Chertron was nearly out of his seat, his eyes smoldering. "He has much to answer for." He made a fist.

Sarion stared at his companion, but he knew instinctively that Chertron was wrong. The Dark Mage was much too powerful to let himself be captured by a Nighton hunting party. If only it were that easy...

"Peace, Chertron. We'll find out soon enough. I want him brought here now." Chensel's voice was controlled, but Sarion knew the First Captain had many losses to avenge. Justice would be certain.

"They'll be here in moments. I'll wait outside for them if you wish."

Chensel nodded, and the sentry left the room. "A

prisoner. Valadire was successful then."

Sarion spoke. "You were right about someone being nearby to control the creatures. Evidently Valadire flushed him out and captured him. This is indeed a good stroke of luck. And foresight."

"Our efforts have not gone without fruition. Not the least through the efforts of yourself and Chertron. Nighton stands together to protect us all."

Chensel would have continued but there was a sharp knock on the door.

"Enter," he said.

Valadire walked in, his eyes intense. "Well met, Captain Chensel. Sarion and Chertron, I heard you both were alright. It gladdens my heart to see you again so soon."

Behind him walked one of his personal guards, and after them a pair of cloaked fighters followed, escorting a shackled man between them. Sarion looked at his face, which was soiled and unshaven. He looked to be fairly young, not much older than himself, with nothing exceptional about his appearance, but his physical condition was appalling...He seemed near death, his skin white, his eyes sunken in their sockets, dark circles branded beneath them. He wore a loose cloak which barely clung to his limbs. He was emaciated and looked like he was starving, his head angled downwards.

"Surely you've made a mistake." Chertron spoke. "This beggar needs food and drink, not an armed escort."

"Hush, Chertron. Let Valadire speak." Chensel shook his head, not taking his eyes off the man.

Valadire spoke. "It might appear so at first, my friend, but do not be so quick to judge." He turned to the Nighton leader. "Here is my tale."

Sarion looked the man over. His health was

terrible, certainly. But there was something else about the man that struck him. He couldn't put his finger on it, but he knew appearances were deceiving at times. *Something* was wrong here. He felt it in his bones...

Valadire continued. "On your command, we rode out to the woods, unhindered. Our purpose was before us and we dared not linger and chance an encounter with the Killworm. We split into two groups and made a sweep of the forest, but it didn't take us long until we came upon signs of a small camp. Tracks led away, and we followed them deeper into the woods. My other group came upon this man, and he tried to pass himself off as a hermit, hiding from the creatures. When they brought him to me I was suspicious, and asked him how he could have managed to elude these predators. I didn't believe his story, and we took him into our power. Once he realized he would be taken, he then told us an incredible story -- that he was an emissary of the Dark Mage sent to destroy Nighton..."

Sarion heard the icy tone in Valadire's voice, and he stared hard at the man, the prisoner's head remaining bowed to the ground.

"Well, what say you, stranger? Few know the name of our enemy. Why were you so quick in naming your intent? Many brave men have fallen. You have much to answer for." Chensel's gaze promised swift retribution. Sarion had never seen the man look so intense. Finally, the prisoner looked up, his eyes wide and staring. It was the look of the damned...

"You're right. I'm guilty of the accusation."

Spittle rolled from his mouth, and beads of sweat covered his brow as if a fever raged within his body.

"So you make no attempt to even defend yourself? Then what say you? Tell us what we need to know and your punishment might be less severe. Where is your cowardly master, one who drives others to spread his evil?"

The man chuckled, although Sarion heard no humor in the sound. "The master? Mine no longer. And I fear not your punishment. My own torment has no match."

Valadire came towards him, lifting one arm. "We found this on him. He told me it's what he used to control the creatures."

A band of some kind was wrapped about his arm, but it didn't seem to have any edges. It appeared to be *fused* inside of his skin somehow. Sarion felt waves of apprehension looking at the odd thing, and his instincts whispered a silent warning to him.

"Beware, don't touch it." Sarion stood, gesturing to Valadire. "I fear some evil is at work here."

The prisoner looked over, as if seeing Sarion for the first time. "Ah, you're the one then." He coughed, and his entire body trembled.

"Valadire, did your fighters hurt this man?" Chensel questioned him, but the Forester shook his head.

"No. He was like this when we found him. I don't know what ails him, Lord Chensel."

Sarion pointed. "What do you know of me?"

The prisoner coughed again, and it took long moments before he stopped. Chensel commanded them to bring water and have him placed in a chair.

The prisoner spoke. "You carry the magic."

Sarion looked over at Chensel, and they matched gazes for a moment.

"What are you talking about?" Sarion pressed him.

"Deny it if you like, it matters not. But it's more powerful than you can dream if you can defeat the Killworm."

Sarion was silent.

"My time is short, so I'll tell you what you want to hear."

Chensel moved closer. "Speak, but don't ask for our trust or forgiveness. You're an enemy of Trencit."

The man shrugged. "I've been sent by the Dark Mage, this is true. But not of my own choice."

The room was silent and Chensel stared at them, giving the briefest shake of his head. Sarion knew he didn't want any interruptions.

"He sent his servants to our village, seeking to enslave us. He was successful." He coughed again, and Sarion spotted blood on his cloak.

"My people didn't want to seek allegiance with him, and so they left us. Then came the ogres…"

Sarion stiffened.

"They took us by surprise, and rounded us up like animals. They never wanted to align themselves from the beginning. They were seeking pawns."

Chensel frowned. "What is the name of your village?"

"Gar-kiln."

"I've never heard of it."

"Deep in the south, beneath the very shadow of the Ridgeline. Past Sharield and west."

Sarion considered his words. The city of Sharield was far south from Nighton, and it was possible there were isolated villages on the edge of the wilderness.

The man continued, although he looked worse by the minute. "The Killworm is dying, and when it breathes its last gasp of air, then so shall I."

"How do you know this?" Chensel asked.

"Don't question me such if you wish to hear anything of use. These creatures were placed under my power. I've failed in my mission. The Dark Mage didn't foresee that the men of Nighton were protected by such magic."

The Rooting of Evil

"What do you mean? We have none at our use, unlike your master." Chensel stood directly before him.

The man closed his eyes, and for a moment Sarion thought he was dead. "Yes you do, although I don't know what it is. You can deny it all you like, but it matters not."

The rod, Sarion thought. Could he feel its presence somehow?

"How do you think you were able to defeat the Killworm? By skill of arms alone?" The man chuckled, the noise horrible to hear, more choking than anything else.

They were missing something here, Sarion knew. What was it? He'd brought the talisman to life, but extinguished its power before anything could happen. He was certain of it...

"You speak riddles. Tell me what you know."

"I know less than you. The Killworm is a magical creature, and can only be destroyed by equivalent magic. Whatever you possess had a hand in its defeat. Otherwise you would all have been lost."

Had the rod worked somehow? Sarion needed to know. "What is the nature of this magic we have? Can you tell us?"

The prisoner shook his head. "You truly don't know? Then I can't help you. I have not the knowledge. I was chosen for this task alone. It's not of my doing."

"Then why not fight the enemy? Why would you serve him instead?" Chensel asked, anger in his tone.

The man's eyes glimmered, and Sarion read the hatred within. He spoke slowly, his voice low. "He sent the Ravenor to our village. It *ate* several of our people as an example for the rest of us. Including Chrissa, my wife..."

Sarion shuddered at his story. The Ravenor? The man's voice was filled with horror at the recollection.

What kind of creature was this thing?

"The ogres threatened to feed my son to it unless I swore to serve the Dark Mage. They took him away. And now that I've failed…"

Chensel interrupted. "If this is true, we feel for the loss of your people and family. But to join forces with him? That's unthinkable. You've traded this for the lives of countless innocent people."

"My son, my son…" He rambled on, coughing while he spoke. "You've never seen the Ravenor. What it can do. It doesn't just eat people. It digests them, slowly. For days…" His voice trailed off and he wept, and it was one of the most pathetic things Sarion had ever seen or heard. What had the Dark Mage had done to this man, his family, his people? And what this man had done to save his own son. The Dark Mage *must* be made to pay for his acts...

"Where can we find the enemy? What is the source of his power? Help us avenge your loss!"

Sarion came forward, knowing that their opportunity was slipping away before their eyes.

"He's found something." The prisoner sobbed, and both Chensel and Sarion leaned close. "Something ancient and powerful, old before even the Giants."

"How do you know this?"

"Because I *saw!*"

His eyes were wide and unseeing.

"He's consumed by the magic. Changed...I was taken to his stronghold in deep Grammore, inside the valley of Murkvale. He did *this* to me, gave me the power to control the creatures that he resurrected. Myself, and others."

"Who are the others?" Chensel commanded.

"I don't know. Several were chosen, but I know them not."

"How do we find this place?" Sarion asked.

The Rooting of Evil

"You will never reach it. Deep inside the forbidden land, the stronghold is guarded by terrible creatures, worse than anything you can imagine. Only powerful magic could give one the chance to gain access. You don't know what it is you even have...And be warned, there are consequences to using magic. Any magic."

Chensel shook his head sadly. "Your tale grieves me, and it's not in my heart to forgive your actions. Ah, but what evil this enemy has wrought upon you and us all."

The prisoner's eyelids fluttered, his face contorted. "It's time, I feel the Killworm's pain. It crawls in the dark, looking for a place to end its life. It only has a few moments left." He weakly lifted one shackled arm. "Doom awaits you all. The choice is yours to make how you end your lives. Find a way if you must...to strike back. Go to my village and free my people. Your vengeance is no less than mine now. I'm...sorry."

And with that his body went into spasms as he coughed horribly. He shuddered one last time and then it was over. He was dead.

Sarion's mind was clear. Perhaps for the first time in weeks. But how would he break the news to the others? Would Chensel go along with his plan, or instead command him to do otherwise? And there wasn't much time left. Things had developed too quickly; events set into motion that would engulf them all. It was the vortex again, the whirlpool which had drawn him in. But now he saw light at the top. Perilous, unpredictable, but a path which lay before him, his choice to either take it or let others show him the way...

"Sarion!"

A familiar voice echoed across the eating hall, and Sarion sprang to his feet in joy. Edward!

"Lad, come here and let me see you!"

His face creased into the largest smile it had worn in weeks. Chertron and a pair of escorts walked behind the young boy, all of them grinning at the reunion. Edward and Sarion met, and he gave the youth a fierce hug, feeling his eyes moisten. It was so good to see the boy after what seemed like years had passed!

"I thought I would never see you again!" Edward's face beamed with pleasure, and Sarion rubbed his shoulders briskly.

"How was your trip here? Did anything happen?"

"No, but everyone's afraid. People are leaving their homes, and patrols are everywhere."

"Our homeland is under attack, as you've heard by now. That's why I had you brought here, so you'll be safe at Nighton."

Chertron came forward, and nodded approvingly. "A fine lad if I say so. I heard he's already good with the blade."

"I practice every day. I want to be in the Western Watch when I get older."

"Keep at it, and you'll be the best one day. Like Sarion." Chertron winked.

One of the escorts spoke. "There were no problems, as the boy said, Captain Sarion. We warned the people in your village, but they insisted on staying. They will not leave their homes, regardless of the danger."

"They're a proud people. I didn't think they would come here." Sarion frowned. "Unfortunately there's not nearly enough men to patrol every town and village. The borderlands are too vast. We can only hope that our efforts will pay off."

"Is it true that they made you a Captain of the Watch again?"

"Yes. I'm afraid my responsibilities have grown. I don't know when I'll be able to work the farm again." He paused. "And I'll be in the field soon."

Edward inclined his head, and now it was his turn to pause. "I know. Until things get better at least."

"But you're safe, so let's not talk about it. And you'll like it here at Nighton. There will be plenty of training masters to work with. For now though, let's get you a bite to eat. I need to rest some more. My ribs are still sore."

Sarion gestured for them to head towards the kitchen, and he felt an immense relief lift from his chest at the sight of Edward again, safe and near. How he'd missed the boy...But he knew this moment of joy was brief, and things would be moving again shortly after the council with Chensel. There would be no time for real rest until the threat from the Dark Mage was over.

"And here we are again, and yet more unseen events have transpired to shake our plans."

Chensel sat in a high chair at the conference table. They had all remained at the western gate for another day, waiting to see if the immediate danger had passed.

It seemed so, at least for the moment.

Several patrols had arrived, including the one escorting Edward. They'd all returned unscathed, which was excellent news, and unexpected. But things in the westland had hardly quieted down...

Sarion was silent, his face thoughtful, as he ate from a handful of mixed nuts. At his right sat Chertron, and Valadire was on his left. No other Foresters were present. These were the only men Chensel trusted with the entire truth.

"Sarion, it's clear that you need to finally meet with King Gregor. He will have sent additional messengers looking for you. They might even be at Nighton by now, so there can be no further delay. You must convince King Gregor to release you back to the Western Watch as soon as permissible. We've gained a respite, but for how long? Some of the news I've just heard is very disturbing."

Was there something he didn't know yet? Sarion questioned the First Forester. "What is it? That bad?"

Chensel's eyes were clouded. "No patrols have returned yet from the south. It takes long days to reach the region as you know, but still there is nothing from Sharield in the past few weeks. This bodes ill."

And yet another confirmation of what I must do next, thought Sarion...

"Aye. It's past time that we need to visit Daregil Keep," said Chertron. "We've done our part here."

"Have we?" Sarion looked over at his companion.

"None would argue this for our friend's sake. He must return to Trencit. For ourselves, there will be no rest," Valadire said as he entered the conversation.

Sarion replied. "But don't you recall the prisoner's tale? Of the evil done to his village?"

"I think I know where your mind is leading you, Sarion, but this is not a task for us. We must wait until King Gregor sends help." Now Chensel spoke.

"I think the king will be sorely taxed in every

direction," Sarion challenged. "He's already suffered the loss of General Charadan. The High Council will be in unrest, and provinces are unwilling to send additional men. Do you really think he's going to strike against the Dark Mage directly, after all this?"

"No, I don't expect him to take such action at this point in time. There's still too much we don't know. My duty is to protect the westland, and I need to have my captains -- both here at Nighton and in the field -- acting in coordination in the defense of our people."

Sarion shook his head. "But through circumstance, choices have been laid before us. Do we fall back on our victory here, and hope King Gregor has the manpower to guarantee victory? I think not...We need to go on the offensive, find a way to defeat our enemy." He slapped the table for emphasis. "I fear the words from the Keeper of Sprechyd Wood. He knows what we face. He said the Dark Mage can defeat us. He already has the power; maybe he's still trying to understand it. The prisoner said so much as well. He confirmed the same thing. Surely this is no coincidence."

Chensel answered. "Perhaps not, but we lack the knowledge and ability to go against him directly. His stronghold lies within Grammore, a region we know virtually nothing about -- no maps, no allies, and only the experiences of yourself from two ventures, both of which ended in disaster. What would you have me do? Send an army into the Lowlands? I will not order such a command."

"No, and I wouldn't ask you to, but I think there are other things we need to pursue, and answers to find. My belief is that all roads lead to Gar-kiln now."

Chensel sighed, rubbing his chin. "I was afraid you would say something like this, Sarion. It has not been out of my mind either. You wish us to search for this village and find the answers we seek. It would be a perilous venture, even if all of the words from the prisoner are to be believed…"

"And what of this creature he called the Ravenor?" Chertron asked.

"We don't know anything about it, but maybe it's left by now." Valadire offered. "The whole village has probably been destroyed as well."

Sarion shrugged. "We don't know either way. But it's a starting point for us. *More* than we've had before. Listen, we can wait here until the leaders of Trencit decide what to do for us, or act on our own and take the initiative. If they exercise too much caution, the opportunity will be lost. The fate of our kingdom might be lost as well. And who will save the westland if not us? This is our home, and we've suffered *directly* from the Dark Mage. If we don't take action, the power of our enemy will spread into every corner of Trencit next."

"These are all assumptions. We don't *know* anything for certain." Chertron pounded the table in frustration.

Sarion disagreed. "We *do* know what we face. We've *seen* it close-up. And I fear that we've yet to see the full extent of what the Dark Mage has waiting to throw against us. Creatures like the Killworm might only be the first assault."

"But they're magical in nature. We were fortunate to have slain it," Chertron insisted.

"True, but we've done it once, and can do it again. We possess the means to do this. It's the rod. I'm *certain* it helped us in some way." Sarion stared at his companion for several moments.

Chensel actually agreed with him. "Sarion, I think you hit on an important point here. All of our knowledge from ancient lore suggests that the monster is magical, and cannot be killed by normal weapons, but we indeed slew the beast. Although you didn't *control* the power of the talisman, you *awakened* it somehow. I've thought much about this. Maybe its *presence* alone was enough to strike the monster down."

"What do you mean by that?" Sarion asked.

"Presence?" Chertron echoed him.

"It's only a notion, but I do indeed think it's possible. Hear me out. This is my belief…" The Nighton leader folded his hands together. "Whatever magic is latent inside the rod acted against the enchanted nature of the Killworm, either by taking it away and neutralizing it, or defending us. It made the creature vulnerable to steel and flame. We don't know how, but we *do* know the result, and the prisoner alluded to as much. If we can trust his words, of course…" Chensel shrugged.

Sarion shifted forward, his eyes intense. "Yes, I think you're right. We can't deny the result." He stood up, pacing about for a moment before continuing. "So if I face more of these things, then I have the ability to fight them. This in itself is a weapon for us to wield, and gives me even *more* cause to seek out the enemy."

Chensel frowned. "I didn't say to seek him out. This is *not* my strategy…however, there is some merit in the notion concerning the talisman. The rod might protect those who combat such creatures. This conclusion we can reach, but as to what its other properties are, we don't know, and by your own trial, you believed it to be too dangerous."

Sarion replied. "Thus you've answered my strongest point. Here is one more reason that I *shouldn't* go to Daregil Keep, and not the least to argue against. Also, it's not something which should leave this room."

They all looked at him curiously.

Sarion remained standing, trying to further emphasize his argument. He breathed deeply. "I fear the magic held within the rod has the potential to destroy the wielder, and unleash power too great to be controlled. This is a perilous weapon to bring into Trencit. It must *not* go to Daregil Keep. My fear is that it might ultimately prove to be our undoing if we attempt to use it as such."

The room was silent for long moments, and then Chertron spoke. "Sarion, you've taken much responsibility upon your shoulders since we first met, tracking the ogre with us into Grammore. You've led us in many ways. No one can deny your loyalty to Trencit and the danger you've placed yourself in, protecting our country and people. But you assume too much here...Shouldn't these matters best be decided by King Gregor and his councilors? They have more knowledge of such matters than we do. We have not their resources. What you're suggesting is contrary to what the king wishes. He's undoubtedly eager for your appearance at the capital. He'll almost certainly send more couriers to seek you out. And now, as Second Captain of Nighton, there's no hiding. You can't *delay* this any longer. How can you prolong what must be done?"

"But I can do *just* that...There is a way."

Sarion stared at Chensel. The First Captain returned his gaze, but said nothing. Sarion lifted a finger, pointing. "Send me on a mission to the south. I'll search for the village of Gar-kiln, and seek help from Sharield if I have to. This is the chance we've been looking for. The Dark Mage has been moving ahead of us at every turn and we must press our advantage. If I'm on patrol in the borderlands, I won't be found by the king's messengers. I could stay in the field as long as needed. Indefinitely..."

Chensel was ready to speak, but hesitated.

Valadire now entered the conversation, having been silent for a while. "I agree with Sarion. The Royal

Armies are tied up in the east. The major houses will be reluctant to send their men off to either front. They'll be worried about protecting their own lands now, and in reality they have a sound argument. Little or no help will come from Daregil Keep. We must act on our own."

The Nighton leader looked at his captain, but still said nothing.

Chertron then spoke. "No, I disagree. A better idea is to wait and not split our strength. King Gregor might be convinced to send Sarion back to Nighton quickly, and come up with a strategy of defense. This notion of yours seems rash at best. We barely survived the Killworm's attack. What if these other creatures are stronger? Or what happens if there are several Killworms? Talisman or not, I fear we would all fall under such an attack. It would be mad to think otherwise."

"We will exercise caution, of course. I would not openly engage such creatures, but use stealth to avoid them. I don't plan on attacking the Ravenor, whatever it is, but avoiding it." Sarion's face was determined.

"And if you find the village, what is your plan then?" This time it was Chensel who spoke. "I command you now, but you also seem fit to act on your own if necessary." His face was stern.

"What do you mean? I haven't even thought past *this* venture yet." Sarion held his hands up.

The Nighton leader's voice was firm. "What I mean is this...if I grant this request and order you on this mission, then what? Do not give thought to entering Grammore again, Sarion. You've escaped twice now. I fear a third such venture. Do *not* tempt fate again. That is my wish, and command."

Sarion nodded, but said nothing.

Chensel now stood, and stared at them all in turn. "Ah, this will not be an easy task for any of us. Surely the king will be angered if Sarion fails to appear at Daregil Keep. I'll have my hands full once confronted about your whereabouts, and I'll be the one looked upon in disfavor. Nevertheless…This is my command then. Your mission is to seek out the village of Gar-kiln, discover what you can, and also find out news from Sharield if possible, although the miles are long and the terrain vast. But be warned -- when messengers from Daregil Keep arrive looking for you, I must tell them the truth of where you go. They might be on your trail."

Sarion shrugged. "So be it. I'll remain in the borderlands then, giving aid to where I may. The rod must not be used."

Chensel nodded. "I've pondered this dilemma, and find that I agree with you."

All eyes were on the Nighton leader.

"I've listened to your words and trust you, Sarion. Your willingness to enter into danger is brave, but also reckless at times. Beware, I say to you. I will send you to the south, to find out what you may and lend aid. If you're able to send me a message on what you discover, then do so. It will be on my shoulders if I decide to withhold information from King Gregor. Mine alone. And you must take the greatest care on your journey. You are the keeper of the rod, and if it cannot be used by our hands, then it certainly must not fall into the Dark Mage's power. Our fate may very well rest upon your shoulders. Choose wisely in all things, Second Captain of Nighton."

"What will you tell the king's couriers, knowing that Sarion is wanted in Trencit?" Chertron asked.

"I'll tell them our need was great, and Sarion is out on a mission of dire importance. I don't think Gregor will agree, and will definitely *not* welcome this news. But was it not he who ordered General Charadan on such a perilous quest?"

"Yes, and one that took his life as well..."
Chertron added.

Sarion remembered the brave leader, and he
wondered as to the similarities with his own situation. It
was unnerving. Would he make the same choices in the
days ahead that Charadan had done, endangering
himself because of his own confidence? Or *arrogance*?
Thinking he can win this battle alone? Admittedly, he
was guilty of brashness at times, throwing himself
recklessly into the heart of the fight, against terrible
creatures. He needed to follow extreme caution, as
Chensel suggested, or else he would be swept into the
vortex which threatened him and pay the final price, one
in which he'd danced dangerously around for weeks...

"The decision is made." Chensel stood. "A
hunting party will be put together, small but capable.
Fifteen strong. Valadire will accompany you as well,
second to your command."

Sarion exchanged glances with his former
companion, who winked. It comforted him to know that
he would be riding with the man again.

"Someone needs to keep you out of trouble,"
said Valadire.

"Shades, *that* will never happen..." Chertron
threw his hands in the air. "I still believe this is a poor
strategy at best. This is certainly in defiance of King
Gregor's wishes. He *will* demand answers, and search
for Sarion. Nevertheless, count me in as well. You'll
need someone with common sense around. I can only
hope I'll be given a reprieve for not returning to Trencit
at once, although unlike Forlern, I wasn't scheduled for
active service directly afterwards. This mission was all I
was told. We'll all end up in the dungeons of Daregil
Keep one of these days, mark my words..."

He cursed beneath his breath, but Sarion grinned
ruefully at him. They had been through so much, and the

reliable fighter was an invaluable companion. Where would fate lead them now?

"Very well. You'll be leaving in the morning. Enjoy another night's rest within the sanctuary of Nighton. I don't need to remind you of what you'll be facing. Ah, the troubles of these evil times. And with Jerol gone, the responsibility is mine now. But it falls on our weary shoulders to be strong and true. For if not ourselves, who then? Good fortune, my friends. I'll be returning to Nighton this evening after I've set everything into motion. New couriers from Daregil Keep will surely be there by now. Farewell." Chensel saluted them, and they responded in turn.

Sarion knew there were preparations to be done, but that would have to wait. For the second time in the past few weeks, he would be leaving Edward behind while he rode into chaos and danger.

"The sky is beautiful. All those stars, and the moon hanging low tonight. Looks like he has a face."

"Indeed he does," Sarion answered. He stood on the wall of the west gate with Edward at his side. The boy had taken the news better this time. He was already on the path to becoming a man. Edward would be protected in Nighton, and offered the best weapons training the fortress had to offer. He would be fine.

But...

Sarion knew their past life was over. Deep down, he realized that his days of quiet on the farm would never return. He hoped that his household would remain safe from marauders. The villagers had mobilized, and all eyes watched for signs of the enemy. The hunters from Nighton had spread the word quickly and the borderlands were on guard. Unfortunately, they were also grievously outmatched. If any of the stronger creatures attacked, they would lay waste to an entire town. Sarion remembered the village of Fledge Rae, transformed into a tomb where horrors now dwelt, the people killed or driven off. Was this the future of the westland if they failed?

They must not let it come to pass...

He sighed, staring into the heavens, wondering what the coming journey would bring. So much had happened recently, and he had trouble absorbing everything, trying to see what it all meant and figure out what the Dark Mage would do next. The forces gathering against them were terrible.

But there *was* hope. Had they not claimed victory here? Slain the Killworm, and brought one of the enemy's chosen servants to defeat? Yes, the day had been theirs. They would not be so easily overcome. Not while he lived and breathed, and others around him as well -- people like Chensel, Chertron, Valadire, and Forlern...What had happened to his fiery-tempered companion? Sarion had been so swept up lately in his own turmoil that he hadn't given much thought to the fighter's progress. Surely he would have reached Daregil Keep days ago, and King Gregor would be waiting for his own arrival. Probably not content even for that. Emissaries would be pouring into Nighton soon.

Yes, it was time he left. But Sarion's heart was at ease with his decision, knowing that *this* was where he belonged. In the westland -- fighting and leading the hunters of Nighton, his comrades in the Western Watch.

He had found his true home again.

And more determined than ever, he felt something else as well. Confidence. They now had a weapon which could turn the tide against the Dark

Mage. The rod, the ancient talisman of power. No, he didn't want to attempt its use again, but if Chensel was right about it having protective properties, perhaps that would be enough. But doubt remained…His hunting and tracking instincts would never permit him to ignore warning signs. None of them really knew anything about the rod, in truth, but *he'd* certainly felt the surge of power. It was real, although latent. And there was a small part of him, a distant voice in his head that told him something else -- that if all else failed; the rod was still a viable weapon, not just a dormant possession, but an active weapon of enormous capabilities. It had tremendous potential. Could he could find a way to control it somehow...

No. Best not to go down that road. Sarion trusted none other in the matter, and *this* had ultimately led him to turn away from Daregil Keep and the King.

For their own protection...

By his actions, Sarion had placed what might prove to be an impossible weight on his own shoulders. *His* alone, as bearer of the rod. Earlier he had told the others about his difficult experience.

Everything -- except for one detail. A very important and disturbing detail, that wielding the power, even for the slightest of moments, had felt exhilarating, enough so that it was a temptation to try again, and had been difficult to release. It had been very strong. So much so, that he didn't want anyone else to face the same dilemma; the temptation to use it. It was so great that he feared that the wielder might capitulate and bring something to life that would devour them all.

No. He would *not* permit the opportunity to occur.

Sarion leaned on the edge of the wall, peering into the twilight which consumed the westland, gazing into his own future and all the uncertainties that waited ahead, unseen.

He was not at peace.

His heart and mind were both restless, churning around in endless circles, and always coming back to the same dreadful possibility -- one in which *he* might give into the temptation to use the powerful talisman, and in the end become the very bringer of doom himself, destroying what he loved most.

The End

This concludes Book Two of the Trencit Legacy.

Book Three, follows the adventures of Sarion and his

companions as they seek out the village of Gar-kiln,

hoping to find answers in the battle against the Dark

Mage.

Paul Melniczek